STEEL HEART

A Jesse Alexander Novel

RJ BLAIN

Copyright

With the Hope Diamond locked around her throat, Jesse Alexander finds herself in the unfortunate position of being a walking national treasure. With the Starfall stone poised to pulse and flood the world with more of its magic, she must figure out how to remove it before she becomes its pawn yet again.

Unfortunately, the stone has a mind—and plans—of its own. Add in a determined tiger, a wolf out for revenge, and an ultimatum to find her clan's missing Starfall stone, and it will take all of Jesse's wit and cunning to survive with her life—and her heart—intact.

Cover design by Daqri Bernardo of Covers by Combs.

Dedication

This one goes out to everyone behind the scenes. Without you, this book would still be feral, I'd probably have rabies, and nobody would have a story to read at all.

Thank you.

Oh, and Charity? Next time, beat me harder so don't end up burning the midnight oil again. Thanks for all your help. I wouldn't have survived writing the feral beast without you.

Chapter One

WHY DID SO many of my problems begin in a bar? I sipped my beer from the corner, kept my back to the wall, and admired the brawl in full swing. Four broken tables, seven stools, and eight chairs littered the floor along with copious amounts of blood and beer, none of which belonged to me for a change.

I appreciated a good fight, especially when nobody died or was at any real risk of being relocated without their permission.

Any other day, I might've waded in and started banging heads together, but after an afternoon of Agent Simmons and Agent Randal tossing me around and otherwise tenderizing me, I wanted to enjoy my beer without a fuss. That I'd gotten tossed around at all, my agents being careful of my shoulder to prevent it from breaking again, counted as a vast improvement.

The instant my duo of bodyguards realized I'd given them the slip following the torture session they called training, they'd turn Charlotte upside down for me. They'd check the coffee shops first; I'd made a point of heading to the cafes following prior escapes to lull them into obeying old habits.

Maybe if the torture sessions had involved weapons and real practice, I wouldn't have minded being tossed around as much.

Tonight, I meant to enjoy my beer, and as long as the brawl stayed on the other side of the bar where it belonged, I'd leave the men and women to their entertainment. Matt, my favorite of the bartenders, joined me, sat down, and set a fresh beer in front of me. "It's been a while since you've been around. Finally ditched all three of your boyfriends?"

"Randal and Simmons are both happily married, thank you."

"That leaves your actual boyfriend."

That problem, named Anatoly Silverston, Ana when he needed to be knocked down a peg or two, had started in a bar, too. It had been a long time since I'd tattooed my mark on him, and he'd accepted my invitation in more ways than one. The resulting chase had spanned years and much of the United States, and I lived to thwart the insufferable tiger at every turn. I couldn't tell which one of us enjoyed our daily spars the most, yet another problem I needed to deal with sooner rather than later.

I huffed, drained my beer, and grabbed Matt's offering. "The tiger is in a meeting. Also, he's not my boyfriend."

Yet. Maybe. Probably. Hell, I had no idea what he was, but refusing to acknowledge him as my boyfriend drove him and everyone around us up the nearest wall, which was why I did it. My interest in the smug tiger was none of their business. Fortunately for the sake of my ruse, the smug tiger spent all his damned time in meetings, which drove me up the nearest wall several times a day.

I blamed boredom.

Boredom always got me in trouble.

Why was I the only one to recognize that critical fact of life? I could've dealt with going to the meetings with Anatoly. Being in the meetings with him would keep me busy. *Something* to do would keep me from wanting to run so the damned tiger would chase me. I couldn't even land a simple gig from a mercenary guild without someone coming up with a hundred reasons why I should stay home where I belonged.

Home should've been in Cheyenne, but times had changed on me again.

I missed my courier rounds, and not even caring for Miracle, who recovered from her illness a little each day, teaching Devil Spawn and Dipshit new tricks, and working with every horse in the palace stables quenched my wanderlust. Of my horses, only the mare Anatoly had given me didn't try to kill me several times a day.

As I'd neglected to name her, she'd started responding to variants of Sweetie Pie and My Precious

Angel, much to the disgust of everyone, myself included.

Oh, well. Sweetie Pie loved attention, and she loved attention best from me, and she put up with my asshole horses without complaint.

No matter how much I loved spending time with my asshole horses, I wanted the freedom to go somewhere and do *something.* Until someone found a way to remove the Hope Diamond locked around my throat, I couldn't even breathe without someone supervising me.

I gave it ten minutes before my agents decided to call for reinforcements and begin a complete search of the city.

A body hit a table, and the table cracked before crashing to the floor. A woman in a suit similar to my agents', pounced with a roar.

"Tiger or lion, Secret Service?" I guessed.

"She's one of your in-laws."

I arched a brow and stared at Matt. "I'd have to be married to have in-laws, and I know for a fact that is not Anatoly's sister."

The day Anatoly's sister came to town, all hell would break loose, something I looked forward to a great deal. Would Charlotte even survive through four Siberians sharing space? Three was bad enough, and I wasn't even the worst offender. I came in last ever since my general containment by the Secret Service.

Then again, left unsupervised, trouble found me with alarming frequency. Hell, who was I kidding?

Even when supervised, I always managed to get into trouble one way or another.

No wonder Anatoly got snarly whenever I left his sight. I'd get snarly, too, in his position.

"You're a Siberian. I've seen enough mate-for-life pairings to know what one looks like. Run all you want, since that's what you tigers do, but it'll be easier on you if you just accept you're delaying the formalization to pull his tail. Anyway, she's a lioness, and she's your handler's backup in the pride. From all accounts, Blossom may as well be Anatoly's sister, you may as well be his wife, and as the lioness is in Blossom's pride, she's one of your in-laws."

Well, shit. I already had a babysitter in the bar, although she'd decided to take some time off to join a fight. Blossom would love finding out I'd watched one of her pride sisters brawl in a bar. It also bothered me that Matt knew more about my life than I did half the time.

One question rose above all others. "I can't escape, can I?"

Why was everyone concerned with my relationship with the damned tiger? If the President, the First Gentleman, and half the damned city had their way, I'd be participating in a wedding within the next twenty-four hours.

I blamed the Blade Clan for my general aversion to ceremonial marriage. Had I chosen to be a man instead of a woman, I would've been wed to Anatoly's sister, however. Permanently. In a lavish ceremony, as the

Blade Clan didn't wed any of their sons often or without good reason. Part of the good reason had been my damned desire for permanency on top of my skills. I still desired permanency. I always would.

The damned tiger, who would one day be stuck with me if anyone, including me, got their way, found the entire situation hilarious. I did, too, but for the sake of my battered pride, I kept a lid on my amusement.

"That's how it goes with Siberians. Everyone's gossiping over how long it'll take for your boyfriend to actually catch you."

"Maybe if he didn't spend so much time in meetings, he might actually manage something more than chasing his tail." Damn it all. I itched to roar in Anatoly's face, sink my claws into him, and drag him off. According to everyone, I was slow to the chase, likely had no idea how to pursue a man even if I wanted one, and would drive Anatoly insane before I decided to settle down.

With him.

If everyone stopped bothering me about it, I probably would take the damned tiger for a walk, make him mine, and return him sometime later. Much later.

"He does seem to have an unusually high volume of meetings lately. What brings you my way, Runs Against Wind?"

Matt numbered among those who knew I'd once been Jesse Alexander, but he liked my Cheyenne flair, or so he claimed.

"Beer, Matt. I worked hard for this beer." I toasted

him and enjoyed the brew's bitter bite. "You know what happened the last time I asked for a beer in that prison they insist is suitable living arrangements?"

"This is going to be good. What happened?"

"They offered me tea, water, or, if I decided to be good for a change, a cup of coffee. One of the assholes even tried to bribe me with chocolate."

I still hadn't figured out what everyone had against a good beer, but nobody wanted to give me even a single drop. Due to living and working so close to the Mayoral Palace, quickly becoming known as the Presidential Residence, Matt understood my plight better than most. Thanks to his potent brews, he'd earned the friendship of most of the Secret Service, who had the sacred duty to keep me and the Hope Diamond out of trouble.

I bet a few were participating in the brawl, which had devolved to poorly aimed blows, drunken laughter, and rolling on the floor.

"They're stooping to chocolate trying to keep you from beer? Damn, they're desperate. What's gotten them on a no-alcohol kick?"

I wished I knew, but I could make a few guesses. "They seem to believe if I have a beer, someone will cause a fight, I might end up knocking some heads together, and otherwise create trouble for someone."

"To be fair to you, that brawl's been brewing for a month, so you can't claim credit for it." Matt chuckled and kicked his feet up on the nearest chair. "Most days, I can't tell if they're friends or not, and well, once the beer starts flowing, the insults start flying, and someone finally crosses a line. And those two? Well, they're friends with just about everyone in here."

Which two? The fight had at least ten participants, and they'd all seemed eager to rough each other up. "If a Starfall stone comes rolling in, I'm leaving, and they can catch up with me in Cheyenne."

Matt glanced at the door. "Your boyfriend's here."

I bowed my head and sighed. "Which one?"

"The actual boyfriend. It seems he has escaped his meeting. You could go marry him now and put an end to the pestering. You could elope. You just have to run down to the courthouse, sign some papers, and go back in three days to finalize it. I give it a month before anyone checks your records and figures out you took the dive."

"You, too?"

"You two are so jealous of each other that until you get official ownership papers, you're going to be insufferable. I'm amused, but I'm concerned for your happiness. A lady with your good taste in beer deserves only the best partner, and you can't go wrong with a Siberian. And when you're happy, you're less likely to participate in a fight in my bar. Or invite your horses in for a visit. He's looking at you like you're the best thing he's ever seen in his life. I thought you'd like to know."

Well, if history wanted to repeat itself in a bar, I had a small roll of tools tucked my belt. Twisting around, I searched for the tiger to find him taking up space in the doorway, still dressed in the suit he'd been wearing last night when he'd been called into the first of his emergency meetings.

I quite liked his dark red tie.

For my peace of mind, I decided to ignore Anatoly's smirk. To be heard over the brawl, I'd have to shout, and I rose to my feet and saluted him with my bottle. "Come have a beer, tiger! I'll even share mine if Matt's stingy."

His smirk shifted to a glare, and according to Anatoly's expression, he wanted to roar in my face again, something I found amusing. My laughter stirred his ire even more. He strolled over, snagged the nearest intact chair, and sat across from me. "You escaped. Again."

I showed him my beer so he could properly admire it. "This is what happens when you come between me and my beer. I told you this would be the outcome. You laughed at me. Then you said what, exactly?"

"I foolishly claimed we'd be able to keep you where you belong. I'm man enough to acknowledge when I've made a mistake. Are you trying to give me premature gray hairs?"

I was willing to bet all my demonic horses Anatoly would only grow more handsome with age and silvered hair. "Am I doing well so far?"

"No gray hairs yet," he reported. "But you're well on your way to accomplishing your goals. I should've guessed you'd gone to the bar first. I tried two coffee shops before realizing I'd made a mistake. I've lost count of the number of mistakes I've made today."

I could make a few guesses. "Didn't take the chance to get dinner while you could last night?"

"That was my first mistake, yes."

Hungry tigers became angry tigers, and angry tigers had a tendency to maul people. "You annoyed the First Gentleman again, didn't you?"

"It's not *my* fault the Bengals picked a fight. Why does he always get mad when I finish fights they start?"

When the emergency meetings turned into fights, *something* was going on, and the last time there'd been any large-scale fights, I'd been on my way to Fort Lauderdale, where I'd unwillingly unleashed the Hope Diamond's lethal powers. "Why did the Bengals start a fight? It's usually the wolves starting the fights. Or the First Gentleman."

Actually, it astonished me anything got done, as the shifters loved nothing more than a good fight.

"They're wanting all the Weapon Clan Starfall stones found, and more have gone missing."

Too many people knew I'd once been a member of the Blade Clan, which meant I could handle Steel Heart without the damned thing taking a hike, which it usually did when someone got their hands on it. Without fail, I'd be sucked into the problem, something I'd avoided thanks to the blue diamond locked around my throat. "If you involve me in that shit, I'm charging you a fortune, Silverston."

Anatoly grimaced. "I know I'm in trouble when you address me by my last name. What did I do now?"

"Meetings," I snarled. "Meetings that I'm going to have to start attending at this rate."

"I argued against it, if that makes you feel better." Anatoly pointed at my throat. "Could you not wear that openly, please? I'm going to have a panic attack every time you sneak out of the palace. You could wear a scarf."

"No. It's not cold enough for a scarf."

"It's never cold enough for us to want to wear scarves. We're Siberians."

"It's like people seem to think I'm going to forget my species if I'm not reminded multiple times a day."

"Have my meetings irritated you that much?" The tiger's smug smile irritated me even more than his damned meetings. "I'm flattered."

"Why is killing you illegal?" I hissed.

"You'd miss me."

"Like hell!" I roared in his face, which did an admirable job of putting an end to the brawl. Someone flopped onto the broken ruins of a table with a weak laugh. The sound drew my ire, and to make it clear I didn't approve, I hissed.

"Don't mind the pissy tigress," Matt announced. "She needs a nap."

"Tenderized by Randal and Simmons again?" Blossom's pride mate asked.

"Is it that obvious?"

"You ran away to a bar for a beer. It was my first guess."

"If you reported to those cretins that I'm here, I'm

returning you to Blossom and Gabe equally tenderized."

Brushing herself off, the lioness hopped to her feet. "You don't remember my name, do you?"

"I think they were still giving me the good drugs when Blossom introduced us," I admitted.

"I'm Beverly. Blossom asked me to sneak onto your detail and keep an eye on you."

How did a lioness sneak onto my detail? "I think you need a beer for being forced to put up with me."

She grinned. "I think you need some formal training where you're not being tossed around like a sack of grain for a change. A workout will do you good. I'm formally trained with a sword, so I might be a decent sparring partner for you. I can also arrange for a good instructor to work with us. I've a few contacts I can impose on."

I sat straighter. "While you're working miracles, can you get me on a local courier route?"

"I can't promise, but I can most certainly try. The pride always needs packages delivered, and controlled work seems far more productive than chasing you down every other day because you're bored out of your mind. Men. They seem to believe they can catch a tiger by her tail and keep her caged at their convenience. I'm a lioness. I know better."

Anatoly hissed at the Secret Service agent. "You're not supposed to be encouraging her."

"There's no reason you can't do your work while you accompany your tigress. She's named Runs Against

Wind for a reason. It's not her fault you refuse to acknowledge that. I've been trying to convince the First Gentleman that a trip is the best medicine for her at this point in time. Her gaudy little necklace will protect her, as we've already seen. It bound itself to her for a reason. What that reason is? Who knows." Beverly strolled over and sat on the edge of the table, snagging Matt's beer out of his hand and taking a swig. "I can tell you this, however. Your tigress is healthy. Her horses are healthy, even the scrawny one with patchy fur. You're worse than a lion with your posturing. And trust me, I know all about lions. Gabe is such a lion."

I toasted Beverly with my beer. "Think you can whip those two old men into shape, Beverly?"

"It depends on why I'm whipping them into shape? Your agents are just doing their jobs. I know it steps on your toes, but they're good at what they do."

For the first time in months, I thought I could do my job well for a change—and for a good cause. At the same time, I could hunt my past, slaughter it, and put it behind me forever. "If the damned tiger is going to be stuck in meetings about a damned stone that grows feet and walks off, then let's go find the damned stone and be done with it already. I've got a Weapon Clan to beat up, too."

Anatoly snorted. "I wasn't all *that* serious about you taking on an entire clan to earn me."

"Too bad. You issued the challenge, so you're just going to have to deal with it. And frankly, they need to be disciplined for losing their damned Starfall Stone.

How better to do it than by kicking their asses before giving it back? That makes my victory all the sweeter."

"Without a Blade Clan sword of your own?" he challenged. "You won't stand a chance, Runs Against Wind."

"I don't need a Blade Clan sword to kick their asses, thank you very much. I'll let that become one of the crowning achievements of my life. When I win, you will surrender."

He growled. "What are you going to do next? Ask for a bow?"

I smirked. "Now that you mention it, that would be nice. You can wear it around your neck, and then I can leash you and prance you around Charlotte at my whim. I'll make Todd shift and ride him while I lead you around. I'll even have Todd dress me up so I'm particularly lovely."

Nothing pleased me quite as much as riling Anatoly Silverston into incoherent fury over my latest jab, and when the bar brawl resumed, he waded in and took his temper out on one of Matt's poor tables. Turning to the bartender, I said, "I'll pay for that one. I goaded him into it."

Anatoly got unreasonable whenever he thought someone might see me when I was looking at my best. Some women didn't like the look of jealousy on their man, but Anatoly wore it well—and only with me.

He thought I wore jealousy well, too.

No wonder Siberians drove everyone crazy. We were well on our way to driving ourselves crazy, and everyone's annoyance at our behavior fueled my need to tug my tiger by the tail.

"That's not necessary, Runs Against Wind. I'll charge the Secret Service. It's their fault for not keeping a better eye on you and that damned tiger."

I laughed, and while word would ultimately reach my aunt and uncle in the Oval Office, it'd be worth the scolding. "Just tell me when you want me to break it up, Matt."

The bartender rose to his feet with a heavy sigh. "I'll go get the stick. I'd like a bar left at the end of the day."

I WORKED out the worst of my nerves putting an end to the brawl, and I even got to spar with Beverly, who wielded a table leg with pleasing enthusiasm. I blamed the felines in us for how our spat turned into a wild chase across the bar, punctuated with hisses and the occasional roar.

The Hope Diamond glittered once near the start of the melee, pulsing with a pale blue nimbus and washing Matt's stick in its light. His beloved baseball bat of bar protection would never be quite the same, but I figured he wouldn't mind its newfound case of indestructible, as not even a table was able to withstand its increased might.

My roaring summoned my secret service agents, and when Randal hissed at me for giving them the slip,

Beverly and I went for them like they were the dessert of our bar brawl menu.

One day, I'd stop trying to pounce either agent; they always dropped me to the floor without delay. To make sure I didn't go anywhere, Simmons sat on me. My roar of disapproval captured Anatoly's attention, who decided the best place for him was seated on my back.

"Damned tiger," I growled.

Randal seized Anatoly by the scruff of his neck. "The easiest way to catch a wayward council member is to catch his lady. While I would've been happy to leave you to your brawl, Jesse, Anatoly is needed in another meeting."

I drummed my fingers on Matt's floor. "I see I'm being cruelly used as bait again. Give me something useful to do, Randal. I'm tired of being bored."

"To be fair to her, she was just watching the fight while sipping a beer in the corner," Beverly announced from her position prone on the floor beside me. "She only got involved when Matt gave her the stick."

My agents glared at the bartender, who retrieved the fallen bat and returned it to its place behind the bar. "The fight ended after she cracked the first table in half with the bat. Also, I'm very impressed my bat survived that."

If he wasn't going to mention the bat had glowed blue in the Hope Diamond's light, neither would I.

While Randal kept a hand on the back of Anatoly's neck, I twisted until I could grab hold of the tiger's knee. "My tiger. You can't take him, Randal. *My* tiger. I will fight you for him. I saw him first, so he's mine."

"You can't stake any claims on him right now, Jesse. He has an important meeting."

I roared at my agent, and I shifted, which made a mess of my clothes, as I'd put on a lot of pounds after recovering from my menagerie of illnesses. After some lessons with Anatoly, with the threat of tiger claws in my ass as motivation to do the job right and without delay, I transformed in less than thirty seconds with my fur growing in last. My agents cursed, and Randal lost his hold on my tiger, scrambling to dodge my massive black paw.

"Jesse!"

I inhaled, but before I could roar again, Anatoly wrapped his arms around my neck and drew my head against his chest. "All right, my beautiful tigress. Easy does it. No mauling your agents. I know you're upset and bored, and I'll look into ways to fix that now that you're feeling better. How about this? I'll take you to the meeting with me, and I'll tell them you're cranky about being separated from me. Those council member busybodies will ask you really nicely to keep the discussion private. You probably know just as much as everyone else in the room, too, so you'll be useful in the discussion, although we'll need to swing by your suite for a change of clothes."

The slight emphasis on my suite reinforced his continual displeasure over having been barred from moving in with me—or being able to move me out of the country's seat of power to his home in Charlotte. On that, we were on the same page. I didn't want to be stuck under my aunt's thumb forever, but she always managed to talk me into staying.

Frequent visits from Anatoly, Todd, and my uncle helped with that.

It wouldn't help for much longer, as I'd rather fight every night with the damned tiger than attend fancy dinners with a strict avoidance of beer. I didn't know what my aunt had against beer, but if I didn't regain my easy access to alcohol, I'd snap. Or bite Anatoly.

Or both.

I figured my asshole aunt wanted me to take a bite out of the damned tiger. I'd already snuck a few nibbles of his throat as taste tests, finding him much to my liking. According to Todd, I was a Siberian to the core, and I'd be leading Anatoly on for at least another year or two before mauling the bastard and taking him for a ride he'd never forget.

I figured my fuse was better counted in days or weeks, as every glance at his throat gave me ideas.

Worse, I already considered him as mine without exception, and I resented when anyone took him out of my sight, especially so he could do something like attend yet another damned meeting.

To make it clear I loathed the situation, I twisted in Anatoly's arms and roared in Randal's face.

"That was even moodier than normal for you," my agent observed, and he wiped his face. "And now I'm wearing your spit. When I signed up for this, I had not anticipated wearing tiger spit."

Anatoly chuckled. "It's a known hazard when you're close enough to get a good look down our throats while we're roaring. She's gotten very good at roaring."

"That she has. Come on, Jesse. How about a compromise. After all of those nasty meetings your tiger has to attend, we'll come back here for another beer, and we won't tell your aunt."

I perked my ears at that.

"Way to encourage alcoholic tendencies," Simmons muttered.

"Simms, she's a merc. Hell, even Todd has had alcohol dependency issues. It took him years to get clean, and he's able to have one or two a week without running afoul of problems."

Ah. Enlightenment struck me.

From the outside, I supposed it did look like I had severe alcohol dependency issues. Flattening my ears, I regarded Anatoly through narrowed eyes.

"Don't look at me like that, Jesse. I like when you get frisky in bars. Good things happen to me when you get frisky in a bar. I'm not a participant in this scheme to curtail any drinking habits. If it lures you into coming home with me, I'll provide a single beer for you every night. That will keep your evil aunt off my back and you get your beer. After all the shit we put up with, a beer a day is basically mandatory."

Randal shook his head. "The no beer rule applies

to you, too, Anatoly. You're at equal risk of dependency issue as her. The President is very much aware of your tendency to look for information in bars while consuming copious amounts of alcohol."

Anatoly hissed at my agent. To distract the tiger from my agent and potentially mauling him, I nipped his shoulder, one part to return his attention to me, one part to make it clear he was mine.

He yelped. I liked the sound so much I nipped him again.

Randal grabbed me by my scruff and did his best to haul me off Anatoly without success. "Damn it, Jesse. You can't maul him right now."

"She's more than welcome to maul me at her leisure," Anatoly replied with a rather breathless tone of voice.

"Tigers," my agent spat, giving another tug of my scruff. "I'll give you twenty minutes alone in your suite to get your need to posture and maul out of the way, but not a damned minute longer. Off your tiger, Jesse. He really does have to go into his meeting. While you're marking your territory in your suite, I'll run a messenger along and make it clear you'll be accompanying him."

As his terms won me the war, I released Anatoly, dragged my rough tongue over his cheek, and released him, pawing at my clothes. One day, I'd remember to strip before shifting. Only a few special pieces, such as the feathers bound in my hair, my beads, my turquoise bracelets, and the Hope Diamond, escaped from my shifter ways.

One set of my leathers tended survive, but the rest of my clothes tore to shreds.

I gave a final swipe at my ruined apparel, picked up the plain katana I carried around as a consolation for my lost Blade Clan weapon, and headed for the door, leaving the others to follow or not as they decided.

Anatoly, as always, caught up to me first, and he rested his hand on my shoulder to make it clear I was his and his alone.

And I, being the foolish Siberian I was, bit his hand hard enough to draw blood to make it clear he was mine and mine alone.

My bite mark on his hand, along with the faint tattoo I'd left on him in Miami, would do to ensure those watching understood I'd claimed him. For now.

Chapter Two

WITHOUT FAIL, I neglected the signs of general exhaustion. True to Randal's word, he locked me in my suite with Anatoly for company. The tiger laughed and flipped his middle finger at the closed door. Then he shucked off his suit jacket and rolled up his sleeves, which transformed him from a handsome man into a breathtaking one.

My urge to bite him grew, and I clenched my teeth to resist the urge.

"They're probably fetching Gentry to make sure we stay put this time," the tiger said, shaking his head. "They're utterly clueless."

Yes, they were.

I padded to the bedroom so I wouldn't assault the tiger and sink my teeth into him, shifted, and snagged my bathrobe, wrapping in its warm, fluffy confines. After careful consideration and a battle with myself, I secured it with the sash. When I emerged to the sitting room, Anatoly had flopped onto the couch to wait for me. He yawned, and I recognized the pinched appearance of his eyes a sign of his exhaustion, likely far worse than mine.

I exhausted myself trying to find some way out of the boredom. He exhausted himself trying to make sense of the United States government and lording over all other felines. I exhausted myself further doing my best to match him. Then, because he was as much of an idiot as I, he did the same.

We were quite the pair.

I flopped on the couch beside him, snuggled close, and invited myself to nestle my head on his shoulder. As always, when we grabbed a few moments of peace, he wrapped his arm around me and dropped a kiss on the top of my head.

My aunt had been the first to kiss me that way, and her affection had broken me. Determined to acclimate me to the idea people could actually love me, Anatoly had taken to kissing the top of my head as a form of greeting or when we snatched a few moments of quiet together. The first time I hadn't flinched, shortly after I'd fully recovered from my illness, he'd told me he was proud of how far I'd come.

I'd cried without understanding why.

I no longer flinched, and I no longer cried, either. I would blame being sick until my dying day for the ridiculous number of tears I'd shed since returning from Fort Lauderdale.

Todd enjoyed teasing me about how I became

easily overwhelmed at the concept of having a family, and the stallion would likely continue to do so for the rest of my life.

Jerk.

Really, it was no wonder everyone got mad when I denied Anatoly was my boyfriend. In reality, I didn't want him as my boyfriend. I wanted him.

Permanently.

I sighed and relaxed against the tiger I needed to hurry up and claim before someone stole him from me. "I want to go into the council and murder them every day."

"Strangely, so do I, but I suspect you have a different reason for that than I."

"Probably."

"Come get your nibbles in before those busybodies interrupt us," he replied, giving my shoulder a squeeze. "You get upset when you don't get your nibbles in, and you haven't gotten your nibbles in for at least a week now. At most, we've seen each other for a few minutes a day here and there, and you've barely snuck in a scrape of your teeth when no one has been looking."

"Twenty minutes isn't nearly long enough," I complained. The process of nibbling the tiger into submission needed at least an hour, and while I mostly focused my attention on his shoulder, neck, and upper arms, I always concluded my session with his mouth.

One of these days, the damned tiger would break my restraint, and he'd only have himself to blame. I had enough experience in bed for both of us, and I enjoyed teaching him how to kiss me right, coaxing him along until he'd become a deft and interesting partner.

Without fail, someone interrupted us before we took it any further, which was my own damned fault.

My damned need to nibble took up a lot of time, and he enjoyed it as much as I.

"I'll neglect to leave tonight, and I'll hide in your suite under the bed until your agents decide it's time for them to guard the hallway. We can escape through the pool and find some peace and quiet in the maze."

The last time I had gone into the maze through one of the pools, I'd about drowned myself thanks to a damned sedative. I'd meant to explore the pools and maze again, but opportunities were few and far between. Taking Anatoly down with me would add an edge to my explorations. It would be a matter of time before Randal or Simmons figured out I'd given them the slip.

I figured my aunt hadn't heard about the pools from Blossom's father, Mayor Longfellow. Or Todd. Or Gentry. Hell, she probably knew, but had decided the only suite suitable for me included a pool.

Tigers loved water.

Had she thought I'd make use of the pools, I would've been kicked out of my suite and put somewhere safer—one with fewer escape paths.

I thought about it as I began my nibbling quest on his earlobe. I growled and gave a tug, holding on with enough force to make it clear I was the one in control.

Rather than being properly intimidated, he chuckled. "I can't tell if that's a yes or a no."

Releasing him, I replied, "I'm game to try. I need a proper nibbling session."

"You get five, I get five, and we'll use the rest of the minutes to take a nap. I don't know about you, but if those assholes don't give me a break soon, I'm going to sleep during a meeting."

Damn. He'd looked tired, but I hadn't expected him to be that tired. Rather than nibble, I kissed his cheek. "Hang in there just a little longer, tiger. I'll hide you under my bed tonight, and I'll pick a fight with my pesky agents to make sure they look somewhere else for you. Then I'll nibble on you, and we'll barricade the bedroom door, then we'll both catch up on sleep."

"Other men might be upset over being rescued by a woman, but I accept your most generous offer of salvation and a chance to get some sleep."

With only five minutes to work with, I'd have to upgrade from nibbles to nips to mark my territory. I started on his throat, which always captured his undivided attention. As always, he tilted his head to give me easy access. Rather than adhere to my usual routine, I aimed for my favorite spot, where his shoulder and his neck met, not quite grazing his collar bone. Had I nibbled rather than nipped, he would've relaxed under my touch. Anatoly yelped, and with a snarl, he retaliated, snapping his teeth at my throat. We rolled off the couch, and I landed on my back with him sprawled on top of me. While I fended him off with a hand on his jaw, I offered him one of my fingers, which he seized with his teeth.

"You are an entity of pure evil." He evaluated our position, which put him on top and in general control of the situation. With anyone else, I would've already been struggling to escape. Instead, I relaxed, tapping his mouth with my finger, which he nipped again. "You test my patience, Jesse."

"When haven't I tested your patience?"

"Good question. I'll think about it. As punishment for such terrible treatment of my person, I'm claiming the rest of your minutes and adding them to my minutes. My turn to nibble, and you only have yourself to blame."

Something about his tone challenged me, and I bit his arm right above his wrist, hard enough he bled. Anatoly yelped again, and I bit down harder.

Mine, mine, mine. Then, to make it clear I would always emerge the victor, I gave the bite mark a defiant lick. Ever since I'd begun shifting, the taste of blood had grown on me, and something about Anatoly's blood appeased the predator within as nothing else did.

Fortunately for him, the wound would close within a few minutes and leave little evidence I'd gotten a hold of him with my teeth. The scent of blood would tip my agents off one of us had bled on something, but they'd likely assume I'd clawed him.

Again.

I had many bad habits, but Anatoly kept driving me crazy. Worse, he encouraged it. Then, as he had no sense of self-preservation, he encouraged me when I landed a good hit and made him bleed.

I gave the spot a kiss to make it all better, as my tiger whined when he didn't receive affection. Then I licked him again to erase the evidence he'd bled from my bite.

"I deserved that," Anatoly growled. Pulling his chin free of my hold, he struck, pinning my wrists to the floor and using his leg to immobilize my lower body. He rested his weight on me, smirked, and kissed the tip of my nose. "You're wearing my blood like lipstick, and I like that."

"You're demented."

"It's such a nice shade on you. But don't be wasteful. You wanted my blood that bad, so at least clean up after yourself."

I licked my lips, well aware he enjoyed when I did such a thing. I didn't understand it, but he liked it, and while tigers couldn't purr, his chest rumbled from his sensual growl. "Better?"

"Much. Now, what am I going to do with you? I have at least seven minutes to enjoy."

"Well, I seem to have somehow gotten pinned. I suppose that means you can do whatever you want with me."

I had pleasant memories of my first time with a man, and I'd gotten lucky, landing one who'd been both aggressive yet considerate, and he'd done with me much as I did with Anatoly. Being coaxed into losing my inhibitions had made the whole night worth my while—and his, too.

I wanted the same for Anatoly, although I'd guessed long ago men had an easier time of it than women.

When he finally let go and gave in, I'd be ready to teach him what I liked and discover what he liked along the way.

"Mhmm." Anatoly adjusted his hold on my left arm, sliding his hand to my elbow. Then, much like a snake tired of being poked with a stick, he sank his teeth into my upper arm. Rather than the blunt, human teeth I expected, the sharp stab of a feline's fangs tore into my skin. I smelled blood, and like I had done to him, he licked me until the wound closed.

"I deserved that," I concede with a smile.

Life as a shifter suited me, especially as I healed much faster than I had before I'd fully embraced my life as a Siberian. Before I could figure out how to escape him, Anatoly relaxed against me, nuzzling my throat. To keep from crushing me, he rolled over and dragged me with him, situating us so my back rested against his chest.

"There," he announced, and he trailed kisses from my shoulder to my cheek. "Maybe they'll forget we're here."

"Unlikely."

"It's worth a try. Maybe they won't notice us on the floor."

"It's worth a try," I agreed, snuggling closer to him.

"If they didn't want us taking a nap, they wouldn't have given us twenty whole minutes."

"Exactly. And I meant what I said. I'm hiding under your bed tonight, and we're going to escape in the maze so we can both get our fair share of nibbling rather than a few nips." Anatoly paused. "I guess those weren't really nips, were they?"

"If you don't tell, I won't, but next time, you better watch your throat, or you'll have to wear a scarf. And if you try to hide it, I'm going to tattoo my claim on your damned forehead."

Anatoly dragged his teeth along the side of my throat. "Remember that, Jesse. I'll mark you from shoulder to jaw, and not even a scarf will hide you're mine."

"I'm tattooing a collar around your throat if you even think about shredding that much of my neck, Silverston."

His laughter rumbled in his chest. "I'll buy the ink, the needles, and the cream to make it permanent."

Tigers. I'd been warned, but I hadn't listened.

We liked it rough, and Anatoly played for keeps.

So did I.

"I keep a kit under the bed, and I've got the ink the same color as your skin. I'll collar you tonight if you keep running your mouth, you damned tiger."

In reality, we'd be dozing or amusing ourselves in other ways, but I'd tattoo another mark on him as soon as he was unconscious and I wasn't—and left unsupervised for the time it'd take to leave my mark. I'd need a lot of the proper sedative to keep him blissfully unaware of me scraping him with my needles to leave my mark on his flesh. Again.

He gifted me with another gentle kiss to my throat. "It's a date. I'll do my best to run my mouth sufficiently to earn such a collar—or nibble you into submission. Either will work."

Pleased I'd be able to steal time with him one way or another, I closed my eyes and basked in his warmth.

THE LOW RUMBLE of Anatoly's growl woke me, and I tensed, preparing to put an end to whatever had disturbed him. He pinned me close, and when I bared my teeth to join him in growling, I got a mouthful of my comforter. Startled, I spit it out.

It occurred to me the damned tiger was likely protesting someone coming to force us to attend his damned meeting. I resented the interruption to my rest, and I rolled over, wiggling in Anatoly's arms until I nestled my chin against his shoulder. "I don't want to get up," I whined.

"We figured that out after your agents fruitlessly tried to get either one of you to wake up," my aunt announced. "They came in and found you two in a rather comatose state. So comatose, in fact, I summoned Cleo and Henry to figure out what was wrong with you two."

Well, shit. The pesky Secret Service agents must

have gotten worried and gone to my aunt at a loss of how to deal with me or my damned tiger.

Hell, I didn't know how to deal with me or my damned tiger.

Anatoly quieted, but he didn't ease his hold on me. "We're not dead."

"I see that. Feel better?"

"No. I was enjoying my nap, and Jesse's tired, too. Go away and leave us alone."

"I'm not going to go away, and I'm certainly not going to leave you alone." When my aunt took that tone of voice, it'd be easier to raise Washington from its watery grave than it'd be changing her mind. Fighting her would unleash mayhem, and I debated how best to annoy her for disturbing my nap. Before I could come up with a plan, she said, "Henry laughed when he had a look at you, and he left without a word, leaving Cleo to figure out what was wrong with you two. Cleo was so shocked Henry just up and left without a care in the world he stared at the door for a solid five minutes before gathering his wits. I can't say I blame him, as Henry takes his mystic duties seriously."

"I figured it out after I looked. I was just gobsmacked he actually left," the donkey said with laughter in his voice. "When the cause of concern is exhaustion and there's nothing actually wrong, it makes sense, Madam President. Henry's got a good feel for Anatoly, and Jesse's obvious. She was conked out so hard I bet they heard her snoring in Atlanta. Now, that snore is cause for concern, but we'll take care of it once she's not worn out. You have a pair of Siberians dancing around each other and no time for them to spend together. That's exhausting for a pair, Madam President. She's been climbing the walls, and the First Gentleman has even said he was worried about Anatoly's temper."

"Tell me in simple terms so I don't have to fret about these two."

"It's separation anxiety. In Jesse's case, she's spent her entire life working, and she's not handling the lack of a serious job well. Anatoly's used to work, and he still has his work, but he's tying himself in knots because she's anxious she's not working. Short form for dense grizzly bears: let them catch up on sleep. Once they're rested, send them into the meeting together, then send them out on a job."

"The Hope Diamond—"

Cleo snorted. "That stone has a mind of its own and likes Jesse. Nobody can steal it, and it's going to defend itself as it sees fit. Until it changes its mind, that's that. Locking her up in the palace isn't going to help anything. Anatoly needs to stretch his legs and get his roaming in, too. I know she's your niece, and I know you like the damned tiger, but caging them isn't going to help. They're so on edge the damned cats were fighting before they settled down for a nap, and they both managed to land some hits. It's just some bruising at this point, but you've got a pair of powder kegs set to blow, and they won't need a combustion zone when they finally explode. Let them sleep it off, then try again tomorrow, but give them both *meaningful* work to do."

"What he said," I announced before snuggling closer to Anatoly and closing my eyes. "Shh, you're noisy."

"Could you at least make it to a bed before doing that? You about gave Randal a heart attack when he found you two passed out on the floor with a faint scent of blood in the air. He'd thought someone had gotten into the room and done something to you."

Ah. That explained my aunt's reaction. "I had to put the damned Siberian in his place again."

Randal sighed. "While I should have guessed, could you both roar next time you're doing that so I know you're just being Siberians as usual?"

Huh. We had been rather quiet during our scuffle.

"I was too tired to roar," I replied. "I didn't mean to worry you. We were too tired to scuffle long, too. I'm sorry."

"Yet you did it anyway, one of you drew blood, and then you decided it was nap time." Randal heaved another sigh. "There's nothing to be sorry about. It's none of my business how you two want to beat each other when you're given a few minutes alone, but could you try to limit the actual bloodshed? I swear, I'm going to need therapy. No matter how often I'm told Siberians are aggressive with each other, I lose a few years off my life when I come in here and smell blood because you two were clawing at each other again."

Anatoly cuddled closer to me. "She gets feisty when

I want to hold her close. One of these days, I might tame her, but I do so enjoy her fight. I also have to be satisfying prey for her when she wants to enter my space. It is a ritual. I've got her nicely tamed for the moment, and if you'd stop talking and leave us alone, she might go back to sleep."

I really would.

"Damned tigers," Cleo muttered.

The donkey had been hanging out too much with Anatoly's mystic, and I grinned, aware he couldn't see my expression. "Where's Todd and Gentry?"

"They're getting yelled at by the First Gentlemen for their failure to contain a pair of tigers. By that, I mean you two," Cleo replied. "They were in here, but Todd started acting weird, then he started laughing, and he left and said we should just leave you two alone."

I needed to thank Todd for having some sense. "And Gentry?"

"He got recruited to wake Anatoly. He roared in your tiger's ear and barely got a grunt. At that point, he started acting weird, too, and left to go talk to Todd. I should go give them both a check. Everyone's acting weird."

The poor donkey likely had no idea what to make of me on the floor in my bathrobe practically wearing Anatoly. "Tigers are warm, Cleo. That's the only defense I need."

"And considering how shit you are at regulating your body temperature when you're tired and stressed, you likely got into a fight because you were cold and couldn't figure out how to ask him to hold you. You can just ask him to hold you, Jesse. He's not going to say no. In fact, the instant he finds out you're cold, he's going to get a blanket, wrap you in it, and hold you as long as you want."

I considered that. "Is he right, Anatoly?"

"Our way is more entertaining, but he's right. If you're cold, I'll do just that, and if that doesn't work, I'll piss you off until you start chasing me so you warm up that way. But I'd probably go get the blanket first."

Anatoly remained as shameless as always. No, even more shameless, as he'd stayed in a protective mode ever since Fort Lauderdale.

To my dismay, I'd grown used to having *someone* hovering to the point where I disliked being alone.

Too much had changed in too little time.

Hmm. "If we keep sleeping on the floor, we're going to be sore." I stretched a leg to discover I'd already crossed that threshold. Something creaked and popped. "Too late."

"Bed or bath?" Anatoly asked.

I wanted both, with him. "Eviction of the others first, then I will decide."

The tiger released me, sat up, and unleashed his loudest roar.

"That's hardly intimidating," my aunt replied. "Really, Anatoly. It's not like you're the only species here who can roar. I'm not going to run just from you roaring. You didn't even rattle my agents' nerves with that one. Are you sure you're quality enough of a Siberian for my niece?"

At Anatoly's growl, I smacked him in the gut hard enough he wheezed. "Leave, or I'll beat the tiger so bad he can't attend meetings for a week." I poked my head out from beneath my comforter, locked eyes with the grizzly, and hissed.

"I'm not sure if that's a punishment or a reward," my aunt admitted. "But if you're hissy enough you're thinking about making a run at me, I see all hope for the tiger is lost. I'll notify the council they're short a Siberian until tomorrow morning. Leave him in suitable condition for the meeting, and be prepared to attend yourself. If you two are going to suffer from separation anxiety of all things, that's an easy enough problem to solve. Really, I'm going to have to have a talk with your mother about this. Separation anxiety, Jesse?"

Even I recognized my aunt's case of severe disappointment. "I like my property where I can easily find and access him."

My aunt blinked, and then she narrowed her eyes. "Are you toying with me, little girl?"

"This is my tiger. I caught him. Get your own tiger if you want one. This one is *mine*."

"And that would be the hyperactive overprotective tendencies of a tigress on display. Madam President, if I may point something out?"

"What?"

"One, her agents scented blood, but nobody found

any on either of the overprotective tigers. This implies the blood was somehow removed. Upon investigation, his scent was only fresh in this room."

While I had expected the lot of them to go overboard, they'd done a sniff test of my suite?

Anatoly sighed.

"I'm aware. Continue," my aunt ordered, her tone implying she'd reached her limit.

"Neither one of them had gone to the pool or the bathroom. Judging from the scent markers, Jesse was only in her bedroom long enough to put on her robe. So, they were probably taking bites of each other and enjoying a fresh treat of tasty tiger."

"For fuck's sake!" My aunt drew in a breath and roared. "You two are idiots, aren't you?"

Yes, we were. Instead of answering her, I glared. She glared back.

"Madam President, please. She's probably trying to tell you to get the fuck out of her hair so she can resume resting, as she's unable to rest without her tiger around. They've been blocked from sharing a home, and at absolute most, they only get a passing nip at each other and limited brawls the few times he's out of meetings. Siberians take their time courting, and they've been nipping at each other for weeks. They probably got overenthusiastic about their nipping before they passed out. That would also explain why the others left while laughing. I'm just slow and dense because I'm used to a damned stallion who would mount a damned tree stump if it got flirty with him."

"I'm so telling Todd you think he'd assault a dead tree," I announced.

"Oh, he already knows. I used that line on him this morning. He laughed, and then he kicked me halfway into next week. I deserved it."

"Anything else you'd like to add to that, Cleo?" my aunt asked.

"Yeah, actually. There is. You can't change her nature, and she was named Runs Against Wind for good reason. Love her for what she is, and stop hoping for what she isn't. Give her a good sword, and not another shady metal toothpick someone probably got out of an alley. That thing is an insult to katanas. I know you want to baby her because she's never been babied a day in her life until now, but she is what she is, and you shouldn't change that. Anatoly loves her because of what she is, not because of what she could have been. She's a Siberian. All caging her will do is make her destroy the cage violently. Now that she's recovered, it's time to stop babying her and start letting her be herself. Let her fly, Madam President. More importantly, let her fall. This time around, she knows we're around to catch her. She's not stupid. She never was. She just didn't know what it meant to have a family, and she's figuring it out. You don't have to cling." Cleo's expression tightened, and then he laughed. "Now I get why those cowards fled. They didn't want to be the one to set you straight. You're going to take me out on a mat and beat me, aren't you?"

My aunt scowled, but then she relaxed, and a smile made an appearance. "That's a fair assessment. And yes, I probably will, but I'll let you off the hook for tonight. All right, Silverston. I'll permit you to move your crap into my house and invade my niece's quarters, but you better take damned good care of her, or I'll remind you why people are wise to fear grizzlies."

Anatoly grunted and covered his head with my blanket.

I raised a brow and poked his shoulder. "You're a pathetic tiger."

"I'm a tired tiger, and I don't want to get beaten up by a damned grizzly today. I got tenderized by one yesterday and this morning."

I growled. "Which one?"

"Gentry," my aunt said. "Some mat time and sparring would do you good, Jesse, so you can take your nerves out on him tomorrow. We'll get out of your hair, and we'll keep your detail outside of the suite tonight. Try not to trash all the furniture if you decide to get violent with him. Better yet, if you absolutely feel a need to go destroy something, have your agents take you to your tiger's home. You can destroy that, and he won't peep a complaint about it."

"Is that true, Ana?"

"To my eternal dismay and shame, it is," he grumbled. "I'd probably like it."

Of course he would. I grabbed the comforter, gave a yank, and wrapped it around my shoulders before staggering to my feet and heading for the warm, soft comfort of my bed. "I'm going back to bed. If you disturb me and your name isn't Anatoly, I may very well kill you."

Anatoly hopped to his feet with zero evidence of being tired and followed me into my room. To make it clear none of the interlopers were invited, I kicked the door closed. "Get out, and stay out!"

We listened until the main door of the suite closed. I couldn't tell if anyone remained within the sitting room, but I didn't care. I sighed and shook my head at their bizarre behavior.

"You're confused, aren't you?"

"Yes, I am."

"They're confused because we've been snapping our teeth at each other for weeks, we haven't mated, and they know it. Unfortunately for us, sex has a distinct smell, and it tends to linger. And don't tell me you haven't noticed when your aunt and uncle have been going at it. The first time you figured out what you were smelling, you stared at them in utter horror."

I groaned at the reminder. "He laughed at me, and he wouldn't stop laughing, and then I tried to decapitate my uncle with a dessert spoon for despoiling my aunt. And I said that. To his face."

Anatoly wrapped his arms around me, blanket and all, and hugged me close before kissing the top of my head. "You were magnificent."

"I was an idiot."

"You were that, too, but you were a most magnificent idiot. I can't look at the First Gentlemen now without cracking a grin. It's one of my few joys in life right now. He comes into a meeting, and I sniff. And depending on what I smell, I either cluck my tongue and display disappointment, or I smirk."

"I better tell him if he kills you, I will kill him."

"Good idea. Can I watch?"

Anatoly enjoyed watching me get my ass handed to me on the mat for one reason alone: sometimes, I won. Ever since my rabbit of an uncle had gotten his ass handed to him, he'd forgotten how to hold back, unleashing his mystic powers and his martial arts on me. When I won, Anatoly savored every moment of my victory, which made me work even harder to win. "All right. What was that nonsense about? I mean, okay. We were passed out on the floor taking a nap, so it makes sense they were worried. But that whole thing with Henry, Todd, and Gentry leaving like they did? What is that about?"

"They smelled blood, which they assume is from a bite, but there was no evidence either one of us had staged a successful seduction. They are aware Siberians mate for life, and they're also aware our bites are how we bond, except we've skipped straight to behaving like a bonded pair without any evidence of having mated."

Right. I was surrounded by idiots. I'd already said I owned the damned tiger. Granted, I'd been delirious at the time, but I'd meant it. "It's so much fun watching them try to convince me you're my boyfriend. I just play dumb, and they drive themselves crazy."

"And the entire time, you're perfectly aware and

content I'm yours to do with as you please. You told them I was yours, anyway. It's not my fault they blame your illness and forgot how damned honest you are. And I am yours, of course. You're also mine to do with as I please, and you display only just enough protest to satisfy our instinctual need to be as difficult as possible. As do I, of course."

"Of course."

"In short, Henry figured out we've been dancing around bonding for weeks, and we've done all the appropriate steps except actually mate. I have no intentions of ruining our fun and ending the chase early. It will be that much more satisfying for us both. But, you've been nibbling at me, bit by bit staking your claim without leaving any actual marks for weeks. I, as I'm a wise tiger who does not mind breaking tradition as needed to win, have been doing the same. We've actively been seeking out a bond and a staking of claims, so it makes a great deal of sense. I'm quite pleased you will be stuck with me for the rest of our lives. I've gotten the better end of this deal, I'm afraid." Anatoly stalked closer, looking me over with a hungry expression. "I'm enjoying the chase, and will be rather unhappy if any interlopers try to end it early."

Sometimes—no, most times—I questioned the tiger's sanity. "And what does that mean for me?"

"It means you may hunt me at your earliest pleasure. I'm no fool, Jesse. Perhaps I'm a virgin, which is true enough, as I honor my agreements, but I'm no fool. You're no virgin, that much I've figured out on my own, but that doesn't change anything. You're not ready for us to take that step. Yet. I'm in this for the long haul. I know you are. You don't need to tell me that. You're not the kind to quit once you decide to do something, and I knew the instant you started sneaking nibbles that you wanted to make sure no one else would claim what you rightfully believe is yours. Of course, I'm going to work very hard to earn my proper bite, which should be brutal enough to leave a permanent scar."

"I have cream for that."

He laughed. "Simple problem, simple solution?"

"Precisely. I also have tattooing needles, and I'm happy to add to my collection of ownership marks to your person."

Anatoly smiled. "As far as I'm concerned, you'd bitten and marked me that day, and I do not care what anyone else says. I don't know what I did to deserve it, but I'm grateful."

At first, I'd feared and regretted tattooing my mark on Anatoly, but time had changed me. What had once been a shame had grown into one of the best choices I'd made in my life. Everything I had become had started with that one short meeting in a bar with Steel Heart as a witness. I still cursed the stone for making a mess of my life with its strong will and determination to roll wherever it pleased.

I grinned. "You're demented."

"I'm that, too."

"You were you. Smug, handsome, and egotistical."

He'd been dark, confident, and interesting, too. He still was.

He smiled but said nothing.

In addition to learning it was all right for someone to show affection for me, I'd begun doing the same for others, even when I found admitting it to be disconcerting bordering on embarrassing. "I like all of those things about you."

"Well, conveniently, there's a lot of things I like about you, too. I would go as far as to say I love them about you, for that matter. I've figured out I'll have to ease you into this, as a beautiful Blade Clan warrior queen such as yourself will have a difficult time handling this. You weren't taught how to be affectionate or show love. It's a part of the clan culture. Like brothers, but still distant."

"Death is our true and constant companion," I recited, the memories of my childhood still lingering despite my efforts to cast them aside. "The only one we were to be one with was our blade and our bride."

"You got a groom instead."

"I got a groom instead," I conceded.

"I'm quite pleased I'm your groom. I'm even more pleased that you're my bride. I still have that document. I've held onto it despite all the whiners complaining about how I should get rid of it. That precious sheet of paper protects you most of all."

I raised a brow at that. "It does?"

"The Blade Clan will want you back, but you're *my* bride, and I am not giving you back. That will put them in a difficult position. They won't kill a man or his bride to take one or the other. That's not the Blade Clan way. I've had long talks with Gentry about this. I've also endured many a beating from Gentry, too. I'll endure many more in the coming days, too."

I tensed. "Why is he beating you?"

"The groom has to wage the wars by their customs. I was not born of the Blade Clan. I don't have a Blade Clan warrior's skills. I need them to prove I'm worthy of you."

"No, you don't. I'll fight them all."

And I would win. They waged wars and fought bloody battles, but I had faced the real world, and I had survived through it with my wit and my blade. Not only would I prove my worth, I would do so with an inferior blade.

No. Actually, I wouldn't. A better idea flitted through my head. I could borrow Gentry's sword and use the weapon that had purchased my life to secure my future. "I have an idea, Ana."

"Should I be concerned? I often become concerned when you have ideas."

"As a matter of fact, yes. I need a new sword, and I know the perfect place to get one."

"You do?"

"I do."

"From where?"

"Gentry, of course. I will use the shorter blade, and you will take the longer one. We will crush the clan with the swords that had been my mother's bride price." I allowed myself to smile. “We won’t defend our future. We’ll aggressively claim it from them. And when we are finished with them, there will be no doubt of my choice at all.”

I was a woman, and they would hear me roar.

No longer would I be ashamed of what I had become.

I had chosen wisely from the start.

Chapter Three

I KICKED Anatoly out of my bedroom long enough to dress in my Cheyenne tribal leathers. To get my way with my grizzly of an uncle, I'd need every weapon I could get my hands on. He wouldn't give up his swords without a fight, and for my fledgling plan to work, I'd need to put up a damned good fight.

I either needed to take his swords or get one that could hold up to a Blade Clan warrior's ruthless strength.

Then again, after seeing what the Hope Diamond had done to Matt's bat, I might be able to make one of my own—if the stone cooperated with me.

As far as I was concerned, if the stone interfered with my claim over Anatoly, we would have words. And I'd come armed with a hammer.

I didn't care how much trouble I'd get into with my aunt and her governmental goonies.

When I emerged, Anatoly had straightened his

clothes and had made himself look as presentable as possible despite having taken a nap in his suit. As I'd been taught how to tie a tie by a mixture of uncles, Todd, and anyone male with a tie nearby, I slapped his hands away and took over the task.

Every time I tied one for someone, I got a little better at it, and I adjusted it to my satisfaction. "I like this on you," I announced.

"The red is similar to my blood after you land a good bite, isn't it?"

I considered it, and I realized he was right. "I keep wanting to bite you. Obsessively. And drag you off."

"Well, yes. We are Siberians, and that is what we do. It's a constant battle, isn't it?"

"We should go beat on Gentry. We'll feel better."

"I agree with you."

I marched to the main door of my suite, opened it, and poked my head outside, startling Randal and Simmons. "Is my asshole uncle still here?"

Randal raised a brow. "Which one?"

"The grizzly one, not that heathen that keeps violating my aunt."

Both agents cracked grins at that and Randal nodded. "He is. He's with Madam President right now. They went to her office right after she left here."

"I need to see him, and I intend on beating him and stealing his Blade Clan swords. Both of them. I'm giving the one to Anatoly, I'm selfishly keeping the other, and we're going to beat up the Blade Clan."

According to Randal's expression, I had lost my mind.

I probably had.

"Let me see if I understand this. You want your uncle's Blade Clan weapons, which he received as your mother's bride price, so you can beat up the entirety of the Blade Clan?"

"Yes."

"But why?"

I pointed at Anatoly. "He's the groom. I'm the bride. They'll try to initiate him, my groom. He is not Blade Clan trained. I am. I figure with him as a handicap, I can give them a fair fight."

Simmons closed his eyes as though the weight of the entire world crashed down on his shoulders.

"Do you need a few minutes, Simmons?"

"How did you go from catching up on sleep to wanting to beat up the Blade Clan?"

"Well, it's their fault I'm in this mess to begin with, they'll beat my tiger if I don't, and they're a threat to my tiger. Mostly, they're a threat to *my* tiger."

Anatoly chuckled and he gave my shoulder a squeeze. "Relax, Jesse. I'm not helpless. Gentry has been teaching me. You can ask them. They've been helping."

Both of my agents grimaced.

"They've been beating you up, too?"

"Ruthlessly, really. It's been necessary, Jesse. I'm aware of how the Blade Clan operates, and I'm aware of how the contracts work. I've known ever since I was young. I became very familiar with the contract terms when it became apparent you'd become the bride and I'd become the groom. I'm not trained to the level someone from the Blade Clan is, but I'm almost to the point where I can hold my own. I've been run around for at least an hour a day, usually when you're asleep. Your aunt's detail keeps an eye on you while I've been working with your agents."

I breathed until the urge to beat my agents subsided. "I want to see what you've been doing to my tiger."

"Well, you're handling this better than I thought," Randal said, his expression easing. "Madam President has been worried, and with your illness, she didn't want to strain you with the amount of training we're putting him through. You're still rebuilding your muscle and endurance, and there has been some concern you shoulder won't handle the strain of weapon training."

However much I hated it, he spoke the truth. "I'll just be rebuilding it more rigorously starting now. If we're going to take on that damned clan, we need to be able to fight together. That means we need to train together. I don't care if you beat me black and blue. And if I break my shoulder again, Henry and Cleo will fix it. Let me repeat myself: I don't care if you beat me black and blue."

"You may not care if you're beaten black and blue, but your tiger does. Your tiger is very jealous and protective."

"And I will beat my tiger into submission if necessary. One round with the sword should put the bastard in his place and remind him I'm not a delicate little flower."

Anatoly grinned. "I look forward to you putting me in my place. I expect you to keep doing so until I knock you flat on your pretty ass."

"Pretty?"

"I think you're very pretty."

I stared at him.

My agents cracked up laughing, and Randal lifted his hand to his ear. "Stiletto to Oval Office," he announced.

Well, that made sure I got a move on, and I stepped out from beneath Anatoly's hold on my shoulder, slid behind him, and pushed him in the direction of my aunt's office. "We have demands we must make of her."

"We do?"

"She has to fetch your clothing and whatever else you need from your house. Also, we need to establish an escape route so we can go hide in your house when this becomes unbearable. I haven't even seen your house yet."

"You will soon enough," Anatoly promised. "We'll sneak over after dinner tomorrow night. I'll make certain there are no meetings even if I have to start mauling people."

"Okay. I can work with that. I will help you with the mauling. It will be a joint venture."

"What happened to getting some sleep?" Randal

asked.

"I can't sleep when I'm worried. Right now, I'm worried. I have a toothpick of a sword that would break if a Blade Clan warrior looked at it wrong. For my peace of mind, I require a real weapon. One that isn't a toothpick someone fetched out of an alley."

That earned a sigh from my agents.

"I can't help it. I'm a Siberian, I'm a mean Siberian, and I'm apparently freakishly jealous over my tiger. And no, for the final time, he is *not* my boyfriend."

"What is he, then?" Simmons asked.

"Mine. Just mine. Period. Stop. If you want to call him anything, Jesse's tiger. Or Run Against Wind's tiger. Whichever appeals at whichever point in time. But this tiger is *mine*."

"Mate is the word you're looking for, Jesse," Anatoly said, his tone light with laughter. "You may as well say it. The word won't bite you. You might bite me, I might bite you, but the word won't bite you."

Simmons snorted. "Might? She's bitten you so many times in the past month we stopped counting. Sometimes, she even tries to hide she's doing it. Drawing blood was an unexpected escalation. It was unexpected enough it hadn't occurred to me a bite had been responsible for the scent of blood."

"She's quite frustrated right now," Anatoly replied with a grin, leaning back into my hands in an attempt to slow our progress down the hall. "She would have preferred a few hours to nibble at her whim, but she got flustered. When she gets flustered, she bites. She just bit me a little harder than she meant is all." Anatoly lifted his arm and pushed up his sleeve, showing off where I'd bitten him. His wound had healed to a faint pale mark. "It was a pure frustration bite."

Like hell it was. I hissed at him and kept shoving him along. "Walk faster, tiger."

"And that little mark you left on her upper arm?" Randal asked, pointing right below where the sleeve of my tunic fell.

Sure enough, a white, healing mark betrayed where Anatoly had gotten a hold of me with his teeth. I scowled. "I'm sure he was just a little frustrated, too. I mean, I'd just bitten the hell out of him. It seemed fair he'd retaliate."

Both agents sighed, and Simmons shook his head. "You two are such tigers."

Anatoly grinned, and then, as he had a death wish, he spun out of my hands, stepped to my side, and kissed where he'd bitten me. "Does that make it all better, my warrior princess?"

I smacked him upside the head. "Idiot. It's your fault I bit you."

"It is?"

"You fell onto my teeth."

"I… what?"

"Fell onto my teeth."

"You know what? I'm not going to ask about that. While we certainly did fall off the couch, I didn't directly fall onto your teeth. I fell onto you."

"That is the equivalent of falling onto my teeth."

"That makes no sense, Jesse."

"If you hadn't tried to squish me, I wouldn't have bitten you. As such, you fell right onto my teeth."

We argued about the circumstances of both of us sporting healing bite marks all the way to the Oval Office, and upon arrival, Randal grabbed my ear and twisted while Simmons snatched Anatoly. While I howled a protest over the abuse of my ear, the agents dragged us inside.

"Why are you dragging them in here by their ears?" my aunt asked. "I just left those two alone to sleep." Then, to my horror, my aunt did a sniff test. "They were not sleeping, it seems. What's going on now?"

Simmons pointed at my shoulder while Randal pointed at Anatoly's wrist.

My aunt rose from her seat, circled her monster of a desk, and strolled over. She took hold of my arm in a light grip and turned it for a better look at my fresh bite mark. "I see someone got a little excited with his teeth."

"She claims he fell onto her teeth and thus deserved to be bitten. He simply retaliated."

My aunt released me, and she examined the bite on Anatoly's wrist. He waved with his other hand while grinning. "Madam President."

"And that explains the source of the blood. And they haven't been entertaining each other in bed, just biting each other?"

"They've been biting each other for weeks, but they haven't drawn blood until now," Randal reported, keeping a firm grip on my ear. "She's begging for a beating on the mat, and she doesn't care if her shoulder breaks. She also doesn't care if we beat her black and blue."

My aunt laughed. "Of course. So, you fell onto her teeth, Anatoly?"

"No, Madam President. I fell on top of her, and she decided that meant I deserved to be bitten."

"And the circumstances of this fall?"

"She bit me."

My aunt tossed her hands up in the air. "She bit you before she bit you? And her biting you the first time resulted in you landing on the floor?"

"Well, I was expecting a delicate little nibble, and she went for my throat like I was a freshly grilled steak. As I was expecting a delicate nibble, she startled me. I went for her throat, because that's what startled tigers do, and we fell off the couch. Then she bit me again. I, of course, had to retaliate with a bite of my own. Then we decided it was time to take a nap, so we took a nap."

"He was warm."

"Are you still having trouble regulating your body temperature, Jesse?"

I shrugged. "He was warm, I was not. I took advantage of him. I refuse to be ashamed of this. I'm going to tattoo a collar around his neck in gold ink. I'm debating on the design."

"No."

"Why not?"

"You already have one tattoo on his person. You've

left your mark. You do not need to leave a third mark. You just bit him."

"It'll fade."

My aunt raised a brow.

"Why are you looking at me like that?"

"Jesse, you bit him over six hours ago. That little love bite would have been long gone by now. You bit him properly. He immediately retaliated, too. I see bites all the time. I know what they look like. I'm quite happy for you, but if you could stop trying to scare years off my life, I'd appreciate it. If I let anything happen to you, your mother will murder me. Just one day without you wandering off or getting into trouble, please. I really thought someone had gotten into your suite and poisoned you both."

Ouch. I hadn't realized we'd been out on the floor for *that* long. "Can the day I behave be tomorrow? I'll go to the council meeting, get beat up by the grizzly, and then go to Ana's to see his house because I've never seen it before."

My aunt pointed at my mark on Anatoly's wrist. "That mark says it's your house, too, and that pesky contract Anatoly refuses to have revoked likewise makes it clear you have a claim on it. That contract is going to be a problem, Anatoly."

"She's mine."

"I'm well aware you're hers. I'm going to be quite pleased when I don't have to deal with you whining about your situation in here. I do question why Jesse is taking her time with you, though."

"She's savoring the hunt, of course. I'm a prime specimen for her enjoyment."

My aunt's brow rose even higher. "Are you planning on seducing your mate sometime this year, or should we hold your union party in a decade or two?"

My face warmed, and I spluttered.

"Right now, we are enjoying advanced lessons on kissing. She's a very thorough educator, and I look forward to more teachings. I see zero reason to graduate until she's showed me everything she can do with her rather versatile tongue."

I covered my mouth with my hands, and my face heated so much I worried I would spontaneously combust despite the lack of a combustion zone.

"I see. Very well. Obviously, I have not been giving you two sufficient time to continue your private education lessons. This is entirely my fault, as I'm an old idiot who forgot how thorough and meticulous my niece can be. Right. All right. Behave yourself tomorrow, Jesse. The meeting will last until two, with a short break for lunch, and then Anatoly is slated to train for three hours. After that, we'll have a family dinner. You can bring your tiger. After dinner, we'll take a trip to Anatoly's house."

"We will?" Anatoly and I chorused.

"Of course. We. You two might attempt to elope. The rabbit might be fast enough to catch you. Gentry can help. Gentry, bring Felicity."

"I'd be delighted to. It's been a while since she's been over for dinner. How about Todd?"

"Yes, that's a good idea," my aunt replied. "Just Todd, however."

My eyes widened. "Not Marie?"

"Marie has been particularly bitchy lately, and she's been saying things I don't like."

I'd learned my aunt lived a life of drama as part of her duties. "What sort of things?"

"She doesn't seem to like you all that much. She thinks you take up too much of Todd's time from the guild and the herd. They're having quite a spat over it, really."

I sighed, but I understood. To Marie, the herd came first—as did her children. I wasn't part of the herd, nor would I ever be part of the herd, no matter how close of a friend I considered Todd. "That's to be expected, I suppose. She's very protective of the herd. As she should be. She's the lead mare."

"Todd keeps a wardrobe of clothing for you in case you need it, and she definitely doesn't like that. She's jealous because you have his friendship, much like a member of the herd, all without being in the herd. You understand a stallion's sense of loyalty and determination, and Todd has few friends who do. Anatoly understands it as well. It is part of being a Siberian. She has regrets she didn't protest your, ah, let me see if I remember how she phrased this." My aunt rubbed her chin with narrowed eyes, which she focused on Gentry.

"She rode him like she owned him, and he went along with it anyway," my uncle replied, his expression neutral.

"Something along those lines," my aunt agreed. "So, be careful around her, Jesse. You'll slaughter her in a fight without breaking a sweat, but she can make things difficult on you. The rest of Todd's herd adores you, as they know you're willing and able to put that mean old stallion in his place. Still, I want you to keep an eye out. I don't trust her at this point in time."

After decades of judging character, I figured my aunt was onto something. "I'll keep an eye out. If she does anything to hurt Todd, well, she won't live to learn from that mistake."

"We're going to have to work on that," my aunt muttered.

"What? It's true. If she's gotten to the stage where she's willing to hurt Todd, her children, and the rest of her herd, I'd be merciful putting her down. Todd won't have mercy on her."

I'd been around Todd long enough to understand some of the bitter truths about the stallion. He took such betrayals seriously, and he wouldn't kill the woman who'd been his wife for decades. He'd exile her from the herd, and then no herd would take her.

Mares needed herds as much as wolves needed packs.

My aunt sighed. "I sometimes forget just how much of the world you've seen, especially when you slip in and out of the shadows, stalking around your own damned house like a thief."

I snorted at that. "This place is too big to be a house. It's more like a maze that happens to have comfortable rooms people tend to stay in for extended periods of time. Anatoly has a house, and I might try to run away and live in it."

"I'm going to have to go with what she said," Anatoly replied. Careful to keep his motions slow and smooth, he pried my agent's fingers off of his ear and freed himself before flopping onto the couch. "I don't mind making this my temporary residence until you get over your overprotective grizzly tendencies. It's hard being an overprotective grizzly, all those instincts demanding you maul anyone who looks at your pretty little niece wrong."

"So many people to maul, so little time," the President of the United States complained. "And then they get upset when I maul. It's just not fair."

My rabbit of an uncle strode in through one of the room's hidden doors, and he laughed. "Who do you want to maul today, babe?"

"Everyone, really. Everyone has just been so damned annoying. And then these two!"

"They were just tired post biting. Next, they'll be tired post mating. Give them a break, babe. They're Siberians."

"Must everyone insist on reminding us of our species? It's not like we're going to forget." Following Anatoly's lead, I eased out of Randal's grip and joined my tiger on the couch. "It's like you want us to snap and rampage."

"That would be fun," the rabbit mystic replied, and he perched on his wife's desk. "If you're going to exhaust yourselves with those little love bites, do try to find your way to a bed first. That way, it's less alarming for your poor, old agents."

My agents sighed.

"You're the reason my agents are exhausted. If you hadn't put them in charge of the Secret Service, they'd be less tired." Part of my containment in the government's seat of power involved them being able to handle their duties as the joint lead agents of the entire Secret Service. The talks of shifting them off my detail had ended when I'd shifted and tried to drag both off while snarling and roaring.

I liked my agents, and I didn't want to lose them to damned paperwork. To make it clear I had no intention of relinquishing them to even my aunt, I narrowed my eyes and hissed at her.

My aunt laughed. "Easy there, little girl. We're not going to steal your agents. I got some paper pushers in to help with their duties. I do want you to meet with some available agents to see if there are any you get along with, but we can ease you into it. I want you to have six solid agents. Nate, you will accept four, with the understanding Jesse's will also be keeping an eye on you."

"Blossom snuck a lioness in. She offered to help tenderize me. And she offered to try to get me back on courier runs where I belong. I like her. I might even remember her name if you give me a few minutes."

Beverly wouldn't mind if I played extra stupid with

my aunt. She dealt with Siberians all the time, and we liked making things difficult by default.

"Randal?"

"It's Beverly, yes, they've met, and she was at that little brawl at the bar down the street. For the sake of our sanity, please lift the alcohol ban. Matt likes her, she generally nurses her beers, and nobody has actually seen her get drunk outside that one incident." Randal glared at me. "And yes, I heard about you drinking after being dosed with a sedative. I'll tan your hide myself if I catch you doing something that stupid again."

Ouch. I rated my agent as more threatening than even my aunt. "Noted. I'll be more inclined to stay put if there is a beer in my evening schedule. I like beer, damn it."

"But can you stop at one beer?" my aunt challenged.

"I usually stop at two. That way, I can be armed with a broken beer bottle if need to while sipping on the second."

"It's true. When I first saw her, she was sipping at a beer. She only lost her temper when that damned rock made a mess of her quiet enjoyment of her beer. But don't mess with her beer. The mercs I'd been following when trying to retrieve Steel Heart interrupted her beer sipping, and she taught them a lesson. Then cleaned out their pockets, lined them up on the bar, and had her turn with me." Anatoly laughed and shook his head. "I'm still stunned you got away with that. How did you even do it? I still haven't figured it out."

"I sedated you with a needle, masked it with a scratch of my nail, and then took my sweet time with you after the rest of the cowards in the bar ran away from that damned rock."

"I like to think Steel Heart recognized you belong to me and led me right to you. Then you wisely claimed ownership, and it ran off, its work done for the moment." Anatoly bumped me with his elbow. "Have I earned being collared yet?"

"No," my aunt replied. "You are not being collared. You aren't collaring my niece, either. If you want to get a tattoo, get one properly, and that doesn't mean using it as a method to maul each other. If you want to indulge in a mauling, do so. If you want to indulge in a mauling that results in children, do so after talking with Henry and Cleo to make sure everything goes well."

I rolled my eyes, as I'd already gotten that talk several times from everyone I knew, including Todd. The foal-obsessed stallion had given me the talk five times. I'd indulged his fretting, keeping my mouth shut that I'd educated myself on safe sex practices from age ten, upon deciding to become a woman instead of a man. It helped I'd picked partners with no interest in supporting unexpected children.

Children tended to end mercenary careers, and I'd wisely picked mercenaries who meant to maintain their career. It helped I'd warned every man I'd been with I'd castrate them if they ditched on their fatherly duties should a child come along. Scratching certain itches worked best when it didn't become a lifelong commitment.

Gentry grinned. "I think she's tired of hearing us old shifters teach her what she probably figured out before she tacked a teen onto her age, Stephanie. And she tries to be so patient about it, too."

"What? It's our job. Her layabout mother isn't here to do it, and don't even talk to me about her father. I've a mind to insert my foot up her father's ass."

"Relax, Stephanie. You'll alarm your agents. When you start talking like that, you start taking action, and her father *is* part of the Blade Clan. And Jesse's 'layabout mother' will kick your ass and feed your foot to you. And, frankly, I know exactly what our sister is up to, you're hiding it from Jesse, and I've a mind to spill the beans just to watch the fallout."

My brows shot up. "You have my attention. All I know right now is that I have my mother's eyes."

"You also have her stubborn pride, willingness to inflict general injury on those deserving a beating, and so many of her temperaments that it's obviously genetic," my aunt muttered. "Gentry, it's like there are two of them, and this is disturbing. Worse, I think she got all the good traits out of the Blade Clan, added in all the good traits from our line, and then magically inherited all of her mother's bad habits. All in all, she's perfection, and I'm not sure Nate's good enough for her."

"Nate is good enough for her," my uncles chorused.

Huh. I relaxed against the couch and inched

towards Anatoly. He lifted his arm to make room for me, and I claimed my rightful place snuggled against his side. "I agree with the rabbit and the grizzly. He's more than good enough for me. I like this tiger, and I will keep him. I may murder anyone who tries to take this tiger from me."

"That goes both ways, Jesse," Anatoly replied.

"Only if you beat me to the chase."

"Why am I not surprised?"

I snorted. "You have a brain, and on occasion, you decide to use it."

"It's true. Splendid male tiger specimens, such as myself, do tend to become quite focused on our duties as splendid male tigers. We develop a very concentrated sense of focus. I'll work hard to make sure you don't have to lift a finger to beat interloping males *or* females. Unless you want to. But since you're you, you will want to. Every day. I'll have my work cut out for me."

As it was true, I shrugged. "Obviously, I need to have a talk with my mother about this. And my father. Preferably in the same room at the same time."

"That might not be a wise idea," my aunt replied with a grimace.

"Why not?"

"Well, knowing your mother, having listened to her rants, and otherwise having done my best to contain her general impulses, should they be in the same room together at the same time, you might bear unfortunate witness to the creation of a brother or sister. My sister is likely the reason you turned out to be a Siberian, as she's got all of the general tendencies of a Siberian while trapped in a grizzly body."

Knowing my aunt liked to yank my chain at every opportunity, I turned to Gentry for verification.

Like his sister, he grimaced. "It's true. She would, and she's not at all shy, and if she thought she could tame your father again, she really would. And she'd likely steal my swords to do it."

Ah-ha. Swords. Somehow, I'd forgotten my real purpose in visiting. "I'm stealing your swords, and I'm going to use the short one, and Anatoly is going to use the longer one, and we're going to beat up a weapon clan. We'll give them back when we're finished."

He sighed. "You would. Are you sure you don't want weapons of your own?"

"If I'm going to shame the Blade Clan, I'd like to do so with a quality weapon. Their pride would never recover if I beat them with inferior steel, Gentry. I'm mean, but I try not to be cruel. That would just be cruel."

"I will temporarily loan you the weapons, but wouldn't it be better to have a blade that better suited you?"

"I have a twig someone picked out of an alley that was shaped to somewhat resemble a katana, and it will probably break if I crossed it in battle with a toothpick," I complained.

"I think I can find you something better than something that crude. But you work well with a katana, and it suits you. You'd be better off with a katana."

"Where the hell am I going to find another katana of that quality?" I complained.

"That katana was a showcase blade, Jesse. I don't think it was ever truly meant to see battle. It was a badge of honor and a gift from the Blade Clan. And while it did see battle—and did well for years—it was always more meant to be a thing of beauty than a thing of war." Gentry shook his head. "I retrieved the weapon and had it reforged." The grizzly lumbered towards the door, cracked it open, and muttered a few words to someone outside. "But since you're ready to wage war with me to get your hands on a good blade so you can keep your tiger, I suppose now is the time you should have it."

"You had my katana reforged?"

"It was too beautiful a thing to waste, and you loved that sword. Of course we had it reforged. Todd helped. He knows the blacksmith who forged the original. The blacksmith was eager for a second chance with the blade, as he'd always found it to be a labor of love more than functionality. An odd sentiment from someone of the Blade Clan, but it is what it is. I think you'll be pleased."

"I will be? Why? I mean, beyond having my sword back."

"Todd says the blacksmith believes this to be the best working of his life, and after having seen the blade, I believe him."

"But the Blade Clan lost their stone," I muttered.

Everyone snorted, and I raised a brow at that, but

rather than asking what they meant, I waited. In time, they'd tell me—or they wouldn't.

I didn't wait long, and Gentry grinned, leaning against the room's curved wall. "Apparently, it 'showed up at the appropriate time' before wandering off. He didn't seem all that disappointed it rolled off on its own business again. In fact, we were informed we could kiss his ass if we thought he'd be 'that damned stone's keeper.' He seems to think it has business to attend to, and he's quite happy letting it attend to its business. He was quite pleased it showed up long enough to assist him in the reforging of your new blade."

"Yet the entire government is freaking out that it can't retrieve the stone to give it back to the same person who just forged that blade?" I lifted my hands, yanked at my hair, and yowled my fury over such rampant stupidity—stupidity that kept Anatoly busy all of the time.

"The Blade Clan, admittedly, is the least concerned over the loss of their Starfall stone. They've adapted a rather casual take on the stone coming and going as it pleases. According to the report, he finished five blades in the time the stone stuck around, which armed their best young warriors. They're happy. If they're happy, we're happy. The problem is with Sunder."

"Sunder?" The name implied it was another Starfall stone, and a worrisome one at that.

My aunt huffed. "I wish you'd stop running your mouth, Gentry. If you'd stop running your mouth, we'd have a few secrets left, damn it!"

"If you had fewer secrets, the little girl here would be far more cooperative, as she'd better understand the stakes at play here. So, I'm solving the problem. It's so much better if she works for us than against us. It's one thing to keep her in the dark while she's ill; the mystics didn't want her being stressed. But now? She's on the prowl, her tiger's on the prowl, too, and there's absolutely no reason for us to not make use of all of the people available. That includes both of them. In their full capacity. Stephanie, she's an adult. I know you want to treat her like a little girl, but she's back on her feet. You can't turn her into a child again. It doesn't work that way."

"I don't see why not."

"That's not how life works, Stephanie."

"It should be." My aunt huffed. "Very well. Jesse, Sunder is a rogue stone. The clan who once wielded it has been wiped out. They lasted a single generation. Sunder's ability was the cause of their demise, as nobody wants anyone possessing a Starfall stone able and willing to destroy anything in its path. The only thing it can't break is another Starfall stone. So, if Sunder ever crosses your path, do not let it touch your weapon. Unless your weapon was forged with a stronger stone, and that stone sees fit to preserve your blade, it will be shattered. I don't know if a Blade Clan weapon can survive Sunder's touch. I'd rather you not find out."

Ew. "I don't like that stone. What does it look like?"

"A smooth, black sphere that has similar qualities to

the Hope Diamond. We theorize Sunder was a piece of the same Starfall stone that made the Hope Diamond. It's quite distinctive, really." My aunt wrinkled her nose. "It's about the same size as Steel Heart. All those stones are. But for now, I'm going to have you focus your efforts on Steel Heart. You're the only one we have with a hope in hell of keeping it from wandering off, as you're a part of the Blade Clan."

The last thing the world needed was another Hope Diamond. One of them created enough trouble, especially for me. "Anything else I should know?"

Gentry and my aunt exchanged looks, and my rabbit of an uncle tossed his head back and laughed. "You two just told her, without a shadow of a doubt, there's something else she should know. You may as well tell her, or she's going to create trouble for you. Remember, she *was* named Runs Against Wind for a reason, and she is not afraid of doing difficult things."

"We lost track of Ferdinand," my aunt confessed. "He's been stricken from Dawnfire's roster, stripped of his rank in the guild, and otherwise blacklisted, but he's a threat. I have no idea where he is. Nobody does. But he's a mad wolf now, and he's a mad wolf who had his eyes on you, Jesse. Keep a watch out. Truth be told, I didn't say anything because you've been using Nate as your personal chew toy, but if he comes around, he'll try something. It's a concern. It's less of a concern now that you're using Nate as your personal chew toy. The situation has changed. He won't be able to use his wolf magic on you."

The last thing I needed in my life was a damned wolf trying to make a mess of things. "What do you want me to do if I run into him?"

"Considering Nate got his teeth on you, and that you got your teeth on him, I want you to play along should you cross paths with Ferdinand. There's not a lot of information on what happens if a pair of wolves try to fight over the same woman with their bite; from my understanding of it, he who bit first wins. Nate bit first, so Nate wins. And since he's been chewing on you probably as much as you've been chewing on him, Ferdinand isn't going to have a hope in hell of establishing a bond with you. I'll write up a contract tonight. Play along, pretend Ferdinand is getting his way, learn what he's up to, and put an end to it. Mad wolves are easily deceived, so you shouldn't have a problem. But there's a catch."

"What catch?"

"I'd rather we keep this from Todd. He's been hurt enough, especially considering his problems with Marie. While Ferdinand was Gentry's wolf, they've worked together, too. Usually on joint efforts between the two guilds. Oh, they had their fights, and Todd has a certain amount of dislike for him now, but still. Todd doesn't want you having to do work as an assassin. To add to the complexity of the problem, once upon a time, Todd and Ferdinand had been friends. Do your work quietly, knowing of Ferdinand's guilt without shadow of a doubt—and don't feel a need to give him a proper mark. He isn't worthy of even your needles."

Gentry heaved a sigh. "However much I hate agreeing with you on this, Steph, you're probably right. Todd wouldn't react well to us asking this of Jesse, either. He's basically assigned himself as an honorary uncle, as it seems Jesse doesn't have enough uncles doting on her."

While it had taken me time to accept having a family, I'd learned I enjoyed the relationships I had with my various uncles, even the damned rabbit.

In the end, Ferdinand needed to be dealt with, and one concern rose above the rest. "Do you think he's bitten anyone against her will?" I asked, my voice refusing to rise above a whisper.

"I know so, which is why I'm authorizing you to use lethal force. I trust you to do what is necessary." My aunt grimaced. "I believe he's tried to, or has, taken more than one woman, which is a good thing for them. The more times a mad wolf bites, the less of a hold he has on the women he's ensnared. I can only hope they'll emerge relatively unscathed once he's killed."

Anatoly growled, which I recognized as his precursor to having a fit over my aunt's edict. I rammed my elbow into his side. "And the women?"

"Do whatever you can for them. He's old, he's cunning, and he's got more tricks up his sleeve than most. It's safer for all of us to assume he'll try something, and that he'll use his every resource—even your compassionate nature. You're the one that got away, and he's aware of your nature and why you operate as you do. That's part of why I've been trying to keep you under close guard. I'd rather if he came to you, he did so where the Secret Service can deal with him—or the guilds. It's a concern."

When my aunt viewed something as a concern, she meant it kept her up at night from worrying. "I can do that. But I'll skip on the contract and take a pardon instead. This one? This one is on the house."

I'd already killed family once under contract, and for all Ferdinand lacked blood ties to Todd, they'd been friends for a long time. To me, that came close enough.

If the situation deteriorated to the point I needed to kill the wolf, I wanted to be able to look into Todd's eyes, tell him the truth, and promise I'd done my work out of necessity rather than money. It wasn't a lot, but in the world of mercenaries and assassins, it would be enough.

Chapter Four

WHILE ALMOST EVERYTHING about my katana had changed, I recognized the hilt as mine, although it had undergone significant modification. The blue fire opals and diamonds remained, but turquoise joined them in decorating the weapon, a nod to the Cheyenne tribe who'd fostered me for so many years out west. Gold and platinum still played their parts in the design, a testament to beauty and strength working together to make a perfect whole.

Gentry handed me the weapon, and when I gripped the hilt, a blue and black gleam ran across the length of the blade before soaking into the fuller. I'd seen Starfall-touched blades before. I'd lusted for one as a child. Steel Heart had touched my first blade—and my second—but neither had shown signs of power. They hadn't been the true, prized blades of the clan.

My new weapon held secrets, and I looked forward to discovering each and every one of them.

"It matches the Hope Diamond," I whispered.

"So it does. I'd noticed that when Todd brought it in. It will zap anyone who tries to take it when it doesn't belong to them, too. I believe it already knows you're its proper owner. I did notice the blacksmith had made some of your modifications to the original hilt permanent."

I stroked my fingers over several of the turquoise stones, which had replaced some of the more precious jewels. "I wonder what happened to the other opals and diamonds."

Gentry took a bundle from one of the Secret Service agents standing by the door and tossed it to Anatoly. "You can't have my Blade Clan swords, but you can have that. It is a thank you gift for having done the Blade Clan a service."

Anatoly caught the bundle with a grunt, set it on his lap, and tore the paper off to reveal a bastard sword. The design of the hilt matched mine, although Anatoly's blade featured more diamond than opal, and the turquoise made a single showing as an accent stone near the sword's pommel.

"But for what?" my tiger asked, training his fingers along the blade's length. A trail of orange and black followed his touch, and every now and then, a spark of green appeared, a match for the light in the tiger's eyes when his passions ran high.

I could only hope Steel Heart had granted Anatoly's blade sufficient power to protect him no matter what he faced.

"Your weapons don't glow like this," my tiger observed, narrowing his eyes. "Why not?"

"Steel Heart favored my blades with strength and durability; I haven't had to sharpen either one since I've had them, and they have seen a great deal of use. I asked what they did, and Todd just shrugged and said you'd have to find that out on your own. The blacksmith, however, is very pleased with them. Hers is better than yours, but not by much." Shaking his head, Gentry took a seat on my aunt's desk and ignored when the President of the United States glowered at him for invading her workspace. "Not even the smith knows what they'll do once in battle. Jesse, while you were recovering, we sent the stiletto over as well. It has been properly sharpened, and your tribe has been notified that the weapon has a purpose. The dagger's dark past should become a bright future in your hands. The tribe sent an interesting message back."

Uh oh. The last time the tribe had sent me something, I'd coughed blood all over a table and made a mess of a bathroom before being hired to murder two of my uncles. "What message?"

"They sent a new feather for you, some beads, and three pairs of moccasins. I replied that you're going to turn into a bird if they keep putting feathers in your hair. As for the moccasins, they expect you'll wear them out with how you roam. They also sent a request for another foal from Dipshit and Devil Spawn. They'd like you to hand deliver the foal so you can join them for some celebrations."

Well, that part would be easy. "I seem to have a mare in foal for some reason, and I have the exact right number of horses. Sweetie Pie, Miracle, Dipshit, and Devil Spawn are the exact right number of horses, except Sweetie Pie and Devil Spawn shouldn't be ridden until they've foaled." I shook my head at the insanity of it all, and how my stallion breaking out and having his way with a bunch of mares had turned into a blessing in disguise. I considered the issue of the feathers, which I wore most of the time. "I'm not headed out west without my tiger, so you're going to have to give my tiger time off work. I also refuse to take the damned train."

My lecherous rabbit of an uncle dared to grin at me. "Your tiger does need to meet with the feline clans out west at some point anyway. We'll plan his visits around your trip to Cheyenne. You can also handle courier work for the government at the same time and any other tasks we might have for you. As for the train, it would be much faster if you were to take it."

"It would also be ridiculously expensive, and the foal needs to learn how to survive the roads and handle the terrain out west. Riding is much better, thank you. You might have to convince Randal and Simmons to wear something other than a suit. Their pretty suits would die terrible deaths on the road, and that would be a pity. They can bring their wives along, too. They might forget what they look like."

My tiger snickered. "We can't take the train anyway, if I'm meeting with the clans. Most of them live a hefty distance from the stations, so we'd be stopping at every station and losing days backtracking. Riding the entire trip is sensible. We'll just have to plan accordingly. Jesse probably knows more about cross-country traveling than all of us combined, and that's including my tendency to drag Henry around wherever I feel like going. I mean, she took me out in a bar like I was a beer nobody had claimed. She knows her business."

"You're claimed," I informed him. "I just made certain you'd remember that from day one."

"Oh, I remembered all right. There's nothing quite like waking up to the knowledge I had my ass handed to me by a woman in a bar who made it clear I was her property. You should have seen Gentry and Todd's faces when I showed them your little love mark. You had them planning my funeral. Well done, by the way. You made them so nervous they tattled to the First Gentleman and the President of the United States."

I turned to my uncle for confirmation, as my aunt and her damned rabbit would toy with me for the fun of it. "Were you going to give him a good funeral, Gentry?"

Gentry cleared his throat, and after a few moments, grinned. "The problem was, we had no idea what that color ink meant on a live body. We had to go do research, as none of us had ever seen an assassin mark someone like that. I'll admit, I was the first one to start ribbing him over having his life and death claimed by a rather notorious assassin. Then for that assassin to be you? He's never going to live this down."

"Which part is he not going to live down? Being suckered in a bar by a woman?"

"Not just a woman, his own bride and mate, and you left him with more questions than answers and a property tag." My uncle raised a brow at me. "We will be having a long talk about your lack of self-preservation skills once you're ready for a good beating on the mat."

Damn it. How had I gotten the family that embraced general violence in an effort to teach someone—me—how to do a better job of emerging from my life's problems somewhat intact? To change the subject back to Anatoly, I asked, "But would you have given him a good funeral?"

"No, because his response to finding out you were Charlotte's premier assassin was to issue that ridiculous bounty so he could beg you to marry him."

I narrowed my eyes and considered my tiger. "You issued the bounty *after* you found out I was an assassin?"

"What man doesn't want a lethal, capable woman to be his wife? I was ready to start begging. But then you ran off on me, and that was just a challenge I couldn't refuse. You just keep getting better and better. Then to be a Siberian, too? I am the luckiest man alive."

Of everyone present, Simmons or Randal might be able to make sense of the madness. As Simmons tended to be even more grounded than Randal, I picked him as the likeliest to help. "Can you explain this?"

"He loves you," my agent replied. "Of course, he would love you no matter what species. He is just a prideful tiger and you're a rare jewel of the shifter world."

My family and friends had gotten to my agents, too. Damn. Before I could come up with a suitable reply to that, Anatoly grinned and said, "It's true. Hope is lost for me. But your aunt isn't going to kick me out at night anymore, so I don't mind at all. I do need to go back to the house to fetch some clothes. I didn't bring anything, as I expected to get into a roaring match with security before being kicked out tonight."

My aunt sighed. "It's like having children again, but they're even worse. Someone go ask the kitchen to make dinner. We'll head over to your place after we have a talk about the current situation, Nate. I could use some fresh air."

With a rather gleeful expression, the First Gentleman bounced for the door. "I'll make the arrangements, and I'll make sure everyone knows Nate is supposed to be here after hours when he's not stuck in a meeting. It can be one of your past owed birthday presents, little girl."

One day, everyone would stop calling me a little girl. I hissed at the damned rabbit's back, but he ignored me as usual. "While you're being a courier rabbit, go tell Todd he needs to get off his lazy ass and make himself useful. He still has a brain. He should come use it for a change."

My uncle laughed and waved on his way out of the room.

"Is Marie the only problem in Todd's herd?" I asked, wondering how the stallion would handle the situation if it went beyond his wife of many years to his foals.

While Todd loved his mares, his children always came first.

"That we know of," my aunt replied. "Some of his newer mares have taken to avoiding her whenever possible, and the foals have generally sided with them. He'll have to deal with Marie eventually, as her attitude is bringing some conflict to his herd—but she hasn't done anything to warrant eviction from the herd or a divorce."

Yet. The word hung unspoken between us. Todd would hold on for as long as he possibly could, as he hated giving up on anyone. I wondered how he would handle the situation as it escalated—and how far Marie would go on whatever mission she was on.

Nothing good would come of that situation, of that I was certain. "And this is because of *me*?"

"Not entirely. Todd is Todd. He's kind and generous with those outside of the herd, and he dedicates a lot of time to his guild, too. You're just a part of the problem. Marie doesn't like to share, and she believes she is owed more of Todd's time and attention. And, if the reports

I've been getting are correct, she's willing to neglect her youngest to make sure he stays closer to home. But that hasn't worked, as the other mares have stepped up to make sure the foals are happy and healthy. This, in turn, has made Marie less than agreeable."

Marie would become a problem, and when she did, I could only hope Todd was able to deal with it rationally.

Stallions didn't do rational all that well. They were all pride and fire, and once angered, I'd rather face an enraged grizzly.

Anatoly got up and put his blade away, before taking my new katana. He returned it to its sheath before setting it aside. Sitting beside me, he wrapped an arm around me and pulled me close. "Try not to worry too much about Todd, Jesse. He's not stupid, he's aware Marie is up to something, and he recognizes she has changed a lot over the years—and not for the better. For now, Ferdinand is the real issue. He knows too much about the inner workings of the government, he's been close to Felicity more than any of us like, and he has a lot of connections from his time working as a mercenary."

"And he wanted to bite me," I grumbled.

"And he is a prideful idiot of a wolf, and he won't care it's been years since he claimed interest. If he gets a chance at you, he will probably take it—not that it'll do him any good." Anatoly growled. "With the rumors of him having bitten multiple women already, he's going to be a big problem. But, him biting multiple women is a good thing."

Anger surged through me, but I quelled it before I growled, snarled, or roared at my mate for even suggesting a wolf biting an unwilling woman could possibly be a good thing. "It is? How do you figure that?"

My aunt eyed the paperweight on her desk like she wanted to throw it at someone or through one of the room's curved walls. "When he's put down like the mad dog he is, he won't hurt them nearly as much. He's stretching his bite's potency across numerous victims—which means all of those victims will suffer less once he's dispatched. He still has sway over them, but not nearly as much sway as he would have over one mate. It's a relief, really. Considering you and Nate have been nipping at each other for a while, Ferdinand has no hope of competing with Nate, and if he has so many bites in place, there's a chance he won't even be able to tell his bite didn't take hold. It'll give you the element of surprise. But, there's a catch."

Anatoly stiffened. "What catch?"

"I asked around and spoke to some wolves with harem packs. Consenting," my aunt replied, taking a seat behind her desk. "The largest harem pack I found had four women in it, and they're structured rather like a lion's pride rather than a wolf pack. The gentleman of that relationship is run ragged all the time because they're very attentive and hungry women. He says after he bit his third lady, his ability to detect his bite went haywire. Just too many emotions and too many women. His solution was to nip his ladies at least once a week, because that keeps his hold on them. And before you lose your temper, Anatoly, they instigate him, just like you instigate with Jesse. It's rare, but some packs form this way, and they're happy, so it's none of my business. We don't judge Todd and equine herds, so we won't judge the rare wolf harem. It's not much different from herd magic, except a mare can leave the herd of her own volition, where a wolf's bite tends to be permanent."

"Some mares can leave the herd of their own will," Anatoly corrected. "It's nearly impossible to leave a stallion like Todd without his consent. He's just got too strong of a hold and general control over his herd."

Life had become complicated again, but some problems had simple solutions. "Is there more to this problem than just Ferdinand needing to be put down?"

"Yes," my aunt answered, but she didn't elaborate.

Interesting. "Gentry?"

"The government has received an increasing number of threats since his disappearance. He's likely involved, as he feels that things should be run differently. He believes wolves have been unfairly treated, but seems to have forgotten all biting species also face the same restrictions as wolves."

Anatoly grinned, tightened his hold on me, and kissed my hair. "This tigress is mine, and I will enjoy using every loophole in the legal system to keep her safe and mine."

I elbowed him in the side. "You have this wrong, tiger. I claimed you first. You're mine."

"I disagree."

I growled, twisted in his hold, and nipped his throat. He yelped, and to make it clear he wouldn't be winning our fledgling dispute, I nipped him again.

Gentry strode over, seized me by the back of my neck, and pulled me off my tiger before I took a proper bite out of his throat. "You're right, Steph. It's like having young children, except they're bigger, even more trouble than the little ones, and can't seem to behave themselves for ten minutes."

"Honestly, I'm impressed they behaved for five. Set her on the armchair over there. That might keep her out of trouble for a few minutes. We'll have to excuse Nate. He's been waiting for this for a long time, so it's expected for him to be excitable. There's no excuse for Jesse."

"Hey," I protested while my uncle dragged me across the room and sat me down in the chair of my aunt's choosing. "Why does he get let off and I don't?"

"You assaulted him in a bar without his permission."

As she had a good point, I looked to Anatoly for help.

"I liked it," my tiger announced. "I liked it so much I'm going to worship her in a lavish wedding ceremony as soon as I can convince her to go along with it. I've seen her in dresses, Steph. She's divine. Do you think I can convince her to wear a white one?"

"She's hardly pure," my aunt replied with a disapproving sniff.

"Hey," I complained. "That's not fair."

"It most certainly is. You should be asking Nate what sort of things you can do to make up for tattooing him without his permission."

"Marry me," my tiger ordered with his best smirk, the one that made me want to lunge across the room, sink my teeth into his throat, and drag him off to somewhere private. "It's my fault I gave her ideas. I treated her respectfully. That's rare in a man, Steph. She just wanted to make sure she got to keep me. And anyway, if she'd asked me, after watching her destroy those mercenaries, I would have said yes anyway. You should have seen her. She was magnificent."

"I've seen her fight before. I'm well aware she's skilled. If you convince her to accept your rather pathetic proposal, I'll have Gentry help plan the wedding."

"Why me?"

"You were whining about how you wanted to adopt Nate. You spent how long chasing him around your guild as a result? You've made it clear you've accepted responsibility for the tiger, so you have to help plan his wedding."

"You are a cruel and ruthless woman, Steph."

"You can make Felicity help with the planning. Unlike you, she'll actually like it."

"You're still cruel and ruthless, but Felicity would

enjoy that, so you're not entirely cruel. You're definitely ruthless, however."

"I try. And Jesse?"

I sensed a disaster in my future, and I wasn't sure how to stop it—or if I wanted to. "What?"

"Half the fun is waiting to give him your answer so you drive him crazy. You want him to worship the ground you walk on, profess his undying love for you, and generally prove he's in it for the long haul. Of course, he's a Siberian, he's already dedicated, and you don't have to worry about any of that, but it's more fun if you drag it out."

"The only wedding I've been to was Blossom's, and I skipped out before they actually had the wedding. If that's what weddings are, can I skip that to whatever part the actual wedding is?"

My aunt's mouth dropped open, and she stared at me with wide eyes. "You've never been to a wedding before?"

"They don't really have them in the Blade Clan," I reminded her. "None of the guard jobs Todd assigned me to involved them before Blossom's."

"Technically, she's already your bride, Nate," my aunt muttered, and her tone implied she'd given up hope for me doing things in a way acceptable for civilized society. While she wasn't wrong, I bristled all the same.

I narrowed my eyes. "You make it sound like I'm a lost cause."

My tiger dared to laugh, and only Gentry wrapping

his arm around my shoulders to keep me pinned in place saved him from a bite to the throat.

"Stop trying to goad my niece into killing," Gentry complained. "She really might."

"She'd only maul me for a little while before getting other ideas in her head. Let her go. I want to see what she'll do." While tigers couldn't purr, Anatoly made a good effort with his attempt, however growly his chuffs emerged. "Admit it, Gentry. She's divine."

"Siberians!" My aunt threw her arms in the air. She then turned on her Secret Service agents and pointed at one of the poor bastards near the door. "Get me a damned court clerk and the legal documentation for civil unions. It's going to take these two idiots a lifetime to sort their mess out otherwise, and my sister really will try to kill me if I don't make sure her daughter has a fully secured claim on her tiger."

"No, Madam President," the agent replied, and somehow, he managed to keep a straight face while disobeying the President of the United States. "Your sister would not kill you. She would merely make you suffer for a while, as we learned from her last visit several years ago."

My mother had visited several years ago? I would've been in Cheyenne, then, but the evidence she truly existed intrigued me. The agent, someone I'd seen around but hadn't learned his name, caught my attention for his ability to withstand my aunt's temper. I leaned back in the chair and tapped Gentry's arm.

"Yes, little girl?"

"I want that agent. He's a badass. He just told her no. He could partner with Beverly. Together, they might take over the country."

My agents somehow kept their expressions somewhat neutral, although Simmons raised a brow.

"Yes, but if he told you no, would you actually listen to him?"

I considered that. "It depends? Why is he telling her no?"

"It's after hours for the court clerks, and it would involve dragging one from dinner in order to handle a non-critical matter, and however much marrying you to Nate would solve some problems, it isn't a critical matter."

I frowned. "I disagree. It's a critical matter. The Blade Clan will beat him because he's the groom and the contract hasn't been fulfilled. He's not ready for a beating."

"How do you know that?"

"He hasn't been training with a sword since he was old enough to carry one. He's not ready."

The Secret Service agents, mine included, exchanged looks, and then Randal cleared his throat.

"What is it?" my aunt demanded.

"It would add an extra layer of protection should this wolf attempt to bite her. It would permit a heightened bounty for any involved with the incident." My agent kept his tone neutral, something he often did when he recognized he said something someone wouldn't like. "It would offer Mr. Silverston certain legal rights as well. You can still plan a proper wedding for them to celebrate when they have gotten around to properly biting each other and making their mating official. It would also put them both at ease, especially should there be another chain of meetings she can't attend. It may resolve some of their anxiety issues, and it would count as a legal claim for them. It would be useful."

My aunt regarded my agent with open suspicion. "Useful for whom?"

"Us."

I laughed. "I'm sorry we worried you, Randal. You, too, Simmons. We were just tired."

"When the tigers are so exhausted they can't be bothered to roar at each other before dancing around each other, it's time to marry them off, leave them alone, and let nature sort itself out eventually. And, I would like to remind you, that if you have legal documentation proving they're a mated couple, you will have to spend less time trying to convince palace staff that it's consenting violence. Ceremonies are currently wasted on the tigress, but she has a solid understanding of legal documentation. When they're ready for their celebratory ceremony, it can be planned at leisure."

Simmons grinned. "It would solve a lot of potential issues later. It would also allow us to push on Head Tiger's Secret Service detail. It would remove his ability to fully opt out of it."

I frowned. "Why are you trying to talk him out of

this? That seems like a way to talk him out of it. From how he acts, he's allergic to having a detail."

"It's coercion. I have what he wants, and he'll have to put serious thought into cooperating with safety precautions in order to get what he wants. I just turned you into the grand prize in a cage match. Also, don't even think about it, Nate. I'm fresh. You're not." My aunt lifted a brow and engaged my tiger in a staring match, which she won after a few moments.

Anatoly roared his displeasure, and Simmons lifted his hand to his ear and said, "All clear. Head Tiger is vocalizing his displeasure over a Presidential edict. Please send for a court clerk with civil union documentation along with required documentation for Head Tiger and Stiletto. Please bring the copy of the Blade Clan contract and a copy of the waivers regarding Stiletto's untraditional documentation."

"I have her birth certificate," my aunt announced, and she rummaged in one of her desk drawers. "I made her mother properly draw the damned thing up last time she was in town. Congratulations, Jesse. You're the first Blade Clan member with an official birth certificate, and we even managed to secure your father's signature as part of your proof for live birth."

My eyes widened. I had a birth certificate? Birth certificates made a lot of the little things in life go much easier, as many places required them to prove identity for purposes of having a good apartment or home. Mercenaries could get through life without them, but with one, I could do a lot more. "That'll make voting a lot easier. And I won't get yelled at every time I renew my courier's license."

"Ah. Agent Simmons? Please request someone to come renew her license while we're at it; it's up for renewal next month, and I'd rather not have to stress about it close to deadline. She'll take herself over for an appointment, and she might even tell us she's doing it."

Simmons passed on the request. "Anything else, Madam President?"

"Begin working on expanding your principal's agent roster, to be effective next month. Also start looking for agents who can work with Nate. They'll need to be ready to travel and be able to form a functional relationship with two Siberians. Put them on a higher pay grade. One Siberian is bad enough. Two will be a challenge. Integrate both teams, as unlike most Siberians, I suspect these two will dislike separation, or so I've been led to believe. While my husband is confirming Nate is allowed in the palace overnight now, please make certain the Secret Service is aware of the alterations to his living arrangements. Offer a bonus for anyone who wants to include checking his home daily for issues on the way to work."

Simmons nodded, opened the door, and slipped outside of the room.

"While I'm working miracles, is there anything else anyone would like from me before we get to real work?"

I raised my hand. "I have a question."

"I have learned to fear when you have a question," my aunt muttered. "What do you want?"

"When can I meet my mother? Do you think she could wrangle my father? I'd like to meet him, too."

It was one of the secret wishes of every child of the Blade Clan to meet his father and do him proud. As I'd defied the Blade Clan in all other ways, I wanted to have it all.

My aunt smiled. "I'll send word to her, although she can be difficult to reach. You definitely got your tendency to wander off from her. But I'll make sure she knows you want to meet her. As for your father, that can be done. Honestly, he's easier to reach than my sister is. But yes, what you want can be done, it will just take some time to make the arrangements."

"It works out that it will take some time." My thoughts turned to Ferdinand and the plethora of problems he would create for everyone. "We have more serious concerns to worry about first."

"That we do."

Chapter Five

THE PRIVATE DINING room wasn't large enough for everyone, which meant we had to use the formal hall. Without hundreds of people crammed into the space, the room transformed me into something small and insignificant. I'd done a good job of avoiding the place, as it held too many memories.

I doubted anyone would fling a dagger at Todd's back, nor did I think I would tango with my uncle again. For his sake, I hoped the gaudy headdress had died a terrible death, as even the thought of the damned thing annoyed me.

It still amazed me how such a brief moment could create so much change. That one little bout with my uncle had made it impossible to hide from the world. It still amazed me the banquet hadn't resulted in my capture or death. In some ways, things would have become much simpler if I'd gone along with the bounty hunters—save Ferdinand.

I could have happily lived without Ferdinand ever taking an interest in me.

I took a seat beside my tiger, stifling a yawn while everyone settled. My aunt sat across from me, which sent an interesting message: she had a lot to say, and she didn't feel like having to raise her voice to be heard. Her lecherous rabbit of a husband sat across from Anatoly, and Todd took the seat beside me. Gentry plopped down next to his sister, and a baker's dozen of Secret Service agents joined us, including my agents.

I found it interesting Simmons flanked my tiger, and I leaned over to say, "Don't let him escape, Simmons. I like this tiger, and I wish to keep him. I'll be very distressed if I can't keep him. You can even beat him a little if he resists becoming my pet tiger."

My agent grinned at me. "We only have to beat him when the President declares it's time for him to go home where he belongs, and as he's been assigned to your living quarters, I don't expect we'll have to beat him for that reason anymore. We do have a training session tomorrow, but I'm sure he'll attend without complaint if you escort him to the gym."

Anatoly sighed. "I'm not going anywhere, Jesse. I'm more concerned you might wander off somewhere. Or have help wandering off. As long as the Hope Diamond is around your throat, you're a target."

The Hope Diamond might really be the death of me one of these days, and as I couldn't deny the accusation, I shrugged. "And if what Madam President has been saying is true, I'm the target of a double dose of it this time."

My aunt nodded. "You are. The Hope Diamond is a constant target, and since it's stuck around your neck, that makes you a target. But, it's also securing your general safety in a way."

I tilted my head to the side and considered my aunt. "What do you mean?"

"The Hope Diamond has a personality, and it is known to zap anyone it doesn't want touching it. You are a far more convenient way to move the stone around. But if they kill you, they'll lose that, so your safety is important to those who want the stone." Something across the room drew my aunt's attention, and she straightened. "That would be the court clerk now. We'll continue this discussion after you've permanently secured your tiger as an asset."

I snickered at that. "You've been demoted to my asset, Ana."

"It's not a demotion. It's a promotion."

Everyone chuckled at that, and I twisted around in my chair to observe a younger woman with a stack of papers in her arms. She strode to the table and dumped her burden on the pristine cloth. "The paperwork you requested, Madam President. Judge Smithson will be along in a few minutes to oversee the signing. He is finishing up some verification work on the other end of the palace at the moment. He asks that you try not to take too long with your review, as he would like to make it home for dinner for a change."

My aunt grinned and reached across the table for the paperwork, which she rummaged through until she found a few sheets, which she reviewed and tossed to Anatoly. "Review that for accuracy, but don't sign until the judge gets here." After a few more minutes, she slapped a piece of paper in front of me. "As the bride of this relationship, you get to tack Silverston onto your name. Since you don't have a middle name, Alexander can become your middle name, so you can keep both rather than changing out your last name, which is what people usually do. That will also allow you to use Alexander on legal documentations moving forward if you want, although I expect your tiger will become upset, as he'll like knowing you share his last name. I've noticed men can get very upset over that. Some women opt to keep their name and make their men change their last name, but I expect you'll be happier this way, as it'll let you get a move on with the rest of your life. Usually, we would have you sign the marriage certificate first, but the judge isn't here yet, so we'll just go ahead and do this. You don't have to be married to change your name, anyway. It just costs more, and I'd pay the fee anyway, just to keep your tiger from having an excuse to roar at me again today."

Anatoly shrugged. "Maybe if you stopped telling me things I didn't like, I wouldn't have a reason to roar at you."

Sometimes, all I could do was ignore my tiger's insanity. Instead of worrying about his posturing, I thought about my aunt's comments. After a few moments of reflection, I realized she was correct. Nodding, I searched for a pen, and the court clerk offered me one. After reading the documentation, I wrote my new name, which was my old name but with Silverston tacked onto the end, and signed in the appropriate places before returning it to the court clerk. "If the tiger gives you any trouble, please roll this up and beat him with it."

She smiled at me, claimed the sheet, and tucked it into a folder, which went beneath her arm for safe keeping. "I'll keep that in mind."

"Hey, what did I do?" my tiger complained.

"You let these people disturb my nap."

He chuckled at my answer. "That's fair. I should have done better to prevent them from disturbing your nap, although I am enjoying the results. You know what these documents are for, right?"

"It's the legalized version of a mating bite," I replied, rolling my eyes over his concern I was utterly clueless. "While I haven't attended a marriage ceremony, I do understand the tax benefits of putting up with you. It also helps post disputes, as we tigers are a species of cat who enjoys things others would be filing domestic violence charges over. The paperwork helps with the species exemption laws for such things. I'd hate to have to bail you out of jail every time you need to show you're a worthy tiger. I also would like to avoid requiring bail because I needed to put you in your place again."

My aunt snickered. "That's one way to view it, Jesse."

"I see I'm outnumbered here," Anatoly muttered, and he faked a sniff. He slid his papers to me. "It looks okay to me. There is no evidence of them trying to marry us to anyone else."

"That would be quite the trick." I took my time reviewing the paperwork, which essentially informed me we would be classified as a legally married couple post signing. As bites held more sway than any government document, I viewed it as a nice way to save some money on taxes later down the road, as the government offered tax incentives for permanent partnerships. "I don't see a line here informing the world I am acquiring a personal slave."

"Marriage doesn't give you ownership over your tiger," my aunt replied, her tone amused. "I had similar thoughts about my rabbit."

The rabbit shrugged. "I would have given it to her if that was what it took to convince her to marry me, honestly. I was a most pathetic bunny then."

"I love that you acknowledged you were a pathetic bunny," I admitted. Then, because I could be just as evil as everyone else when pushed, I did a sniff test. "I'm not sure you've been doing your duties, Mr. Male Rabbit."

My aunt tossed back her head and howled her laughter. "She got you with that one, babe."

"Good little tigress. I will have to figure out a suitable reward for that one. I will do my best to rectify my cruel mistreatment of my wife."

"In the privacy of your chambers, if you please," I replied, careful to keep from either laughing or grimacing and ruining my attempt to hold my own against the rampant pervert.

"I don't please, but my wife makes me behave."

Unable to help myself, I rolled my eyes. "Why did you pick a rabbit?"

"He cried, and damn it, I *really* can't stand when prey I can't eat cries."

My uncle leered at my aunt, and I dropped the papers and rose to lunge across the table to end his perverted ways. Anatoly grabbed me around the waist, yanked me to him, and sat me on his lap. "Easy there, my beautiful tigress. Despite appearances, you actually *do* like your uncle despite him being a terrible First Gentleman."

"I'm not a terrible First Gentleman. I'm perfection."

Todd heaved a sigh, stood up, and flicked my uncle with a finger between the eyes. "That is for making Jesse want to kill you."

"See? Even the stallion is on my side."

The First Gentleman laughed. "I love that we're surrounded by Secret Service agents, and not a single one of them even thought about protecting me from such a cruel assault."

My aunt snorted. "That's because you deserved it, and the last time they tried to help you, you electrocuted them. They've learned to just let you handle your own problems unless it looks serious. Now, settle down. As soon as the judge gets here, well take care of the signing and have one less problem on our plate. Then we'll talk serious business."

"Serious business that involves the majority of your detail, the current leaders of the Secret Service, and a few extras?" I asked.

"I would have brought the entirety of the Council into it, but between my rabbit and your tiger, we have all the information we need to discuss the situation. They can relay to the Council once we're done with discussions here—and the Secret Service overflows with intel we may need for this. I've found it's sometimes best to just bring them to the table and make use of their expertise."

The more I heard, the more worried I became. "And all of this is because of one rogue wolf?"

"Not precisely. You'll find out soon enough." My aunt straightened. "Ah. There's the judge now. Jamal, come witness these signatures so we can get to the rest of our evening and you can go home to the wife for dinner. How are you?"

"Pleased I'm doing something other than look over murder cases, thefts, and arsons. There's been a plague of them lately," the older man complained, stepping to the table. "You finally convinced Silverston to settle down?"

"Convinced? They're trying to give her detail a heart attack. They got nippy with each other, wore themselves out, and passed out so hard Gentry roaring in their ears didn't do jack shit to wake them. I'm just providing the legal documentation so you don't end up with a chain of cases of them being accused of domestic violence when they're flirting with their teeth. I'm saving you from a great deal of paperwork."

"Tigers," the judge complained. "It's simple. Sign on the appropriately lines, print your name below the signatures, date the form, and pass it to the witnesses. You need one witness each. I recommend the President and the First Gentleman. They're considered unassailable witnesses. Mainly because no one is stupid enough to question either one of them on something like this."

I had no idea who the judge was, but I liked him already. I took up the pen again, found the appropriate lines on the form, and filled it out before passing it over to Anatoly. "Sign so I can claim you as my slave."

Anatoly chuffed his amusement. "We just went over this, Jesse. This is not a slave ownership paper. It's a marriage certificate. But, if it makes you feel better, I'll pretend I'm your most loyal servant."

"Servant?"

"I get paid as a servant."

"What am I paying you? Damn it, I already signed! Nobody told me I had to pay him." I pointed at my aunt. "You tricked me."

"Why are you pointing at *me*, little girl?"

"This was your idea."

"You're paying him with your love and affection. He'll probably accept bites or nibbles as currency."

I considered that. "Then I've paid him in advance."

My aunt's expression turned thoughtful. "Yes, I would say you're correct. Payment has already been rendered, Nate. You're now a serf at absolute best."

With a shrug, my tiger signed the papers and slid it across the table. "She's worth serfdom, so I suppose I must accept these terms."

"You better," I grumbled.

Anatoly smirked at me, and I hissed at him.

My aunt took her time with her signature before handing it over to my uncle. "Jamal, please have this record sealed from the general public. Until certain matters are handled, it's a safety concern. Have it flagged as having to be unsealed by you with my direct approval, and mark the file as belonging to the Silverstons. That will help cover their tracks somewhat. As soon as a certain matter is resolved, I will have you unseal the records."

"Understood, Madam President."

After five minutes, some discussion over certified copies to be held in the President's safe, and some pleasantries, the judge and court clerk left. As I expected all hell to break loose, I kept a close eye on my aunt. "What's going on?"

"The Secret Service has vocalized concerns over an assassination attempt on many upper government officials, along with the guild leaders of major mercenary bands in the city. As the people insist on voting in my favor, there are those who wish to end my Presidency through any means necessary."

"Do you think Ferdinand is involved?"

"I think it is probable, as it would fit his goals rather well. He wanted to take over Dawnfire, but my brother is a stubborn old grizzly who has no plans on retiring, and whenever he's out of action, his wife takes over, which had made things difficult because she would need to see me often."

While I didn't see Felicity often, she hated being separated from Gentry for more than a few hours. "Let me guess. She's why Charlotte was picked as your residency."

"It had something to do with it, yes. Felicity doesn't ask for much, but she wanted to be closer to home without having to shirk on her duties to the government. I liked being closer to family, too. Charlotte has all the infrastructure we need, and it is generally considered to be in a safe location."

"And this is why you've been treating your residence as a dungeon?"

"In part. The other part involves your mother and my death if I let anything happen to you. When she signed with the Blade Clan, the thing she wanted most in life was a child. And it seems she's developed some of your Siberian instincts, probably infected with them while you were still in the womb. The last time she came for a visit, she was muttering under her breath over how she planned to take over the entire Blade Clan so she could reclaim her male. Your father is hunted. I would feel pity for him, but I've been educated about how the Blade Clan operates, and I have a feeling your father is a lot like you."

Todd chuckled, and he reached under his seat and pulled out a long box, which I recognized as the Cheyenne's chosen container for their stiletto. "Be very careful with this, Jesse. It has been sharpened by the smith from the Blade Clan, and it has come into contact with Steel Heart. Steel Heart ran off, as it likes to do, but I've been told to tell you that this is yours, and it will take care of you until the end of your days."

I took the box, set it on the table in front of me, and opened it. The stiletto gleamed in the overhead lights, and the fragment of the blue diamond in its hilt gleamed with a blue light before darkness crept into its heart and washed over the stone. The Hope Diamond warmed against my throat.

"Steel Heart woke its stone?" Careful to avoid the sharp edge, I lifted the stiletto out of the velvet-lined box and examined its edge. Blue and black sparked from the point. "Why does the Blade Clan smith deal with you so often, Todd? He reforged my katana, and he forged a blade for Anatoly, too. And then to do such work on the stiletto?"

"It's a matter of trust. He also feels responsible your blade broke when you needed it the most, although he confessed the blade was better meant for a wall ornament than seeing the sort of heavy use you put weapons through. He hopes your new blade serves you well. As for your tiger, he says it makes up for some of his suffering, having to put up with a stubborn tigress such as yourself."

Anatoly snickered. "You know you're something else when even the Blade Clan's premier smith pities me, Jesse. Pass word along the line that I'm the luckiest of men, Todd. And I am. I have her as mine in all ways now, and I am on a mission to put her in a white dress. You can help with the dress's design."

Todd looked me over. "She'd look like a scrawny goose if you put her in a pure white dress, Nate. Go with an untraditional color. She'll be stunning, and you can be a black swan beside her. Don't hide her colors through traditional nonsense."

I twitched. "A scrawny goose? Couldn't I be a scrawny swan instead? Why does he get to be the swan?"

"Nobody with half an iota of sense screws around with a goose *or* a swan. You're a power couple. And, anyway, blood is near to impossible to get out of a white dress. A pastel tone works well with you, but a good crimson would suit you better."

My tiger kept on snickering. "He's saying blood is a good look on you, Jesse. He's not wrong, but he's questioning your purity."

The paperwork must have broken his brain, and I stared at him. "*What* purity? I was literally bred to kill people. I don't think there was anything ever pure about me."

"You were actually conceived because my sister wanted a child, and she wanted a father who could donate superior genes to her cause. She is now obsessed with your father. I'm sure she'll be after you as soon as she tames herself a Blade Clan warrior. He's being a challenge, I believe. That, plus she hasn't asked where you are, so I haven't seen a need to tell her. I'm sure she'll figure it out eventually. You should be thanking me for sparing you from that nonsense for so long. Getting them in the same room together might be problematic, however."

"Why problematic?"

"My sister won't let him leave, and then I'll have to explain to the Blade Clan why it lost one of its best men to his own damned bride." My aunt snickered. "It'll be a wonder to behold, really. I'll plan it so you can enjoy the entertainment, too."

Somehow, I'd been born into the craziest family in the entire United States. "Should I be concerned?"

"Honestly? Only if you try to escape your mother when she comes for you."

I turned to Gentry. "Should I be worried?"

"Only if you're not successfully acclimated to positive attention before Jenny gets a hold of you. She will hug you into submission, and she'll cry the entire time. Then she'll beat anyone who embarrasses her because she cried. Your mother is a piece of work."

Well, I'd definitely inherited a few things from my unknown mother. "Who in this family isn't?"

I earned the ire of two grizzlies, and my lecherous rabbit of an uncle howled his laughter. "She got you good with that one, babe. Let her have it without roaring her head off over it. It's not like she's wrong about it. I'm a prime example. I tried to give you an escape through offering you the Miller name, but all you did was corrupt me into being as bad as any Adams man."

Gentry covered his mouth and cleared his throat. "You make a good point."

Something behind me caught my attention, and my aunt rubbed her hands together. "The kitchen angels are waving to inform us they're ready with their culinary offerings. We'll talk after we're all a little less hungry and prone to biting and roaring at each other."

I wondered what sort of disaster loomed on the horizon for my aunt to be unwilling to discuss it until she'd had a chance to take the edge off her standard grizzly irritability through food. I'd find out soon enough, although I already regretted taking part in whatever waited for me.

It would be a long night, of that I was certain.

Chapter Six

FRIED CHICKEN, mashed potatoes, and gravy did an excellent job of taming my aunt, and five heaping plates fell prey to her appetite before she signaled she was ready to brief me on the various problems plaguing the government. Within an hour, the problems would plague me, too, but at least I'd be involved in Anatoly's work rather than pacing around like a caged animal who hadn't seen the light of day in years. Even my horses had adapted to life in the stables better than I'd anticipated, but only because someone had talked me into letting the Secret Service train with Dipshit and Devil Spawn.

Anyone who could ride those two demons could ride anything, and my horses demanded perfection. I even got to monitor the lessons, and when I thought an agent wasn't doing their best in the saddle, all I had to do was speak a single word to give them the ride of their lives. Devil Spawn wouldn't enjoy being removed from the training roster, but I wouldn't risk her or her foal. Dipshit would amuse the Secret Service while Devil Spawn enjoyed being spoiled and doing halter work to train promising agents how to handle an intractable animal.

"Did you miss lunch?" I asked my aunt, staring at the pile of bones littering her plate. I'd barely managed a quarter of what she'd inhaled, and I already regretted my act of gluttony.

"Unfortunately. We got caught up in a meeting, and then I got pulled out of my meeting because my niece and her tiger were found on the floor, dead to the world."

For some reason, I doubted I would ever live that down. "It's your fault for restricting my beer intake."

"Beer would not have been good for you, especially since you can't seem to keep from catching every damned cold the country has to offer. But we can negotiate on your beer supply tomorrow."

Anatoly chuckled. "If she won't give it to you, I will, but I'll only provide one, plus an empty bottle you can use as a weapon if anyone tries to interrupt your enjoyment of your drink."

"Now we're talking. Deal. I want it so cold it's at risk of turning to ice—without actually turning to ice."

"I think I can manage that."

With the important problem of my beer solved, I focused on the real problem at hand: Ferdinand. "Gentry, what exactly is going on with Ferdinand?"

"After you were taken to Fort Lauderdale, he began

acting strangely. Within a month of our return, he refused to show for duty and disappeared. That is when I took steps and had him stricken from the roster. He's still missing, but I'm concerned because he showed interest in you—and in the Hope Diamond. Unfortunately, there are a few other details that are really bothering me."

"It involves Marie," Todd said with a slow shake of his head. "Before Ferdinand's disappearance, the other mares spotted Marie having a long discussion with Ferdinand. She was attempting to do this on the sly; she went somewhere my mares usually don't go, except Kari and some of the newer mares are more adventurous than the others, my daughters included. They ultimately spied on Marie, and they came to talk to me about it."

Well, that changed things. "Marie seemed so nice, but that was years ago."

"Yes. Years ago, she was quite nice and generous. Times changed. But she's still my wife and lead mare, so I have to handle this delicately. I have no proof of treachery, but I question her choice of company. I love her as much as I love my children, so I want to think the best of her, but I cannot deny what my other mares witnessed. *Something* is going on. I suspect she wants to help Ferdinand acquire you, as acquiring you would make most of her grievances disappear. But that would be a betrayal of the herd, as I have never revoked your status as an honorary member of the herd. You're not the only non-equine with the status, and I've welcomed men and women alike as honorary members, but you're the only one she doesn't approve of."

Poor Todd. "I'm sorry. I've caused you trouble again."

"I'd say Marie and Ferdinand have caused the trouble, and you're just caught up in trouble others make for you, as usual. I'm right, you're wrong, so simmer down and accept it."

Damned stallion. "I can still be sorry."

"No, you can't. It's not your fault, so you're just going to have to accept being guilt-free for once in your life."

I scowled, but before I could reply, Anatoly kissed my cheek. "Pay attention to me and not him. I'm much better than some randy old stallion."

His breath on my skin gave me inappropriate ideas for the dinner table. My conquest of his person would begin the instant I managed to kick all of my agents out of my suite for the night, and we'd roar enough to keep the whole damned palace awake for the entire night before I was through with him. "But he is a pretty stallion, you have to admit."

My tease earned me a scrape of teeth on my neck, and I sucked in a breath.

"She's going to have you for dessert," Todd warned.

"If you two could wait until after we're done here and have a chance to head over to his house, that would be great," my aunt added. "You don't have to mark your territory, Nate. You're technically married to her now. You don't have to posture to keep Todd aware she's yours."

Todd chuckled at that. "Courting tigers are so much fun. You just have to look at one of them, and they get so damned jealous they can't see straight. I'm not going to steal your woman, Nate. I have already endured a very thorough rejection from your tigress. I am in no hurry to suffer through another. Of course, you might want to impress upon her the proper usage of her tattoo needles."

"She used her tattoo needles in a perfectly acceptable fashion," Anatoly replied. "I'm just a thorough man who takes his time when challenged by a capable woman."

"Nate, stop flirting. Todd, stop encouraging him to flirt. We have a lot of serious business ahead, and inflating her ego isn't that business, however challenging and worthwhile that task might be." My aunt smacked the table with her hand to make it clear she meant business. "First, there's the issue of the rebellion threat, which I'm beginning to believe Ferdinand is a part of—and by nature of her behavior, possibly Marie."

Todd sighed. "You know where my herd's loyalties lie, and the instant there is evidence of this, she will be cut from the herd bonds without hesitation. That is one thing I do not allow or forgive in the herd. But she has been argumentative as of late, and if you want to question her, I suspect you'll need a charge and a warrant.

Which would make it clear she is no longer fit for my herd. I will continue to hope you are wrong."

"You've been together for a very long time," my aunt conceded. "For your sake, I hope I'm wrong as well. That leaves the issue of Ferdinand. Jesse, this is going to be the most trouble for you."

"And me," my tiger growled. "I'll rip the bastard apart if he lays a finger on her."

"Yes, yes, assuming she doesn't rip him apart first. Considering how much you two have been fawning over each other for weeks, he has no chance in hell of securing a proper bite on her—and if he has taken as many women as we suspect, he won't be able to tell if he's successfully bitten someone, Jesse included. That gives us an opening."

"If it comes to that, I can infiltrate his pack, gather data, and do my job without any issue."

"There is the issue of a legal bounty. One needs to be established to keep you legal. You don't have to claim it, of course, but the existence of the bounty would make it a sanctioned kill, and you would be able to handle the matter without a lengthy trial. If he bites you, it would fall under self-defense, anyway."

I shrugged. "Do whatever you need. Which guild will handle it?"

"I will have an open bounty issued on a national level. Dawnfire will be the primary contact, but Lancers' Alliance will be the secondary contact. I have a list of guilds in every major city in the United States that will also be sent notice of the bounty and can send the body to Dawnfire or Lancers' for verification."

I grimaced. With a national bounty, Ferdinand wouldn't last long even if he did manage to get through the Secret Service, my aunt, uncles, Todd, and Anatoly to somehow nab me. It would take more manpower than Dawnfire had used when my damned tiger had put a bounty on my living head. "Maybe we should discuss the type of force it would take to get to me if I happen to stay in the palace like I'm supposed to."

"Enough to substantiate the rumors of a potential rebellion. I do think that their target is the Hope Diamond, which would give them potential power in a rebellion situation—if they can figure out how to use it. Unfortunately, while we have rumors of a potential rebellion to work with, we don't have a timetable, we don't have a specific target outside of the speculation they want the Hope Diamond, and we don't have a motivation. It's possible those from Fort Lauderdale wish to rebel, but so far, it's been quiet on that front. My visit went well, and there's been a lot of progress integrating the surviving residents into the modern world. I don't think they're organized enough to mount the kind of assault required to damage the palace. But, I am concerned it is linked to what woke Fort Lauderdale in the first place."

One day, I'd be able to remember the pair I'd killed without grimacing over it. Of all the assassinations I'd handled, I regretted the necessity of their deaths the most.

I still feared my family would truly realize I had been the one to kill them, and turn on me like I'd turned on my traitor uncles at the ocean's shore with the Hope Diamond as the only witness of my deeds.

Anatoly prodded me in the side with his elbow. "I don't know what you're thinking, but your expression promises it is something I won't like. If you're worried about the assholes, we're only upset you weren't able to stab them sooner, and that you were so badly hurt in the process of stabbing them. Your shoulder still isn't fully healed, and you keep getting sick no matter what we do. Cleo and Henry can't figure it out, either. And yes, that's probably part of why our Presidential dictator is so against us going out for a beer. She's worried you'll sniff alcohol and get sick."

"It's true," my aunt admitted. "As far as I'm concerned, it's a miracle you've gone a week without having a case of *something*. Stop catching colds. That's an order. I'll even relent on you having beer as long as you're not ill."

"So I can have beer as long as I'm not sick?"

"I can accept those terms, but try not to drink yourself under any tables. Keep it to one or two, and the instant you get sick again, you're not getting beer again."

"Is there any beer in this place?" I demanded.

My aunt laughed and raised her hand, which someone would interpret as an order to bring me a damned beer.

"So, if Ferdinand shows up, should I play along or just try to kill him at the first opportunity?"

"Convincingly protest," my aunt ordered. "And cut off his family jewels should he try to do anything other than bite you. Obviously, I'd prefer you get information first, but if he does try something like that, I want you to use every weapon in your arsenal to castrate him."

"What she said," my tiger announced.

"Is there a specific method you'd like me to use to dispatch him?"

"Quickly. His death could ripple through his bites, and I'd rather not torture his victims unnecessarily," my aunt replied.

Of everyone at the table, I worried my uncle would suffer the most, and I regarded Gentry with a frown. "And you?"

"He wants my job, and he probably wouldn't mind killing me or my wife off to get it. Does that help with your guilt somewhat?"

In a way, it did, but in a way, it didn't. I scowled, uncertain what to say.

"Don't mind the little girl," my aunt said, clucking her tongue at me. "It took her how long to accept we weren't upset over her for what happened in Fort Lauderdale?"

"She just cares," my tiger said, and he rewarded me with a kiss on the cheek. "Go ahead and worry, but we're not going to turn on you for doing unpleasant but necessary things. Ferdinand has changed over the years, and not for the better. His threat to bite you was only the beginning of his downfall. Those mean old grizzlies have had plenty of time to work through their feelings on the matter, and that mean old stallion over there was on board with finishing him off the instant he threatened to bite you against your will. Next time, Todd, just kill him."

"It wouldn't have been legal."

"It would have been legal the instant Jesse verified he'd threatened to bite her, and you know it. Just like it would be legal to put me down if I threatened to bite Jesse without her permission. Of course, I've been goading her into biting for months." He shrugged. "Wolves could learn from us Siberians. By the time we get to biting, it's clear both desire the partnership."

"Also evidenced by you both signing the paperwork without even a second thought on the matter."

"It protects her."

I shrugged. "He's my tiger, and if little pieces of paper help prove that, I will sign the pieces of paper."

"Well, tonight, do try to properly bite him after we get back from retrieving his clothing." My aunt pointed at Anatoly's throat. "You want your bite visible, as you're making it a very public declaration you own him. That little nip counts, as it scarred rather than healed, but it's best if you continue to secure your claim. How many times did Noona bite her wolf before she was satisfied, Nate?"

"I stopped counting after five, as I try not to think about my sister mauling some damned wolf."

"Don't listen to Nate, Jesse. He likes Gerard, and

Noona beats anyone who says anything negative about her chosen wolf. That poor wolf has his hands full, because she loves children, so every time one of theirs gets old enough to start toddling, she's out for his blood yet again. Nate, you should invite their entire brood to town so they can meet your mate. By that, I mean you should really invite Noona before she invites herself and you earn a beating. I'd rather keep the bloodshed to a minimum."

My tiger sighed. "I'll send word as soon as this mess with Ferdinand is resolved."

"Excellent. Jesse, should Ferdinand look like he intends on becoming violent with any women he's bitten, use excessive force. While I'd like intel, I won't have it at the cost of an innocent woman's life."

"Understood."

"Until we learn more, there's not much left to discuss regarding him. He knows a great deal about the inner workings of the government and mercenary guilds, so he has been classified a significant threat. Do what you can, Jesse, but your safety and the safety of his bitten women come first. Ideally, you'll be able to play him, dispatch him with little harm to his women, and be done within a week." My aunt shifted her gaze to Anatoly. "You will do your best to refrain from unnecessary hysterics."

Todd and Gentry stared at my aunt like she'd lost her mind, and my rabbit of an uncle joined in. My tiger laughed. "You're asking for a miracle there, Steph. There will be necessary hysterics, and I'll have them daily until that wolf is dealt with. Jesse should be authorized to attend all mandatory meetings moving forward."

"Ideally, we flush him out and do a live capture, Nate. That means having her somewhere a little more accessible on the palace grounds or nearby—with a stronger detail. Randal?"

"I'll have a team put together tonight, including Beverly. I believe Blossom also has some other candidates she thinks might work with the Secret Service."

"Interview them, and if you think they're suitable, bring them in for training and see how they do with Jesse. A Siberian and a pride of lionesses will make for a strong team if they work well together. I recommend against putting the lionesses with Anatoly, unless you want Jesse fighting with them constantly."

"I have some candidates in mind, mostly men to keep Jesse from picking fights with them. The women will be chosen specifically with Jesse's temper in mind."

I considered my agent's concerns, and after a few moments of consideration, I shrugged. "I'm probably going to be unreasonable about this. I should be sorry, but I'm not."

"You're supposed to be unreasonable about your mate," my aunt replied. "Courting pairs are usually trouble, but it's a simple enough problem to work around. Same-gender teams help. It keeps the in-fighting to a minimum. Typically, we'll bring in mated wolves or other species to fill out a detail when necessary, as these individuals are less likely to trigger fits of jealousy and general posturing. You're more laid back than other Siberian women, much to your detail's general relief. Anatoly is also more accepting of other men around you."

"I see no need to be jealous of married men with more experience in the Secret Service than most details combined, and I only want the best watching over her." Anatoly sighed. "We're essentially inviting Ferdinand to come take her."

"Essentially, yes. That's exactly what we're doing. If we didn't believe he has a pack of unwilling women, I would deal with him in another way, but for their sake, we need his ego, greed, and attention on Jesse, who is their best bet for escaping relatively unscathed. Jesse, you remember how to contact the Secret Service if needed?"

I wrinkled my nose at the memory of Randal and Simmons taking turns with me on every damned type of phone in existence making certain I knew how to place a call to the emergency line if I got into any trouble without my agents around. "It would take severe head trauma for me to forget at this stage."

"Good job, Agent Randal, Agent Simmons. If you can teach her other tricks as well, you might even have a good principal before you two flee into retirement."

My agents laughed, and Simmons dismissed my aunt's criticism with a wave of his hand. "Her ability to handle solo situations is superior to most principals, and I expect she'll be a quick study once her shoulder is fully healed. Because of her shoulder, we've been focusing on her strengths rather than her weaknesses. Considering what you want her to do, I think we've made a good choice with how to handle her training. If your goal is to allow an opening, we should lower her active number of agents conditional to her staying here. That should create the type of opening you require and lessen the risk to active detail members."

"Agent Randal?" my aunt asked.

"We can use the opportunity to train her proper detail, assuming this goes to plan. With the Hope Diamond's inclination to protect her, she's probably safest with this change to her detail. Simmons, you want to take her next shift? That'll free me to make plans and track our quarry's associates."

"I'll take her primary shift, and we'll have some of the night owls work the evening shift. Madam President, how many openings do you want us to leave in security?"

"Enough to allow her to sneak out to her favorite bar and offer opportunities for any conspirators during the short walk," my aunt ordered. "Try to use your new freedoms somewhat responsibly, Jesse."

I huffed, as there was nothing responsible about deliberately turning myself into a target for a damned wolf I already wanted to disembowel given a single opportunity. As disemboweling would take too long and hurt too much, I'd have to settle with ripping the bastard's throat out, but I'd savor the final seconds of the bastard's life. "That means I can't take my tiger with me."

"You would be correct. Outside of the Secret Service and close friends who come here often, few are aware you're being heavily courted by your mate, so chances are, Ferdinand is unaware of your relationship developments. That works to your advantage. Don't draw attention to any of Nate's bite marks. The same applies to you, Nate. Use makeup to cover yours as needed."

"I don't want to cover—"

"Cover it," my aunt ordered.

"But—"

"Cover it."

"You can't win, tiger. Just surrender, or be beaten by two grizzlies, a rabbit, a stallion, and some Secret Service agents. That's how they operate here. I've learned this from months of them hovering over me. I suspect some of them are wanting to have some mat time with you because you fell on my teeth today."

"I hate how right you are," my tiger grumbled. "Fine. I'll cover it. For now. I'm doing this under protest. Also, can I fall on your teeth again tonight?"

"Really, Ana?"

"I enjoyed such a good nap after I fell onto your teeth. If I sleep that well again tonight, I might be functional tomorrow."

When I thought about it, he had a very good point. "You might be onto something. We'll talk about it tonight."

"With our teeth?"

"Sure, with our teeth, you idiot tiger."

He laughed.

My aunt heaved a sigh and rubbed at her temple. "If you could stop trying to find ways to get my niece to bite you again at the dinner table, I would appreciate it. Anyway, you're supposed to be going along with this under protest. You wouldn't be a suitable mate for my niece if you liked the idea of her handling this one solo. I don't like the idea, either, but I understand the necessity of it—and that she's our best chance to rescue his other victims. If there weren't innocent women involved, likely bite victims, I would have a bounty out for his head already. You can posture after Ferdinand is dealt with."

"I'd rather deal with him myself." Anatoly huffed. "But he'd just run, because he's a cowardly wolf and knows I don't like him."

"Now that we've talked about that unpleasant business, there's the issue of the missing Starfall stones. Jesse, should you cross paths with Steel Heart again, try to keep a hold on it. The Blade Clan has been the quietest about their missing stone, especially as it presents itself for its smithing duties, but the other clans are not as fortunate. They want their stones back, and they want their stones back now. A lot of meetings have been about trying to figure out how—and why—all of those stones disappeared at the same time. It's speculated that someone has stolen them, but we haven't determined for what purpose."

I shrugged, as it seemed obvious enough to me. "If

you have a rebellion in the works, they want the stones to forge weapons. That's the obvious answer."

"Except the stones typically will not function for someone who is not of the appropriate bloodline," my aunt replied.

"But how many people actually know that?" I countered.

Everyone stared at me, and I rolled my eyes at their blatant oversight. "You missed what was right in front of you, haven't you? For most people, researching Starfall stones is pointless. We know what they do, we know they can randomly burst, and we know they create magic. Beyond that, nobody really cares about specific stones unless they're turning them in for a reward. Why would anyone care about the clan Starfall stones outside of their use to create excellent weapons? Even the books that do identify and discuss the stones don't mention a lot about who can make them burst. You have to do high-level research—or be a member of the clan—to have access to that information. I'm assuming the upper branches of the government have done the research required, especially if the clans are requesting help to recover their Starfall stones."

My mate snickered. "I'll confess, it hadn't occurred to me to think of it from that angle—mostly because everyone is always after the damned things and the clans are notorious about protecting them. Nobody actually considers how the stones are typically attuned to someone of the appropriate bloodline. But that does beg a question."

"What question?"

"Why you? Why not another member of the Blade Clan? Why does Steel Heart seem to show up where you go?"

"How the hell should I know? It just shows up and makes a mess of my day. Mostly. I'll give it some credit, if it hadn't wandered into that bar, I probably wouldn't have made use of my tattoo kit."

"I rather like the stone for that, really."

My aunt sighed. "You're hopeless, Nate."

"I will admit, I had a bad moment or two when I realized I'd gotten branded with an assassin's mark, but I do rather appreciate what the ink means at this stage of my life. Granted, it could mean she's waiting to kill me off herself, but some risks are worth taking."

My tiger would drive me crazy one of these days. "What is the probability the weapon clans are part of the growing rebellion risk?"

The First Gentleman shook his head. "None. They want their Starfall stone back, and the mercenary companies won't work with traitors, and they've been hiring them left and right; whomever returns the stones will get a weapon forged with their clan's stone. If they were part of the rebellion, they would be forging weapons for it, not chasing down their stones and trying to prevent someone else from using them, losing them their place as premier warriors for hire. Now, the possibility does exist that they'll be coerced into participation, but so far, that doesn't seem to be the case."

Well, that was something. "And the Council?"

"The Council is scrambling because there's talks about integrating a representative from every class of mystic into the group for better representation; it would allow the Council to be more effective, rather than making guesses at what the mystics need from the government. Right now, mystic requests come through me, and I present them to the Council and various branches of government as required. It's impractical. The shifters have an edge in legislative matters because they're organized. The mystics would need to elect a representative for each grouping of magic, but it's something we've been discussing. The next election will bring the matter up for vote, and there will be a special election should the measure pass for the mystics to vote in their specific local officials. The local government will then select who represents them in the Council."

That sounded like a nightmare, and I considered how I might best rescue my tiger from his responsibilities. "This is going to make a great deal more work for the Council, isn't it?"

Once again, my lecherous rabbit of an uncle shook his head. "Not as much as you think. After everyone settles, it should save a great deal of time. I expect Henry or Cleo will ultimately represent healer mystics, as they both have an excellent reputation. It'll likely be Henry, because Henry is a known entity. Depending on who is voted in, I wouldn't be surprised if Cleo was given the nod to represent evocative mystics; while he is primarily a healing type, his combustion talents are the most stable among mystics, and he understands the delicate balance required to control evocation abilities on a government level. His work with mercenaries would make him an ideal representative."

I foresaw a disaster in future meetings. "But how would the local mystic representatives even know to suggest either one of them?"

"Henry travels with your tiger often, and he handles mystic affairs when his healing services aren't needed; he's a known entity among many city mystic circles. As for Cleo, while Todd typically stays close to Charlotte, he does have a reputation, and Cleo is often part of that reputation, especially as he's a donkey male in a horse herd. That has a certain status, as he's the only adult equine male who is a full part of the herd as a full adult. After age twenty-five, Todd's colts tend to band together in a male-only herd until they establish herds of their own. How many of your colts are part of a familial herd now, Todd?" the First Gentleman asked.

"They're thirty strong, although two of my colts are looking to form their own herds soon. We're allied herds as well, which is somewhat against herd tradition. We're stronger together, and we all know it. I also give my colts access to Cleo as needed."

"Where *are* Henry and Cleo, anyway?"

Todd laughed. "Probably at home enjoying the rest of their night off. After dealing with you two lazing about, they were ready to blow their tops, so we sent them off to do whatever it is mystics do when they're not taking care of their obnoxious charges. I'm sure they'll be back in the morning to bother you and check for new bite marks. Try not to maul each other too severely tonight."

"I'll try to limit falling onto her teeth to once or twice. I wouldn't want to tire her out too much."

Tigers. "How can I get a sedative for a tiger if they went home? I think this tiger needs a sedative."

Todd leered at me. "I'm sure you'll figure something out."

"Please keep your perverted ways to yourself, Todd. Dare I ask if there's anything else I should know about?"

"Beyond the typical idiots upset they got on the wrong side of the law, nothing special. Same shit, different day," my aunt replied. "It just happens today's shit also has a dose of Ferdinand and the possibility of rebellion to add some spice to our lives. Spice I could live without, mind you. Just be careful, Jesse. I trust your judgment."

I directed my attention to my lecherous uncle. "If she thinks *my* judgment is sound when I view another living being as a dessert for my enjoyment and have issues with marking his person without his permission, she probably needs a vacation. As for Ferdinand, should he show up, I'll make sure any of his plans die with him," I swore.

If I had anything to say about the situation, all Ferdinand would become was a bitter memory.

Chapter Seven

ANATOLY NEEDED to retrieve things from the Council meeting hall, and in a bid to keep from wasting extra time, I took my new moccasins, feather, and beads to my suite, intending to meet everyone else at the bridge spanning the lake surrounding the mausoleum I now called home.

It amazed me how much could change. While I had built a home in Cheyenne, I'd never viewed it as anything more than a place to stay with the comfort of having the tribe nearby. The former mayoral palace, transformed into the seat of power for the entire United States, had somehow become a central pillar in my life.

Randal went with my tiger, and Simmons kept close. As everyone seemed to believe my tiger would create problems somehow, they went with him, giving me breathing space. I regarded my agent with a raised brow. "I've lost most of my shadows, but I don't even have an urge to run away this time."

"You were promised beer, and you have a tiger to warm your bed tonight. It's all about having the right incentive. Frankly, I'm amazed it took this long for new arrangements to be made."

"You knew?"

"It's rather obvious. We were expecting a more vocal and violent snapping of tempers rather than some over-enthusiastic nipping and a nap. Still, this will simplify matters for everyone as soon as other matters are resolved."

Ferdinand. "I don't suppose you know anything more than what we talked about?"

"Unfortunately not. Nothing that's been confirmed. As far as we know, there are at least five women in his pack at current, but there could be more. We're judging that figure from missing persons reports and sightings of Ferdinand in the area, but they're unconfirmed speculations. Should he come for you, and you opt to try to help them, you'll have your hands full. You'll need to be careful and make certain you play along. That will not be easy. Also, expect any failed bites to hurt; it's not common, but there have been women involved in feuds between rival males with multiple bites. The bites all hurt until a victor is decided and the other bites have been erased."

"Erased? How?"

"The victorious male will bite over the prior bites,

or the rival male is killed. That's all we can tell from our reports. He'll try to put you through hell."

I scowled at that. "I can handle some pain."

"It will be more than just 'some' pain. The sole account we have compares each bite to the aftermath of a broken bone."

Ouch. "That's going to make this assignment less than pleasant."

"And you'll likely be mauled by your tiger as he reclaims his territory. We'll try to mitigate that, but that's probable. Siberians are more territorial than even a wolf, and we suspect he'll be unreasonable until any evidence of a rival having bitten you is completely erased. And he might not allow anyone near you until he's satisfied." Simmons scratched his head. "It'll be a mess."

"But for a good cause."

"Still. I want you to be careful. It goes against everything I've worked for to just let this happen."

"But you see the necessity of it."

"I see that you would go out of your way to deliberately get picked up specifically to make certain that any allegations of taken women are resolved. And that's why we're ultimately going with it—because you're correct to do what you can for their sake. And we have enough circumstantial evidence to believe it's probable. In your shoes, I would do the same."

"And that bothers you, because you're rather like my aunt. You want to wrap me up in a soft, warm blanket and keep me safe."

"You very much enjoy soft, warm blankets, and it's a pleasure to provide them when we notice you're cold again. Although honestly, I'd rather provide you with your tiger, who will be happy to bring you a blanket, because you're happiest when you can snarl at him at your leisure. When you aren't giving us the slip, you're a pleasant principal."

"Did you hit your head the last time you were tenderizing me?"

Simmons laughed. "No, but I'm amused you're concerned I have a head injury for enjoying that I'm part of your detail."

"I'm not the easiest person to get along with, and I have a bad habit of roaring, wandering off, and creating trouble for you. And this time, we're basically throwing me to a wolf. On purpose."

"Well, our work has not been boring. And however much I dislike tossing you to a wolf, you're the best person we have to handle that specific problem. Between the Hope Diamond and his previous interest in you, the wolf will want you alive. That's a key consideration. If they want the Hope Diamond, they need you alive—and once a wolf decides who he wants, he's difficult to deter. This is extra protection for you. The advantages of going along with this far outweigh the disadvantages. And, we're wise enough to know if you found out about the situation and we tried to bar you from helping, you'd find some way to help anyway, which would result in a even worse mess to clean up later."

I really would. "I'm more impressed Anatoly actually went off on his own."

"He knows he gets to stay with you tonight, and this is more efficient."

The Secret Service loved efficient. My tiger did, too. Efficient meant he had time to do what he wanted, and as of late, the internal workings of the government had been anything but efficient. "I keep trying to figure out ways to rescue him from those damned meetings."

"Once the current issues are resolved, I'm sure his schedule will ease. It's just a lot of problems at once."

"And I am part of at least half of them," I muttered.

"Jesse—"

The twang of arrows leaving bowstrings heralded a thump. Pain flashed along my upper left arm before numbness crept towards my shoulder and fingers. I reached for the hilt of my katana, freed it from its sheathe, and turned.

Simmons slumped beside me, and I registered the presence of arrows protruding from his chest and throat, the life already fading from his eyes, my name on his bloodied lips.

I had seen death too many times to deny the truth of it. Nothing I could do would save him; the arrow to his throat alone, severing through his spine, had brought a swift and merciful end. He wouldn't feel his pierced heart fail to beat, nor would he have registered more than a moment of confusion before the darkness had come for him.

I had no idea who the men down the hall were, but I expected they'd gotten in the same way I had long ago, hitching a lift with supply shipments coming into the building.

They would not be leaving except in a body bag. My blood dripped to the tile, mixing with Simmons's as his pooled on the floor. Rather than take the easy route, the six men abandoned bows for swords, and they stepped forward to engage with me.

My katana's blade erupted into black and blue flames, and heat washed over my hand although it didn't burn me. Around my throat, the Hope Diamond likewise warmed.

Nothing would bring Simmons back from the dead. Nothing could.

I understood, then, why the Blade Clan did as they did, simplifying life to a series of contests and the endless cycle of life and death, removing as much emotion from our existence as possible.

In the blink of an eye, I understood Simmons wouldn't be coming back, and the pain of it crushed me far worse than even the moment my uncle's blade had torn into my shoulder. It reminded me of the grief of watching the abused horses I couldn't help die, but far sharper and deeper.

I could only think of one thing to do: crush those who had killed my agent and forever taken him from me.

For a time, I would escape from the brutal emotions seeking to tear me apart from within.

It didn't matter if my left arm went numb. I didn't need both arms to kill them. I would fight to my final breath to ensure they all went down with me. The days of my childhood, such as it was, surged back to renewed life.

The first to die would be the taller man, the one who'd first gone for his sword of the lot, leader by action. Much like severing the head from a snake, I would begin with the most dangerous part and cut my way towards victory.

I came in poised to slash the fucker's throat, switched my grip on the textured hilt, and ducked beneath his swing before running the bastard through the gut, twisting the blade as I yanked it free. Death would be a long time coming, and to make certain he wouldn't be bothering me again, I slashed through the muscles of his forearms to prevent him from gripping a weapon. If he wanted to gnaw my ankles in his death throes, I'd enjoy kicking out his teeth. With one threat neutralized, I went for the next in the line, a fool of a man too stupid to realize death would come for him next at my hand.

Sometime before dispatching all of them, the numbness spread to my chest, making it difficult to keep a hold on my katana. A solid hit knocked the blade out of my hand, and I reached for my next possible weapon, the stiletto I held for the tribe.

It, too, burst into blue and black flames. I should have retrieved my katana, but I could only focus on one thing: making sure each and every one of the bastards paid for Simmons's life with theirs.

Losing the katana gave them harder, longer, and more painful deaths, and a better person would have regretted extending their suffering. I did make certain to finish them off after they no longer posed a threat to me. Panting, I stood over their bodies, more of my blood dripping down my arm.

Ferdinand chose that moment to make his appearance, stepping around the corner with a smug expression on his face. "You're as spectacular as always, I see. It's been a while, Jesse. You've become more beautiful over the years."

I wanted to end his miserable life, but I remembered. Before he could die, I needed to discover the truth. My gaze dipped to Simmons's body, and my anger surged. I swore to never forget, and I would make certain Ferdinand lost everything.

Even if it meant pretending weakness to accomplish my goals.

I'd just stab the bastard a little first with my stiletto, hope the wound became infected, and that he suffered for months before dying a slow, agonized death.

Keeping my hold on the weapon would prove the trick, as the numbness insisted on spreading despite my wishes to stab Ferdinand a few times for his part in Simmons's death. I panted, struggling to maintain my balance, a chill seeping through my body.

"It won't take much longer for the sedative to kick in," the wolf promised, stepping just outside of my reach. "While I'm sorry about the agent, it was a necessity. You'll understand that soon enough."

I'd heard that bullshit from the uncles I'd assassinated, and I refused to believe it. "What do you want?"

"What I've wanted for years. I'd ask you to keep from being difficult, but that's part of your charm. I like my women tough. This is a fight you can't win. Not this time. I'd rather you didn't make this even more difficult on yourself."

I gave it another minute or two at most before I lost the ability to stay on my feet, a mix of the drug and blood loss. Throwing a stiletto wouldn't do much good, but would be an act of defiance that might leave a mark. I adjusted my grip on the blade and tossed it at his chest. As expected the wolf side-stepped, although the weapon's tip did scrape against his arm before clattering to the floor.

He laughed, regarding his arm with an amused expression. "Just what I expected of you. Defiant until the end. I'm going to be generous, Jesse. The first bite hurts the most, so I'll take care of securing you as mine as soon as you're properly sedated and easy to handle. I'm a lot of things, but I'm no fool, and I won't give you even a single opening. Not this time."

Anatoly's bite hadn't hurt hardly at all, but I kept my mouth shut. I forced myself to take the steps needed to make it to Simmons's body. Ferdinand stayed out of my reach, and something about his expression changed.

Had I not known better, I might have assumed he was concerned.

I dropped to my knees beside my agent's cooling body. He'd fallen on his side, his neck twisted so he faced the ceiling. Reaching over, I closed his glazing eyes. My eyes burned. Some said the strong didn't cry, but how could I not?

I couldn't bring him back.

In the distance, the sound of steel clashing on steel warned me Ferdinand hadn't come alone. I could only hope everyone else fared better. As nothing could bring my agent back, I drew in a deep but wavering breath. I pressed my hand to Simmons's still side, clutching his suit in a fist.

Ferdinand would see my acts as weakness. I knew better.

To the fallen, I made a vow, and I would find satisfaction in the complete ruin of everything Ferdinand held dear. His plans would fall to ruin along with his accomplices, and I would tear him apart while he believed his bite could defeat me.

I hoped whatever foul magic he attempted on me hurt. It would only fuel my vengeance and focus me on what I needed to do.

The chill continued its steady march, and when my vision finally dimmed and I swayed under its influence, Ferdinand grabbed my arm and hauled me to my feet.

I remembered nothing else.

Chapter Eight

FERDINAND, as expected, lied. He woke me right before he bit me, and he did it to savor the moment. As warned, it hurt, and my tiger's bite on my arm burned. Ferdinand picked a spot above the Hope Diamond's setting to mark his territory, and he made sure he drew blood so his wolf's magic could work.

Except it didn't.

Every place my tiger had nipped and nibbled heated to the point of pain, a reminder of the weeks I'd spent cultivating my tiger in preparation of making him fully mine. The bite mark on my throat burned, but nothing else happened. The discomfort faded to something close to tolerable, and to play along with my new role as an infiltrator in addition to Ferdinand's killer, I slapped my hand to the still-bleeding bite.

I wanted to scowl, but I widened my eyes to feign weakness.

He smirked, and he pulled away, sitting straight in

his seat. It took me a few moments to realize we were in a private cabin on a train. I wondered how he'd pulled the stunt off, although the answer seemed obvious enough: he'd allied with people at the train station to smuggle me on board somehow. I expected an incident nearby, likely on another train at Charlotte's station, had provided the necessary distraction. He had the blinds down on the windows, making it impossible to tell where we were. It didn't matter; I wouldn't have been able to tell much from the scenery anyway.

"You will be quiet, you will cooperate, and you will do as told. When I introduce you to the other members of our pack, you will treat them well. You are the lowest in the pack, and you will stay that way, as while you're now one of my mates, I have no intention of producing offspring with a cat. It would send the wrong message to the pack. However, tigers are well-known for ferocity in protecting young, and that will be your role in our family. You will protect the children of my wolves, and you will do so with pride."

Well, that was something. I wouldn't have to abandon my duty to find out his plans by prematurely slaughtering him if he even thought about getting randy with me. As he'd ordered me to be quiet and cooperate, I clenched my teeth, aware of every single time my tiger had scraped me with his teeth.

I'd need to have a talk with somebody about the potency of the bonding magic I'd been exploring, as my tiger had left countless, invisible marks on me.

No wonder tigers got territorial; in any other situation, I would have snapped and mauled Ferdinand for subjecting me to such discomfort. Instead, I used it as fuel for my mission.

Ferdinand would pay dearly for Simmons's death, and I would add to his punishment for making me even more miserable in the process. I'd present the wolf's head to my uncle on a platter, and I'd give the rest of the body to my tiger. If I found proof Marie was involved, I'd bury her in a hole so deep nobody found her for years, and I'd brand my assassin's mark to the bone so everyone would know she had deserved her death for her traitorous deeds.

I already regretted not having secured guaranteed payment for my work, although my aunt would pay upon demand.

The money would come in useful, especially if the women of the pack were being used—and treated like—broodmares for the wolf's pleasure. No matter what the women decided once I finished with Ferdinand, they would have the funds needed.

I'd just mooch off my tiger when I found my way back to him. I would also swap roles and hide under his bed for a while.

"Good. I'm glad you understand how things will be. Nobody will really miss you, so I suggest you accept your new role. Once you've proven your loyalty, I might even allow you off your leash a little."

Bastard. I wanted to hiss and roar at him, but until he asked me to say something, I needed to play along. I regarded the otherwise empty train car with a frown.

"I booked the entire car, although our compatriots are currently in the dining car retrieving something for you to eat. They were waiting for me to wake you and seal you to my pack. Otherwise, they would want you put down so they could acquire the stone that way. I had to remind them that it's easier to transport a live woman than a dead body, and we have no guarantees the stone will remain cooperative should you be killed. You're lucky I have an interest in you."

While he'd told me to be quiet and cooperate, he hadn't told me I couldn't display disgust, and I curled my lip in a silent snarl at his egotistical proclamation.

The bastard dared to laugh. "You'll be an excellent asset to my pack. You'll learn your place soon enough. As I do with all new members of the pack, I will bite you once or twice a day to ensure your loyalties are secured. The first bite is the worst. After a few weeks, I will reduce my claims to once a week, and it won't have to be on your throat once you're appropriately scarred."

Fortunately, there were ways to remove most types of scars, and I'd beat however many mystics required to make it happen. As telling him to go fuck himself with his own teeth wouldn't help my plans, I remained silent.

Three men with trays entered the train car, setting their bounty on the pair of tables near the front, which had enough room for everyone. Ferdinand gestured for me to head over, and I took my time, aware of the lingering sedatives in my system. I swayed with my first few steps, but I made the rest of the walk with my head held high.

I didn't recognize them, and I hoped they realized I carved their faces into my memory, so they would pay their share of dues for their part in Simmons's death.

"She'll cooperate with you for what we've discussed," Ferdinand announced. "As she's mine, you will take all due precautions to make certain she's returned to me alive and in good condition when the time is right. In the meantime, she stays with my pack, and you can verify her presence as promised."

The wolf's phrasing led me to believe he meant to keep me in the dark as long as possible. In a way, he disappointed me; I'd hoped he would have made some part of my job somewhat easy.

No matter. I appreciated a challenge, and I wouldn't put him down until I had the proof needed to keep my name pristine.

"Jesse, eat. Once we're home, you'll find you'll be working for your supper or you'll go hungry. Enjoy while you can."

I could see the idiot controlling his pack through revoking access to the basics. As I hadn't been told I could speak up, and I needed to maintain my strength if I wanted to do my job well, I sat, investigated the offerings on the trays, and selected a plate of chicken and steak for myself, baring my teeth in challenge if they didn't like my choice.

"Tigers have quite the appetite," Ferdinand

explained. "And bites are tiring for the recipient. Feed her, and she won't bother you."

Oh, I would bother them. I would just take my time about it. But when I was finished, one thing was certain: their deaths would be so brutal people would grimace at the mere mention of their demise.

FERDINAND TOOK me to wolf country, and when we drew close to the station deep in the heart of Tennessee, he dressed me up in jeans, a button-up denim shirt, and a cowboy hat to help cover my more distinctive appearance. Instead of asking me to take out the beads and feathers from my hair, he pretended they didn't exist.

I wondered at that. The feathers and beads gave me a unique look, marking me as someone affiliated with a tribe, something that could identify me and send word back to Charlotte.

The feathers would draw attention, which was a double-edged sword. Until I finished my job, I didn't want word reaching Charlotte of my whereabouts.

I couldn't afford to hope that the feathers and beads were somehow encouraging people to forget about their presence. I wished they could help me forget the feel of Ferdinand's bite. My skin skill crawled.

I wanted my tiger, but I couldn't afford to have him show up, not until I finished my mission. When he did arrive, I had plans. It would take a lot of his bites to remove the slimy memory of Ferdinand's teeth breaking through my skin. A persistent ache lingered everywhere my tiger had touched me with his mouth, but I welcomed the discomfort.

It helped me ignore Ferdinand's bite and reminded me why I needed to play along with the wolf's plans.

Much like in Charlotte, the streets of Knoxville were clogged with horses, wagons, carriages, and people, making it easy to disappear into the crowd. Nobody paid Ferdinand any mind, which led me to believe that, unlike in Charlotte, the wolf had gone out of his way to just be another face among many.

Wise traitors did that.

After over two hours of walking, Ferdinand gestured to a two-story home. "This is the pack house, where you will stay when you are not with me. You will not leave it without permission or if one of the pack bitches orders you to. If you behave, you'll earn a bedroom, but for now, figure something out. I'm sure they'll have extra bedding you can use in the meantime."

I fought my desire to get on with the assassination portion of my job, grateful he'd told me to be seen rather than heard. Given leave to speak, I'd regret my words within moments of speaking them.

I would have a few words for my uncle about bad choices regarding his former second-in-command.

Ferdinand guided me to a town house in a rattier part of town, although the building seemed in better shape than its neighbors. Making the assumption he skimped on the property to give him more funding for his traitorous plans, I heeled as I'd been told and struggled to keep from snarling at the bastard wolf. He climbed the short flight of steps to the front door, unlocked it, and headed inside, waving for me to follow him inside. "Rachelle!"

A heavily pregnant woman with limp brown hair and a gaunt build waddled into the home's entry, which consisted of a bench, a shoe rack, and a side table stacked with opened letters. To my amusement, there was a dish filled with letter openers, something I could weaponize in a jam.

I flexed my hands so I wouldn't grab one and end Ferdinand's pathetic life right then and there.

"Ferdinand?" the woman asked, and she averted her eyes. Her posture screamed prey. Her scent claimed she was a wolf shifter. She sniffed the air, and she tensed.

I couldn't imagine a wolf woman appreciating a larger predator coming into her turf, not when she had an unborn puppy to protect.

"This is Jesse. She is now part of the pack. She will do whatever you need her to do. Send her on errands, do whatever you want with her. She isn't to leave the house without me or at your order. She isn't to have a bedroom until she's proven herself, so put her anywhere else you see fit. If you're not sure where to put her, have her pick a spot. I would tolerate the attic, if necessary."

According to Rachelle's expression, she couldn't

believe what she heard, but she bobbed her head in acquiescence.

What choice did she have? None. I abhorred wolf magic, but I couldn't even growl over it, or Ferdinand wouldn't believe his bite had worked. I expected he'd tear my throat too often for my liking. His bite—and all of Anatoly's marks—still ached. My shoulder injury and recovery gave me an edge; I'd adapted to far worse pain sustained for longer than I hoped I'd be stuck with the wolf and his pack.

"Good. I'll bring the monthly food budget in tomorrow, adjusted for the extra mouth. She's at the bottom of the pole, and you won't have to worry about any children with her. While I've staked my claim, there won't be any hybrids." The way Ferdinand spat the world implied he'd rather drown any offspring with mixed heritage. "You'll find her competent and useful, and I bit her to protect the pack. For all she's unsuitable for mating, she's the best out there for being the pack's guardian. She's an experienced mercenary with a specialization in touchy guard jobs. Despite her unfortunate species, she will do her job well. I will be back daily to secure my hold on her, so do let the other ladies know."

Rachelle bobbed her head again, and I got the feeling she fought the urge to dip into a curtsy. "Of course. What time can we expect you tomorrow?"

"Around noon. I expect her to require a few days to settle, as she is unused to the restraints of pack life. She is a more solitary creature."

"Creature?"

"Tiger," Ferdinand snarled.

I clasped my hands together so I wouldn't go for the bastard's throat then and there.

One day, he would learn—very briefly—that there would be nothing more terrifying and lethal than a scorned tigress. I would make his death so quick, yet so brutal people would whisper of his fate for years. Fantasizing about his demise helped maintain control over my flaring temper.

There would be no roaring, not until I'd finished my work and could roar out my frustrations for my mate to hear.

Once I worked out the worst of my irritation, he would soothe me. He always did, no matter how annoyed he made me with his egotistical posturing. He might soothe me by instigating more roaring and a spat, but I would emerge better for it.

When I finished roaring, I expected the first quiet minutes alone would lead to doing what I couldn't yet bear: mourning my lost agent.

I missed Simmons, and the awareness he wouldn't be clawing his way up the walls to find me stabbed deeper than any blade could. I clung to my rage. I would need it to get through the next few weeks—or however long it took me to crush Ferdinand.

"A tiger?" Rachelle asked.

"A tiger," Ferdinand confirmed. "Do with her as you wish. Consider her your servant. I have work to do."

Without another word, the wolf spun on a heel and left, and I glared at his departing back. I waited until he closed the door to bare my teeth in a silent snarl. Controlling my expression, I turned to the pregnant woman but didn't speak.

"Well, come on then. He does this to anyone who is new, even the wolves. He leaves his new mates waiting a few months to make them desperate before changing his mind. He enjoys his dominance, but he'll be kind enough as long as you do as told."

He'd be long dead before he even thought about doing such a thing with me. Rather than correct her, I mimicked the way she'd nodded.

"I wonder what we did to deserve him guarding us," the woman muttered, and she shook her head.

I read between the lines: he didn't care for any of them, which matched how he tended to use people. He'd used people even in Dawnfire, something I'd remind my uncle about when I found my way back to Charlotte. Then again, he might get off without a peep from me.

By the time I made it home, I'd need time with my tiger, and yelling at my uncle would take away from my time with my tiger.

I focused my attention on the wolf, taking note of her paler complexion and slender, gaunt build. While Ferdinand claimed he'd account for my presence, I'd take the bare minimum to make sure any pregnant women could benefit. She needed more than she was getting, but with my current orders and my need to play dumb, I had no idea how to help her.

Worse, I worried she was only the start of my domestic woes.

While I had lived on the streets and struggled to get by, I had always been accepted with Todd and his guild, flitting in and out of their lives with an expectation of being welcomed.

She had a home, but my nose told me living in it scared her—and that my presence changed things. For her, I expected change terrified rather than comforted. Change added uncertainty. Change created problems.

Change likely hadn't opened any doors for her.

Ferdinand would have changed everything with his first bite, leaving her an unwilling prisoner forced to do his bidding.

Fucking wolf. Fucking wolf magic.

I should have said the same about Anatoly's tiger magic, but I'd never felt a need to obey him. He treasured my defiance. He enjoyed when I tried to best him. He loved when I bested him, and he encouraged my triumphs the same way he coaxed me into craving physical touch and affection.

Being bound to him wasn't a prison. Binding him to me also wasn't a prison.

I'd stepped into a cage, but my resolve strengthened.

When I left the cage, I would emerge with a pack of freed wolves, and I didn't care for their names or reasons for being part of Ferdinand's pack. I wouldn't take note of them beyond the bare minimums to get by. I would pay close attention to Rachelle.

The others would be caged birds to me, ones I meant to set free.

Simmons would have approved, however much he would find my quest for vengeance unsettling.

He hated when I killed, but not because he believed murder and assassination to be a man's work. No, I'd seen through my agent, too late to do me any good.

He'd just wanted me to be happy, something I struggled with on a good day.

Killing everyone who had taken my agent from me would make me very happy—until the grief settled in again and threatened to choke me.

Rachelle regarded me with a frown. "You're pretty calm about this. The new ones usually aren't."

I forced a smile. "He will regret his bite."

He wouldn't live to regret it, but he would regret it all the same, as would any allied with him.

"That's a toast I would raise my glass for. Since he directly ordered, I can't give you a bedroom, but you're welcome to take whatever space you otherwise see fit. I'll leave it up to you if you want to meet the others. We try to keep to ourselves unless we know Ferdinand won't be around. He doesn't like when he thinks we're banding together." Rachelle sighed. "No surprise there. You'll get used to it. You'll find overt defiance is impossible, but we have our moments. Once."

I understood; they defied him as they could, exactly once before he ordered them to never do such a thing again, and the wolf magic would enforce it. Like me, her throat bore a fresher bite, likely a few days old but healing well enough.

Slower than my tiger's bite on me had healed.

"One day, once will be enough," I promised.

"Or so we pray," she replied, gesturing deeper into the sparsely furnished house. "Come with me. It's not much, but the pack's house is our home, and it's safe enough."

From her tone, I gathered it was only safe for as long as Ferdinand wasn't around, and I wondered if there was anything I could do to change that for her—for them.

One way or another, I'd find out.

Chapter Nine

A WAIF of a woman with pale hair stalked after me, and I debated if I wanted to ignore her, growl a warning, or go for her throat and establish I wasn't prey for her or anyone else. Rachelle halted, raised a brow, and engaged the woman in a staring contest, which she won after a few tense minutes.

"Ferdinand bit her," Rachelle whispered.

"I guessed as much from the rage in her eyes. She looks ready to burn the house down if you gave her the right Starfall stone and a few minutes alone. I like it. He finally brought someone who might be able to do something about this. Fucking fool."

Well, that simplified things. I reevaluated my initial impression of her. I couldn't reveal I might be able to light the house down given a few minutes alone without the help of the Hope Diamond, although I'd be tempted, given a week of the incessant ache from my tiger's bites. "I'm Jesse."

"Lauren. I'm five or so months along, I'd like to kick that wolf in the nuts, and any time you want to play cards and discuss the best way to cut his dick off, let me know."

"I'll keep that in mind."

"What's her orders?" Lauren asked, planting her hands on her hips and again meeting Rachelle glare for glare.

"Apparently, she is a tiger, and she is to protect the pack."

"A cat with a bunch of dogs? Is he trying to start a fight? He's not going to be able to handle a cat, and I don't care how good he thinks he is with wolf magic. He's going to find out what happens when he bites off more than he can chew, and she don't smell like he's been taming her in other ways."

I'd do more than kick him in the nuts or cut his dick off if Ferdinand tried, but I kept my mouth shut. While Lauren seemed like a potential ally, I wouldn't know for certain until I had a chance to watch the pack of women.

"I've been told I'm to manage her."

"That'll be interesting. How does someone manage a cat? Cats live to be trouble."

Rachelle shrugged. "Well, he did bite her. That will ensure her general behavior."

"He's going to get kicked in the nuts and have his dick cut off by the time that cat is done with him. I just want to see it when she breaks free, snaps, and kills the bastard."

"She's been bitten, Lauren."

"Don't matter. He can barely hold onto the pack he has, and adding a cat to the mix isn't going to make things easier. He's going to have to bite her every day if he wants half a prayer of making her do what he wants—and it'll make it easier for us, too." Lauren circled me in the confines of the hallway, and she touched one of the eagle feathers dangling from my hair. "You're native?"

"Not quite, but I was gifted with these from a tribe." It would take longer than any of us had to explain the odd relationship I had with the North Cheyenne tribe. When I headed out west again, I'd have to ask the elders if they'd lost their minds when they'd sent me more beads and another feather. If their base criteria involved me living up to the name they'd gifted me, I supposed I had earned every feather and bead I wore.

Heading west with my tiger would go a long way to restoring me to the person I wanted to be, although I expected the trip would be long and difficult on a good day.

"Huh. And you're supposed to guard us? Why would he care about having us guarded? We're trophies. It helps set his rank here having an extra mate, but beyond that, we're evening entertainment and extra mouths to feed."

For that alone, I'd enjoy killing Ferdinand.

"Don't let anyone else hear that, Lauren," Rachelle warned in a hushed tone. "No matter how true it might be. You know some of them are ordered to snitch, and that's no fault of theirs. Don't set Jesse up for a fall, not when she doesn't know the ropes yet."

"Fine. Where is he having her stay?"

"Not in a bedroom," Lauren replied, her tone bitter.

"The upstairs linen closet is large enough for a body, and we can move the towels out, so she can use the shelves for whatever she needs. Can't do much about the lack of light in there, but at least she'd have a space, and it's not a bedroom. If you tell her to pick a spot, she could wander up and take it, and we'd be all right, it's not like we have all that much extra to store in the other rooms."

"Jesse?"

A closet would offer me a little privacy, and I'd stayed in worse places while working a job or traveling the United States. "I suppose I will go wander up and pick a spot that seems like a closet." The expected answer left a bitter taste in my mouth, but I would convert the space to my haven, make it mine, and use it to continue my plans to crush Ferdinand and his willing accomplices.

"Then it's settled. Can you deal with everyone else, Lauren? Perhaps they should give Jesse space for a month or two, as she's not just a cat, but she's a rather large cat—and Ferdinand would not be pleased if we fought each other."

According to Rachelle's tone, a mix of wary and disgusted, in-fighting had plagued the pack before.

"We ain't fought nobody in months. Why? We're all stuck up the same shit creek without a paddle or a boat. Maybe she'll shift for us and give us something new to look at."

I needed to practice shifting, especially partial-body shifts. I'd need my sharp claws to properly tear out Ferdinand's throat, and my efforts needed to be masked through other activities—like entertaining a bunch of captive pack women.

"He told her she couldn't shift as far as I know," Rachel murmured, looking me over. "We're only allowed to shift for official pack gatherings. He doesn't want to lose his hold on us, and it's harder to maintain his bite when our wolves are out."

"What do you mean it's harder to maintain his bite? I thought wolf bites were permanent."

The two women exchanged looks and shook their heads. "Not precisely," Lauren replied. While we have to obey his direct orders, his hold on us has been getting a lot weaker. We're at the point we can think for ourselves again."

"You can *think* for yourselves?" I'd heard enough about wolf bites to realize obedience was required of the bitten victim—and a woman *could* bite a man, but men typically did the biting. I hadn't thought the wolf's magic could be so strong it could circumvent the ability to remain an individual.

"It's like being wrapped in a towel and drowned," Rachelle replied, and deep lines cut across her brow. "All that mattered was making certain he was content.

There was no room for anything else. Every woman he bit has made it easier. I don't drown anymore. The compulsion is still there, and I have to obey, but I can see the world around me again."

Holy shit. No wonder everyone had believed there'd be no rescuing myself from Ferdinand when I'd been at high risk of being bitten. "That's terrible."

"It is, but one day, we'll be free. The day he bites one too many women, he'll lose us all. We'll be *free*," Lauren whispered.

They'd be freed a lot sooner than they likely dreamed possible, but I still worried what would happen upon Ferdinand's death. If they cared for Ferdinand, what would their grief do?

If they felt even a fraction of my rage over Simmons's death, they would tear me apart.

Then Anatoly would tear them apart for their role in my death.

Things could get messy in a hurry.

"Well, until then, we're stuck."

Lauren checked over her shoulder. "Order her out of the house every day. She's a cat. She'll go crazy if she stays cramped in a closet surrounded by a bunch of hormone-crazed bitches."

"Lauren," Rachelle warned.

"What? It's true. Is Ferdinand going to up the budget? He didn't last time."

No wonder the women seemed gaunt; if he hadn't given them extra money to fill an extra stomach, they probably shared among themselves as much as they could.

"He said he'd bring extra tomorrow."

"Really? Do you think he's really going to do that? All he has to do is keep us alive. Nobody cares about us beyond that. They don't care about our pups, either. They don't even care we don't want this. Nobody cares."

"Lauren."

The woman scowled, bowed her head, and huffed. "Fine. What do you want me to do?"

"Tell the others Jesse needs time to settle, and we'd be better off if we didn't have an infuriated tiger in our midst."

"Yeah, I guess a few hundred pounds of angry cat would make a mess of the place, and he'd make us fix it. I'll let them know. We don't have enough meat to keep a tiger fed, though."

"I won't eat much," I promised. It wasn't a lie. While I could eat the palace stocks barren, I'd take only enough to keep moving one foot in front of the other. Once I finished Ferdinand off, I'd gorge.

I'd gone hungry before. I could do it again. Life with my family and my tiger hadn't made me go completely soft.

After a few weeks, I'd be courting trouble, but I'd do my best to make sure the women got the excess my share would include. With a little luck, Ferdinand would remember tigers could eat a lot and plan accordingly.

"I thought tigers ate a lot."

We did. "I'll be fine."

A little hunger wouldn't hurt me, and if I needed something, assuming I could get permission to leave the damned house, I could go out of the city and try to hunt something. I hadn't learned the finer points of hunting as a tiger, but it beat starving to death without putting in some effort.

Maybe I could find a particularly slow and stupid deer to eat somewhere in the woods.

Both women eyed me like they weren't quite willing to believe a tiger could live off a light diet without eating them.

"I'll show her the upstairs," Rachelle muttered. "Can you check what we have in the kitchen and how much of a budget we still have?"

"Will do." Lauren left me with Rachelle, and the woman sighed.

"She seems rather rebellious," I observed.

"She was taken second, and Ferdinand picked her because he likes snuffing out our fire. We were hoping the next one would free us all, but no such luck."

As I couldn't tell Rachelle his bite couldn't stick on me, I feigned dismay. What else could I do? "I'm sorry."

"It's certainly not your fault. You don't want to be here, either."

While I didn't want to be in Tennessee, far from my tiger, I needed to be there. I would bide my time, and when the time was right, I would act.

Somehow.

THE CLOSET WOULD TEST my patience, but it was the best space that wasn't a bedroom in the entire house, unless I wanted to share the attic with a bunch of bats and their guano. I questioned how the wolves tolerated the mess right over their heads.

Fire simply didn't happen outside of a combustion zone without the help of magic, but I'd expose one of my darker secrets to torch the place and bask in the warmth while it burned. With the Hope Diamond, which remained locked around my throat, I could make it happen without anyone believing I was the responsible party. The Hope Diamond could do anything.

It could torch a house that Ferdinand used as a prison.

In good news, I could stretch out in the closet. In bad news, I ran a high risk of bashing my brains out on the shelf over my head, which was bolted into place. There was a sufficient gap between the door and the shelves I could, if needed, stand in the closet and access the shelving space. I doubted Ferdinand would bother with any of the basics, but Rachelle had refused to listen to my request to leave the towels alone, as I didn't own anything.

She brought enough bedding to make a comfortable enough nest, and she left me to my own devices.

Staying distant would help my cause, assuming I

could get close enough to Ferdinand to learn more about his plans. While I appreciated a good challenge, I worried I'd have to do my investigations following his death. Within a few weeks, I would have a good idea of life with the pack, the precautions the wolf inevitably took to hide his treason, and a better feel for the women under his heel.

To prove I had nothing to hide and benefit from the light in the hallway, I left the closet door cracked open, burrowed in the blankets, and settled in to wait. After battling cold after cold, with the added bonus of a busted shoulder, I'd gotten in a lot of practice at biding my time and behaving. Instead of consoling myself with the necessity of the murder I planned, I reminded myself of the bitter past and why I needed to choose mercy over satisfaction.

There'd be no proper tattoos; I lacked the needles and ink. Peaceful sleep wouldn't overcome my victim before I finished him off, either. *Them*, if the suspicions about Marie proved to be the truth.

For Todd's sake, I wanted her to be innocent, but everything pointed to the same place: she had played some part in my agent's death. If my understanding of the situation was correct, Ferdinand had been marked as suspicious long enough he wouldn't have been given any relevant information on the inner workings of the palace. Marie, through Todd, would have been able to access current intel to a certain degree.

Particularly, she would have known something of

my activities, and would have been able to help them pick a good time for their move.

I would always wonder if luck alone had spared Randal from Simmons's fate, as any other day in the palace, he would have been with me. Then, half of the arrows that had killed Simmons would have found their mark in Randal.

I would have carried the burden of both their deaths to Tennessee.

Had Randal survived? Had anyone gone after my aunt? My uncles? The pain of my tiger's nips, nibbles, and bites offered the reassurance he'd survived whatever had happened at the palace. Not knowing bothered me more than the discomfort of Ferdinand's bite, which hadn't seemed to heal like I expected.

I would blame my tiger for that, and I'd enjoy sinking my teeth into him and dragging him off somewhere once I found my way back to Charlotte. Contemplating what I would do to and with my tiger would occupy a lot of empty time, I expected. Creating elaborate plans to drag him off, evading everyone in the process, would need a lot of care to do right. I would need several hours of uninterrupted time, somewhere we wouldn't be disturbed, and at least one of his ties, preferably the red one.

I bet I could do a lot with him and his red tie.

My thoughts of my tiger distracted me for all of five minutes before the reality of my situation crept in again.

I'd expected women. I hadn't expected starving

pregnant women. However difficult my job became, I refused to fail. I wanted to snap, head back to Charlotte, and find out if everyone was all right. Ferdinand and his accomplices had attacked my home. After so long adrift, the thought of them sullying what I finally had birthed a rage as strong as the one burning over Simmons's loss.

I would torch everything Ferdinand held dear.

A thunk at the door jolted me from my thoughts, and I opened my mouth to ask who it was when sparks burst off a dark surface. The pitted, dark stone hit the door again and bounced into my nest.

My eyes widened, and before the Starfall stone could draw unwanted attention from one of the pack's women, I snatched it up. Memories welled of the moment the stone had bounced across the bar in Miami, coming to a halt in front of me. Waiting. Casting flecks of light and flame off its surface.

Steel Heart.

It warmed my hand, although its light died away.

While faint, the memory of the stone inducing my first shift surfaced. It had warmed me then, too. Everything that had happened until I'd reached the forest remained lost, but I appreciated recapturing even a single moment of finding another facet of my true self.

While Ferdinand had taken everything from me except my beads and feathers, he'd given me a belt with a pouch on it, a common enough accessory to make my outfit seem authentic. It would make a good hiding place for Steel Heart and some other stones I picked up, which would give me an excuse to have it. Any rock I could fiddle with and rub would convince him of my innocence, or so I hoped. If he spotted Steel Heart, he would know its nature.

He'd been involved in the initial hunt for the stone.

I placed it in my pouch and tied the drawstrings to prevent it from wandering, although I had no doubts it would leave confinement if it wanted to. After all, it had found its way into the house, up the stairs, and to my closet.

If Ferdinand discovered the stone's presence, the ruse would be up: I would have to eliminate him to protect my clan's property—and to keep him from finding a way to weaponize it. Possessing the Hope Diamond was problematic enough, but it burst at its whim.

Steel Heart had a long history of bending to the will of men. I wondered if it would listen to a woman if circumstance demanded I find a way to put the Starfall stone to use. I couldn't forge a sword, but I could do some serious damage with a butter knife. I bet the rock could turn a spoon into a dangerous weapon.

Scooping out Ferdinand's eyeballs and feeding them to him might appease the beast within for a few moments. Then again, if I gouged out his eyeballs, I'd have to spend even more time with him. No, brutal and swift would be my best bet. Unless he died before he comprehended I'd turned on him, he might find some way to retaliate.

Simmons's death reminded me of an unfortunate

truth: a good assassination left no chance for the victim to do anything other than die. I'd built the entirety of my career on such deaths.

Unlike Ferdinand's accomplices, I'd do my dirty work alone.

In time, when my agent's death settled to a bone deep ache rather than a cutting edge, I might view his last moments with a twisted sense of pride.

He'd been so dangerous and skilled they'd needed so many to ensure he died.

Maybe Ferdinand needed an army to do his vile work, but I would become a one-woman army determined to erase everything he stood for. I would find some way to use the Hope Diamond to accomplish my goals.

And Steel Heart, too. That Starfall stone would create problems for me.

My clan would want it back, and they would eventually find me. Would hiding it in a pouch and holding it close work? It would be my first plan until I found something better—or the stone decided it no longer desired my company.

Without my tiger, my friends, or my family, I hoped the stone would stick around. I found some twisted comfort in the Hope Diamond's presence locked around my throat. While it inconvenienced me more often than not, the necklace had transformed itself into something of a friend, too.

It refused to leave me, although I didn't understand why.

I still struggled to understand why others hadn't given up on me, especially among my family, who had searched for me on nothing more substantial than the knowledge I existed. Gentry's admission he'd hunted for me, his missing niece, continued to amaze me long after the fear of discovery had faded away.

My tiger's dedication to an unknown entity still flummoxed me. He hadn't even been the one to forge a commitment with the Blade Clan, but he'd taken up his sister's responsibilities without question or complaint. No, he'd done everything with his typical ego and pride, turning what should have been a burden into a matter of honor.

That *I* had become the woman he'd promised himself to only made him prouder and even more egotistical.

To him, he wasn't meeting some obligation forced upon him.

I was a prize worth winning.

In the dark quiet of the closet, I feared my thoughts would drive me insane long before the pain of the conflicting bites.

As always, I became my own worst enemy.

THE IDEA of a fire capable of consuming entire buildings left me awed.

It also offered me additional insight.

Everyone believed the Hope Diamond could do

anything. When it burst, cities fell—or came back to life after decades frozen in time. Time had caught up with Fort Lauderdale's residents, bringing as much tragedy as it had joy.

I wondered if Ferdinand's betrayal extended to even then, when I'd been taken for the Starfall stone before. If he had been involved with the stolen courier horses, it would mean something went on larger than a growing rebellion wishing to displace my aunt. The possibility of the connection bothered me.

Ferdinand would have had plenty of time and opportunity to work with my deceased uncles to secure the Hope Diamond from the National Archive. Had he not been sent to Knoxville, he would have been in the perfect position to disrupt any efforts to locate the stone.

While I hadn't been asked to prove he'd been involved with my uncles, I'd do my best to discover the truth. Everything I'd witnessed thus far confirmed his guilt, but it would be better for everyone if I learned how extensive his betrayals were. I finished most of my food, leaving a few token scraps to help convince Rachelle I truly didn't eat much, something I'd have to do every day to maintain the ruse. Water would keep my stomach from gurgling much.

It would be a long time until I got to indulge in another beer, and I might go for a full keg after dealing with Knoxville and a damned wolf I couldn't kill quite yet.

To prevent any of the wolf women from having

even more reason to dislike me, I went to the kitchen, cleaned up after myself, and listened at the doorway leading to the dining room. They talked about me, and their pity annoyed me enough I returned to the library to keep from growling. As soon as Ferdinand's body hit the ground, I'd make it clear they had no reason to pity me.

I'd teach them they had no reason to pity themselves, but I couldn't reveal that truth to them. Not yet.

Soon, but not yet.

I picked a comfortable chair, picked up the book about cars, and read about engines, the laws of the road, and the practices of a safe driver. Little of the old ways remained, with asphalt and concrete being maintained on the main thoroughfares and leaving the rest of the country to fend with dirt and stone.

Would I like a world without horses, swords, and the grit and grime of the road? Trains and their set schedules offered convenience, but I found true freedom in the saddle, riding where few others dared. I'd survived through winters making rides between towns, aware a single accident could result in my death. My horses would likely die, too, although they stood a better chance of survival in the wilds than I did.

I'd never tested my ability to light fires beyond what was necessary to live in Wyoming on my own. Luck had contributed to my ability to survive at my home, which I missed, despite the harsh winters and hard work.

The memory was almost enough to make me smile.

Not long after I'd moved into the area determined to settle down with my two black demons, I'd gotten lucky; a patch of mud in the land I'd staked as mine had become more than just a wet spot in the ground. In the month after, it had turned into a proper spring. With some shovels and help from the locals, who would invite me to their tribe in the following year, I'd built a home around the spring.

The horses loved the water, as did I. It had an odd taste, but it warmed, and none of us had ever gotten sick from drinking it. When drought hit, which happened often enough it was a way of life among the tribe, I invited everyone and their animals to drink, as it never seemed to run out, although it took some time to quench everyone's thirst.

I figured the spring, which welled up inside the cozy comfort of my cabin before draining out through a stone-carved channel to turn into a trickle of a creek, would be the first place I'd take my tiger when I dragged him west to meet the tribe.

I held onto the thought as another lifeline to get me through the following days.

I would need it.

Chapter Ten

FERDINAND BROUGHT extra money as promised, but the ten dollars wouldn't go far, not for a month. To complicate my already complicated plans, his second bite hurt worse than the first. Not only did it throb in my throat, the heat of my tiger's claims burned hotter, a reminder I'd already dedicated myself to someone else. After twenty minutes, it ebbed to a tolerable amount, but I shook in the aftermath.

Rachelle tried to convince me things would improve, but I doubted it.

We fought different battles, and she didn't have someone dedicated to her and only her. Within the first twenty-four hours of captivity at the pack's house, I'd learned a few important truths.

Every last one of the women, most of whom remained nameless to me, deserved someone who valued them like they deserved. Ferdinand cared nothing for them; from the brief snippets of conversation I overheard when I wasn't hiding in my closet, he viewed them as status symbols needed for a wolf to live the high life in Knoxville.

He who mated with the most bitches climbed the social ladder faster. Having the appropriate rank in the city would aid his efforts and put him in touch with others who might share his goals. I expected having a rank as a lead wolf in the area would offer him financial benefits as well. With his experience in Dawnfire, Ferdinand might be able to establish—or take over—a mercenary guild. In exchange for offering mercenaries reliable work, controlling contracts to keep them fair, and otherwise guaranteeing better pay, guild leaders levied two percentages, one that went into the guild coffers, and another that lined their pockets.

Todd posted his jobs after guild fees, his cut, and taxes, which made it cash-in-hand, something many guilds didn't do. As far as I knew, Dawnfire did the same. If Dawnfire *didn't* do the same, I would have to have a talk with my uncle and yell at him until he made the appropriate changes. I'd even face off against his wolverine of a wife.

She worried me a lot more than he did.

On the third day of captivity, Ferdinand bit me twice, once in the morning when he brought an extra ten dollars to aid in feeding me, and again in the evening, when he dragged me to the library, sat me down, and gave me a beer.

I accepted the bribe, as his bites were supposed to make me more docile and inclined to do as he wished.

The extra calories would do me good, but I'd be crawling to sleep it off in my closet. Taking off the cap, I set it aside and took a tentative sip.

Bad beer beat no beer, so I took another sip and pretended to enjoy his favor. He sat nearby, and he looked me over. After a few minutes, his gaze landed on the Hope Diamond. "Once we are finished with the stone, you will find life will be a little more pleasant for you. Not as pleasant as you would wish, but more pleasant than it is now. I recommend you get used to the pack, as you will be with them for the rest of their life, however long or short that might be. I would rather it be longer. You served your guild well, and you have been loyal for all you're misguided."

I sipped my beer, and as he hadn't ordered me to speak, I remained silent.

"For the next few weeks, you will do everything Rachelle wants. I have given her permission to send you on errands, and she will have very specific instructions for you for every outing. Tigers do not handle captivity well, and this should keep you somewhat contained until I require you. More accurately, I require the Hope Diamond, and it is much easier to move when it cooperates with you. You add strength to my pack, and your affinity with Starfall stones adds to your value. You will never return to your old life, but you can have a good life here. Your behavior now will also ensure the pack's comfort."

Even when I'd been much younger, I'd built the entirety of my reputation on my desire to help and protect. That Ferdinand would use that against me didn't surprise me in the slightest.

I wondered if he understood he sat with an assassin, and that I would enjoy my work far more than I ever had before. Guilt would haunt me over the man's death, but only from fear of how Gentry would handle the reality of what I did. And if I found evidence of Marie's involvement, I worried for Todd—and I worried if my relationship, however odd it was, would survive through such a storm.

My aunt wouldn't turn her back on me. Even at my sickest, she'd visited me every day. On the days I hadn't been able to stop from crying no matter what I did, she'd held me and stroked my hair. She'd also called for my tiger, pulling him out of countless meetings of importance.

Because of her, I'd begun to understand what it meant to be loved by family, but she'd built the foundation of her work on Todd and his ready acceptance of everything I was.

I couldn't understand why anyone would want to betray my family and friends. They gave so much for the sake of others.

Taking another sip of my beer, I regarded Ferdinand with as neutral of an expression as I could muster under the circumstances.

"It's only for a few weeks. In time, you'll become used to me. You might even like me after a while. You'll certainly need me because of my bite soon enough.

The faster you accept the reality of your situation, the happier you'll be."

I wouldn't be happy, not until I returned to my tiger and my family. Almost grateful he hadn't given me permission to speak, I glared at my beer bottle, as I wasn't idiot enough to glare at him.

The last thing I needed was a third bite in a single day adding to my troubles.

"You'll understand the necessity of what I do soon enough. You might even respect my hard work. You understand hard work. I have a few rules that you are to abide by that not even Rachelle can overturn. She knows of these rules, so she will not put you in an unfortunate position. You can view this as my first gift to you. You will not leave the Knoxville area without my direction. However, should you be particularly well behaved, I will permit you to shift and hunt in the neighboring forest. To keep you healthy, I will permit a hunt once a month, although you'll accompany the pack on these ventures. A solo hunt will be the best reward for your cooperation. Your boundaries are an hour's walk away from the border of Knoxville. Second, you will not go to any bars. Should you behave, you will be given some beer at home. You have problems with bars."

Sometime soon, preferably before the estimated 'few weeks' Ferdinand kept hinting at, I would beg, plead, and whine until people stopped mentioning my tendency to find trouble in bars. Steel Heart had found me twice in a bar, and it had done more than create just a little trouble.

It had brought change with it, change I didn't want to live without.

The stone's weight in my pouch comforted me despite the burn of my tiger's bites and my awareness of where Ferdinand had bitten me.

"Third," Ferdinand announced, holding up three fingers. For that dramatic flare he liked, he stared into my eyes and waited to draw out and savor the moment. "As tigers of all species make excellent guardians, you will be in charge of protecting my children. Rachelle is due soon enough, and you will handle all tasks she requires of you. Do you have experience with children?"

As he asked me a direct question, I couldn't defy him through refusing to answer. While I didn't consider myself qualified to be a parent, I'd helped with the tribe's youngest enough times to be confident of the basics, so I nodded.

"Excellent. They're all new mothers, so you can help teach them how best to care for the babies. If you know of anything I can do now, tell me."

What an asshole. He'd impregnated how many of his mates without having any idea of how to care for them? But, as he'd asked, I'd do what I could to help them. "They will need extra meat in their diets to go with some additional vegetables. The babies require substantially more to be healthy." I'd seen how much they'd eaten—or how little. They left no scraps, and I worried they'd taken the little I hadn't consumed to stave off their hunger.

"Extra meat? Where did you hear this?"

"It is customary in the tribe. When a woman is showing and is confirmed pregnant, she is given the lion's share of the meal's bounty to ensure her good health. While there was enough for a normal woman, they could use larger portions." That I had to explain this at all infuriated me. "They have a good track record of having healthy babies. The tribe has a mystic healer who helps with the delivery, but they're usually strong and healthy."

"Usually?"

I shrugged. "It gets lean in the winter in Cheyenne, and the mothers who deliver in the spring sometimes have a hard time of it when food is scarce."

Ferdinand dug into his pocket, pulled out a hundred dollars, and handed it to me. "Give that to Rachelle to add to the monthly budget, then."

The gesture wouldn't save him when I finished gathering the information I needed, but I took the money and nodded to indicate I would obey. A hundred wouldn't do much, but it would help—especially if I kept maintaining my lean rations.

"None of your trouble, and don't even think about attempting an escape. You're mine, and that's that. You'll like life with me eventually, but you're as stubborn as they come, so I expect I've got a lot of taming to do to make you worth your while. For now, don't cause me any trouble." Ferdinand rose, and without another word, he left.

I finished off his beer and raised my empty bottle in a salute to his departing back. Letting him go took more will than I liked, but he made it out of the pack's house intact. Taking the bottle to the kitchen, I left it on the counter as I'd been told to do if I ever came across one. After taking a few minutes to breathe and control my temper, I went off in search of Rachelle, finding her in the sitting room with most of the women in the pack. I offered her the bills. "From Ferdinand for the food budget."

Every last one of the women stared at me like I'd grown a second head, and Rachelle took the money with a shaking hand. "But how?"

"I told him someone did a better job of making healthy babies than he did, but more gently."

Lauren snorted. "That would do the trick. You tweaked his pride without pissing him off? But how?"

I shrugged. "He asked me for my advice, I gave it."

"But why ask you?"

"He asked me what I knew about raising babies, and I guess he believed I know my business."

That got their attention.

"Do you know how to raise babies?" Rachelle asked.

"I know enough of the basics I can help after the delivery, though I don't know anything about delivering human babies. Now, if you've got a pregnant mare, I can help you with her. But I know how you're supposed to hold them when feeding, how to support their heads, how best to change their diapers, how to make sure they're sleeping right, and how to go about doing the normal things. I won't be much help if a little one gets sick, but I can handle the basics readily enough. If you want help beyond that, I know nothing of children, unfortunately."

"Well, at least someone in this joint will know what to do at first. Ferdinand won't let us get a midwife until it's time, and even then, we don't really know what's going to happen."

It disturbed me I might really be the one who knew the most about babies and their care in the room. "I told Ferdinand you needed more meat and some extra vegetables in your diet, and that was when he gave me the money to give to you."

"Would you mind helping with the shopping for this tomorrow?" Rachelle asked.

Every extra minute spent in the pack's house reaffirmed my need to slaughter Ferdinand. I wanted to flex my hands, but I fought to remain relaxed. The women didn't need my fury adding to their stress. "Of course."

The woman smiled. "Thank you. You look tired. Is there anything we can do for you?"

"Do you think he'll come around every day?" I asked.

"Without fail. He wants to keep you bad enough he's willing to bite you several times a day to cement his hold on you. He'll probably do this for up to two months. I'm sorry. If we could stop that, we would. He did it to all of us, except me—and he didn't do it to me only because I was his first." The bitterness in Rachelle's voice reflected in her expression. "The only time he might not come around every day is if he has a meeting with someone. He gets some woman in from Charlotte every now and then, and he drops what he's doing when she comes to town. She usually is off back home on the next train out."

Maria. The woman's admission, when considered with what Todd's other mares had witnessed, made the odds seem likely who was coming to Knoxville —and why.

I hated traitors. I hated traitors who wanted to hurt my family. I especially hated traitors who even thought about doing anything to my tiger. The only one allowed to bite, claw, maul, or otherwise disturb a hair on his head was me.

"Do you think she'll be coming soon?"

"Oh, probably. A month doesn't go by when she doesn't come on down for a visit, but don't you worry none. He doesn't bring her around here. Ferdinand says she wouldn't understand pack life." Rachelle shrugged. "I thought she might, but he knows her best."

No, Marie was a lot of things, but she understood how pack life was supposed to work. She would have seen the women and reacted poorly. She'd toss me in a ditch to die without remorse, but she didn't view me as a victim. She viewed me as a threat.

For Todd's sake, I hoped it was some other woman

from Charlotte. In reality, I needed to prepare for the worst.

Once, I'd considered her a friend.

If she showed up, death would come for her with a swift and merciful hand. She would deserve neither, but I would walk away without betraying my oath to myself. No matter how much the tiger in me wanted her blood, there would be no suffering.

Only death.

"I'm sure he knows her best," I conceded. "Is there anything I can do?"

"You've already done so much," Rachelle protested. "Go rest, we'll take care of the chores. You look tired."

I was, but until I finished my painful work, rest would be an elusive foe.

FERDINAND DID a good job of limiting the number of weapons the pack could access. He allowed a few knives for cooking, but I was under the impression those three, old blades were sacred to the women. With Steel Heart in my possession, I might be able to make the cutlery something dangerous in their hands.

Having Steel Heart could only help if I could get my hands on the knives without anyone catching me, and I learned early on bored, pregnant wolves had erratic schedules.

I lost track of the days along with the number of Ferdinand's bites. My tiger's marks continued to brand my soul, ensuring I couldn't sleep or even breathe without thinking of him. The need to tear Ferdinand limb from limb intensified with each day, but I controlled my impulses through careful counting and controlling my breathing while meditating.

The Blade Clan had taught me many tricks to find internal balance so I could focus only on my weapon and the art of death. Somehow, I'd circled back to my youth, although many of the memories of my childhood remained buried, pushed aside as I found them more painful than they were worth.

Deep within a sleepless night, an opportunity stirred on the heels of a larger-than-normal dinner, courtesy of Ferdinand gifting the women with a large roast to reward their good behavior—and mine. I'd taken the scraps as always, making sure they got more of the meal while I left the table closer to starved than not.

I could last a few more weeks. I needed to for the sake of the unborn.

To escape my closet without waking anyone in the adjacent rooms, I crawled out and to the stairs, careful with each placement of hand and knee. While faint, enough moonlight spilled in through the downstairs windows to guide me to the kitchen. I listened to make certain none of the women were aware before retrieving Steel Heart from its pouch. The stone shed a faint light, enough for me to poke through the room in search of the knives they cherished.

I hoped the Starfall stone understood what I

wanted and transformed the knives into something they could use to defend themselves if needed—and provide them with the strength to act despite being the victims of a wolf's bite.

Without any real idea of how to use Steel Heart, I touched the Starfall stone to each of the blades. If the stone did anything, I couldn't tell. It took a few minutes to restore the kitchen to exactly how I'd found it, and I returned to my closet aware I had done what I could for them.

The little things would get me through the next few weeks, and I would cling to every possibility of a better future possible, not just for myself, but for the true victims of Ferdinand's scheming. The pack deserved better, and while I still hadn't learned their names and didn't want to, I wanted them all to have better days ahead of them.

They needed what Marie had, a strong family to cherish them. That Marie would throw away all the good in her life from petty jealousy angered me most of all. She had so many children who adored her, many sisters in the form of her fellow mares within the herd, and everything else most women wanted in life.

Only a fool like me would reject a man like Todd.

Then again, I hadn't been a fool at all. Instead of Todd, I'd won myself an egotistical tiger. Todd would have wrapped me in a blanket to keep me safe, caging me when I wanted to prowl. Anatoly would try to wrap me in a blanket, and he'd get away with it from time to time, but he'd poke me to hear me roar, run so I would chase him, and expect me to run so he could have his fill of the hunt, too.

But while Todd would never be the right man for me, he could show the women how a good man treated a woman.

My heart hurt for everything Marie would lose if my suspicions were confirmed. The longer I thought of it, the more likely Marie would come visiting from Charlotte, carrying the broken hopes and dreams of her loyal husband with her.

The pain of the mare's treachery cut deeper than the dueling sets of bites using my body as their battlefield.

I didn't want Marie to come and force me to do the unthinkable.

I didn't want to lose Todd's friendship.

Retreating to the safety of the closet, I resumed my hunt, waiting for the moment Ferdinand slipped, paid a visit, and said a little too much—or I tired of the hunt, finished him off, and did record research to try to piece together his plans.

In either case, the wolf's days were numbered, and I hungered for his blood. He wouldn't live long enough to scream, but some prices were worth paying.

Chapter Eleven

BY THE SECOND week of my stay with Ferdinand's pack of trophy women, I'd learned two critical things: his Charlotte informant would make or break him, and her information would determine the dates of his plans. Ferdinand hadn't meant for me to overhear any of his hushed conversation with a cloaked man outside of the pack house's front door, but he forgot about the study on the second floor, the one few used and held volumes of books about living off the land and other things survivalists might need to know to remain breathing.

"When will we know?" Ferdinand's guest hissed through clenched teeth, but the sound carried to the window I hid near. I thanked the sky for the bright, sunny day, which had coaxed me into throwing open the curtains to read a book about identifying toxic plants.

"The day after tomorrow. The train gets in at noon,

and we'll meet at sunset. The train will leave in the early morning. We'll make our plans then. Our courier will be ready for them. She's adapted to my bites well, and while resentful, she's settling in. She is well liked in the pack and has proven to be a good addition to it."

What an asshole. All I'd done was make sure they got a little extra food, something any half-decent person would do for a group of abused pregnant women with no choice in their lives. I curled my lip in a silent snarl. I didn't deserve to be praised for helping to provide them with *food*.

For that reason alone, I'd slit his throat while looking him in the eyes, and make certain the last thing he saw was my hatred for him while he failed to draw another breath. I'd spend the rest of my limited time in my closet, practicing how to transform my hand into a lethal paw armed with sharp claws.

I should have practiced earlier, but I wouldn't beat myself up over it. Extra pain wouldn't have helped me control my already flagging temper. I focused on breathing and remaining quiet while I listened in on their conversation.

"Assuming she survives."

"She better. I'm loaning her to you only so you can use her to burst the Starfall stone. That's it. I will come for you myself if she doesn't live. She is mine."

I scowled at that. The only man I'd ever allow to stake any claim over me had fiery orange and pristine white fur with perfect black stripes, a temper the match of mine, and more loyalty than he knew what to do with. I'd have to make sure he left work long enough to test my temper every day, but none of my life's plans involved staying with a traitor wolf and his accomplices.

"I'll make sure she's as safe and shielded as possible during the transfer. We've already done some tests that seem to work for what we need, so she should emerge mostly unscathed. Any decent mystic should be able to care for her in the aftermath. You'll have to retrieve her yourself from the site once we're finished. Getting her out is your problem."

"I've already made arrangements for that," Ferdinand replied. "How is the rest coming together?"

"Assuming the new intel is good, we'll be ready within two weeks. More time is better if we can manage, but we'll have everything in place then."

"I'll do what I can."

"Where will you be meeting her this time?"

My eyes widened, and I froze, afraid to breathe in case they became suspicious and stopped conversing outside the pack house's front door. If I could get to her first, I'd create a break in their plans. They needed information. Killing their informant would put a kink in whatever their plans were—and I'd be free to deal with Ferdinand sooner than later, too.

I'd play dumb when he discovered his informant had refused to show or no longer lived. Either would work. Ideally, I'd learn what she had to say, but it could go to her grave and do less harm if she managed to pass word to Ferdinand. I waited, taking care to keep my breathing silent and steady.

"The clearing off the trail from the crater. If you've time, come."

"I don't, not today. We trust you to get what we need for our venture."

A pity. Had all three of them been in attendance, I might have considered just killing them all and asking questions of the bodies. As it was, I might get a two-for-one special if Ferdinand beat the informant to the site. But, if Marie was the informant, she'd show early.

She hated being late, especially when society demanded she be late for the sake of fashion. If she showed up and told me she'd caused so much pain and heartache because Todd made her attend things late, I'd believe it without question.

The fool woman, throwing away a perfect life from greed and jealousy. I didn't want anything from Todd beyond his friendship, something I would treasure even if everything fell apart.

I wanted to cry, but beyond a few stray tears, I couldn't seem to figure out how to grieve for everything I'd lost. Sometimes, I turned a corner and expected Simmons to be there, a disapproving scowl on his face for having given him the slip again.

"Then it's settled. I'll send a messenger if I can't meet you after the train departs; it's possible. I need to take the pack out. It's been a while since the ladies have had a hunt, and it's upsetting them."

"It can wait a few days. We can't do anything for

two weeks anyway, unless there's something she tells you that's important. Let's plan for three nights after your meeting in the same place and skip the messenger."

"I can work with that. I'll send a messenger if it's critical. It should just solidify the window, so I don't expect it'll be critical. We've already got the supplies to our staging points."

Damn it. I wanted to know what the staging points were; if I could find those, a single telegraph or phone call could put an end to the rebellion before it could begin.

"Good. Don't let that tiger of yours escape."

"She's got so many of my bites on her she can barely see straight. She's docile, so don't you worry about that. Within a week, she won't be able to breathe without my consent."

I'd enjoy the moment my claws tore through his flesh and ripped the life out of his body.

"Good. Keep her docile. Bring her by train to the first staging point when the time comes, then you can handle your part."

Ferdinand grunted his consent, and I wanted to snarl curses that they hadn't mentioned the location of their staging point.

After heaving a sigh, the wolf replied, "I already have the tickets, as we can wait there however long is necessary. I've a place remote enough to avoid detection until we're prepared."

Well, if he had the tickets, I could find them and

get the location that way—after I slaughtered the traitor. I wanted his accomplice, but the best I could do was remember his nasally, obnoxious voice and hope I ran into him again later.

The two men exchanged pleasantries before the cloaked figure departed. I returned my book to its place in the study, headed to my nest, and hid in the closet so when Ferdinand came to bite me again, I could feign having been asleep, something I did with such frequency I worried the other women. I rarely slept, but the ruse served me well.

When he came in and asked Rachelle where I was, she would say I was probably in my closet resting. He, as always, would assume his bites wore away at me, pull me out of the comfort of my bedding, and tear into my throat again.

Ferdinand didn't waste much time with Rachelle before ordering me out of my nest so he could take another chunk out of me. My tiger's marks burned as hot as usual whenever the wolf attempted to use his magic on me, but I breathed through the pain despite wanting to scream or roar. I couldn't afford to blow my cover, and he hadn't given me permission to make a sound.

"Do as Rachelle tells you." Without another word, he left me in the hallway, my blood trickling down my neck.

I waited for the door to slam downstairs before allowing a single growl.

My time had come, I just needed to wait until the day after tomorrow.

What felt like an eternity passed before the time came to deal with the first of the traitors on my list.

As though somehow understanding I needed to be out of the pack's house before I went mad, Rachelle, with a little encouragement from Lauren, sent me out on a pointless little errand to fetch her some herbs I doubted she really needed and didn't want to waste the limited budget on. To give me the chance for some fresh air, she handed me a precious five dollar bill. With a smile, she told me to take my time. She issued the order where the other women in the pack could hear her. For all I remained an outsider to them, they watched my back anyway.

Then, as she seemed to believe I might get lost, she gave me directions to all of the markets in the city and told me where the interesting sites were, including the Starfall crater at the edge of town. Her smile turned sly, and she hinted everyone who came to Knoxville should see it at least once.

The other women agreed, but Lauren said, "I wouldn't mind a worry stone. It might help on the bad days."

If asked, the pack could claim I'd been sent out to the markets—all of them—and tasked with finding a worry stone for Lauren.

I would somehow repay them for the opportunity I needed to begin my bloody work despite their lack of awareness of what I meant to do.

On my way out the door, I grabbed a scarf to hide the Hope Diamond and pocketed the only weapon I could, one of the steel letter openers the women used to keep from breaking a nail. No one would miss one of the dozen littering the entry's table. I figured they'd had the same thought about weaponizing the pieces of metal.

Unlike them, I had Steel Heart. I could only hope it or the Hope Diamond would aid my cause. If not, I'd shift and deal with the first of the traitors that way. Once certain the Starfall stone was covered, I headed down the steps, pausing long enough to listen to Rachelle's instructions for her latest batch of herbs, which she wanted to use to make stew.

It would be a challenge to keep Marie's blood off Rachelle's herbs, but I would figure something out. Somehow. At least I wouldn't have to worry about Ferdinand. If he asked where I was, they would all tell him the same story.

In several hours, I would return with the herbs Rachelle had requested, paid with the small petty fund Ferdinand offered his women. She would make certain dinner included the herbs I'd purchased. The women would, if he showed up for dinner, thank me for running the errands.

No one in the pack, save for Ferdinand, cared what I did. Ferdinand only cared that I did as he ordered, which meant staying in the pack's house unless ordered by one of his trusted pack women to run an errand. Then, in an act I viewed as pure defiance, they'd concocted an excuse to send me out.

I hoped they savored the moment. It would become their freedom within the next few days.

Unbeknownst to them, their defiance would become death in my hands. First, the informant, likely Marie, would die. That evening, she would fail to show, thus damaging Ferdinand's plan. Thanks to Ferdinand, I wouldn't have to work hard to find her.

Because Marie was Marie, she would arrive early. I couldn't imagine the pair of traitors wanting to delay their meeting.

The information Marie carried, likely from snooping on Todd's work, would die with her.

I left the pack's house, headed for the market the pack had recommended closest to the crater, and purchased everything they'd asked for. With a little haggling I managed to get a waterproofed pouch for everything, which solved the problem of Marie's blood. With a single touch of my tribe feather, I could purify my clothes and hide the evidence of my scent.

It would serve as a precaution, eliminating my trail at the market. I made certain to set the precious herbs down so they wouldn't be caught up in the tribal magic before purifying my clothes and removing all of my scent markers. After I dealt with Marie's body, I would invoke the tribe magic again to eliminate as much of the evidence as possible.

For my plans to work, Ferdinand couldn't discover the cause of Marie's failure to show up for their meeting. I wanted him to suspect betrayal.

If he suspected betrayal, he might change his plans —and Todd, Gentry, and the rest of my family might be spared from his treachery. Or, at least spared long enough for me to eliminate the wolf's threat and warn them of the ploy.

Their knowledge that something was in the works offered me hope we might all make it out alive. Well, most of us.

Of all of the ways I'd killed someone, I'd never used a letter opener before. I expected it would be dire, grisly work giving the mare a more merciful death than she deserved. Without understanding how herd magic worked, I didn't want her suffering to hurt the others.

They didn't deserve to share Marie's misery.

It took me over an hour to reach the meeting point, where the city made way for untamed land. At some point in the city's past, it had fallen prey to a Starfall stone, and I skirted the crater's lip. The landmark reassured me I'd found the right spot, although I still needed to hike for another ten to twenty minutes to reach my goal.

There were a lot of good places to hide the body in the stretch of woods, and I wouldn't even need to work all that hard to make it happen. The crater with its loose stones would serve well. I could bury her beneath a deep pile of stone without having to do more than some manual labor—or deliberately trigger a landslide on one of the more questionable slopes.

I retrieved the letter opener from my pocket along with Steel Heart, wondering how my clan made use of the stone to imbue weapons with its power. On the surface, it remained ugly, pock-marked and pitted without any luster hinting it was a marvel of the world.

In my hand, Steel Heart warmed, and sparks danced over its dark surface, much as it had in the bar in Miami.

I missed that dive of a bar. I missed my tiger. I missed my odd collection of family and friends. After I killed Marie for her treacheries, would Todd forgive me? Part of Marie's death would boil down to vengeance; she'd played her part in Simmons's death.

Equines didn't understand long-term vengeance all that well, although Todd did possess stubborn tendencies and could hold a grudge.

Once I hid Marie's body, once I gave Rachelle the herbs she'd asked for, I would retreat to my little closet space, close the door, and try to mourn for my agent. Killing Marie wouldn't bring him back, but her traitorous ways would die with her. She wouldn't just die for her part in my agent's murder.

I'd listened enough to Ferdinand to understand she'd betrayed everyone I cared most about—and that they surely had intended for Randal to die as well. They'd planned to kill both of my agents to make it easier to get to me.

Randal accompanying my tiger may have saved his

life, but I wouldn't know until I returned to Charlotte. I could only assume my tiger had survived, as his marks still burned, battling Ferdinand's morning ritual of taking a chunk out of my throat. Given another few weeks, the consistent pain would likely make me snap and go on a rampage, and I would slaughter the source of my discomfort.

I hated working on a tight schedule, and I hadn't found enough information on Ferdinand's affairs to kill him off quite yet.

I needed to keep holding on and pretending Ferdinand had a hold on me. I had until the pack met for a hunt to get the information—or I'd have to hope I could find records after his death. I expected he would die before I found out what I needed to know.

Killing Marie would begin his end, although I worried what price I'd pay for her death. My relationship with Todd would inevitably change.

I went beyond inconveniencing him to striking a huge blow to his herd.

Ultimately, I needed to stop accepting responsibility for the choices of others. I hadn't made Marie betray Todd. She'd done that all on her own. I would swear in front of a mystic, proving the truth of my words.

If I didn't deal with Marie, their scheming might kill them all.

I would deal with Todd with my head held as high as possible, despite my apprehension and fear.

I would never be able to forgive myself if I allowed the mare to live when she sought to destroy everything

—and everyone—I cherished. Reminding myself of what she intended to do, that she intended to give Ferdinand information to better help his efforts to dismantle the current government, made it easier for me to resume my march after selecting a suitable place to hide her body after I finished my dirty work.

Steel Heart sparked again, and the letter opener's blade darkened to deep blue. After a few moments, the blade returned to its original shade, although something about it had changed. I refused to question the Starfall stone's gift, and I returned it to its pouch. Muttering a thanks under my breath, I resumed my hike, following the creek from the crater through the woods until I came to the outcropping of rock that marked the turnoff for the meeting place.

The hike took me along a deer trail to a clearing beside a larger stream. As expected, Marie had arrived early, sitting on the rocky shore, sheltered from the sunlight beneath the boughs of a young oak.

Marie's eyes narrowed, and then she smirked. "Ferdinand does have a sense of humor, doesn't he? Sent you to keep me company until he could arrive, did he?"

She wouldn't learn from her mistake, but I shrugged to play along with her. After weeks of dealing with Ferdinand, I didn't have to work hard to keep my expression neutral.

Marie's gaze locked on my throat, and while I wore a scarf, it didn't do much more than hide the bastard's bites. Her brows furrowed. "He said he'd bitten you, but he's torn you up badly. I'd told him not to hurt you.

He said biting was necessary, but that it wouldn't be an issue. That is worse than I expected."

If I hadn't known she disliked me for ruining her picture-perfect herd, I might've fallen for her sympathy. I wanted to believe her, but I didn't. "I guess he paid you a lot to sell out Todd?"

"I didn't sell out my husband."

I shook my head. "You didn't know?"

"Didn't know what?"

"He means to kill the guild leaders in Charlotte. Active and former guild leaders need to be eliminated. He can't afford to allow them to live. They know too much. Lancers and Dawnfire are in the first wave to be eliminated." Technically, I lied, but I believed every word of it.

Everyone I knew would die if they wanted to completely destroy the current government, which I assumed was their main goal.

Marie narrowed her eyes. "You lie."

I shrugged. "Why would I lie? He doesn't care about anything other than his goals. If you want your herd to emerge intact, I recommend you make sure Todd isn't in Charlotte when Ferdinand begins his plans—if you can get back to Charlotte in time without being caught."

"That's no problem. I have a train ticket for tomorrow morning. That'll give me almost a month to plan." Marie scowled. "That would be like Ferdinand. No matter. I'm strong enough to keep the herd intact until Todd recovers, should there be a fight like that. I will make certain Ferdinand remembers my husband isn't to be killed. Driven out of Charlotte should suffice."

Bingo. While I'd known the group needed two weeks and Ferdinand had discussed something happening in a few weeks, I'd narrowed the window to between two weeks and a month. The timeframe was much easier to work around than an unknown, and after I finished with Marie, I could work on exposing more of Ferdinand's plans and notifying the Secret Service. "I wish you the best of luck convincing him to leave. You'll need it."

"He will. Herd before guild."

Poor Marie. I'd seen people like her, blind in their fanaticism to their cause. "I'm not usually allowed out. Walk with me for a while? It'll be a few hours before Ferdinand comes." I'd figured that much out from his schedule, which only allowed for a short meeting with Todd's mare between his other treacherous tasks.

She rose from her seat and dusted off her skirts, an outfit Todd liked on his wife and she wore often.

I would hate staining the pale fabric with her blood, but it would make a suitable burial shroud for her when I hid her body beneath piles of stone. If Ferdinand decided to use his nose, he'd discover I'd been at the site, but I would do what I did best, lying to him and playing stupid.

Marie frowned. "He doesn't let you out much?"

"I'm not useful to him or his pack. I've been told I should be grateful he allows me to serve. I don't have a choice in the matter. That's how wolf bites work, Marie. You should know this."

"I've heard rumors…"

"Well, they're true rumors." I allowed my bitterness to emerge in my tone, aware I needed to convince her of my unwillingness to cooperate. "A wolf's bite is law. I may not disobey. Neither can any of the other women in his pack."

"A necessity. Everyone will be better off for your sacrifice, although I am sorry. I hadn't thought a wolf could truly take someone's free will."

I didn't believe her, not when she struggled to hide her smile.

When I didn't say a word, she shrugged. "You'll see soon enough."

I pointed into the woods in the general direction of the crater, far enough off the beaten path no one would see—or hear—when I put my letter opener to good use. "What's over there?"

"You must have been cooped up a long time if a bunch of trees and a meadow are actually interesting to you. There is a pond and a stream; there are a lot of those here. The meadow is nice enough, I suppose. This way. There's a deer track." She headed in the direction I had pointed without waiting to see if I followed.

How often had Marie come to see Ferdinand that she knew the area so well? How did she keep leaving the herd unattended for so long without drawing Todd's suspicions? The stallion would be able to tell me, assuming I made it through the next few weeks intact and sane.

People could go mad from long-term pain, and the constant pressure from so many bites already drove me closer to the line than I liked.

A quick, painless death would serve my needs, and what happened to the bitch's body after might keep me from snapping for a while. Drawing in a steadying breath, I tailed her, the forest around us still, as though it held its breath waiting for the moment I lived up to my name and struck, adding another body to my tally. I wouldn't add to my guilt despite carrying plenty around already.

I maintained my oath to kill only those deserving of their deaths. I would maintain my oath to kill with mercy even when mercy wasn't deserved. I couldn't send her to painless sleep, but I would improvise. I could only hope Steel Heart's dire gift would give my letter opener the strength and sharpness needed to severe her spine in one blow. If not, my tiger claws would do the job, albeit not as cleanly or mercifully as I would like.

The deer track meandered through old trees, and sections of it had been destroyed long ago. Charred husks of trees promised some form of destruction had rained down. I pointed at one, which had been reduced to a tree-shaped chunk of charcoal. "Do you know what happened to these trees?"

"Starfall," she replied, and she gestured in the general direction of the crater. "It was a combustion stone, and fragments still litter the forest. When they burst, trees burn and end up like this. But since it's not a combustion zone, the fires don't spread far." Marie joined me, crouched, and picked up a stick, poking around at the soil. "This one is new, so there's a chance the stone is still here. It will sell for a lot, and I know Ferdinand is a skinflint."

Marie's kindness in her final moments would haunt me, but I couldn't forget or forgive her treachery and intent to harm those I loved.

Because of her, Simmons was dead.

My fingers closed around the letter opener's handle, and I freed it from my pocket. Steel Heart's sparks danced over its edge. I supposed Todd had kept my secrets well; a wise woman wouldn't have turned her back on a known assassin. Ferdinand likely knew parts of my identity, but I couldn't tell if he believed me a good mercenary or if he knew about my darker work.

A letter opener shouldn't have had the strength or sharpness needed to fully sever a spine in a single blow, but the weapon cut deep, slicing through the bone at the base of Marie's skull with so little resistance my hand thumped into the back of her neck. I firmed my hold on the handle and gave a twist to be certain of my kill.

Bone cracked, and her body slumped to the ground. As that somehow didn't seem enough, I slit her throat. Between the two injuries, she didn't last long, and I hoped the damage to her spine prevented her from feeling the life flee her body—if only to spare the members of her herd.

I waited for her eyes to dim and begin to glaze before rolling her over, checking her pockets. The hundred bucks wouldn't get me too far, but I'd be able to return to the market on the way back to the pack's house for something a little better than just a pack of spices.

The pregnant women didn't eat enough as it was, and while it wouldn't help much, it was better than nothing.

I waited for her neck to stop gushing blood before activating the feather in my hair and erasing the evidence of my crime. The magic, as though understanding I killed for more than one reason, cooperated and cleaned the body as well. It reminded me of tribe honor, and how they, too, took brutal steps for justice.

I wondered how they would feel about me when I came to them and confessed my many sins.

As I wouldn't have much time once I got her body to the crater, I rolled her onto her back and carved my mark deep into her forehead, making certain the letter opener dug into her skull. My anger over the pointlessness of my agent's death surged, and I took my fury out on her body. It didn't help. It couldn't do much of anything at all, but it unleashed some of my misery over my situation.

Her corpse didn't care what I did to it, and the brutal marks I inflicted on her, some to or through the bone, would leave a message throughout the years.

The broken ruins of her body would serve as evidence of acquiring justice and preventing more misery in my family. A deep, relentless part of me grieved for Todd, who wouldn't know the how or why of Marie's death until I found the courage to tell him.

I harbored some hope he would understand when I told him she had played her part in Simmons's death. No matter how hard I tried to forget, I remembered the feel of his cooling skin as I'd closed his eyes one final time.

Pain deeper than any of the bites plaguing me surged, and I slammed the letter opener into her breastbone, yanked it free, and continue to stab her until my arm burned from the effort and I panted. Then, when I couldn't bring myself to pierce her again, I dropped my weapon, sat beside her body, and cursed.

Something dark rolled to me, and when it touched the letter opener, the metal turned black and crumbled to dust, leaving a smear on the leaves, barely distinguishable from the soil. My eyes widened at the smooth, polished surface, much like a child's marble and darker than an overcast night in the heart of winter.

Sunder.

Having Steel Heart show up at the pack's house had been daunting enough, but the black Starfall stone terrified me; its ability to destroy rather than create set an even fouler omen than the body cooling beside me.

With a trembling hand, I picked it up. I expected a chilly, lifeless thing, and its warmth startled me. Unable to think of what else to do, I put it in the pouch with Steel Heart, hoping the theory Sunder wouldn't destroy other Starfall stones proved to be the truth.

Then, as I couldn't go a day without bitter irony biting at my heels, I spotted the smoldering fragment of a Starfall stone among the leaves, flickering between red and orange. While nameless, its power awed me, a flicker of flame where nothing could otherwise burn. It had played a part in Marie's death, and I took up her stick and poked the fragment. The red darkened, much like a cooling ember. I expected to get burned, but I reached for it anyway. While hot, it had cooled enough to handle. Much like the fragment in the stiletto, the Starfall stone was more of a jewel than a rock, a red diamond waiting to burst into flame again.

If it burned me, I deserved the pain. I put it in the pouch with the other two Starfall stones, wondering what I would do with it.

Maybe once I freed the pack, I would take the women somewhere peaceful and quiet and show them a fire, allowing them to capture moments of peace in a world that cared too little for them.

Maybe I'd give it to Todd after telling the truth of how his wife had perished at my hands.

Maybe I'd keep it to remember my sins.

I rose to my feet and hauled Marie's body through the forest towards the crater, where I would hide her deep beneath the stone and soil, where no one would find her until it was too late for it to matter.

WITHOUT A SHOVEL, I couldn't traditionally bury Marie's body, but I found a good spot to dump her into the crater and roll stones onto her corpse. It took me at least an hour to cover her, but enough loose stone fell off the crater's side as I worked to mask her final resting place. After making sure the area seemed disturbed by nature rather than someone hiding a body, I activated the feather to clean my clothes and remove the remaining evidence of my sins.

The magic warmed my skin, as though the feather understood what I had done and why, accepting the woman's death at my hand. I'd have to ask the tribe about it later. I'd never had such a reaction from the feathers following acts of self-defense. Perhaps the nature of the eagles had something to do with it.

They, like me, were predators.

On my way out of the crater, I picked a smooth stone for Lauren and put it in my pocket with Steel Heart, Sunder, and the unnamed fragment. If the Starfall stones had any mercy in their cold hearts, they'd do something to the rock to help protect the pregnant woman and the rest of the captive pack. I didn't expect anything from the rocks, but I hoped for something to help the women when my plans came to fruition and Ferdinand died.

I returned to the market and browsed the goods, purchasing extra fresh herbs along with a large bag of potatoes and a disgusting number of carrots. Neither would help pregnant predators as much as I wanted, but bad food was better than no food, and I had no idea when Ferdinand would feed them properly again.

Then, taking the remainder of Marie's money, I purchased three chickens and two large beef roasts. The women would have to hide the excess meat from Ferdinand, but it might make a difference for them. I wanted to purchase one of the live chickens for the eggs, but the damned dictator of a wolf wouldn't let the women keep it—and he'd probably eat the hen while making them watch.

When I killed Ferdinand, it would be with my claws, and I would savor the feel of his throat tearing beneath my first, lethal swipe.

I lugged my ill-gotten gains to the pack's house, and Rachelle met me at the door. "Ferdinand was here."

Of course. If it weren't for bad luck, I would have no luck at all. "And?"

"I told him I had sent you to the market for herbs, and that I wasn't sure if some of them were still in season, so that I expected you to take a while, as you would check every market before accepting defeat. He believed this, as it seems you have a reputation of doing things like that."

I supposed I did. "I used the time to acquire some extra funds and get some things for the pack." Per Ferdinand's idiotic rules, I needed to wait for Rachelle's every order, and she invited me into the house with a wave of her hand. I lugged everything to the kitchen and set the bags on the counters. "I hope you have a place to hide this."

"Easily. He doesn't check the refrigerator or the freezer. He doesn't particularly care. Thank you for making the most of your time out today. I appreciate it. I'm sure the others will, too."

As a general rule, I limited my interactions with the others to the point I still only knew two of their names. At Ferdinand's demand, Rachelle managed me, but she kept her distance, too. I played my part in that, hiding at every opportunity.

I wasn't a wolf, I would never be a wolf, and I wasn't a part of their pack, for all Ferdinand deluded himself into believing he controlled me and that I was.

The incessant ache from my tiger's nips, nibbles, and bites might drive me insane long before I killed the bastard in a few days—forget the estimated few weeks I had needed to last for. Fighting my desire to snap at the woman, I sighed. "Do you need me for anything else?"

"No. You look tired. Go get some rest. When Ferdinand returns, I will tell him you walked across most of the city to find the herbs, and I'll cook something nice tonight so he can see for himself. He's a foolish man at times."

At times? Rather than argue with her, I excused myself and shuffled up the stairs to the hallway closet I'd claimed as my nest, crawling inside and closing the door. The tight space and the darkness served as reminders of everything I stood to lose if I couldn't put an end to Ferdinand's plans. Killing Marie before she could give Ferdinand extra information might help my cause.

It might force his hand.

If her death forced his hand, I might be able to do *something.* If he began to make a move, even without the information I needed, I would tear his throat out and ransack through any properties he had in the area. I was aware of one townhouse, a nice place that he rarely invited his women to. From my understanding of the situation, those invitations usually led to a child. I tried not to think too hard if Rachelle was the first to be issued such an invitation. If she wasn't the first, what had happened to the other women and their children?

The more I learned about Ferdinand's treatment of his pack, the harder it became to leave him alive long enough to learn more.

I worried for the unborn. Perhaps time with Todd, Gentry, and Anatoly had spoiled me, but even with my help in increasing their food budget, no one ate as much as I thought they should. If my tiger discovered how little I ate and how much weight I'd lost in the past few weeks, he would become a terror hellbent on destruction. I would enjoy the show, but I couldn't afford having him—or any of my family—come close to Ferdinand.

I had no idea how many in the city were in league with the wolf. Once I had a better idea of when things would happen and where Ferdinand's allies were, I could make a plan.

Simmons would have been proud of me for stopping and thinking through the consequences of my actions for a change. Considering how much time I spent lurking in the pack's house and hiding in the closet I'd claimed as mine, I'd had too much time to think about the consequences of my actions, both past and planned.

I burrowed into the blankets, but I couldn't bring myself to cry for Simmons. The tears refused to fall.

My work wasn't done, and there would be time for my grief once I made sure all of Ferdinand's schemes fell to dust.

Chapter Twelve

SOMEONE KNOCKED on the closet door, and as it wasn't yanked open with a growl, either dinner was finished or Ferdinand had demanded my presence. If they had cooked one of the roasts, dinner would be served long after nightfall, and Ferdinand would have discovered his meeting with Marie unexpectedly cancelled. I yawned, wondering how much time I'd spent in the darkness, my tiger's bites a constant reminder of the wolf's treachery. Making any of them wait would cause me trouble later, so I squirmed in my tiny space and pushed open the door.

Rachelle waited, an apron covering her heavily swollen belly. "Ferdinand is here, and he is upset over something, but not so upset he is putting a stop to dinner. Unfortunately, he has decided to join us."

Unless the wolf stalked at her heels, he wouldn't hear her complaints.

"For dinner? He has?"

"He brought a roast, which is currently in the oven with the roast you'd purchased. He said to make both, and we'd eat well tonight."

The oven and stove, a marvel mixing technology and Starfall magic, had a stone buried somewhere inside allowing combustion. The technology somehow controlled the flame's temperatures, which were usually fueled with coal unless the stone burst, in which case it produced its own flames on demand. It was the only luxury Ferdinand had offered the women beyond having a roof over their heads.

I questioned the stove—and where he'd gotten so prized a Starfall stone.

"He brought a roast?"

"A large one, too. I showed him the potatoes and the carrots you had gotten along with the herbs, and explained again you'd gone out on an errand for me, and it was my fault you had been gone most of the day. Then I had told him I'd gotten a roast with some of the budget since you'd gotten such a good deal on everything else, and that I'd sent you out to choose it—and that you'd gotten a good deal on that, too. It somehow calmed him. I'm not sure why."

Unknowingly, she'd provided me with an alibi for Marie's failure to show at the meeting. If I kept playing dumb, maybe the wolf would slip and tell me everything I needed to know before he breathed his last.

"How strange," I mumbled, crawling out of the

space and straightening my clothes. While the feather's magic would have eradicated my scent, the closet would have restored it enough to prevent suspicion. "He's been calm?"

By calm, I meant non-violent, and judging from Rachelle's sigh, she understood my meaning. "So far. He said his evening plans seem to have been cancelled, so he would spend the time here discussing our future tonight."

With a little luck, he'd slip and reveal a timeframe of what the future would hold so I could figure out how long I needed to keep the bastard alive. Marie's failure to show for the meeting while her scent was still present might change everything—or nothing at all.

I would find out soon enough.

"I'm sorry," I whispered.

"Why are you sorry? It's not like you want to be here. None of us do. We do what we must, and that is that. Like you, we would leave if we could." Rachelle pressed her hand against her stomach. "I want a better wolf for my child."

I wondered what life would be like for them when Ferdinand died; I hoped the relief from the pain would be enough to let me finally rest. At a loss of what to say, I shrugged and followed her downstairs.

The list of things I needed to do intimidated me, with finding a telegraph station, mystic courier, or telephone taking the top spot. A telephone would work best, as I would be able to notify the Secret Service—

and my tiger—of my whereabouts without any delay. While some parts of the city had electric poles, I had no idea if they were wired for telephone service—or if the telephone system connected to Charlotte.

The courier network would be able to help me.

Ferdinand waited in the dining room, and I lowered my gaze, reminding myself I needed to stay silent unless spoken to. Under no circumstances could I growl or roar at the bastard. Depending on his mood, he might add yet another bite to my throat.

"Sit, Jesse. Your part in this will be over soon enough, then you can have a little more freedom. I know you're having a hard time right now. Rachelle told me you ran a lot of errands for her today across the city. How do you like Knoxville?"

I wanted to be home in Charlotte, but I fought my urge to snap my teeth for forcing me to exchange pleasantries with him. "Knoxville seems nice. The markets are interesting." They were, too; Charlotte had markets similar to the ones I'd seen in Knoxville, although Charlotte had specialty markets for live animals, where I could've gotten live beasts from most of those I'd spotted on my hike across the city today. "I almost got a good deal on a live hen, but I wasn't sure you'd allow one."

There. That would aid my cause. Ferdinand thought he knew me. I would've wasted at least an hour humming over the live hen, and I spoke the truth; I had wanted to get her to provide eggs for the pack.

"The next time Rachelle sends you to the market, I

have no problems with a live hen or two for the pack. How much for a live bird?"

According to the expressions of the women, Christmas had come early for the pack. They held their breath as though afraid their luck would change.

"A young hen would have cost ten, but I could have gotten chicks for much cheaper. We could have gotten five chicks for ten dollars, but there is always a chance of a rooster with a young batch of chicks." I'd overheard that gem from one of the shoppers who'd gotten a rooster that way. I thought a rooster with a few hens would be an excellent investment for a while to have extra chicks, and then the rooster could have been eaten—or used to keep producing chickens for the pack's consumption. "I saw goats for sale, too."

"I like goat cheese," Lauren announced. "I know how to make it. I know how to make butter, too."

I admired Lauren's bravery. Most of the women wouldn't say a word without Ferdinand's permission.

"The price of a goat, Jesse? The yard in the back should be big enough for a goat and some chickens."

"We'd need two, a male and a female; they won't produce unless they have kids. You'd want to get a male from a different breeder than the female, and a female looked to cost about seventy. The males are cheaper. They need fresh alfalfa, and they need to be kept separate from the chickens if you want the milk. I didn't listen much more than that." I'd only listened in long enough to figure out Ferdinand likely wouldn't consider such a thing.

"The yard's big enough for both, and you ladies can build the pen for the chickens. I know a farmer or two. I'll have one look over the back yard and set that up for you. A few goats and some chickens might keep you occupied." He narrowed his eyes and looked me over. "Cows?"

"I didn't look at the cows except for the roasts. Where would we put a *cow*?"

He chuckled. "As practical as ever. Very well. I'll send you out tomorrow for a box and some chicks, and you can set them up in the backyard. That's walled to ten feet, so they should stay put. I'll leave the money with you. How long until dinner, Rachelle?"

"Ten to twenty minutes," she replied.

"Good. That's enough time to discuss business before we eat. I need to take Jesse on a trip three weeks from now, and we should be back within a month. As such, we'll do a pack hunt tomorrow afternoon into the evening after she's come home with the chicks. We'll have a feast to properly welcome Jesse into the pack. Oh, you may as well get a hen or two to go with the chicks, so they can be producing right away. It's been a while since you've ladies have had any fresh eggs, as it's hard to get out every day."

What was Ferdinand up to? Had Marie's failure to show done something to the man? Had he figured out I'd been the one behind her disappearance? Had her disappearance somehow pleased him? I could see that; he played games because he could. He could have been testing if I'd gone to the market, knowing I had the skills needed to pull off the mare's murder without breaking a sweat.

I had, but I wasn't going to tell anyone that.

Rachelle's eyes widened. "We can really have chickens?"

"You will be required to butcher the excess chickens for the dinner table, and I'll find someone to teach you how—or we can hunt them during pack hunts. Whichever you prefer. I verified Jesse's advice with a midwife, and I have made an appointment for someone to come in a week or two to help with the babies." Ferdinand raised a brow, turning to me. "You continue to surprise me. I had no idea just how valuable you truly were until I verified your knowledge. I do want my sons and daughters to be strong, of course."

Liar. "I'm glad I could help."

"While the yard isn't large enough for a horse, there's a stable not far away with a riding ring, and if you continue to do well, I will acquire an animal for you. That will make errands in the city easier for you, and you can play courier when I need messages sent. If you're particularly well behaved, I'll send you to neighboring towns and cities in Tennessee and let you stretch your legs. You have a lot to prove to me first, though."

I raised my brows at his offer. "I'd like a horse."

"You're obsessed with horses. I've seen what you will do for yours. For now, chickens and goats will have to amuse you. Try not to get too attached to the ones you'll have to eat."

"I've raised goats, and I enjoyed killing the obnoxious ones. They were delicious."

"I hadn't considered raising goats to eat. I'll ask about how they're butchered and perhaps call in some favors if it's not something you ladies can handle on your own."

I could butcher a goat faster than anyone else in the tribe, and I didn't damage the hide when I did it. The task wasn't one of my favorites, but if he wanted the extra goats to make it to the dinner table, I could make sure the women knew how to do the job—and how to butcher any damned men who got in their way at the same time. "I can take care of that. I've done it."

"Have you, now?"

"There wasn't anyone else around to butcher the extra goats for me, so I did it myself. I'm proficient, and I know how to skin and tan the hides, too."

"You just one useful little kitten, aren't you? Good. When you're looking for chickens tomorrow, see if you spot any promising goats. If so, purchase them, and I'll find a place to board them until we're ready for them to live in the backyard."

I nodded.

Ferdinand pulled out his wallet and handed me a stack of bills, and some included hundreds. "Use this to buy everything tomorrow, and you may as well do some grocery shopping while you're at it, as you seem to know your business. Be back no later than one in the afternoon so we can go on our pack hunt. After the hunt, I will be very busy until it's time for my trip, although I will check in daily."

I read between the lines: he meant to maintain his bite despite his preparations for their scheme. Careful to open the pouch only enough to slip the money inside, I stuffed the bills in with my Starfall stones. "I will."

The limited freedom would give me some time to prepare for Ferdinand's death. It took several deep breaths to force myself to relax, but I managed.

Something chimed in the kitchen, and Rachelle, Lauren, and one of the other women left the dinner table, signaling dinner would soon be ready. I hope Ferdinand enjoyed his dinner.

It would be his last.

THE NEXT MORNING, I endured two more of Ferdinand's bites, and it hurt so much I almost ripped his head off in the entry of his house. Only the suffocating waves of pain kept me from growling. I needed several minutes to recover enough to get on with my day and fulfill my promise to set the women up with livestock. I went to one of the other markets they'd told me about, browsing through the selection of birds and goats until I found some promising candidates. To my delight, the vendor was willing to deliver to the pack's house, as he delivered bottles of milk in the afternoons and evenings for people on that side of the city. When I told him where the pack lived, he nodded. "I have a customer on that street."

As he had to deliver milk there anyway, I bought several bottles for them to enjoy along with an entire flock of chicks, all mystic-confirmed to be hens, their mother, and three other hens that got along well together. Then I went to a different vendor, bought a rooster, and dragged the cage over for delivery.

He laughed. "Smart woman. Anything else you need delivered tonight? I figure I can make some space."

I checked his mystic-cooled box of meats and pointed at a variety of nice roasts and three birds ready to go into the oven, bought three of his assorted boxes of vegetables, and a variety of herbs all to be delivered.

That would make certain they had plenty to eat until the pack women adapted to Ferdinand being gone. After paying, I went on the hunt for some goats, picking two adult white females and a black and white male from three different breeders scattered across the market. They didn't like me much, but a single warning growl convinced them they should listen.

Damned goats. I'd never gotten along with damned goats. They liked pushing my buttons.

Herding the animals cost me an extra hour on the way back to the house, but I made it for the deadline, and their damned complaints would drive me insane by the end of the day.

Ferdinand waited for me, and his brows raised at my three acquisitions. "Well, in good news, the backyard is available for their use temporarily, and I had someone bring supplies for a week for them already along with a watering barrel. Take them around back, set them loose, and get ready to go. You'll get a chance to stretch your legs as a tiger, which might soothe your temper some. You look ready to eat one of your new pets."

"Goats," I spat, allowing my disgust to leak out. Taking the animals around the house, I found the gate, and Rachelle opened it for me from the other side. I gave her the lead lines and made sure the little bastards stayed in the yard where they belonged. I returned to the front of the house after the woman secured the gate closed. "They looked healthy enough, but they're not prime stock. They should make good enough milk, but you won't want to breed them for show."

"I'm sure they'll taste just fine when the ladies get tired of taking care of the goats. I'm sure the ladies won't take long settling the animals. They're not the type to care too much about things like that. Did you get any chickens?"

"They will be delivered tonight along with some fresh milk, vegetables, and herbs. I got some hens, a rooster, and a flock of chicks."

"That will keep them busy."

I expected chaos.

With more patience than I expected from him, he waited for the pack women to get ready. I spent an hour listening to Ferdinand ramble about the history of the townhouse and its yard, which he'd gotten through some arrangement with another wolf pack. I assumed he'd coerced or killed the other pack off, leaving the property for him to claim.

Wolves didn't play fair.

Making the pregnant women walk alone sparked all the fury I needed to get through the rest of my afternoon, and I followed along like I was supposed to, taking care to keep from staring at Ferdinand's back. If he detected my hostility too early, I'd be in for a rough fight.

I'd lost a lot of weight skimping on my meals and making sure the pregnant women got as much as I could manage. It hadn't been enough. Rachelle still seemed gaunt, as did the other women. The exercise wouldn't do them any good unless the pack hunted after I finished sending Ferdinand to his grave. I'd find out soon enough.

Quick and brutal would work best for me, and then I'd wait for the ramifications of my actions to hit hard. I figured it could go one of two ways: the women would shift and tear me apart, or they'd be too deep into shock to do anything about me, after which they might still tear me apart.

I supposed they might celebrate without tearing me apart, but I'd learned to expect the worst and be pleasantly surprised when something good happened. If I took advantage of their shock, I could make a run for it, but I couldn't bring myself to abandon them.

They'd been stepped on too much. I would face my

fate with pride and dignity—and if they didn't kill me in the aftermath, I'd do my best to help them if I could.

I'd seen the relief in their eyes when they realized they'd have better and more food on their table, and that relief hadn't been for themselves. Life would become complicated, but I would find some way to make everything work out.

I always found a way to make life complicated, and I'd done well enough surviving. Once Ferdinand was dead, once I didn't hurt so damned much, I could work with the women and do something good for a change.

Ferdinand led us outside of the city to a thick forest, lush and ripe with prey. A herd of deer scattered from where city and wilderness clashed, promising the wolves would have a fresh trail to track with good meat at the end of their efforts.

"Here's good," Ferdinand announced. "Go ahead and shift, ladies. I expect it'll take Jesse longer, as she's a late-age shifter, and she's never had an easy time with her transformations."

Fury over his criticism gave me all the encouragement I needed to force my hand to change into a paw armed with lethal claws. Warmth radiated from my pouch, and blue sparks danced over my charcoal fur.

Ferdinand turned, and I closed the distance between us. In three strides, I reached him, and by the time he'd turned to face me, I stood in striking range. Black smoke coiled from my pitch-black stripes and engulfed my paw. The sharp tips tore into the wolf's throat, and I put all my strength into my one blow to make it count.

The bastard's eyelids fluttered and blood gushed from the jagged wounds, where I'd exposed pale bone. He crumpled, and his throat bubbled as his body struggled to draw another breath. In death, bodies twitched, even ones with severed spines, as muscles spasmed and the body became nothing more than organic matter destined to rot.

I stared down into his unseeing eyes, and I smiled.

Chapter Thirteen

THE WOMEN DIDN'T KILL me, for which I was grateful. I would have made easy prey for them, as Ferdinand's death created a flare of pain so intense I forgot how to breathe. While I swayed, I somehow remained on my feet. Then, like a receding tide, the agony faded to something manageable, a burn that afflicted my entire body.

That, too, ebbed after a while. I still hurt, but I could tolerate the discomfort.

I waited, and the women stared at me in shock, Ferdinand's blood still dripping from my claws and seeping into my clothes. The bite marks Ferdinand had inflicted on my throat throbbed to the beat of my heart. Without the wolf's desire to claim me driving his magic, I held hope the wounds would finally begin to heal. It would take time, but I would make certain they didn't scar. Somehow, I would circumvent nature and erase all evidence he'd ever touched me with his teeth.

By the time I was finished, no matter how many mystics I had to hire, there would be no evidence left of the bastard's attempt to steal me from my tiger. Not only would I erase evidence of Ferdinand's bites, I would eradicate him from history.

I almost regretted I'd refused to accept a proper contract for the bastard's death. Had I, I would've demanded bonuses from my aunt for putting up with the wolf's stupidity. Then I would've demanded extra bonuses for any and all anguish Anatoly had faced during my cooperative incarceration with the wolf pack.

Maybe I'd demand a bounty payout anyway on top of whatever they'd offered to mercenaries and bounty hunters for my retrieval, assuming my aunt had moved forward with her plan as we'd discussed. I hoped so.

The first thing I'd do with the money involved the removal of any scars, and then I'd share it with the women in Ferdinand's pack, making sure they had a solid future. As that wouldn't be enough, I'd recruit help from my family and stubborn friends to make certain they had a good life beyond their unfortunate imprisonment in an unwanted pack.

Ferdinand hadn't even comprehended his plans, foolish in all ways, had been doomed to fail from the beginning.

The wolf had gone against my grizzly of an aunt, my tiger, and his former guild master, and he'd lost.

I had claimed Anatoly the day I'd met him, and I had obsessed over the tattoo I'd left as a warning to other assassins. I still did. He was mine in life, and he was mine until death. If anyone tried to take him from me, I would use the scar above his wrist and my assassin's mark to justify the hell I would rain down on any responsible.

Ferdinand's death was only the beginning.

I'd have to explain to Todd, the one last, albeit terrifying part of Ferdinand's demise. I held some hope he'd understand about Marie. He'd already known of her behavior. I would have to hope he would progress through the stages of grief without our friendship being sacrificed in the process. If I couldn't get through to him, my aunt would talk to him.

So would others.

I could only hope Todd's relationship with me and my tiger survived the upcoming days—and that I somehow managed to deal with Ferdinand's wolves before they snapped and killed me if the power of the bastard's bite overwhelmed them.

So far, so good. They hadn't turned on me yet.

The wolf's body cooled at my feet, his blood still flowing from the jagged tears across his throat. The surprise in his expression pleased me. He'd bitten me so many times he had believed, right up until end, that I belonged to him.

I had never belonged to him, but the rest of the women of his pack had.

They hurt, too.

I straightened, aware of the crimson dripping from my claws to the ground, darkening the soil. All I could do was test the turbulent relationship I had with the pack of wolf women freed from Ferdinand's bite. "I know someone who can help you."

Todd would never forgive me for inviting a pack of wolves into his herd, but Marie couldn't pay for her crimes anymore, and he could undo some of the damage she had caused with her machinations.

In a way, I resented the circumstances leading to so much suffering. It would be hard forgiving the stallion for making a home with a pit viper, but I did believe she had fooled him as much as she had fooled me—even with my aunt's warning of her possibly treachery. Still, it would be a long time until I let go of what Marie and Ferdinand had done.

I still needed to unearth her body and move it somewhere better than beneath a pile of stones to keep the animals off it. If given a choice, I wouldn't bother, but I wondered if Todd would want her body back.

We'd lost so much because of her.

I still remembered closing my agent's eyes for the final time, his skin cooling in death. Had Randal survived? Had anyone?

Ferdinand had done a good job secluding me from the world and coercing me into obedience through threats. The stench of fear from the women he'd claimed as his own, so many of them pregnant, had brought me into line, as had my aunt's request to dig for more information on the bastard.

The wolf women had been stolen, too.

I reminded myself of that, and I would continue to do so until the whole mess was behind me.

Instead of fear or anger like I expected, I smelled blood and anguish, and I wondered how I'd fix the damage I'd done to them through Ferdinand's demise.

I lifted my chin, and I repeated, "I know someone who can help you."

Todd loved women, and Todd loved children. Wolves and horses would bicker, they'd fight, and things would become insane in the manor he called home, but Ferdinand's children would have a stallion for a father and a childhood worth remembering.

I'd beg it of him if needed.

And if, for whatever reason, Todd did refuse, I would turn to Anatoly for help.

Todd was the better choice.

He understood women and children.

"Who?" Lauren asked. I almost smiled at the edge in the woman's voice, unable to do anything other than admire her. While she had bowed to Ferdinand's magic, she had found ways to fight the bastard, dodging his orders through loopholes and subterfuge. She'd been in the background, nudging and suggesting when Rachelle should let me off my leash a little more, helping to give me the opportunity to rid the world of Marie.

Both of our actions had led us to the moment I'd turned on Ferdinand and ripped this throat out with my claws.

To make it clear what I thought of him, I turned

and mule kicked his body hard enough his corpse rolled over. "I know a stallion. I killed his lead mare, the woman who was his informant from Charlotte. Ferdinand had betrayed him and our friends. Stallions live for foals, and they don't necessarily care if they are horse, wolf, or something else. He will welcome you."

"The woman Ferdinand had been meeting was this stallion's mare?"

"She was before I killed her for her treachery."

Because of Marie, I would never again see Simmons or any of the other Secret Service agents who'd lost their lives protecting their principals. I could only assume others had lost their lives. I remembered the sounds of combat.

In that, Ferdinand and Marie had lost.

Their ploy had brought destruction, but they had killed the wrong people. They hadn't killed me. I refused to believe they had killed my family. I wouldn't stop until everyone connected to their scheme fell, no matter where in the United States it took me. I would finish what they had begun.

I flexed my hand, and my tiger's claws shrank back to human fingers. One day soon, I hoped everything would stop hurting all the damned time. Returning to Charlotte and sequestering myself with my tiger for several days might help, too.

Lauren growled, drawing my attention back to her. "This stallion has been betrayed, too, then."

"Yes, he was betrayed. He's respected in Charlotte,

so Marie would have been able to get good information for Ferdinand."

"You speak of the Lancers' guild leader, then. The black stallion who rules over Charlotte. Rumor says he is close friends with the other guild leaders in Charlotte, despite their status as rivals." Lauren's expression eased. "I've heard of him and his prowess. He has many foals and a strong herd."

"He's an egotistical asshole, but he loves women and children in equal measure. He will dress you as queens until you find your feet, and he will sing praises at you until you believe him. And then he'll treat your pups as his own, because he doesn't know how to do it any other way."

They could trust Todd. I could, too, although I would be braced for his wrath when I told him of his mare's fate and how I'd killed her for her betrayal.

For all I'd found balance between my lives as Runs Against Wind and Jesse Alexander, I still remained the Water Viper, and I'd tattooed my mark on her brow to declare the kill as mine. Per my aunt's request, I'd left Ferdinand's body untouched. If anyone found her, they would know her killer long after her flesh decayed away. I'd carved my serpent to the bone, making sure her skull declared her guilt, as I only killed the guilty.

Some things I refused to change.

Of all of my kills, of all the bodies I'd left rotting in my wake, I walked away from Marie's body without remorse or shame.

I would stare into Todd's eyes and declare I'd taken

her life with pride, no matter the consequences. I foresaw it going one of two ways. He'd either ruffle my hair and tell me I'd gotten worked up over nothing, or he'd storm off and come back a few days later before ruffling my hair and telling me he understood.

Either way, the bastard would ruffle my hair, because he liked screwing with Anatoly.

Lauren frowned, and she looked me over head to toe before focusing on my bloodstained hand. "You're sure of this?"

"He would have taken me into his herd without question for all I'm a predator, too. I am not suited for pack or herd life."

"Tigers have clan siblings," Lauren replied. "That's similar. Their clans function as packs in a way. But you are right. It is not the same, and you're not suited. Ferdinand was a fool, and he deserved his death."

The other wolves murmured their agreement, but the stench of their fear still hung heavy in the air.

"If I can get to a telegraph station, this will be over quickly."

"It can? Why do you think so?"

"I'm a Siberian, and my mate is on the Clan Council."

It didn't hurt my aunt was likely flipping her lid, I didn't want to think too hard about what Anatoly was doing, and my uncles, both grizzly and insane rabbit, would be neck deep in the hunt, too. The attack would have solidified their purpose, and not a one of them would quit until they won.

If Todd joined in, along with both Lancers' Alliance and Dawnfire, I pitied Ferdinand and his little army. The pair of grizzlies would clean up half the mess without help, the damned rabbit with a predatory side would take care of the other half, and everyone else would complain they'd been robbed of their chance to join in the slaughter.

The wolves stared at me with wide eyes.

Lauren recovered first, and she pointed at my throat. "But Ferdinand bit you."

"While painful, these bites mean nothing to me. I've already staked my claim on my tiger, and a weak bastard of a wolf can't do anything to me. I faked it, Lauren. I pretended he had influence over me. I did it all for this moment, all so I could take what I learned of his plans and destroy everything he's worked for. I still need to figure out where he intended to take me and what his full plans are, but I've learned enough."

The timeline for him to act needed to be enough, along with my knowledge that he needed the Hope Diamond to succeed.

The damned fool, even after death, sickened me.

"And we will help you," she announced, and she shot a glare at the other women. "We all will. We are not broken. We will never be broken. And we will undo some of what he has done now that we are free."

One by one, the wolves nodded their agreement.

Well, that would make things a little easier. I turned to Rachelle, aware her baby was at the highest risk and she needed safe, easy work—and a lot of good meals.

"You will handle communications. I will not endanger your baby. We will give you work, but it will be work that keeps you and that puppy safe. And I will find that little one a father worthy of both of you."

I'd always thought Paulus would make a good father, and he had a lot of years left in him, too stubborn to give up the ghost and die. He probably danced at death's door for the fun of it—and to give his guild master gray hair.

Sometimes, I pitied poor Todd for what he had to put up with.

"I had always heard tigers are the most stubborn of shifters, but you are more stubborn than I expected. To endure so many bites all as part of an act? Some of them still bleed."

I touched the bite from earlier in the morning, and sure enough, the damned thing still bled. Sighing, I shook my head. "They'll heal, and I'll beat every mystic I know until they strip the scars if I must. It'll take time, but they'll heal. A real bite scars quickly." As I'd already told them the truth of having a mate, I showed them my upper arm and the faint white mark branding me as Anatoly's. "Ferdinand ignored this scar because it's so much like all the others I have, isn't it? But this is where my mate bit me. I bit his arm, too."

I had plans to bite Anatoly a few more times to make certain nobody doubted my claim. After I finished biting him, I'd drag him off for something far more intimate and long overdue.

"Clever tiger. Everyone else bites the throat. You

had scars on your throat, too. He must have believed your tiger hadn't marked you at all."

My damned tiger had marked my soul from the day I'd met him, I just hadn't realized how deeply he'd sunk his claws into me until later. Then he'd marked me ruthlessly with his nips and nibbles, invisible bites, but bites all the same. I supposed for tigers, intention mattered more than anything else.

In a way, I had to thank Ferdinand for confirming everything I hadn't wanted to believe because of fear and uncertainty. For all I was I killer, I was a killer capable of loving others.

I loved Anatoly.

I loved my aunt.

I loved my uncles, for all they drove me crazy whenever I crossed paths with them. I loved Todd, too, despite the ups and downs we'd faced over the years.

Through them, I loved the parents I'd never met. When I found my way home, I would ask my aunt about my mother again, but I wouldn't ask for just information.

I'd demand a meeting, and I wouldn't let them distract me from it. I didn't even care if bringing my parents into the same room together resulted in a brother or sister. If anything, I desired having a brother or sister.

That my parents would still want each other after so long meant I'd been born from something more than just a contract, that my mother had found value in my father and their time together, and that my father had found worth in my mother, too. I'd ask for a chance to have what I'd always believed impossible.

I'd stop being my own worst enemy.

My thoughts returned to Anatoly, who'd haunted me from the day Ferdinand and his accomplices had taken Simmons from me along with so many others. "He's going to be quite angry."

"Who? The stallion? Your tiger?"

"My tiger, Anatoly. If he gets his hands on Ferdinand, he will tear his body to pieces, I expect. While roaring."

The women exchanged looks, and after a while, Lauren grinned. "Do you think he could get here before the bastard rots too much? I'd pay to see that."

My worries of them hating me for killing their mate evaporated. "We could toss him in cold storage and let him thaw after my tiger gets here."

"Or we could just hack him apart and feed the fish. There's a river nearby."

"He might poison the fish," I countered.

"That's true. I vote we just leave his body to rot. Let the vultures have him. He deserves nothing from us." Lauren joined me, and she kicked Ferdinand's body. "And if your mate becomes upset over those marks on your throat, we'll correct him. What do we do now?"

What could we do? I thought back on my life as a mercenary and a courier. Knowledge won wars, and the best I could do for my family was provide as much information on the wolf's plans as possible. That left us with one choice. "We raid wherever Ferdinand has an office, get all of the information we can, and find out how deep this rabbit hole goes. Depending on what we learn, we'll make plans. There are plenty here who hate Ferdinand. We can recruit their help to stop whatever plans he has."

"He was after the government. He wanted to bring in new powers, and he wanted to be a part of that," Lauren replied. "He meant to change the presidency first. It surprised me when he stopped talking about his goals after bringing you to the pack's house."

"I'd guessed that when he attacked Charlotte, likely attempted to murder the President, and kidnapped me. But this goes deeper than just that, and I plan to figure it out—and destroy everything he built. That will be my revenge for what he has done to us. And your final revenge will be to live happily without him. I know a good wolf with a strong pack who would love to have you and your baby, Rachelle, and I know other good wolves without mates who would love your children like their own. And there's always the herd with Todd, too."

Paulus and the many other single wolves in the guilds of Charlotte could offer everything Ferdinand had not.

It occurred to me that somehow, despite the circumstances of my birth and the life I had led, I knew a lot of good people who could transform disaster into hope.

I grinned, wondering which one of the women would win Paulus, much to *his* shock and astonishment.

Compared to Ferdinand, Paulus would be a treasure they'd fight over.

"You know a lot of people."

"Trust me on this one, I find that as unbelievable as you do. If you think what I've told you is bad now, wait until you meet my family."

It would be chaos.

Lauren's expression saddened. "He targeted us because we don't have families."

"Well, I do, and I'm happy to share them with you. Maybe you've lost your mate, not that he was a good one, but you won't be alone. That much I can promise you."

Even if I had to adopt them all myself, they would never be alone again.

They'd suffered enough.

We took everything except Ferdinand's clothes, and we went to the townhouse he'd claimed as his own, the one place he kept from his misfit pack of disgruntled women forced to serve because of his bite. They'd learned of its location through subterfuge.

Ferdinand hadn't told Lauren she couldn't follow him, and she'd ghosted his steps late one night to learn where he lived.

The place reeked of rotting food, sweat, and sex, and the other women snarled at the evidence of even more betrayal.

"Would you like to go back to his body and tear into him for a while, ladies?"

"No, but I want a mystic to make sure I didn't catch anything," Lauren grumbled, shaking her head. "What a dick. He may have bitten more women, then. Or just hired some whores, I guess."

A desperate wolf would hire whores, but he'd learned how to force his pack to attend to his every desire. I'd escaped his lust, but only because he'd wanted to break me first. His delusions I would beg him for the pleasure of his company would haunt me for a long time.

The doubt in Lauren's voice would haunt me, too. "Does it feel like he brought anyone else into the pack?"

"No, it doesn't. He never managed to ensnare you into the pack, though. We'd wondered about that. He forced you to stay in the house without you being in the pack. We couldn't make sense of it. For all we could tell, he believed you belonged to him."

"I'm a stubborn tiger with zero desire to be bound to him in any shape or form. I'm just sorry there wasn't anything I could do to help you sooner."

"Smart woman. No, we don't blame you for resisting him. We only wish we could have, too. And we definitely don't blame you for anything. You did what we thought was impossible. I'm grateful you accomplished the impossible."

Arguing wouldn't help matters, so I forced my thoughts back to business. "Let's tear this place apart.

If you find anything regarding the government, let me know. I can deal with it—or I know who to contact. Does this area have phones, or will I need to find a telegraph station?"

"Yes, we're connected. We got lines last year. We can call most major cities, but the call quality is poor. Ferdinand said he has a phone."

A phone changed everything. Calling the Secret Service would light a fire under my aunt's ass faster than a Starfall stone. "I need that phone."

Rachelle waddled off and waved her hand. "I'll look for the phone and give a shout when I find it. I can't read, anyway—but I've seen a phone before."

She wasn't the only wolf who couldn't read, and they joined the heavily pregnant woman in her quest for the device. None of them could, which made the pack's house the perfect place for Ferdinand to store research material without worrying about the women figuring out his plans.

"Okay. He probably has an office in here some—"

"Phone!" Rachelle announced. "In here."

Well, I wouldn't complain about early access to Ferdinand's phone, although I would have preferred a few more minutes to prepare and to think about how to explain everything that had happened over the past month.

I went in the room where Rachelle proclaimed there was a phone to discover a paper-filled office. "Thank you, Rachelle. This is probably going to be where we figure out what he's been up to. Do you want to get off your feet?"

"I'm fine so far, but thank you. I'll help the others tear this place apart. I bet the bastard has cash squirreled away somewhere. Once we find the money, I'll take care of feeding us properly. I was worried he'd make us eat those poor goats and the chickens. They're such sweet animals." Her expression soured. "We'll eat properly at the pack's house. You, too. You must be starved. You've eaten so little since you've joined us."

I was, but my stomach took mercy and didn't gurgle a demand for food.

"I'll have to tell them somewhere where we'll be. What's the best place?" I asked.

"The pack's house, I guess. We're all comfortable with it, and it's clean. You know the address?"

"I know it." I couldn't get out of wolf country fast enough, and if I had my way, I'd never step foot into Knoxville ever again. I went to the phone, picked up the receiver, and put it to my ear, bracing for a dead line.

The tone left me weak from relief, and I sat in the chair before the overburdened desk, and spun the rotary dial as I'd been taught. After a click, the phone rang.

"Secret Service dispatch," a woman's voice answered. "Please identify yourself."

I drew in a deep breath and prepared myself for the chaos. "It's Stiletto. I'm in Knoxville, Tennessee, and there's a pack of women with me who also require assistance."

"Please stay on the line, ma'am. We are now in process of tracing your call. What is your current situation?"

"Pissed off, mostly. Ferdinand, formerly of Dawnfire, is dead. Marie, one of the wives of the Lancers' Alliance's guild leader, was likewise an accomplice. She is also deceased. There is something planned for three to four weeks from now, but I'm not sure what, but they plan on using the Hope Diamond for their plot. There's paperwork here that needs to be sorted through which might tell us more."

The papers would tell me more, and I was relieved I wouldn't have to play stupid even a minute longer.

"What is the current status of the Hope Diamond?"

"Around my neck as usual," I complained. "I am also in possession of Steel Heart and Sunder."

The stones would cause me problems, but in a way, I appreciated their presence.

They shined whenever I felt truly alone, as did the Hope Diamond.

Sunder, however, scared me. Whenever I looked at it, I got the feeling it hungered, and it wouldn't stop until it devoured every weapon in the world. I wondered if any Starfall stone could protect against its power.

I wasn't sure I wanted to know.

Assuming I wasn't able to stop Ferdinand's plan or

otherwise dispose of his prized weapon, I had plans for Sunder.

"I will make your primary agent aware, and I will have him dispatched to your location immediately."

"Agent Randal?" I asked, unable to keep the waver out of my voice.

"Agent Randal is still your primary agent, ma'am. I regret to inform you Agent Simmons was killed in the line of duty. He was given full honors at his burial."

I closed my eyes and sighed. "I was with him when he died. I'm aware. I didn't know if Randal had survived."

"While Agent Randal was injured, he has since recovered and has been working on finding you."

"Have you gotten a trace on the call?"

"We have confirmed you are located in Knoxville."

I told the woman the address of the pack's house and how to get there. "We're going to get as much information as we can from one of the conspirators. They wanted the Hope Diamond as part of their plan."

"Understood." The woman barked orders, relaying my information to someone nearby. She also gave marching orders for Randal to head towards the Knoxville area along with a team. I waited until she finished before saying, "There are numerous women who were bitten by Ferdinand against their will. Thirteen, I think. At least several of them are pregnant. Can you request Cleo and Todd? They're…"

I hesitated, unwilling to call them damaged despite it being the truth. They'd gone through too much.

"Traumatized," the woman supplied. "Yes. We have been briefed on the consequences of a wolf's bite and what happens to women following the death of their mated wolf. I will put in the request, and I will find others who should be able to assist with your situation. Were you bitten?"

"I would call myself unpleasantly tenderized, pissed, and so help me, if my tiger isn't with Randal, I will not be happy."

She chuckled. "Understood, ma'am. I am certain someone will ensure that Head Tiger accompanies your agent to Knoxville. He has been an active participant in the search for you."

I bet. "Tell him I'm fine, please. It won't help much, but he may be a little less growly."

"I will do that, ma'am. I—"

The woman yelped, and the line clattered. I wondered who had barged in when word had spread I'd called in.

"Jesse?" Anatoly growled.

"Don't you growl at me," I replied, and to make it clear he shouldn't push my buttons, I hissed at him.

He hissed back.

I narrowed my eyes. "I am reserving my roar for when I can do so in your face."

"And mine will be louder. By far."

In his dreams. I had weeks of frustration to work out, and unlike in Fort Lauderdale, I wasn't near dead from illness and injury. "I'm fine. Bring me my agent. I took care of the problems personally, but I need you to do me a favor."

"Anything."

"Marie was involved."

Anatoly sighed, and in his voice, I heard defeat and grief. "We know. Todd knows. He figured it out when she abandoned their youngest foal and left town following the attack. Nobody has been able to track where she went; she'd hop trains, go somewhere, get on a train again, and move on before anyone could catch up with her. He's beside himself with rage and grief. His little girl doesn't understand why one of the other mares has taken over her care. The herd's a mess, and they've been doing a lot of soul searching—and learning if anyone else was involved. None of the other mares were. Just Marie. She was still in the herd when she died."

That bitch. "I dumped her body, buried her with some rocks, and I regret I showed her even that courtesy after I finished her off. I carved my mark her forehead right down to the fucking bone."

"I'll let Todd know. Is that what you wanted?"

"She had a clean death. Frankly, I should've drawn it out and made her suffer. She betrayed Todd."

"And she forgot you deal with traitors in one way: you kill them. Are you all right?"

"I'm all right. I was tenderized, but Ferdinand was an old and stupid wolf. He couldn't even draw me into his pack. He's bitten a lot of women. Some are pregnant. I thought Todd might help."

"It'll be good for him. How many?"

"I don't know exactly. At least five? One's due soon. I asked for Cleo. He's good. Ferdinand wasn't taking care of them. They're malnourished, Nate. I had to convince him he should feed them more, but they haven't eaten enough."

Using his nickname would send a message, one that went beyond my usual formality with my tiger, especially as I reserved Ana for when I teased him.

Anatoly sighed. "I'll make sure they're taken care of. Forced?"

"All of them."

"And you?"

"I'll heal. He didn't want to sully himself on a damned cat."

Anatoly growled at that. "You've earned ten bites and anything else I feel like doing to you for that comment."

Damn. I grinned at the thought of my tiger finally snapping and going for me like he meant it. I planned on enjoying every moment of it. "It's nothing a little time won't fix. I ripped the bastard's throat out, took his stuff, and left him to rot. I'm now in his house looking through his shit and using his phone."

"Good. You're sure you're all right?"

"As I said, I've been thoroughly tenderized, but I've been through worse beatings. I'll be back in shape before you figure out how to get your ass on a train and get here. Ferdinand and his asshole accomplices intend to take on the government using the Hope Diamond. How, I'm not sure exactly. I'm presuming something combustible; he had a lot of books about various technology that used combustion."

"We'll be ready for them. But I'm coming for you. It'll be twelve hours, roughly. It depends on when the next train leaves. But it won't leave without us. Someone was calling the station when I came in."

"How did you get in there so quickly, anyway?"

"I'm wired because I told them if I didn't hear about you immediately, I would kill somebody. I only get looped in about anything involving you, but that's all I wanted. There's a lot of chatter on the line right now. I was just down the hall on my way to a meeting. I have skipped the meeting. I'll toss the First Gentleman into the crater if he tries to make me go to that damned meeting."

Anatoly snarled, the phone clattered, and I wondered who'd get the receiver next. According to the snarls, growls, hisses, and other feline displays, Randal had barreled in and wanted a piece of my tiger.

Waiting bore fruit, and whoever had won the battle for the phone panted.

"Are you finished?" I asked, careful to keep my tone mild to keep my tiger somewhat calm, assuming he'd kept hold of the phone.

"For now," Anatoly replied. "I'm sitting on your agent. It's my turn with the phone, and I refuse to relinquish it to anyone. You're *mine*."

Tigers. My tiger, in particular, would need a great deal of nibbling and cuddling to calm down. "Yes, yes. Go catch your train and bring my agent with you. I have to finish robbing this house, and then we'll meet up at the pack's house. Don't be late." I sighed. "I want a hug, and I want my nibbles. But my neck hurts because Ferdinand tore up my throat thinking that'd actually work. It didn't. And I don't care how much it costs, not a single damned one of these will scar. I'll kidnap your mystic if I must, damn it. I'll assault the damned President of the United States if needed!"

"Everything will be fine. If Henry can't and your aunt doesn't coerce one of her mystics to take care of it, I'll take care of it. How bad is it?"

"Every time he couldn't get a bite to stick, he'd try again. He assumed they were working a little, and that he just had to bite me enough times to make it stick. And they just don't heal. Well, they're healing now."

"Because he's dead. How badly does it hurt?"

I wouldn't tell him the nips, nibbles, and bite he'd decorated me with had hurt more than Ferdinand's pitiable efforts; he'd beat himself up over it before adding a few extra bites to the mix because he could. "It hurts. I've dealt with worse. My shoulder? That was worse."

"I'll be there soon. I'm going to give the phone back to the dispatcher so we can catch the train."

"Tell Randal I'm okay."

"I will. And you better still be okay when I get there."

The phone transferred hands again, and the dispatcher asked, "Will you be safe until a team can reach you?"

"I should be. We're going to lie as low as we can, but we'll be ready if anyone tries anything."

Without Ferdinand holding the entire pack of women hostage, I could do what I did best: fight.

We exchanged a few pleasantries before hanging up. Turning to Lauren, I said, "We tear this place apart, and after, we will go to the pack's house. If anyone interferes with us, retaliate. Violently. You are wolves. Show them you are not prey. If the pack house isn't safe, we'll go to a hotel and pay for it with Ferdinand's money."

They bared their teeth in a wolfish grin promising blood and misery to any who crossed them.

Ferdinand had damaged them, but they weren't broken.

It was a good start.

Chapter Fourteen

FERDINAND HAD KEPT ALL of his illegal dealings locked in an iron safe, but not even three inches of metal could bar me from gaining access. My anger provoked the Hope Diamond, which devoured the iron in a shower of sparks. Sunder joined in, and what the Hope Diamond didn't consume, it did. The Starfall stones gleamed blue before darkening. The wolves stared, their mouths hanging open while blue and black smoke finished engulfing the safe and leaving only its contents in its wake.

"Do you think that counts as a burst?" I asked, waving my hand to in a futile effort to clear the air. It took almost twenty minutes for the scentless haze to dissipate. A stack of papers, a pile of cash, and a shocking collection of Starfall stones littered the floor, spilling everywhere without the iron walls of the safe containing them. I went for the stones first, which glowed in a rainbow of colors beneath the light of the Hope Diamond.

I assumed they, too, belonged to some weapon clan or another. At the rate I was going, I would be the sole owner of every weapon clan stone in existence. I slipped the stones into my belt pouch with the others, discovered they wouldn't all fit, and crammed the rest into my pockets as the damned things refused to leave me alone.

Rachelle peeked into my pouch. "Why would Ferdinand want those Starfall stones? They don't look special."

"They belong to various weapon clans. All part of his ploy to destroy the United States government, I presume."

"That fool."

The possibility—no, probability—of Ferdinand being involved with the original theft of the Hope Diamond bothered me. It colored my thoughts, adding a dark miasma to everything that had happened. My heart still hurt whenever I witnessed my horse's struggles to recover from her sickness. Adrian had kept his word, but she had just gotten to the point she could be ridden again before Ferdinand had kidnapped me and taken me to Tennessee. "If Ferdinand is involved with what I think he is, I've seen horses sick from whatever it does. It's very hard for them to recover. It took a lot of help for Miracle to survive. She did, barely. If they weaponize this thing like they want, a lot of people will die."

If anything could weaponize that mysterious toxin, it was the Hope Diamond.

"We'll stop them," Lauren swore. "I won't see that bastard's plans survive. Not now."

Without Ferdinand's bite on them, the women could once again exercise true free will. For that alone, coping with my time in Tennessee had been worth my while. I wished I could kill him over and over again, once for each time he'd stolen someone's life and forced her to do his bidding.

All I could do was focus on the little things: because he'd bitten so many, they'd escape his death with little consequence—I hoped. I'd obeyed his commands for their sake, enduring bite after bite while pretending I wavered a little more, faking obedience to keep his ire from landing on the true victims of his crime, the women of his pack.

I never wanted to smell so much fear again.

"I don't know how involved they'll let us be. But we'll try."

While it would be rude, I could leave right before they were scheduled to arrive, acquiring horses and beginning a mad dash across the country.

Taking the train would be faster.

"Who is coming?"

"A very small army of stubborn people, I expect. It'll probably include my mate, who is a Siberian tiger, my aunt, who is a grizzly bear, my uncle, who is also a grizzly bear, and my other uncle, who is a rabbit. He's the most blood-thirsty rabbit to plague the United

States, so you watch out for him. The stallion who will take care of you and your puppies will probably be coming. Marie's stallion. Todd's a good man, although he's definitely a whore of a horse."

"We're used to a whore of a wolf," Lauren replied with a shrug. "We don't mind an honest whore, truth be told. It's men like Ferdinand we don't want. We're like sisters now, and while we didn't like the wolf, I wouldn't mind remaining a family. A herd would let us do that. But with a good man this time, not…"

"Not Ferdinand." I nodded. "I expect a lot of people will be coming, and it wouldn't surprise me if Todd comes along. He'll want to bring you into his herd right away so you can settle and have stability. He won't want your babies to be stressed, and if you're used to a pack or herd environment, he'll want to sustain that. Without Ferdinand, will the pack bonds survive?"

The women shook their heads.

"The pack is already falling apart," Rachelle admitted. "He had to bite us once or twice a week to sustain the pack's bonds."

That helped explain part of why Ferdinand had gone after my throat so often—not because he thought he lacked control over me, but trying to force me into his pack so he could control me even more.

I regretted having killed the man so mercifully. A thousand more deaths might have balanced the scales. Undoing his plans would have to be good enough.

With so many Starfall stones to identify and deal

with, I'd have my hands full for the next few days. I considered the documents, which likely consisted of evidence of Ferdinand's wrongdoing. The entire lot would have to go with us until someone could read it all.

That someone would be me until Nate, the Secret Service, and my family arrived.

Having a family who cared for me still confused and unsettled me.

When would I feel worthy of them? Would I ever feel worthy of them?

Life had been easier before I'd discovered what it meant to be loved by someone—and to love them in return.

I shook my head to clear it, crouching beside the papers and stacking them together to make sure none were missed. "Then that settles that. We'll wait for them to arrive, and we'll play it by ear. Find something we can carry these papers off in. We'll try the pack house first, and if that isn't safe, we'll figure something out. We only have to hold out until tomorrow."

Tomorrow couldn't come soon enough.

FERDINAND'S DEATH took a toll on us all, and while we managed to transfer all of the paperwork out of the house in a bunch of boxes in one trip, exhaustion stripped us of our ability to do anything more than make dinner, take care of the goats and chickens, and find somewhere to sleep. Returning to my closet bothered them, as there was nothing preventing me from sleeping somewhere more comfortable.

I simply smiled and promised I'd grown used to the space, and that I was too tired to move the bedding.

One day, I would tell them all of the various flops I'd occupied over the years as I'd roamed, and how I'd crossed most of the United States on foot or horseback. I would regale them with tales of the time I'd caught a tiger by his tail in a bar in Miami, resulting in the poor bastard chasing me all over the United States because I hadn't had the sense to accept I had worth.

I woke to breath on my throat, which startled me into roaring. The roar led to swipes and growls, and the growls led to snapped teeth and blood. Anatoly's chuckle rumbled in his chest, and the bastard tiger sank his feline fangs into my shoulder near my neck, one of his favorite spots for nipping and nibbling.

It hurt, I bled, and while tigers couldn't purr, he did his best to imitate the sound. "Good morning. How is my tigress doing?"

"You just took a chunk out of my shoulder, and you're asking how I'm doing?"

He licked the fresh wound, and he chuffed his pleasure. "I want to bite you a hundred times and leave my marks all over your skin, a claim no one can refute. I want to keep you close so no other man can look upon you without hearing my warning growls. A leash might work, but I'm willing to endure being handcuffed to you."

I yawned, surveying my nest within the closet, which realistically lacked the room for both of us, although he'd done his best to invade my space. Unlike Ferdinand's bites, Anatoly's had already faded to a minor discomfort. "You can't bite me a hundred times right now."

"Right now implies you would allow me to do such a thing."

"If you bite me that many times, I'm biting you that many times."

Todd stuck his head through the closet door and shook his head. "And people wonder why Siberians maul each other. Apparently, extended courtship reduces tigers to mindless sex fiends worse than even equines. There are a lot of upset people downstairs wondering if you're all right, as everyone here heard you roar before it fell deceptively quiet. I was sacrificed to come up and investigate. Should I report there was a mauling or flirting?"

I considered my two options. "Can it be both?"

"It can be both," Todd replied with a smile, one that promised everything would work out despite all that had happened.

"Both. And I don't want to hear any damned whining about bloodshed."

Todd chuckled. "I'll let them know. Are you all right? Can we be selectively upset about bloodshed?" The stallion pointed at my neck, which hadn't healed all that much since I'd passed out in my nest in the closet. "We're all rather upset over that bloodshed."

"I'm fine. Is Cleo here? The pack needs him. Henry should help, too."

"He's here with Henry. They just finished checking on my new herd of wolves. I can't believe you suggested I add a pack of wolves to my herd, Jesse. Did you forget I'm a stallion?"

"I picked you because you're a stallion."

His smile widened to a grin. "The wolves will be all right, mostly." After a moment of hesitation, his expression sobered. "Two will likely lose their pups. Cleo is going to help them as much as they can, but the pups are close to death, and it would take a miracle to save them at this point."

I wore a miracle, although I didn't know how I might convince it to save two unborn children. "We could try the Hope Diamond. Do you think that might help?"

"Nothing we try will make the situation any worse for the puppies. Cleo believes malnutrition and stress are the main factors. None of you are healthy, though despite having endured a mauling, you're in the best shape."

"I'd be sorry, but I'm not. I played along to help them, just like I was supposed to."

Todd reached over Anatoly and ruffled my hair, just as I expected from him when he wanted to reassure me everything would work out. "Of course. That's what you do. Thank you for requesting me. I've never seen so many women cry at one time just from being brought into the herd. I asked the mares to be prepared to welcome them. They did just that. The instant the ladies realized we were genuinely willing to take them in, they had a breakdown. Henry has been dealing with that and checking in on them while Cleo has been trying to figure out how to save those puppies. The women want them, so he'll do whatever he can. Wolves and equines together will be interesting, but we'll make it work. I've already promised both women I'd take them for a ride they'd never forget if they lost their puppies. They want to be mothers."

I hated so much tragedy, and I hoped I could make the intractable diamond locked around my throat do some good for a change. In the meantime, I could solve one problem. "I was thinking you might introduce Rachelle to Paulus."

Todd's eyes widened. "I'll be damned. Aren't you just a clever little tiger today? Now, being serious. How are you doing? Cleo took one look at your throat and started cursing. He started counting the bites, and he stopped after thirty. I've never seen him quite so speechless before. Or so angry."

"I was angry, too. I took it out on Ferdinand's throat. I won't say I'm sorry because I'm really not sorry. Did you get to the papers?"

"Your aunt is going over them now, and she's making plans."

"And Randal?"

"He saw your throat, pitched a fit, and has been fuming downstairs ever since. Gentry made him leave so you could sleep. Nate's been guarding the doorway of your nest, but it seems he got tired of you resting. Henry said you were wiped out and needed more sleep—and that you'd appreciate Nate being the one to wake you. Henry's upset that you were mauled, and so is Cleo for that matter. Considering how fast your wounds are healing, they should be gone by the end of the day. Cleo doesn't think any of them will scar, as he believes you're so damned stubborn you won't scar unless it's a scar you want to keep. I tried to tell him that wasn't how scars work, but he kicked me. He then blamed the Hope Diamond. Then he blamed himself, should your stubborn pride and the Hope Diamond fail to do the job, he'll take care of it himself—or coerce another mystic to take care of it."

"He should thank the Hope Diamond for making his work easier." I'd abuse the damned rock if needed to make my claim reality.

Given a few days, I'd feel sorry for the Hope Diamond, as it would have to put up with me at my worst.

"I'll make sure he knows that. I'll go let everyone else know you're busy flirting with your tiger and will need at least an hour to settle. No naps," he ordered.

I hissed at him.

"No naps," he repeated.

Anatoly's position over me kept me from biting the stallion as a rebuke for trying to tell me what I could and couldn't do. Laughing, Todd retreated, leaving me alone with my tiger.

Anatoly pinned me beneath him and wiggled the

rest of the way into my closet. "You can't escape me now."

Between his weight and the closet's confines, he was correct. The situation put him in nibbling range, and I began with kissing my favorite spot on his throat. Touching his skin soothed me as nothing else had since Ferdinand had gotten his filthy hands on me. I skipped the rest of my nibbles and nips and went straight for a bite.

While I'd forced my hands to shift before, I hadn't figured out how to force my fangs to make an appearance. My teeth ached, Anatoly sucked in a breath, and I tore into his skin deep enough he bled. My tongue likewise underwent a transformation, and I dragged the roughened surface over his skin to capture every last drop of his blood.

"Is my tigress hungry?"

I growled and licked him again.

"I'm taking that as a yes."

Once the bleeding stopped, I sighed, wrapped my arms around him, and held him close. "We should take a nap."

"I want to, but I really need to get you downstairs before Randal loses his mind. Everyone else is bordering on losing their minds, too. The only reason I won the right to wake you up was because you're mine, and I threatened to have a temper tantrum of the likes they've never seen before. They're just going to have to learn to deal with that."

After losing Simmons, I didn't have to wonder why

Randal was at risk of losing his sanity. I'd worked through most of my grief for my agent already, with acceptance coming on the heels of a solidified plan of vengeance for his senseless murder.

His memory still hurt, but I thought it would be an easier burden to bear in the upcoming days.

"All right. Let's get this over with so we can go take a nap. I'm so tired."

"You're tired because you've been fighting Ferdinand's attempts to bite you. I bit you solely to make sure any of his attempts to lay claim were fully erased. You're *mine.*"

I was, but he was equally mine, too. I nipped him to make it clear he was my tiger. "As if I'd let some stupid wolf mate with me."

"And for that, I'll forever be grateful."

Randal and Anatoly fought for the right to curl around me, and the pair, both sporting fur coats, rolled through the pack's sitting room, destroying the table and several of the chairs while they battled to be the supreme male. I observed, too tired to stop them.

I regarded my aunt with a raised brow, yet another yawn slipping out. At a loss of how to deal with them, I gestured towards the pair.

My aunt huffed. "Your tiger has been tying himself in knots. Your agent, as soon as he was recovered enough to comprehend he'd lost his partner during the fight and you were taken, has likewise been tying himself in knots. When they haven't been conspiring to escape and find you on their own, they have been fighting with each other. Nate has been trying to convince Randal that he holds no actual responsibility for what happened to his partner, and Randal has been trying to convince Nate he was actually responsible, and that Simmons might have survived if we hadn't separated then. Basically, your agent keeps groveling to your tiger, and your tiger isn't having any of it. They both forget you'd planned to be taken in the first place. Losing Simmons wasn't something any of us expected, although we lost a lot of good men and women that night."

Unless I took care of the problem, they'd keep fighting. Despite my exhaustion, I waded in, grabbed my tiger by his tail, and seized my agent's scruff. "Enough, both of you!"

Anatoly roared at me, and Randal did a good impression of a dog's whine.

"Idiots, both of you. Idiots! You can share." I sat, crossed my legs, and patted my knees. "Share nicely. I'm too tired for your posturing."

After an exchange of swipes, the cats cooperated, and the pair used my knees as their chin rests. Once they settled, I scratched them both behind their ears. Randal purred and closed his eyes. Anatoly bit my finger hard enough I bled, and then he licked me. Once satisfied I wouldn't bleed to death from his bite, he closed his eyes, too.

Within moments, the pair slept.

"Are you all right, Jesse?" my aunt asked, and she gestured at my healing throat.

I pointed at Anatoly's fresh bite. "This one is a good bite. I like this one. The rest will heal without scarring."

"Scars don't work that way, Jesse."

"They do now. You can pay the bill if they don't cooperate with my wishes. I have plans for the Hope Diamond that involve a hammer if it doesn't cooperate with my wishes."

"I see you've decided you're getting your way even if you have to go to extreme measures. I suppose scars do work that way when I'm footing the bill and bullying my mystics into making it happen. Please don't try to smash the Hope Diamond with a hammer. While I should be upset over you dictating what I'll do, I'm rather proud you're being assertive without one of us having to pressure you into it. I'll take progress where I can get it."

Knowing my aunt, she wouldn't be happy until I took over the entire world, which went directly against how a good assassin operated. On the other hand, claiming a Clan Council member for my mate would end my days as an assassin—for the most part. Jobs would still come my way, like the unofficial one that had resulted in Ferdinand's death. The Water Viper would appear often enough to remind people of my deeds, but no so often I'd be easy to track.

It would do.

I wouldn't miss much about my life as a killer for hire.

"They're sleeping on me," I observed, stroking my hand over Anatoly's head. "How bad has it really been?"

"It's been pretty bad. If I thought I could put Randal on leave for a while without it breaking him, I would. Simmons had been partnered with him for a very, very long time. It'll be hard finding someone who can take his place. I butted my head into the Secret Service's business and told them they'd wait until you were found before searching for someone who might mesh with him—and with you. But I did get a concession from Nate to cope with a pair of agents."

Hell had frozen over within the last month, and I'd missed the show. "How did you sell that to him?"

"I told him his agents would also be available to help *you*. That convinced him."

Of course. I should have known. "How bad was the attack? I only saw part of it, and then I slept through the rest. What happened to my sword?"

"It's with us, and it wasn't damaged. I had it checked over, and Nate's been carrying it around like a lifeline. We lost a lot of good agents, but all of the principals survived, which we're considering a miracle at this point. Rebuilding the damaged sections of the palace has already begun, and we've identified most of the conspirators. We haven't caught them all, but we had identified Ferdinand and Marie early on. As expected, Todd took the news hard. He was particularly concerned you would overreact should you deal with Marie. Which you have, and he's relieved he won't have to deal with her himself. He even admitted he was being a coward, but he didn't want to kill someone he's loved a long time. You spared him a great deal of anguish, for which he is grateful. Anyway, we were aware of forces gathering in the cities you'd mentioned, but we hadn't realized their goal, which the papers you found revealed."

"What is their goal? I mean, beyond killing you and taking over the United States. I'd figured that part out on my own. Obvious, really."

"To weaponize nuclear energy. That's the power source mystics use to provide electricity to Charlotte and many other cities. The mystics limit how toxic that method of power generation can be. I don't really get how it works, but I've been promised it isn't an issue as long as it's properly contained and mystics maintain the system. So, we believe they're trying to weaponize that toxicity. The symptoms Miracle suffered through match what the mystics predict would happen to horses when exposed. It's different when humans are exposed to it. So, she was probably used to transport this weapon and was left to die like the other horses."

The thought of my little mare hurt, especially as her coat had only barely begun growing back in. I didn't even know what color she would be when she fully recovered. "Are my horses all right?"

"They're fine, even Miracle. She's turning out to be a gorgeous little chestnut, possibly a buckskin. Her coat is coming back in patches, and it'll be slow going. Right now, she's mostly gold, but the few hairs of her mane and tail that have come back in seem dark. Nate wanted to bring your horses with us, but it would've taken too long to get them boarded, and we'd already delayed the train enough. We got Miracle boarded, but that's it. She's under guard at a nearby stable, so you can see her later. I asked for someone to bring your other horses along on the next scheduled train out, so they should be here tomorrow. Up for telling me what happened?"

I nodded, and I began from the moment the attack began, glossing over nothing, not even my agent's death. In some ways, I hated acknowledging Simmons wouldn't return despite having witnessed the life fade from his eyes. Nothing would bring him back, but I'd never imaged it would be so hard to let someone go.

My aunt scowled at my mention of the drug on the arrow and Ferdinand's daily bites in his desperate attempt to control me and the Hope Diamond. "What a fool."

"Which part makes him a fool?"

"All of it."

"Are you being a biased aunt or honest?" I'd learned early on to ask, as my aunt, for all she ruled over the United States with an iron paw the size of a dinner plate, had certain ideas about how the world should view me, despite my long history as an assassin for hire.

She scowled. "I'm being honest."

"This time, she is," Gentry announced, striding into the room and pausing long enough to drop a kiss on top of my head. "Your neck looks like Ferdinand put it through a blender. Good job disposing of him. I've been told I'm not allowed to mutilate his body, as that is a crime. I'm very unhappy with these law-abiding busy bodies. I couldn't even get them to turn around for five seconds. That said, even when we planned for it, we need to work on you getting grabbed out from under our noses. You're bad for my blood pressure. I'm going to have your agent run you through every damned training session to get you into shape and make certain you're better able to defend yourself." My uncle raised a brow and stared at Anatoly and Randal. "I see you've been collecting cats."

I pointed at the black panther. "You haven't been taking care of my panther, Gentry. He's tired."

"And what about your tiger?"

As there was no point in hiding my claim over him, I dug my fingers into Anatoly's fur. "Would he let you take care of him?"

Gentry laughed. "All right. That's a fair point, little girl. How are you feeling?"

"Much better now, thank you. Is Randal going to be all right?"

"He'll be fine. He's been pushing himself hard, and losing Simmons hurt. Once he confirmed you were safe, he reached his limit. Don't worry yourself. Your tiger will be fine, too, although I can't help but notice you two have gotten aggressive with your teeth again."

"My neck offended his delicate sensibilities. I've noticed he has very delicate sensibilities. Give me something to do, Gentry. Something useful."

"I can do that. We have hundreds of pages of papers to read in a short period of time, and two of the more literate among us seem to be sleeping on the job. You can do their work until they wake up, then you can have your turn taking a nap. If your neck hurts, I'll go fetch Henry to fix it."

"It's fine, but I refuse to let any except the one scar." I pointed at where Anatoly had bitten me. "This one stays, and I will be very upset should anyone try to remove this one."

"Tigers," my uncle spat in disgust before turning on a heel and marching out of the room.

"Don't mind Gentry," my aunt said, sitting on the floor beside me. "He's upset there's no one left here for him to kill. He'll get over it eventually."

"I thought grizzlies held grudges into eternity."

"We hold grudges until death, and we like it best when we are the cause of death. If what we've learned is right, we'll be wading through blood and bodies before this is over. He'll get his satisfaction soon enough. I'll even save a few for him. This is the beginning of the end. I will see to that personally."

I feared she was right.

Chapter Fifteen

PAPERS RULED MY LIFE. Instead of delivering them for hire, I read, shaking my head over the insanity. Ferdinand, in his madness, had taken everything he'd learned from working within a mercenary guild, applied it to how he thought a government should operate, and had sought to reshape everything in a guild's image. Every level of government was up for hire, with the President of the United States being the one who decided who would win the important roles, earn the best keep, and dodge being little more than an expendable grunt.

Everything about the new system screamed impending war, a war that would pit mystics and shifters against each other. If Ferdinand's plans succeeded, the prominent mercenary guilds of Charlotte would be scattered and destroyed, and the Clan Council would be eliminated, its members murdered so the old way couldn't infect the new order. The mystics would face a similar fate, with any mystics in higher seats of power losing their lives to prevent their corruption from tainting the group's version of the future.

The attack on Charlotte accomplished so few of Ferdinand's goals, save for one critical piece: their acquisition of the Hope Diamond.

Had my aunt not asked me to play along to learn more, they wouldn't have gotten that much. In a way, her request had become our saving grace. My time as a captive had won us a great deal—and had bought the pack of wolf women their freedom.

I flipped through the pages, setting aside the ones that repeated their main goals and added nothing new to our information on their plot. While Ferdinand held a high role, we missed a critical piece: the identity of the true mastermind.

Someone as foolish, stupid, and cowardly as Ferdinand couldn't be the mastermind. I refused to accept we'd lost so much to someone so damned stupid. The evidence he was close to the top surrounded me, and the Starfall stones I'd discovered in his safe supported he might, in truth, be the one behind so many of our problems.

It made me wonder if he'd been a traitor all along.

It made me wonder if Marie had been traitor all along, too.

"You look like I've taken your sword and refuse to give it back," Gentry announced, crouching in front of me. "What's on your mind?"

"You have taken my sword, and you refuse to give it back," I reminded him.

"You can have it back tomorrow. Today, you get to keep resting with your tiger and your agent. In the morning, you can have your sword back and resume giving us gray hairs. I figure if I hold your sword hostage, you might not run off."

I considered that. "Did Todd bring that cute little gun of his?"

"He did, actually. He grabbed most of his weapons, and then he decided he may as well look stylish—and be armed if we have to fight in a combustion zone."

"Fetch Todd, and make him give me his gun. If I can't stab someone, I wish to have the right to shoot them."

My uncle sighed and shook his head. "We're not in a combustion zone, Jesse."

"I don't need a combustion zone, Gentry. I have the Hope Diamond. The damned gun will work." Of course, the Hope Diamond wasn't the reason the gun would fire, but I meant to keep that secret close to my heart in case I somehow became separated from the Starfall stone.

Most of the time, I forgot it hung around my neck. And when I didn't, the stone made certain I didn't take it off—and prevented others from removing it. It got in Anatoly's way more than it got in mine, but I found his frustration with the gaudy thing amusing.

He really wanted to nibble beneath the setting and stake a claim there.

"That is one of the scariest things I've heard in a while, Jesse, and that counts that damned wait to find out if Stephanie had kicked the bucket on me during the attack."

"I did not kick any buckets," my aunt growled from across the room. "Don't fill her head with nonsense."

Gentry drew in a deep breath, and I slapped my hands with the papers I'd been reading to my ears to protect myself against the grizzly's roar. The thunderous sound woke Anatoly and Randal, who jumped to their paws. Their snarls and roars added to the cacophony. Sighing, I dropped the documents and snagged their scruffs before my uncle earned a mauling.

The large cats quieted when I tugged on their fur, although Anatoly hissed at Gentry.

"You're an idiot," my aunt announced, her tone filled with her disgust. "Did you have to wake the other idiots?"

"Yes. You about lost your damned head, and it was just damned luck Henry and Cleo were around in the aftermath."

Uh oh. To all appearances, my aunt looked fine, but shifters deceived people often. What didn't kill them outright wouldn't keep them down forever, but scars happened—unless a mystic erased them. To offer the illusion of stability, mystics would've removed any scars from my aunt within minutes of them forming.

I engaged my aunt in a staring contest, one I refused to lose.

"Don't you look at me like that, little girl."

Gentry wasn't the only one who could roar, and I unleashed one, baring my teeth as the sound died away to make it clear she didn't frighten me in the slightest. Anatoly tensed, and Randal twisted around and tried to lick at my hand, probably to convince me not to attack the President of the United States.

"Having been on the receiving end of her ire, she really will dance with you, Stephanie. You know this. I know this. She definitely knows this, and she doesn't care she's still mauled from that damned wolf. Not only will she dance with you, she's just like her mother, which means she doesn't know when to quit. That means Henry and Cleo will have to nurse you both back to health, as you both have a lot of frustration to work out. I'd also like to point out that Nate *will* dance with you, too, because that's what a male tiger does when his mate picks a fight with someone bigger, older, more experienced, and generally nastier than she is. And yes, Stephanie, you're nastier. You don't fight fair, and we all know it. I'm glad you don't fight fair, which is why you're alive, but she isn't up for a full spat with you."

Like hell I wasn't. I shifted my glare to Gentry, and he raised his hands in surrender.

My aunt sighed. "While I'm old, I'm not at any risk of falling over dead. I'm quite healthy, thank you."

"You weren't quite healthy three weeks ago." Gentry wrinkled his nose. "I'm impressed your killer rabbit hasn't come barging in here ready to knock heads together to make sure you've recovered properly."

The First Gentleman chuckled and strolled into the room, and he paused near me long enough to ruffle my hair. "If you really want to work your temper out on my wife, give it another week. And don't you even try to pretend your leg is fine. I caught you limping this morning, Stephanie."

"Damn it." The President of the United States flipped her middle finger at her husband. "Next you're going to start patting my head and asking me if I'd like a cup of tea so I can settle down."

My rabbit of an uncle knelt beside Randal and scratched my agent between his ears. "I just might. If your little girl of a niece can learn to tolerate us being affectionate with her, I'm sure even an old grizzly like you can learn a new trick. She didn't even try to bite my hand off that time. Good job on tearing out Ferdinand's throat, and even better work on disposing of our other problem. We've recovered her body, and we dealt with her to Todd's specifications."

I recognized trouble when I heard it. "To Todd's specifications? Wait, how did you find her body?"

Todd entered the room and snorted. "Nate took a few minutes to think like you, and he suggested you would try to hide her in plain sight, but you wouldn't want her scent to betray her burial site. The ladies mentioned something they'd overheard, so they directed us to the crater. Henry and Cleo spotted the disturbed slope, so we figured Marie was probably beneath it. We were right. Anyway, I asked she be given a somewhat tolerable burial, but that was only after the rest of my requests were refused." The stallion joined me, sat down, gathered the papers I'd dropped, and stacked them in a neat pile. "While you were dozing, we took turns visiting her body, and we were rather impressed with your determination to make certain your mark would be noticed long after death. What did you do to her? Did you take the Hope Diamond off and use it to carve your mark into her forehead?"

"No, but that would have been a really good idea, and I regret I hadn't thought of that, not that I can get the blasted thing off. But if I *could*, I most certainly would have abused the Starfall stone's powers to do just that." I released the two large cats, figuring Gentry could defend himself if they got snappy. I reached over, and as Todd liked to ruffle my hair, I patted his head. "Are you okay?"

"Better than I thought I'd be," he admitted. "Having the wolves to care for helps. They're all crashed out. Cleo and Henry want to borrow you and see if you can put that stone to good use."

"Which puppies are in trouble?"

"Rachelle's are in the most danger, and Gillian's is in pretty rough shape, too."

I sucked in a breath. "Rachelle's? But she's so far along. Wait. *Are*? There's more than one?"

I wanted to return to Ferdinand's body and tear him to bits. I growled, and when a growl didn't suffice to express my disgust over the wolf's destructive choices, I hissed. I'd save my roaring for when I had no other options.

The Hope Diamond would get a very rude wakeup call if it didn't get its ass in gear and do something good for a change. However much I appreciated some elements of its existence, including my ongoing life despite impossible odds, the suffering it'd wrought far outweighed the rest of its deeds.

I didn't want either of the women to lose the children they'd fought so hard to keep.

"When Cleo figured out the puppies were in trouble, he took a closer look and realized she's carrying twins. Twins are hard on a woman in the first place, and she's been abused. That's no fault of hers. And she's late enough into her pregnancy Cleo is thinking about inducing labor and hoping he can rescue them and get them through the next few weeks. Their chances might be better." Todd sighed, a pained and defeated sound. "But he hates losing little ones, and he's getting desperate."

"The Hope Diamond has a mind of its own, but maybe it'll help." I got to my feet, and I patted the large cats before pointing at my aunt. "Play guard cats and sit on her if she tries to leave. She's obviously trouble."

My aunt snorted. "That's cute coming from you, little girl. I'm not going anywhere. I still have at least a hundred pages of bullshit and treachery to read."

"Good. Anatoly, if Randal tries to escape, sit on him."

Gentry laughed. "You're in a mood today, Jesse. If you think those two are going to let you out of their sight, you're deluded. I'll keep an eye on Stephanie. Take those troublemakers with you so they don't whine. I'm tired of the whining. And don't listen to anything Stephanie says, either. She's as much of a whiner as your mate and agent. Once your neck heals, you're going to get flattened on the mat and cuddled into submission. I expect the rabbit will do the majority of the flattening, as he has half a chance of giving you a good run in your peak condition. And make no mistake, we need to get you back into peak condition as soon as possible." The grizzly glared at the stacks of papers taking over the sitting room. "This is just the beginning."

I was so tired of every disaster ultimately becoming the beginning of yet another disaster. "The next time I decide to mark a damned tiger in a bar, I'm skipping straight to unlawful possession of another living being and moving to a quiet cabin deep in the woods to prevent discovery."

Anatoly chuffed his amusement and rubbed his head against my leg to mark his territory.

My aunt raised a brow. "And what are your plans for this damned tiger you plan on finding in a bar?"

I pointed at Anatoly. "This tiger, specifically. He's an easy mark. And I have all the tools I need to make the bar clear out so I can tattoo him at my utter leisure."

"Your sense of humor is evil. I thought you should

know this." My aunt shook her head and heaved a sigh. "Try to make one of those damned Starfall stones do something useful for a change. And for fuck's sake, keep Sunder contained. Also, as I'm a bitch over all bitches, if you want to hear Gentry scream like a girl, show him Sunder."

I reached for the bag of Starfall stones I kept nearby.

My uncle lifted his hands and made a gesture against evil. "No."

Smiling over having nettled him, I said, "It seems happy enough to stay in the bag. They all do."

I'd been given a bag large enough to hold all of them, made of thick, good leather with loops to tie to my belt.

My aunt snorted. "That's because you're holding the Hope Diamond."

"I don't see what that has to do with anything. Well, except we're fairly certain Steel Heart exists because of the Hope Diamond."

"All of those stones exist because of the Hope Diamond. That's the most popular—and probably accurate—theory. They've all been recorded having a similar miasma to the Hope Diamond. Especially your stiletto, which has a shard of the original diamond."

Crap. I'd forgotten all about the stiletto. "Did you find it?"

"It's with your sword. We saw it'd gotten some use; you used it after you were separated from your katana?

I'm assuming the Hope Diamond has something to do with its unexpectedly sharp state."

I nodded and played along with her assumption. "I even got a hit on Ferdinand, but it didn't do me a whole lot of good. Should've poisoned the damned thing before throwing it at him."

I wonder if scratching the bastard, however lightly, had contributed to his inability to make his bites work on me. I discarded the idea as absurd. No, I'd shrugged off his pitiful attempts because I'd already marked my territory, and I'd done so of my own volition. More than that, I'd done so years ago.

It would take more than a mad wolf to disrupt my claim on Anatoly.

I released my anger, gave myself a good shake, and reminded myself the dead stayed dead. Ferdinand could wallow over his failures in his grave. Under no circumstances would I allow his interference to ruin my future.

Some things I couldn't change, but I would change what I could and refuse to let go of what I needed in my life. Somewhere along the way, Anatoly had gone from a want to a need. It had taken me a long time to arrive to that conclusion, but I would try my best to keep my regrets from drowning me.

Regret and fear had already claimed too much from me.

My aunt offered one of her gentle smiles, a rare enough sight I focused entirely on her. "However satisfying his immediate death would have been, what you did is better. Go see if you can make that damned rock do something useful for a change. Let's keep this from becoming even more of a tragedy if possible."

If possible. So much of our lives had been based on those two, terrible words. Nodding, I braced myself for a fight with a damned rock. "Where's Cleo?"

Todd got to his feet and headed for the hallway. "He's with the women. I'll take you. Gentry, keep that damned pest of a sister of yours out of trouble while I'm gone."

That made my aunt scowl, but she didn't argue, which warned me something was going on and that I'd have to start peeling answers out of people. First, I had more important things to attend to. As expected, Anatoly and Randal followed. The two big cats snapped their teeth at each other, and Anatoly won the dispute with a single shove of his far larger shoulder.

"You're a jerk sometimes, Ana."

My tiger huffed and nipped my hand.

I flicked his ear.

He took my entire hand in his mouth, applying enough pressure with his teeth I'd add a few more scars to my tally if I attempted to escape without his approval. Since I wouldn't escape without extra bloodshed, I kept walking, treating my hand as an unconventional leash.

Todd wrinkled his nose. "I can't believe you're letting him get away with that."

"Well, he won't be going anywhere without me

knowing about it this way. He's my property, and I want to keep careful track of my property."

"Technically, you're his property, as he still hasn't filed that damned form to dissolve the Blade Clan contract."

"Is there a reason he should file that form? He's not escaping me, Todd. I've decided I'm keeping this tiger. I look forward to thoroughly educating the clan about why they should take care with my tiger. I will repay every bruise they give him tenfold. It'll be violent."

"Sometimes, I have a very difficult time thinking you, who first came to my guild looking for work and meshing with the bodyguards, could be capable of that much violence. Then you surprise me. Again. Stop that. You're bad for my peace of mind."

I could believe that easily enough. "Unknowingly harboring an assassin tends to make a mess of things."

Todd balled his hand into a fist and thumped the top of my head. "You're as much of an idiot as Steph sometimes. I didn't mean it that way. I mean you get into trouble, and as a result, my peace of mind vanishes for a while. That, plus I have to be on guard because there's nothing as unpredictable as a tigress on the prowl. Considering you're armed with the Hope Diamond *and* Sunder? Maybe we should put you in charge of the United States."

"No," my aunt snapped from the sitting room.

"What she said," I added, cursing the grizzly's sensitive hearing.

"What, Steph? Nobody would push her around

with that damned stone around her neck. And stay in there, damn it! Don't give Gentry reasons to want to beat me."

"Then stop trying to give my niece my job. I do have a Vice President."

She did? I stopped, turned, and returned to the sitting room. "Wait. You have a Vice President?"

"It's traditional for the United States to have a Vice President, Jesse." My aunt set aside her papers and arched a brow. "You're a voter. You even voted in the last election, doing your legal duty. It's right on the ballot who my Vice President is."

Narrowing my eyes, I turned to Gentry. "Is there actually a Vice President, or did she eat the poor bastard?"

"You know her Vice President," my uncle replied.

Damn. "Is her Vice President going to beat me for not knowing?"

"Not particularly. Since it's too dangerous to go abroad, the Vice President is on call if the President requires help; mostly, the Vice President needs to stay up-to-date on current events, but generally? The Vice President is ready to take over if needed, and may someone have pity on the United States should my sister be removed from her position and the Vice President takes over."

Like many others, the last time I'd voted, I'd checked off my aunt's box because I disliked unnecessary change almost as much as the rest of the country. Somehow, we'd found something that generally worked without pissing off the extremists, and nobody —except Ferdinand and his goons—wanted to rock the boat.

"Okay. Who is the Vice President, then?"

"My wife," Gentry admitted.

My mouth dropped open, and I floundered at the thought of the wolverine taking over the United States should something happen to my aunt. "That's a *disaster*."

"I know, right? It had been a hoot during their first campaign. Some people still call Steph President Adams because of that. It's fun watching Steph get offended because she very much appreciates being a Miller. She thought she'd escape the burden of being an Adams."

My aunt heaved a sigh. "I really thought you knew."

"But Felicity doesn't have Secret Service agents. Why doesn't she if she's the Vice President? Am I the only person who sees something wrong with this whole thing?"

Gentry grinned at my question. "She kept sending them back fully tenderized, and after a while of asking nicely to be left alone, the Secret Service decided to leave her alone. She usually has a pair shadowing her, but they're very good at hiding in plain sight."

I narrowed my eyes, debating how my aunt could possibly pull off having a detail for the wolverine. I could only think of one way for my aunt to pull it off: the Vice President was unaware she was being guarded.

"Gentry has Secret Service agents masquerading as mercenaries, doesn't he?"

"I knew you were a smart one. As a matter of fact, yes. I do. I'm a bad friend."

Gentry rolled his eyes. "She also has Secret Service members in Todd's guild, too. We work together to make sure people of interest are protected during general work. Also, Felicity is aware you're up to no good as usual, but as she hasn't caught you in the act, she's ignoring it. She thinks you're cute, Steph. Also, as fair warning, she might try to steal the little girl here for a while. The last I heard, it was 'to teach that poor little girl what normality actually is.' I got my ass handed to me when I laughed."

"Felicity, your wife, and technically one of my aunts because of you, is the Vice President of my actual aunt? And nobody in this country saw anything weird about that?" I bowed my head and sighed. "I didn't even look at the Vice President part, honestly. I am a bad voter."

"I think most voters don't care who the Vice President is, because I'm too damned mean and stubborn to die. Don't beat yourself up over it, Jesse. Felicity is a great Vice President. If I need time off, she just takes over, browbeats anyone who gets in her way, and goes back to doing her own thing. And my bunny does a good job of taking care of the Clan Council matters."

The bunny in question shrugged. "Americans don't really care how the government is run as long as they feel their freedoms have been properly preserved, we don't push our luck with taxes, and we keep things running the best we can all things considered. The various attacks on Charlotte haven't even done any damage to the Presidency, despite the destruction. Hell, the locals love it. Destruction means rebuilding, and rebuilding means a boosted economy and job security. And since the attacks have been mitigated to government officials and members of the Secret Service, nobody cares. Personally, I think they should," the First Gentleman complained. "Go see if you can take care of those puppies, Jesse. There'll be time enough for you to wrap your head around the idea that Gentry's wife is the Vice President later."

Right. I hesitated, afraid of my inability to do more than yell at the Starfall stones and hope one of them did something useful.

I hated feeling so damned useless.

Todd snagged me by the back of my neck and pushed me along. "This way, Jesse. I know how you can talk once you decide it's time to start solving problems. You can figure out what's going on after the women are looked at. I doubt that damned rock will make itself useful, but I've given up guessing what it will and won't do. It seems pretty determined to stick near you, so maybe it'll play nice."

"Since when have any of the Starfall stones played nice?"

Anatoly lashed his tail and swatted Todd's leg. The stallion raised a brow and engaged my tiger in a staring match. Randal pressed against my leg and purred.

Men.

"No posturing. I'm too damned tired for your posturing. Ana, behave."

Anatoly flattened his ears and bared his teeth at me.

I sighed, and Todd hauled me down the hallway and up the stairs. "Henry? Cleo? I've brought the woman, and she's got the rocks."

Henry poked his head out of a nearby bedroom. "That's got to hurt. Do you have to hold onto her neck, Todd? She hasn't healed much yet. She's been through enough."

While Henry hated people in pain more than most mystics I knew, I raised my brows at his concern.

Before I had a chance to reply, Todd shoved me forward. "Take her. She's fine. Anyway, what's a little bloodshed between friends? Maybe if I help her bleed a little, the Hope Diamond will burst and make everyone around as healthy as I am. And Cleo can tell you just how healthy I am."

One day, Todd would finally finish driving me insane, I'd go for the nearest weapon, and we'd have another fight. And because Todd was Todd, I'd probably end up face down in the sand with a busted shoulder. Again.

I had a bad habit of screwing up my shoulders, and I needed to do something about that.

"Freakishly so," the donkey grumbled, emerging from the same bedroom Henry occupied. "Let her go so she can do whatever it is that stone might do. I've put the ladies together in here since there were two beds, and it'll be easier to keep things quiet for them. The babies improved a little since we got the women fed and let them rest, but it's going to be touchy, especially for the twins."

"Why can't I kill him again?" I complained, flexing my hands at the thought of how easy and relatively painless I'd made Ferdinand's death. A moment of surprise, a few gurgles, and a few labored breaths hadn't been enough suffering.

"Quick and merciful beats leaving him with an opportunity to surprise you," the donkey countered. "Get your ass in there, Jesse. I don't want to lose those puppies, and I don't know if there's anything else I can do for them."

I heard the dismay in the donkey's tone, and when I glanced at Henry, he shrugged.

Hope remained a cruel and terrible thing, capable of breaking even the strongest people in its fickle grasp. Hope could, in its stubborn way, lead to the greatest of triumphs. It could also lead to the bitterest defeats.

I tired of losing. Peeking into the room, I regarded Rachelle and one of the quieter women, who hadn't looked as far along as some of the others, who to all appearances, slept peacefully. "Are they drugged?"

"No," Cleo replied. "I used a mystic trick to help make certain they slept. At this stage, there's not many medications I'd be willing to try. Their babies are just too delicate. Even a mild cold could kill them."

How could life be so fragile? Why? I doubted I'd ever understand the give and take of life and death.

Stepping into the room, I went to Rachelle first, stabbing the nearest stool with my foot and dragging it close so I could sit. I placed the bag of Starfall stones onto my lap, opened it, and rummaged inside. Every weapon clan's stone served a different purpose, but of them, I thought Steel Heart might be the best suited for what I needed.

Something about it brought people together in unexpected ways. I had a mother who apparently prowled for my father and a father who hadn't picked another woman because my mother lived somewhere out there. Without the damned stone rolling around and doing what it wanted, I wouldn't have met Anatoly as I had.

Unlike the Hope Diamond, which had more destructive tendencies, I viewed Steel Heart as a tool of creation.

Perhaps it could forge lives for the unborn children who fought to enter the world, despite the circumstances of their existence. I removed it from the pouch and placed it on Rachelle's stomach, at a total loss of how to convince a rock to do what I needed.

Before I could open my mouth, the Hope Diamond glowed with a gentle orange light, which spread into the room. Every other time I'd witnessed it glow, it'd been blue and black, shedding a potent miasma warning those of its more treacherous nature. Much like cool, soothing water, the light flowed over my skin before bathing everyone in the room in its luminescence. It faded, and I shrugged, picked up Steel Heart, and returned it to the pouch with the other stones. "The Hope Diamond has opinions."

Cleo rested his fingers against Rachelle's throat. "Their vitals are already better. Not perfect, but better."

"How much better?"

"I won't be awake all night wondering if they'll die. But we'll have a lot of work ahead of us getting them fed and in the best shape possible for their birth. I'll still stay up all night to keep an eye on them and do what I can to make sure Mom's healthy for delivery, but I won't be standing vigil waiting for them to die. Henry?"

He leaned over the other woman, brushing his fingers against her brow. "No change."

I got up and went to her, taking Steel Heart out of the pouch and setting it on her chest. As it always did when I wanted to use it for some purpose, the stone glowed with a gentle light. "Now?"

The mystic frowned, and deep lines creased his brow. "Nothing."

"Will the baby live through the night?" I whispered.

"It would take a miracle," he admitted, shaking his head. "There's only so much we can fix, Jesse. We can't reverse long-term starvation. No fault of hers, no fault of any of them. They can't eat food they don't have, and none of them knew what they needed to eat. They told us what you'd done to try to help them. You're the only reason those babies had a chance at all. They would have died earlier if they'd sustained the diet they were on."

"But I did so little," I protested.

"You did enough to give them a chance."

It wasn't enough. I hadn't been able to cry since I'd arrived in Tennessee, not really, but frustration and the smothering helplessness of the situation conspired against me. After everything, I didn't want any of the babies to die.

Nothing had been their fault.

I dumped out the entire bag of Starfall stones, wondering which one might be able to do the impossible. Could Sunder severe the chains of death and allow the baby to live? It hadn't hurt me touching it. It seemed to dislike weapons altogether.

Maybe it wanted life to continue without the threat of weaponry to exist. Maybe we'd been wrong to fear the stone all along. Maybe it could do what Steel Heart hadn't been able to do. I sniffed and set the dark stone next to Steel Heart.

"Sunder?" Todd asked. "Why did you pick that one?"

I swallowed in an effort to take control of my roiling emotions. "Maybe it hates weapons because it likes life. Maybe it wants to make miracles and stop ending lives."

Maybe the Hope Diamond had performed a miracle for the twins and had left us to figure out how to help the other baby on our own. Maybe it believed we could make a miracle.

Maybe it didn't understand what I needed it to do. I dumped the rest of the Starfall stones on the bed and reached for the clasp of the Hope Diamond. The clasp separated, and the heavy stone dropped away. Expecting the rock to change its mind, I swept Steel Heart out of the way and placed the jewel on the woman's chest.

I held my breath, wondering what to do to convince the stone to help. There was no physical change in the stone or the woman, and I bit my lip hard enough it bled.

"Easy does it, Jesse," Henry said, reaching over with his free hand to pat my arm. "It's not a lot of a change, but things are already looking a little better." The mystic narrowed his eyes, redirecting his attention to his patient. "Just enough of a difference to get the baby through the night. A chance is better than no chance at all—and that's all the miracle I could ask for. We'll have a busy night, Cleo, but I'd rather have that than the alternative."

"Take your stones back, Jesse. I think they've done all they're going to do, and this was what we were praying for—just a chance."

I'd seen how hard both mystics would work with the prayer of a chance in the past. I wiped my eyes and nodded. "Shouldn't you keep the Hope Diamond with you?"

"No. That stone wanted to be with you for a reason. Let's not annoy it trying to separate you. It might zap us and pull a Steel Heart."

The last thing we needed was the Hope Diamond wandering off. Heaving a sigh, I retrieved the necklace and clasped it around my throat. "You can now confirm I'm out of my right mind. I put it back on after I got it off."

"Hey, think about it this way. The stone let you take it off. It's not as heartless as some think. You're a good woman, Jesse. Go back to your family and learn what you can. We'll take care of the babies and make sure their mothers are ready for train travel. They'll be best off in Charlotte. That way, we can recruit an entire army of mystics if needed, to make sure these babies make it into the world alive. We won't give up on them," Henry promised.

I nodded, and I retreated back to the sitting room so I could do my part to make sure their children had a world worth living in after they drew their first breath.

Chapter Sixteen

ACCORDING to the train tickets my aunt found, Ferdinand had meant to take me to Rock Hill, North Carolina, the last train stop between Augusta and Charlotte. From there, he had notes regarding Fayetteville, Asheboro, Greensboro, and Hickory, all excellent mid-sized cities if a rebellion wanted to stage a rebellion and converge on Charlotte from all directions.

A few stubs of train tickets to Whiteville stupefied us all. Why there? Once upon a time, the train had gone all the way to Wilmington, but the city had long since fallen into the sea.

Anatoly and Randal, who had shifted back to human after I'd left the room shared by the sleeping pregnant women, flanked me and read over stacks of documents, too.

No matter how many times everyone else focused on Rock Hill, the mentions of Whiteville—and Sandy Creek, a coastal town overlooking the ruins of Wilmington and its fellow victims of the ocean—bothered me. It wouldn't cost us much to go to Whiteville; a train left for the town every day, as it served as a coastal junction to help people get around the eastern seaboard of the United States.

Sandy Creek reminded me a lot of the Fort Lauderdale situation, although not even the Hope Diamond could restore those lost, but it could propel the drowned city out of the waves and restore the land. Would it? I had no idea. I didn't want to know, either.

The reawakened Fort Lauderdale caused enough problems. I wasn't sure what the rise of another lost city would do if anything.

But, if I could convince them to go to Whiteville, I could ask around at the station about the town and what, if anything, made it special. A little knowledge could go a long way, and locals often knew the important things. Preparing for a brawl, I straightened my shoulders and said, "We should go to Whiteville first. Nobody would expect anyone from Knoxville to go to Rock Hill from Whiteville. You can start some rumors about you traveling directly a day later, and we'd be on the wrong set of tracks incoming into the station to see who shows up." I waved the copy of the train schedules for North Carolina in the air. "The Whiteville train arrives thirty minutes before the Knoxville train, and we'd have plenty of time to transfer to the Charlotte train, even considering Miracle needing to be moved around."

I couldn't wait to see my horse, who was waiting for

me in a nearby stable. Tomorrow, I'd be reunited with her, and in a few days, I'd be able to see my black demons. The first thing I meant to do was ride Dipshit, have the stallion tenderize the hell out of me, and enjoy my tiger pampering me after my stallion taught me a few lessons about why it wasn't wise to neglect stubborn stallions who enjoyed a good fight.

Everyone stared at me as though I'd grown a second head, and I heaved a sigh. "What? It's a good idea. There's just too many references to Whiteville to ignore it. I realize it's not a good staging point for Charlotte, but obviously *something* is going on there, and maybe we should look into it."

Anatoly smiled, captured my hand in his, and kissed my knuckles. "It's not an unreasonable request. I'm just not sure what could be important there. All Whiteville has is a few carriage stations, a large train station, and a bunch of inns and stables for people riding through. It's got a very small local population, and they're all in the hospitality business. The town exists because of the various types of ground transportation that goes through there. It probably just makes a good place for them to converge before moving on. Nobody would think anything of large numbers of people passing through there. Large numbers of people pass through there all of the time."

"Then it won't hurt anything if we go look."

"It won't. We're way ahead of the schedule for this," my tiger conceded. "What all of this doesn't tell us is how they plan to accomplish their goals beyond a few thousand people, the Hope Diamond, and their weapon—and I'm not sure what that weapon will do beyond make people sick."

"Does the weapon have to do more than that?" I asked.

"No, it really doesn't—not at the scale of what that thing might be capable of doing. Where they'd gotten the material to build this weapon is a mystery, too. Ferdinand didn't have anything on it beyond the infrequent mention of transporting something of importance."

"He had an accomplice. I heard his voice. A nasally, nasty sounding man who wore a dark cloak and kept his features obscured."

"I bet I know who he is," my aunt said, wrinkling her nose and snorting. "Before Richmond began going under, there was a Secret Service agent who matches that description. He used to be on my detail, but I fired him for having less-than-ideal ethics."

"How would he know Ferdinand?" I asked.

"Through me," Gentry admitted. "I've taken him to Richmond to see Steph, so they would have been able to talk—right along with the assholes."

I grimaced at the mention of the uncles I'd assassinated at the behest of the government. My shoulder still ached, especially as I hadn't been able to use it much during my captivity. I'd need to go through a lot of therapy to restore my strength, but until all of Ferdinand's conspirators died and the weapon was destroyed, I couldn't afford to whine about the discomfort. "That means the chain could end there? That this cloaked figure could be the other head of the rebellion?"

"Things are rarely that simple, Jesse," my aunt replied. "I wish that were so, but we have no way of knowing yet. We'll have to question some of the survivors."

Gentry growled. "You assume there will be survivors. They tried to kill you."

"They tried to kill you, too," my aunt retorted.

"They almost succeeded with you. They didn't almost succeed with me."

If I let them fight, they'd never stop. "Todd, please give me your gun."

The grizzlies kept snarling at each other and failed to notice my request. The stallion rolled his eyes but handed me the weapon. I checked it, loaded a single bullet, and considered my targets. I raised the weapon, cocked it, and cleared my throat. "If you two don't behave, I will fire."

My aunt's gaze landed on me, and she raised a brow. "You'll wake everyone in the house if you fire that thing in here, little girl."

Well, at least she didn't act like it wouldn't fire. "If you two don't stop arguing, I will fire. I will waste a fortune of Todd's bullets, which will upset him. You will go to Whiteville, and you will go to Whiteville without whining about it. We will have dinner at a nice inn, and the ladies will enjoy a scenic train ride. They will be safer if we approach from an unexpected direction, and you will have your Secret Service agents make official plans for us to go to Rock Hill on that train on that day, and you will have the train officials behave as though we are on that train while we're headed to Whiteville on an entirely different train. You will do this without complaint. Also, I'm keeping your gun until we're back in Charlotte, Todd."

Todd handed me his box of ammunition. "I only brought a hundred bullets with me, so try to make them last."

I accepted his gift with my free hand and set them beside me. "So, what'll it be, Aunt Stephanie?"

"Well, at least you didn't go calling me Madam President. That's when I know you're really pissed at me." My aunt scowled before flipping her middle finger at me. "Fine. We'll do it that way. I'd be a pretty terrible aunt if I got angry at you for doing exactly what I wanted you to start doing. I would have preferred if you hadn't decided to use a gun to prove your point, and I'm disgusted my agents don't even care you're armed and dangerous."

I regarded my aunt's agents with a raised brow.

As one, the men smiled and shrugged.

"I think they're on my side, Aunt Stephanie."

"They probably are. You're being the sensible one in this room. Very well. We'll go to Whiteville in the morning, assuming it's safe for the ladies to travel. I'll even make sure all of those damned chickens and goats come with us, too. I bet Todd is eager to build homes for his new pets. Aren't you, Todd?"

"My manor will become a barn, but I'm all right with this. I can't take away their baby chicks, Steph. The wolves are smitten with them. They're even smitten with those awful goats. Jesse, you need to stop picking demonic animals. Those three goats are terrible animals that hate everyone."

I didn't believe the stallion, as I'd witnessed the three demonic goats loving all over Lauren and nuzzling her for attention. "They aren't terrible animals." Satisfied my aunt intended to cooperate, I uncocked the weapon and removed the bullet from the chamber, returning it to the ammunition box.

"The one bit me."

Right. Goats had four hooves, and Todd had something to prove to any rival male, even livestock. "Well, what did you do to deserve it?"

"Why do you always think I've done something to deserve it?"

"I know you, that's why." I stacked the remaining papers I hadn't read through in a box, which I placed near the door. "Come along, Ana. There has to be a couch or something we can nap on. I'm tired, damn it."

"You're tired because you're undernourished. Go eat something before you have some quiet time with Nate," my aunt ordered.

My tiger linked his arm with mine and pulled me in the direction of the kitchen. "I'll take care of her, Steph. I'll try to return your niece to you in a better mood."

"Not rested?" my aunt asked with amusement in her tone.

"If only," my tiger whined. "Alas, she needs rest, and I will just have to wait for her to be at her best."

As I had no intention of waiting forever, and it would probably take that long for me to get back to my best, I planned to wait long enough for a room somewhere warm, safe, and private. Those three criteria would test my luck and patience, but I figured I could handle somewhere private at the minimum.

First, I would finish what I had set out to do, and then I'd worry about enjoying the rest of my life with my tiger.

My tiger fed me so much I fell asleep the instant I sat on a soft surface, and I somehow made it to the train station without being aware of going. The hustle and bustle of the station filtered through my daze, and an odd pressure behind my knees and against my gut offered a clue or two. Someone had gotten the bright idea to toss me over a shoulder and carry me, something that drew a great deal of unwanted attention.

Damn. One good meal had reduced me to a comatose mess. Judging from the suit, my tiger had taken responsibility for me despite there being several better candidates for the work, including both of my uncles. My position made biting Anatoly near to impossible, and I growled my dislike of my situation.

Todd peeked around my tiger and grinned at me. "Look who decided to join us. Feel better?"

"Why did you allow this travesty? Where's my horse? You could have just tossed me on my horse."

Todd pointed, and I spotted my patchy-coated Miracle with my aunt, who held her reins while talking to her husband. She'd dressed in casual clothes and wore a hat. The lecherous rabbit did a good impression of Secret Service in his black suit. Todd, too, wore a suit. "Why are the men all dressed up while my aunt looks like she just came from a farm?"

"She likes confusing people."

That she did. "Is there a reason nobody woke me?"

"Well, Nate did try to wake you, but he's now the proud owner of a baker's dozen of fresh bites, you clawed him up, and his other suit will never be the same. Henry patched him up, but you went for him like you meant it, and you even shifted your hand to a paw to better maul him. After you finished mauling him, you cuddled against him and went back to sleep. We tried a steak, cut into swallowable pieces and seared for your enjoyment. You devoured it, snarled, and went back to sleep. After that, we decided to just move you without waking you. There's been enough bloodshed this morning."

I didn't remember that. "Did I do that, Ana?"

"You sure did," my tiger replied, and he laughed. "I've got a beautiful set of claw scars over my chest. I made Henry use your cream on them."

Wow. "You need to have Henry examine your head.

You used my cream for that? If you wanted me to use my cream, I could have tattooed something nice on you. Like my mark. Again. On your chest." I liked the idea a great deal, as I wanted the world to know he belonged to me, especially if he took his shirt off.

"We have discovered tigers *can* purr in the appropriate situations. After you clawed me, you purred over your handiwork."

"I purred?"

"It was this rather lovely growly purr. You were so happy you'd marked your territory. I couldn't just let it heal, so I got a hold of your cream and made use of it. I'll get you some more," he promised.

Obviously, I'd lost my mind after a good meal. "I'm a terrible person."

"You're a perfect tigress. You were just claiming your territory. It's Todd's fault. He was trying to help me escape your clutches. You didn't handle it well."

"You shouldn't have tried to escape me, Ana. This is obviously your fault. I can walk now."

"Why bother? We have like twenty feet to go until we board. Then you can sit next to me and resume using me as your throne."

I had a throne? "When did I get a throne? Shouldn't my aunt get a throne? At most, I'd be like a rejected princess or something."

"You're not a reject."

"But I'm not really a princess. My mother doesn't rule over anything."

"Your mother rules over anyone and anything she

decides is hers," my aunt complained. "I'm concerned you're picking up bad habits from her."

"But I haven't met her."

"Magic. I'm certain of it. She boobytrapped me with magic, and it has infected you, turning you into a copy of your mother. I suspect your oddities are your father's contribution. I'm going to have a talk with your mother about this. This is all her fault. Only my sister would give birth to a Siberian. Gentry, where is she, damn it?"

"Probably hunting for her mate, because she's a grizzly, and she has decided who her mate is. He is likely sensible, as he's a traditional member of the Blade Clan, so he wisely evades her."

"Wisely?" My aunt growled. "Wisely, my ass. Jenny's off doing whatever it is Jenny wants to do. And next time she shows up, I'll teach her a thing or two about letting her offspring run amok."

"I don't run amok on purpose," I protested.

"On purpose. You still end up running amok."

I sighed. "Put me down, Ana."

"We're going twenty whole feet. You're fine where you're at."

"I'm really not. Your shoulder is digging into my gut. I can walk."

"It's only for twenty more feet."

When Anatoly decided to become stubborn about something, he refused to listen to reason. I could go with his flow, or I could maul him. Either option benefited me, as him carrying me ensured he wasn't going anywhere. Mauling him would establish my place as the superior tiger of the relationship. I growled, concentrated, and forced my hand to become a paw with sharp claws perfect for adding a new set of scars to his back.

Todd grabbed my wrists, putting an end to my plan. "Hey!"

"You can't maul your mate in public. You'd make us miss the train."

"He started it."

"I'm sure he did. You still can't maul him right now. It was your idea to make us go to Whiteville, so you're going to have to deal with him carrying you around. You've mauled him enough for one morning."

"It doesn't count if I don't remember it."

"It counts."

I growled and contemplated mauling the stallion, but Todd won in the brute strength department. "I'm awake. I can walk."

"I'm sure you believe you can walk," my friend replied, and he kept my hands captive until we boarded the train and located our seats. Anatoly dumped me onto my seat and Todd kept my hands captive until my tiger took over restraining me.

"Thank you, Todd. She's quite feisty this morning. I don't know what's gotten into her, but I like it."

"Predatory instincts kicking in after a good meal and rest. She'll probably give you trouble for a few more days until she's confident of her next meal happening at regular intervals. That was a lecture I've heard a few too many times."

Cleo joined us, caught sight of Anatoly keeping my hands captive, and laughed. "More like we'll have to lock Nate up. She's itching for a meal of tiger, and her delicate sensibilities have been sorely offended. She has claims to stake, and this morning was just a warmup for the rest of her plans, I'm sure."

As I couldn't deny the accusation without turning myself into a liar, I shrugged. "It's been a rough few weeks, and I need to make it clear that he's my tiger."

"We know, Jesse. The wolves also have realized he is unavailable for their entertainment. Anyway, they have Todd for entertainment. They don't need your Siberian." Cleo shook his head and took the seat behind me, and Todd joined him. "Henry is with the ladies in a different car. So far, so good. Everyone's doing better than yesterday, although Todd's budget feeding them is going to break his bank."

"Hardly," the stallion replied, making himself comfortable in his seat. "That damned goat is more of a threat to my wallet than the women. They want their chickens and goats to have the best home. Buying steaks is far cheaper than it'll be building homes for those animals. If they don't get a good home, it'll be another mass meltdown. I'm already expecting another mass meltdown because the mares are all at home preparing for the new arrivals. The mares attacked my wallet for yarn so they could start on baby blankets, they might cut down half a forest getting new cribs built in time for the new arrivals, and it's a damned good thing some of my layabout colts decided to move out, as I needed those rooms for the new ladies. I'm going to have to add an extension at this rate."

Anatoly laughed, leaned over to kiss my cheek, and released my wrists. "Make Steph house some of the colts until they're ready to get on with their lives."

"No," my aunt announced, and she took the seat in front of me. "I don't need a herd of randy colts making a mess of my house. They'll try to seduce the palace staff."

"Well, they're young, male, and have discovered they're male," Todd replied, his tone amused. "They know the meaning of the word no, but they're so handsome women don't say no for some reason. I even taught them to use condoms unless the lady wishes to become a mare in his herd. I've done my fatherly duties properly, I assure you."

"They even hold doors open for others," Cleo added.

"No. Todd can do his fatherly duties to help his sons meet appropriate women to establish herds and get their start in the world. He could fetch a good amount of money if he sold them as plow horses, I'm sure." My aunt snickered. "Some of those black studs would make excellent carriage horses."

Todd laughed. "I don't know what I did, but I'm sorry."

"You tried to seduce my niece."

"Hey. Nate's trying to seduce your niece. Yell at him. She declined my generous offer."

"That is because she has at least one grain of common sense in her thick skull. And anyway, if I didn't give the tiger my approval, he'd cry. Apparently, I can't stand when Siberians cry almost as much as I can't stand when that damned rabbit of mine cries."

The damned rabbit in question strolled down the aisle towards us and raised a brow. "What did I do now?"

"Cried when I wasn't sure I wanted to court you."

"That'd break any man's heart, babe."

My aunt grunted. "You manipulated me with your tears."

"It must be so hard knowing you have a heart." My uncle sat and twisted in his seat to regard me with a smirk. "You can probably get your tiger to do whatever you want if you cry. He absolutely cannot stand when you cry. It's the most effective tool in your arsenal. Do not be afraid to use it. The trick is to use it sparingly."

"You're an awful rabbit. You should not be giving anyone advice," I replied.

"I see Steph has been giving you lessons in social graces again."

"I need lessons in social graces? But why? I've found stabbing people who upset me to be very effective and far more satisfying than talking with them."

"Steph, did you have to? She used to be so polite."

"Yes," my aunt replied. "Just be glad she only

demanded we go to Whiteville. I'm not sure I'm woman enough to tell her no at this point in time."

Well, if she was stating she couldn't tell me no, I could think of something I'd like. "I need another horse and a dagger to go with my new sword. I also need my sword returned to me. Where is it?"

"You have a gun. You don't need your sword right now."

"I need my sword."

My uncle whistled to someone and pointed at me. A Secret Service agent handed me my sword, in a bejeweled scabbard I didn't recognize. While it still possessed a mix of blue fire opal, diamond, platinum, and gold, fire-orange and black stones were included in a roaring tiger motif. Upon closer examination of the hilt, the tiger and dragon design remained, but the dragon had been restyled in turquoise and the tiger reminded me a lot of Anatoly, fire bright and fierce. "Someone has been fiddling with my sword again!"

"That would be the sword's maker. He showed up a week after the attack and borrowed it. It came back with a new scabbard and some adjustments. He wanted to do an integrity check of the blade," Todd explained, reaching around the seat to point at the pommel stone. "He replaced the pommel diamond, too. The picky bastard wasn't happy with it or something. This one is better."

I examined the pommel stone, frowning as it had changed, its color frightening close to that of the Hope Diamond. "But the old one was beautiful."

"It was not beautiful enough, apparently. I've given up trying to convince that one of anything. He's more stubborn than a damned rock. He thinks the adjustments this time should make up for the previous sword breaking as it did."

"But you said it would have broken anyway."

"Don't try to understand a swordsmith's pride, Jesse. Your old sword broke, and that's that. He's very upset it broke. Anyway, there's your sword. The stiletto is in Charlotte under lock and key. You'll get it back when we're back in town. Try not to cause any more trouble, okay?"

"I'll try," I promised. I set my sword beneath my aunt's seat, and to make sure nobody made off with it, I looped the belt around my ankle. "It probably won't happen, but I'll try."

My uncle laughed. "Well, she's honest. Don't ask for the impossible, Todd. She wouldn't know how to stay out of trouble if you sat her down, gave her a manual, and explained it step-by-step."

As it was true, I shrugged and amused myself looking out the window at the busy station while waiting for the train to depart.

Chapter Seventeen

DELAYS PLAGUED OUR TRIP, and we arrived in Whiteville late the next day, resulting in us having to wait almost a full day for the next train to Rock Hill. With Sandy Creek a short enough ride from Whiteville, I could give Miracle the exercise she really needed, slip off while everyone was fussing over the delays, and make excuses as soon as I figured out why Sandy Creek kept getting mentioned in Ferdinand's files.

A list of dates and nothing else wouldn't give us the answers we needed, and unless I got lucky asking locals about the seaside town, someone would have to go take a look.

There was no reason that someone couldn't be me.

Randal and my tiger, the busybody he was, got drawn into the heated discussion over the delay, leaving me unsupervised. If they'd wanted me to stick around, they wouldn't have left me alone. I strolled to the stable car and grinned when my horse whinnied a greeting. I spent a full ten minutes stroking her and promising she was the best of little horses before leading her out of the car.

My agent looked about like he was about to lose his mind over something my aunt said, and I gave it five minutes before my tiger snapped. His growls drew Gentry and Todd into the argument, and I shrugged, leading my horse away from the platform to one of the maps pinned on the wall. To my delight, the map included ride times between the station and nearby towns.

To my dismay, it would take a full day—or night—to reach my destination. I grunted, wrinkling my nose.

One of the station attendants approached and asked, "Do you need help, ma'am?"

I pointed at Sandy Creek's listing. "Do you know anything about this town?"

"Oh, yes. Of course. That's a fishing village now. It used to be a major waypoint, but the coast has infringed on it again, and it's actually moved closer to us. The maps haven't been updated yet." The attendant reached out and pointed at a lake substantially closer to Whiteville. "Sandy Creek is now located here. The coast line has come in an additional ten miles except for some odd outcroppings here and there. Parts of the original Sandy Creek are still intact, but the residents are ready to move out at any point in time. The waters there are particularly dangerous because of all the sunken buildings. They have something called the Creek Bore there, and if you're looking to see something interesting, you go there."

"Creek Bore?"

"If you put even a toe into the water, it will suck you out into the ocean, and you'll never be seen again. That's the Creek Bore. On a still day, the water boils where the tide is at its most violent, and that goes right to the churning waters. It's particularly bad there; you can see the ocean's fury. Out beyond the still waters, the waves can get taller than most buildings."

Damn. I'd have to make a point of dragging my tiger there one day to see it. "How far to the new Sandy Creek?"

"Three to four hours at a good trot. A courier can do it in two if they're in a hurry."

One day, Miracle would be a good courier horse again, but I'd take the slow but safe route. Nine hours would get me back to the station by morning, and it wouldn't take long to figure out if something was amiss near the new Sandy Creek.

Nobody could hide a large force of people, and I'd be aware of them arriving in such a small town.

I regarded my aunt, uncles, mate, and friends bickering away on the platform, shrugged, and asked for directions on how best to get to Sandy Creek. The attendant told me how to reach the edge of town, which would put me at the start of the road to Sandy Creek.

I wandered to them with my horse, tapped my

tiger's shoulder, and said, "Money, please. I'm hungry. Miracle's hungry, too."

Without missing a beat in his prized and heated debate, he got his wallet out of his jacket, pulled out several twenties, and handed them to me. I waited to see if he would ask me to do anything like suggest I should stay put. When he didn't, I shrugged, and decided his willingness to pay me to go feed myself was evidence he refused to lose whatever he was arguing about. After a brief listen, I determined they were arguing if they wanted to wait for the direct train for Rock Hill or purchase horses and just ride there. I left the platform armed with enough money to make it to Sandy Creek, board Miracle for a few hours if I needed, and grab a good meal on the road.

I waited until I made it out of the station to mount, and then I gave Miracle rein and a nudge. She pricked her ears forward and shuffled into a brisk walk, sliding through the crowd departing the station to find somewhere to spend the night until the next trains left out in the morning.

Once outside of Whiteville, Miracle transitioned to a ground-eating trot, something most courier horses did without prompting. Her ears, both pricked forwards, pleased me.

Like me, she liked to work, and I wondered if she had missed the road as much as I had. I monitored her, but she kept trotting with no sign of distress. I'd have to thank Adrian, Henry, and Cleo somehow for the effort they'd put in to make sure she could be a healthy, happy horse again.

As the sun set, the Hope Diamond gleamed, offering Miracle enough light to see by while she followed the road towards Sandy Creek. I passed through several towns on the way, and I stopped in each one long enough to offer my mare water and a light snack and a breather. At the same time, I found someone to ask about Sandy Creek.

Most, like the station attendant, told me the town had moved due to the ocean's ever-growing temper. As I approached Lake Waccamaw, something in the air changed. For so late at night, the town was abuzz with activity, and curious, I reined Miracle in at the first carriage station I found.

One of the attendants, an elderly woman who needed the help of a cane to walk, looked me over warily. "Your horse sick, too?"

My eyes widened. "What? No. She's not sick." Not anymore. "Is there an illness going around?" If a plague was spreading through the local population, I'd be bolting right back to Whiteville to warn my aunt. If it was limited to horses, then I'd be poking my nose around.

I remembered what had happened to the other courier horses, and if I could get a hold of those behind their deaths, I'd enjoy putting Todd's gun to work.

Such filth didn't deserve my blade.

"There've been bodies."

"Bodies?"

"Human and horses, some with no hair at all and awful boils." The woman pointed down the road in the direction of Sandy Creek. "A few have made it here from that way, and then reached the edge of town and fell over dead."

"And they had no hair?" The memory of Miracle becoming bare-skinned and losing her mane and tail would forever haunt me. Her relentless will to live had saved me, and I wanted to turn around and send her somewhere safe, somewhere she'd never have to endure such torture again.

"It fell out even as they walked."

My rage sparked to life. "Where?"

The woman once again pointed in the direction of Sandy Creek. "We aren't allowing anyone come through from that way now, and we're trying to keep people from going that way."

"Got a courier here?"

"We do. Why?"

"I need to send a message to Charlotte." I'd piss off Felicity, but I figured there was nobody better for the job than the Vice President—and there'd be zero chance of the rest of my family catching on until I had a good look. "What's the name of this town?"

"We're Little Waccamaw, named after the lake that way. We think this mess is coming from Sandy Creek. One of the bodies had a letter."

"I'm a courier, although I'm not on route right now. Do you still have the letter?"

The woman's expression brightened. "You can read?"

"Yes, ma'am. I can."

"Come, come. Nobody here can read more than the schedules, you know? The youngins who can read head off to the city and they only come back for visits, not that I blame them. We know a few words and numbers, but nothing like in that letter, and we didn't know who to send it to. Barb! Barb!" The woman hobbled towards the neighboring inn. "Barb, I've got me someone who can read her letters here. Bring that thing Patty-Jo found."

A rotund woman waddled out of the inn waving an envelope over her head. "I've got it right here, Jolene. That little girl can read? You look pretty tired. What's a little thing like you doing all the way out here?" Barb held the envelope out to me, and I took it. While the Hope Diamond continued to glow, neither woman seemed to register the stone's presence. Inside, blood-splattered parchment informed the recipient "the cylinder" was on route to Charlotte through Whiteville to Lumberton before passing through Rockingham. One date marked when the cylinder was scheduled to arrive in Lumberton, which is when the first test would occur, and it required a special shipment. The initials HD offered me the only clue I needed.

I held a treasure in my hand, and the messenger had died much like my little bare-skinned mare would have died if she hadn't been given a miracle and a new lease on life.

"Do you have paper and a pen here?" I asked, fearing I'd have no way to ensure the message got to Dawnfire with the needed information.

Barb turned and headed into the inn, returning a few minutes later with a pad of paper and a pen. "We keep a stock for couriers," she explained.

"Thank you. I'll pay you for the supplies."

She waved me off. "You're a courier, even if off duty. We send the bill to the government if you've a message to send while off duty."

I needed to kiss the ground my aunt walked on. I copied the message, and I wrote a letter to my aunt with an explanation of what it meant and how it connected to Ferdinand and his conspirators. Closing my eyes, I drew in a deep breath. If anything could protect the precious letter and make certain it reached Gentry's wife without incident, it would be the Hope Diamond.

The stone seemed to have half a clue about the important things, so maybe it could identify the traitors and make sure they wouldn't get their hands on it. The necklace warmed against my throat. When I lowered my hand with the precious letter, the paper shimmered. "Do you have an envelope?"

"That I do." Barb returned to the inn, returning with an envelope and a jar of glue so I could seal it.

After putting the letter inside and sealing it, I addressed it to Dawnfire for my aunt, added my name in the sender's space along with Waccamaw, and drew a deep breath. "Where's your courier station?"

Both women pointed across the street, and I dismounted, walking Miracle over and knocking on the door they indicated. A young man answered, a familiar enough face I pointed at him, and his eyes widened. "Runs Against Wind, if my eyes don't deceive me!"

It took me a minute to remember the fellow, who possessed a tongue-twister of a name he claimed came from Scotland. Fortunately for me, he'd liked me enough he didn't mind if I called him Leo rather than lose thirty minutes doing my best to keep from sounding like an idiot. "It's been a while, Leo."

"I'd heard you'd about got yourself killed not long ago, but you're looking in good form. Odd horse, though, but I bet she runs like the wind despite that coat."

"I rescued her from a bad owner, and she's been getting fit. She's game for a brisk walk through the woods, though. I need this sent to Dawnfire on the fastest relay you can get me. The courier should only give it to Felicity Adams. Gentry Adams, Stephanie Miller, and that damned rabbit of a First Gentlemen are also on the allowed list. If the courier runs into Anatoly Silverston, he can receive it, but he must be slapped with the envelope first."

"You want a courier to slap a Clan Council member with the envelope?"

"And have the courier tell him the slap is from his mate."

Leo whistled. "You landed yourself a Siberian tiger?"

"I took pity on him."

"You deserve a good man, not that trash you tended to shack up with. I was wondering if you'd ever settle, but that's not settling at all. That's taking the most wanted bachelor on the market."

I grinned at Leo's description of my former lovers, having forgotten I'd regaled a group of fellow couriers with some of the more awkward tales of their lack of prowess. I hadn't told them what I'd been doing in those days, allowing them to believe I'd been an unofficial courier all along. "I've had some good ones over the years. Those stories just aren't as much fun to tell between circuits."

"True enough. Ever get to shifting?"

"Sure have."

"Hot damn, you're on a roll. What species?"

"Siberian."

"Well, that would have made you the most wanted bachelorette in the entire country for all of the ten minutes you stayed single before you were hunted by Silverston."

I laughed. "Not quite. We are Siberians. We had to posture and fight first."

"That's true? I thought that was just a running joke."

"It's true. We're pretty violent. Every damned time I look at him, I want to start a damned fight." I couldn't stop grinning at the thought of my tiger and how he'd react when he realized I'd given him the slip. "I'm actually starting a fight right now, and it's going to be a good one when he catches up with me. Anyway, this is official government business, so make sure we get a good relay going; wire a warning we need a non-stop chain to Charlotte, if you've got a wire here."

"I've a wire here, and I've a fresh horse. I'll hit the road as soon as I get the confirmation they're ready for me. Who should the bill go to?"

"President Adams."

"Right up to the top? Must be some message."

"It's important. You got a classified stamp?"

"As a matter of fact, I do."

"Stamp it."

"Wax seal, too?"

"If you've got a warmer."

"We're fully kitted. Give me ten minutes, and you'll be on your way."

"That's great. Thanks, Leo."

As promised, it took him ten minutes to get the wax warmed so he could seal the envelope with an official courier seal, send a wire to set up the relay, and prepare the letter for its long ride to Charlotte. His horse, a tall, leggy bay mare, snatched at the bit when he went to bridle her, and she stamped the ground, eager to hit the road. "Beautiful mare, Leo."

"I took your advice and went south for a horse. I caught her on the tail end of winter when she was hungry and cold, and convinced her she liked to be fed and kept warm in exchange for outrunning the wind. I can't match your asshole blacks, but she comes close. Maybe we can try a race sometime?"

"Catch up with me in Charlotte, and we'll race some horses. I'll even coerce some equines into shifting for us and competing."

"Who do you know who'd let you do that?"

"Oh, just the guild leader of the Lancers' Alliance. I'll beg one of his sons to give his father some competition. It'll be fun. I'm positive I can coerce him into it."

"I would pay good money to watch you try."

"It's on, Leo. Catch up with me in Charlotte sometime, and we'll do just that."

"Not going back to Wyoming yet? That's your usual haunt. You'll kill my success record if you stick around here, Runs Against Wind."

"I'm mostly off circuit right now, so your record is safe. My shoulder's still busted up, and my little mare here needs some conditioning before she's ready for the road in earnest. We're just getting some exercise tonight, and that business came up."

"Isn't that the way it always goes? You take care of yourself. I'm assigned here for the next three months, but I'll come up to Charlotte and see if you're in town then."

I saluted him, swung into the saddle, and got out of his way. He touched his heels to his mare's sides, and she bolted straight to a gallop, charging out of the small town as though a pack of wolves nipped at her heels. While he'd said he couldn't match my blacks, I bet the mare would give Todd a run for his money and then some, and while Devil Spawn liked chasing the wind, I doubted she'd beat the bay on a short track.

Few could match my horses in an endurance run, but they worked as hard as I did.

I'd have to condition them for long rides again, but they'd find their stride soon enough, assuming their age didn't start catching up with them.

In reality, I had no idea how old my black beauties were, and I dreaded the day they showed signs of being ready for retirement.

Once Leo and his horse were out of sight, I followed after him at a trot, went far enough nobody in town could see what I was up to, and circled around to bypass Little Wacammaw in search of the cylinder someone planned to use as a weapon against my home and family.

I FOUND the first body not far from Little Wacammaw, and the poor bastard and his horse hadn't been dead long. Miracle trembled, and I stroked her neck, wondering if I should tether her and walk on foot. I dismounted and searched the man's corpse, finding another letter similar in content to the first. Several hundred dollars filled his wallet, and I took the money, as I didn't want it falling into the hands of anyone who had tortured and killed so many horses for the sake of triggering a civil war.

While it wouldn't bring the poor chestnut back to life, I stroked her head and wished her spirit well.

When I straightened, I unholstered Todd's gun,

loaded the chambers, and dumped extra bullets into my pocket so I'd have enough rounds to kill every last one of the bastards responsible for the horse's death.

She'd deserved better than a slow, torturous demise.

I mounted and angled Miracle in the way it looked like the fallen pair had come, relying on the Hope Diamond's light to navigate the forest. Within a few minutes, I found another horse's body, the corpse at least a few days old and still wearing its tack. I gave the corpse a wide berth, curling my lip in a snarl over the waste.

A trail of bodies, man and horse alike, led me east. The glow of a small fire, likely birthed by some Starfall stone or a small combustion zone, guided me the rest of the way, and the presence of several sick, dying horses told me everything I needed to know.

The men at the fire would die, and I'd abandon my ethics for quick, humane, ruthless, and unexpected. I dismounted, as I expected the sound of gunfire would terrify my mare. I tethered her to a tree trunk, crept closer to be in good range, and counted corpses unaware they breathed their last.

Six men would die, and I'd practiced enough in Wyoming with every gun I could get my hands on I'd make sure they'd all die without having to reload Todd's colt. Setting my stance, I raised the weapon, picked my target, and fired. The weapon bucked in my hand, and I switched targets, cocked the pistol, and fired again.

Two shots, two bodies.

Shouts of alarm and screams broke the quiet of the forest, and without remorse, I picked my target, waited for my victim to stop long enough for me to be sure of my aim, and fired again.

His body fell, too.

The three remaining victims scattered and attempted to flee, but they couldn't outrun a bullet. No one could.

Around my throat, the Hope Diamond glowed with a red light, as though it took delight in the blood I'd shed. Maybe later, I would hate myself for what I'd become and done, but with the bodies of tortured horses around me, with the memory of Miracle's suffering still too fresh in my mind, I refused to feel anything other than satisfaction over their swift demise.

Miracle trembled but stood her ground, and I praised her for her bravery, kissing her nose. "It's all right, baby. They'll never hurt you again." I untied her reins and tossed them over her head so I could mount.

A seventh figure rose and bolted for the forest, and my mare screamed a challenge, bolted from my hold, and charged towards the camp. She crashed into the man. He screamed, but not for long.

Miracle reared and slammed her hooves into his fragile skull, ending his life with a crunch. Then, because once wasn't enough, she trampled him until I gathered her reins and pulled her away.

She blew air, stretched her neck towards the body, and snapped her teeth.

"Easy, Miracle." I pressed my hand to her chest,

which was wet with blood. Afraid she'd gotten hurt trampling her foe, I checked her legs, but she had emerged from her rampage unscathed. She snorted, but she backed down, although I read her body language as ready, eager, and willing to stomp on the corpse some more.

To keep her out of trouble, I tethered her to the tree and examined the body.

It didn't take me long to discover a metal tube which fit the description of the cylinder, and something about it made the hairs on my arm stand on end. Then, with a furrowed brow, I examined the bodies of the men I'd shot to discover they, too, were covered in boils and had lost most of their hair.

I didn't need anyone telling me the bitter truth: I carried death in my hand, and I would share their fate. How long it would take, I had no idea, but I feared the worst.

Miracle would be my best chance of getting rid of the weapon before it could kill anyone else, but I balked at the idea of exposing her to whatever it was that did such a good job of killing horse and man alike. I wanted to set her free so she could run and live, but if I did, would I make it to the ocean before the tube's contents killed me and anyone else it came into contact with?

Some choices weren't choices at all. Hating myself for what I needed to do, I shoved the tube into my pocket, wondering how something no longer than the length of my hand could create so much misery. Then I untethered Miracle and prayed to the uncaring, unknown gods for forgiveness for what I had to do.

I expected the ride to the ocean would be my last, and my loyal, precious little horse would see me through to the bitter end.

I touched my heels to her sides, and we galloped towards the churning sea.

Chapter Eighteen

I STRUGGLED to believe something as insignificant as a metal tube could ruin everything I held dear. In the hours since claiming it from the band of traitors, a headache tore through my skull and brought dizziness and nausea in its wake. I tasted fouled blood, a promise I lived on borrowed time.

It was all I could do to point my horse east and find the ocean so I could search for the Creek Bore. It would serve my purpose, and I wished good fortune on the station attendant who told me of the spot and what to look for.

Miracle galloped without floundering, and the Hope Diamond gleamed with a bright light, which infused my horse. I hoped it protected her from what would kill me—and had killed the men determined enough to kill themselves transporting the tube towards Charlotte to destroy everyone and everything I loved.

Disbanding all mercenary guilds and implementing

martial law would bring chaos and rebellion. Killing the top mercenary guilds might lead them to success.

None of them would live to learn from their mistakes.

I refused to regret killing them for what they meant to do. If given a chance, I would slit the throats of any who willingly participated in a scheme meant to murder my loved ones, my family, and my mate.

Miracle slowed to a walk, whinnied, and turned her head to bump her nose against my knee. The salty scent of the sea teased my nose, promising we'd soon reach my goal. I leaned forward and stroked my hand over her short, patchy and bristly coat. With time, she'd truly heal—assuming I could get her away from the weapon's lethal reach. Assuming the Hope Diamond wasn't protecting us from the tube's vile influence. Todd would help Miracle if she escaped its influence alive, and he'd repay my debt to her for having carried me so far on such a hopeless venture. It didn't matter how things ended for me. He knew I loved my horses.

He'd remember me through her.

So would Anatoly.

They would treasure Miracle as much as I did.

Had another choice presented itself, I would've taken it without hesitation, fighting for survival despite the impossible odds I faced. But no other ways had bubbled to the surface, not without sacrificing others.

There were a lot of people between me, Anatoly, Todd, and my family. Those people had families, too. They had lovers. They had friends. People like sweet

Leo, a passing friend and hard worker, would die as well.

No matter what, the tube and its lethal contents needed to be destroyed. I couldn't afford to give anyone an opportunity to reclaim it and use it. I couldn't allow them to find more Starfall stones and have them breathe life into their vile weapon.

The lethal ocean and its devouring waves could take the weapon far from human reach. My aunt's name for the damned thing still bothered me.

Nuclear power sounded so pure and innocent to me.

It was anything but.

In the light of the rising sun, I guided Miracle to the ocean's jagged shore. I searched until I found the abandoned town of Sandy Creek and the promised Creek Bore, dismounting near where the currents transformed into a hungering beast, devouring anyone foolish enough to dip even a foot into its depths. In the Hope Diamond's light, which spilled out over the ocean as far as I could see, the water boiled as claimed, stretching out to where light gleamed over massive waves that broke before cascading down and settling as its fury calmed when it reached the shore. I set the tube onto a nearby rock to buy enough time to set my mare free. I lifted my hand and brushed my fingers against the Hope Diamond wrapped around my neck. With a mind of its own, the Starfall stone did as it willed, but it sometimes listened.

Maybe it would listen.

Maybe it would gift my mare with a vibrant life, one without illness. If I could, I would have taken Miracle's lingering pain onto my dying shoulders and bought her a chance for a better life. I would take whatever illness the tube inflicted on her with me until the sea claimed me and the weapon as its own. Seizing the diamond, I clutched it until the metal of its setting bit into my skin along with the many diamonds encrusting its surface.

My blood seeped into the deepest crevices of Embracing Hope, and through the gaps between my fingers, a bloody light shone.

Miracle snorted, turning her ears back. Her white-rimmed eyes betrayed her fear, but as she had from the day she'd first carried me, she endured.

For me, she'd done more than endure. She'd given me her life without condition or regret. She repaid my compassion for her with unconditional love, something I still struggled to understand.

There would be no chance for me to learn, not now.

But I would send my mare to those I cared for the most, and I would hope she would be enough to convince them I'd made my choices for their sakes. For mine, too. With my free hand, I fumbled with my sword's belt, loosening it and securing it to her saddle. Todd's prized colt went into a saddle bag with the ammunition.

I kept the letters I'd found. The couriers would send

word to Dawnfire, and they would have time to act. They would be able to prepare.

They would have the dates, the times, and the places where treachery would happen.

Through her, my voice would reach beyond my watery grave and whisper of my love for them. While too late, if I ever had another chance, I'd make sure they heard, from me, that I loved them and hadn't chosen as I had without doing my best to claw my way back to them.

I stepped away from Miracle to keep her safely out of range of the tube and its wretched contents, I picked up my death in my free hand. I tightened my grip on the Hope Diamond.

The stone's dark miasma continued to pour in the gaps between my fingers, reminding me of a simple truth.

Where a Starfall stone went, catastrophe surely followed. When a Starfall stone glowed, wise men ran.

If it would save my beloved Miracle, if it would give me the strength to dispose of the weapon meant to kill everyone I loved, I would dance in its light and beg it to burst. I would allow it to devour me if needed, to earn enough of its favor to save my mare, my mate, and my family.

Asking a stone to help a horse counted as an act of folly, but I'd found the end of my road, and I didn't want the animal to share my fate. "Please," I begged in a raspy voice. The taste of blood intensified, and I wondered what had torn my throat up so much it bled.

Or if I bled somewhere deeper.

The Hope Diamond's dark miasma shrouded my hand, and sparks of blue danced over my skin. It reached out for my mare, engulfing her before she could do more than whinny her alarm.

The darkness faded in the time it took me to suck in a breath.

I barely recognized the mare left in the wake of the Hope Diamond's display of power. Instead of a paler coat, the golden we thought would eventually color her coat to dun, she'd become a black beauty of a horse, the match of Dipshit and Devil Spawn. She remained small but otherwise perfect in every way. A pale gleam drew my eye to her brow, and a blaze the same shape as the Hope Diamond graced her brow.

"Find Todd," I ordered, hoping the mare would remember the stallion and the first of the commands I'd tried teaching her. Devil Spawn understood the order, although she rarely obeyed, and while Dipshit would obey, he'd find some way to surprise me—and Todd—by the time he finished being an asshole.

Miracle backed away and made a low, distressed sound, but she whirled and ran the way we had come.

I hoped she found him or ran away long enough I'd be far out of her reach before she returned to find me. Either would work. She'd be safe. Those I left behind would search for me and find her. Todd would care for my horse, and he'd recognize her from her small size and spirit. Her new blaze would give him pause, but he'd figure out she was mine. And if he didn't, Anatoly would.

My katana and his pistol would be all the clue they'd need, although my mate would smell me on her, unless the Hope Diamond's dark light had erased all evidence of my scent. I wouldn't put it past the stone.

It had a mind of its own.

With luck, the sea would claim us both. The Starfall stone, capable of shaping an entire continent, might change the ocean, too. Could it calm the churning seas beyond the questionable safety of the shores? I doubted anything could, but I'd seen enough miracles to understand it might be able to do anything, even bring back the dead.

Everyone believed nobody could be brought back from the dead, but the longer I lived, the more I wondered. If any stone could, it was the Hope Diamond.

Perhaps it brought so much destruction to so many to pay the price of saving lives—or bringing them back from death's door. I'd been to death's door once. While recovering, plagued with more illnesses than Cleo or Henry could readily count, I had vague memories of the mystics warning Anatoly I still might die despite having survived through so much.

Of the memories of my illness, that one had remained with me.

Anatoly hadn't taken the news well. Until then, while I'd heard Anatoly ask favors of people, he'd never begged.

He'd begged for them to do what they could.

Begging wouldn't do me any good, but if I'd thought begging might help, I would've asked for everything. I wanted it all. I wanted to destroy the metal tube and its lethal contents, and when I finished my work, I wanted to return to everyone I cared for—and who cared for me.

I hated the necessity of what I needed to do, but I saw no other choice. I couldn't justify sacrificing so many others for a chance of survival, not when one death, mine, would protect everybody else. Some choices in life weren't really choices at all.

I would go to my grave with a clear conscience, my integrity intact despite breaking the one promise I cared about over all others.

Except I knew the truth Anatoly might never learn: I'd truly done my best to survive.

I wanted to, but I couldn't.

My survival could become his death—and the deaths of everyone else I'd learned to love.

Releasing the Hope Diamond, I headed for the outcropping of large rocks extending into the sea. It marked the start of the tearing current, and the place I'd go to reach where the seas churned and killed any foolish enough to fall into its cold embrace. I expected death would strike without hesitation or remorse.

As long as I lived long enough to destroy the tube with the Starfall stones in my possession, it would be enough. It wouldn't take long for the tide to take me where I needed to go. Sunder would take care of the rest, the Weapon Clan Starfall stone that warriors feared.

If Sunder couldn't break the tube, nothing could—and Sunder hungered for metal it could destroy. With a single touch, its work would be done.

I removed the other Starfall stones from the pouch and set them on the beach beyond the sea's reach for someone to find. As fate enjoyed playing cruel games, I bet the damned things would follow me to my death, as there was nothing the Weapon Clans' Starfall stones liked to do more than linger in my shadow.

Maybe they'd hold a wake over my drowned body before going off and doing whatever it was semi-sentient stones did once their target of choice kicked the bucket. Perhaps they'd have some tea and chat about every stupid thing I'd done in my life.

Steel Heart, in particular, could kiss my ass. It'd brought my mate to my door, he'd tempted me, I'd tattooed him, and the cowardly thing had run away. Then, as it couldn't leave well enough alone, it'd rolled right back into my life and brought even more trouble with it. I credited it for helping to save the unborn. I assumed all the stones had played some part.

This time, nothing would bring Anatoly to me.

My mate needed to fight a different war, one of equal importance. He'd understand he needed to prepare Charlotte for the onslaught of traitors. The battle would go to him, the mercenary guilds, my aunt, my uncles, and everyone else who would have to rally the city's defense. I held the traitor's main weapon, the one that would destroy everyone and leave their conspirators free to take over.

It wouldn't exist for long.

Clutching Sunder in one hand and the tube in the other, I jumped into the Creek Bore and allowed it to tear me out to sea.

WHILE THE OCEAN appeared to boil, the water's chill tore into me. Somehow, I gasped with my head above water, caught myself, and took another deep breath before the current dragged me under. I battled my instinct to struggle. I needed all of my strength for when the tide tossed me into the raging ocean beyond the safer waters near shore.

Then and only then would I use Sunder to destroy the weapon, far enough from shore its toxic influence might not poison the land. I had no idea if it would work, but I would hope for the best. That hope was all I had left.

My life's final task wouldn't take long.

Without mercy, the current jerked me out to sea, spitting me out where monstrous waves crashed, spraying white froth everywhere. I broke the surface long enough to gasp before water slammed me down and drove me towards the deeps.

It would do. Nothing, especially not me, would survive long in the violent waters. Sunder and the Hope Diamond would disappear with me, although I expected both would somehow find their way back to shore and bother someone else.

Life had a bad sense of humor, and I pitied the poor bastards stuck with the stones, although despite its destructive nature, I rather liked Sunder. Of all the stones, it sought to destroy what might hurt those I loved the most.

I brought my hands together.

The ocean exploded around me, countless bubbles seething in the water. A bright light blinded me, and the pressure of the Hope Diamond around my throat vanished. The waves caught the setting and the Starfall stone, tearing them away from me.

Blue and black consumed the sea, and a pressure built around me, worse than the burn of my air-starved lungs. Terror should have consumed me, but instead, I found something peaceful and calming, spreading through me from somewhere deep within my chest.

The tube broke apart to nothing, falling through my fingers to disperse, forever lost.

Miracles could happen, although I wouldn't see the aftermath of the one I'd wrought with the help of a dark Starfall stone most were wise to fear. As death would come for me soon enough, I opened my mouth to whisper thanks. Instead of water, pure, crisp air swept into my mouth.

The Hope Diamond burst in a pulse of pale blue light, and the bubbling ocean froze around me. Ice crackled, chilling my skin as it spread. The necklace hung, the same as I remembered in the watery temple on the outskirts of Fort Lauderdale. I reached out my hand for the jewel.

The setting's clasp shattered, and countless pale diamonds fell into the sea and disappeared into the depths, passing through the frozen waters as though it were air.

I closed my fingers around the Hope Diamond, brought it to my bloodied lips, and kissed its faceted surface. While I still breathed, I tasted the blood and understood I died.

Unlike so many I'd seen perish over the years, I wouldn't beg. From the moment I had turned Miracle east towards the shore, riding her at a gallop long after any other horse would have fallen over dead, I'd been prepared.

For those I'd loved, I would have given so much more than my death. Had it been an option, I would have lived with them and for them, ready to battle for a future with my tiger and friends and family.

I waited for the end, and my only regret was my awareness that there wasn't a future with me in it.

THE OCEAN HATED ME, but it didn't want me to die. Whether afraid of the Hope Diamond's wrath, the Starfall stone had a mind of its own, or Sunder had opted to use some unknown power, I'd never know. Instead of dying in the churning waters, I choked on my own blood on the stone shore while gentle waves lapped at my feet. I breathed, and something rattled in my chest.

I lacked the strength to do anything about my situation, which ultimately meant I'd die a slow, painful death on land instead of a quick, merciful death in the violent waters. I'd emerged bruised and aching, but I couldn't tell how much of the pain came from being battered in the current, tossed on shore, or from the tube's lethal presence.

I just couldn't do anything the easy way, not even die.

The clatter of rock on rock warned me I wasn't alone. I should have done something other than struggle to breathe. Not breathing would put an end to the pain, providing a permanent escape. I thought about it and tried to hold my breath to help myself along, but my body refused to obey.

It kept breathing.

My own damned body hated me and didn't want to die.

I needed to have a long talk with my lungs about why it wasn't ethical to torture people. A clean death, quick and as painless as possible, was the way to go. I'd have to remember that the next time I went into battle. Swords through the eye brought quick deaths, as did severing the spine. Gut wounds took longer. I'd have to try to spare the time to slit my victim's throats if I somehow survived through hell.

Maybe I could retire, catch my tiger, and hide under my bed with him.

Maybe there was a future with me in it after all.

Hot fingers brushed against my throat, and someone grunted, a masculine sound, but not one I recognized. I'd heard my tiger, Gentry, and Todd grunt often enough I'd never forget them.

"You were born stubborn, little girl," a man announced, and he pried open my fingers, retrieving Sunder before taking the Hope Diamond from me. After he checked the necklace, which had seen better days, he located my belt pouch and put both of the Starfall stones inside and tied it closed. "You could have just used Sunder on shore and dropped it into the tide, you know. I will have to teach you how to think things through a little better, I see."

Something about the man's voice, deeper than most, sparked a memory of long days and roaring flames, a marvel in our often cold world. I still wondered how the Blade Clan had been able to control flames hot enough for metal to melt, but I'd been too entranced by the flickering orange and red to ask questions.

One by one, memories filtered through the pain-induced haze.

It occurred to me I'd seen something like my katana before in that distant forge, but it'd been a raw blade with no hilt, flawed and destined to be destroyed. Blade Clan warriors weren't supposed to beg for anything, but I remembered.

I'd cried that something beautiful would be destroyed because it wasn't perfect.

Instead of melting it back down, the blacksmith had indulged me, and the imperfect blade had been spared.

I'd learned about mercy that day.

I opened my mouth, and I coughed before croaking, "Blacksmith."

"You remember my voice." In his statement, I heard pleasure. "Yes, I am our clan's blacksmith. I noticed you left Steel Heart with the other clan stones. It is sad you left it behind."

At least I could justify *that* action. "I didn't want it to drown, too."

The blacksmith chuckled. "It is a stone. It cannot drown, but I am sure it will be appeased that you cared for its fate. You should be more worried for yourself. I need to move you, and this will hurt. I will tend to you until your mother comes, and then she will beat me for not tending you well enough, I am sure."

My mother? "Why?"

"You are my greatest forging, and your mother gets upset whenever she catches wind you have done something else to hurt yourself. You are very good at hurting yourself, I have noticed."

I was his *what*? "You're…?"

"Who else to tame you than your own father? The rest of the clan could not handle your fire, so they tossed you into my forge and ordered me to teach you. From your first breath, you were determined. You were so determined only I could rein you in and charm you into learning our ways. We broke many traditions in your early days. I cannot take my eyes off you for even a moment, can I? No, I cannot. Have children, the Blade Clan suggested. Take a bride. I picked a grizzly and bred a Siberian. What have I done to our world? And yet, you remain my greatest forging despite your tendency to create trouble wherever you go. Brace yourself, my little girl. This will hurt. If I could take that from you, I would, but I cannot. Try to bear with it, and I will do my best to return you to your groom in as good health as I can. You still breathe, so I am certain you are too stubborn to die this time."

I meant to reply, but my father worked an arm beneath me, and the world vanished in a flash of pain.

I HAD A MOTHER AND A FATHER, and they bickered worse than anyone else I'd met before in my life. When I was coherent to watch them, they dedicated themselves to their verbal sparring without reservation. If I gave them knives, I worried someone wouldn't walk away alive.

They bickered over the strangest things. The first argument, my father worried I wouldn't like the blanket, which was blue. My mother thought it matched the Hope Diamond, and she refused to accept the red one he'd picked out.

I lacked the strength to tell them a blanket was a blanket, and I'd take both.

Sickness, as always, made it hard for me to get warm.

The next time I caught a plethora of colds and everything else the world had to offer, I wouldn't complain. I also held a new admiration for what Miracle had endured.

She had tolerated dancing at death's door a lot better than I did, and I spent most of my time fighting to keep from screaming or crying. On the screaming front, I fared fairly well. I cried more than I liked, one part from frustration, the rest from the relentless onslaught of pain.

Sometime after I'd washed up on the shore, my father found my horse. Miracle stood vigil over me whenever my parents looked the other way long enough for her to sneak into the abandoned cabin they'd taken over. She usually nuzzled my cheek and made certain I understood I wasn't alone.

She also tried to bite my father and mother whenever they forced soup down my throat. Nothing settled in my stomach well, and pain stabbed through my teeth and jaw every time I tried to eat anything. After every meal, my little mare managed to drive my father away for a little while, and she stood tense guard, stomping her hooves on the wood floor until I recovered enough to reassure her.

Time lost meaning, but every time my mother visited, she brought news and information, and she often wore the blood of those she'd dispatched on her one-woman mission to end the rebellion and seek revenge for my piss-poor condition. To her, if they hadn't been ambitious, greedy bastards, I wouldn't have had to prove I was truly my mother's daughter. That meant every last one of them needed to die.

It didn't help I was also my father's daughter.

Unlike me, my grizzly of a mother, who reminded me a lot of my aunt with a softer face, did not follow anyone's rules other than her own. Her rules said she preferred to rip her foes apart limb from limb. If she was in a mood, she'd use one of the limbs to beat her next target into submission before dismantling her prey into four or more pieces.

My mother terrified me sometimes, and her behavior offered a few insights on how I'd become a Siberian.

She had eyes only for my father, and she was right to fight him—and fight for him.

I'd somehow turned her natural inclinations into magic.

My tiger would love my mother for that.

When I dozed off or feigned sleep, my parents spoke of the weapon I'd destroyed in low voices, and they'd recover enough letters to identify who they needed to trick to turn the tables in my family's favor.

Then I learned a secret about my father; not only could he forge weapons, he had a steady hand and had mastered the art of forgery, too. In another man's script, he changed the entire face of the war, concocted lies about the weapon, and had my mother plant them. When she finished her work, he took over, gathering the clans to participate in the inevitable battle brewing.

I missed a great deal of the planning and had vague memories of skirting death's door without understanding why I couldn't seem to get any better. I lived, but I didn't heal.

When rest didn't help my body recover, my father dragged me out of the cabin, gave me a wooden stick, and beat on me until I found the strength to fight back. Miracle snorted her disapproval of his methods, but unlike rest, I could breathe easier when I held a weapon and pretended I might match the man who'd played a part in my life.

After the first spar, such as it was, my mother wandered off and didn't return, which bothered me, as my hazy memories refused to provide more than fragments about her; my memory failed more often than not right along with my ailing body.

The day I managed to scramble onto Miracle's back, we left the cabin and headed for Charlotte.

Either I healed or my tolerance for misery grew, but I survived the ride. Along the way, the weapon clans joined us until we created an army that marched on the United States' seat of power.

The government wouldn't appreciate the chaos so many clans would bring to the city, but at least we could claim we were on their side for a change. The clan stones remained in my pouch, and representatives from every clan visited me to confirm I possessed their stone.

They liked to glow in the presence of their clan's elders, but none of the stones seemed inclined to return to where they belonged. Sometimes, the Hope Diamond gleamed and sparks played across my skin, a warning the stones were to stay with me. I had a vague memory of my father attempting to fix the necklace, but he'd abandoned the effort, instead turning it into a bracelet and securing it with a piece of leather strap until he could find a way to repair it—or make a new setting for it.

He got snarly if anyone suggested they should examine the priceless Starfall stone.

I suspected my father transformed into a cat of some sort, but he'd only tell me he wasn't a Siberian like me, and that I was the pride of our family, as there was no better species for me to be.

I thought he needed to tone back his biased attitude.

The Blade Clan joined our motley army last, and the tigress within me roused to the challenge, and I snarled rather than greet any of the men. Some I vaguely remembered, idolizing them before I'd taken a different path in life. The clan's elders looked me over, and the bastards dared to smile at me.

I hissed in reply.

"Please forgive my daughter. She is surly. The enemy's chosen weapon made her quite ill. It is a testament of our ways she lives to tell the tale of how she defeated even the ocean."

Biased bastard. Miracle snorted, and if horses

could roll their eyes, I suspected my mare would have. She tossed her head and gave herself a shake as though hoping to dislodge my father's nonsense. I wished her luck with that. Stroking her neck, I relaxed in the saddle, grateful I no longer coughed blood often.

Henry and Cleo wouldn't be happy when they figured out I would once again put their magic to the test. My tiger wouldn't be happy, either.

"Only you would sire a daughter and set her out to change everything. You were just as much trouble as she was from the day you were born."

Well, at least I could blame my father moving forward. I regarded the elder, a man so old I wondered if he'd witnessed Starfall personally. Some first generations refused to age much, like Todd. Others lingered, their bodies old and tired but resilient against death's call.

My father smirked. "Show him Steel Heart, Jesse."

He hadn't used my name often, and I had a faint recollection he'd been the one to encourage me to take it. Suspicions rattled around in my head, as he'd encouraged me to like pretty things, like the katana's flawed blade and a name suitable for both a boy and a girl. While tempted to argue with him because I could, I removed the Starfall stone from the pouch and displayed it on my palm. It decided to roll up my arm to my shoulder, where it hid beneath my tattered hair.

"It likes her," my father said with an utter lack of sympathy for the elder who likely wanted his damned rock back.

"I see that. How is she?"

"She will fight to the death to prevent the clan from beating on her groom as is proper, and she will probably take us all out with a spoon should she feel we plan to test his prowess. During some of her less lucid moments, she informed me what she would do to us. I found it charming and amusing."

"Well, she was raised to do the fighting. A friendly spar, then, so we can test his mettle without perhaps quite as much of a beating as he might otherwise endure. It can be part of our celebrations when the bodies of our enemies feed the Earth in our wake. I've been tasked to ask if she will be our standard bearer in the battle to come."

"The clans may rally around her, for she carries the hearts of all of our clans with her. But no literal standard. It would tire her, and her little horse will be tired by the time we arrive. She is quite serious about guarding her rider."

"I will have the clans send their best for the guard, and we will dance to the stars so that our jewels might illuminate the way." The elder's gaze fixed on the Hope Diamond. "We are honored."

"We are," my father agreed. "Are we ready to ride to war, Elder?"

"We are ready."

"Then we ride."

Chapter Nineteen

A WEEK after the Blade Clan joined the other weapon clans, we swept through Charlotte and brought death with us. The Hope Diamond's first burst illuminated the entire city in a blue and white. Then, as though it'd been hoarding its dark miasma for years, unleashed its fury and marked those it disliked with an inky black, coloring their skin. Those doomed to die shed shadows filled with blue-white sparks, drawing attention to them no matter where they tried to hide.

Had I not known what they'd meant to do, I would have felt guilt for the slaughter. Knowledge mattered.

They'd meant to subject everyone in the city to the same destructive toxin I suffered from, without pity or remorse.

They didn't deserve the mercy they received, delivered at the hands of the Weapon Clans out for vengeance that their Starfall stones had been stolen for such evil.

Someday soon, I expected someone to dub Charlotte the City of Change. War hadn't done my home any favors, and what had once been quiet residential neighborhoods become war zones. The Blade Clan swept through, leaving death, destruction, and hope in their wake. The Hope Diamond, which liked to wrap itself and its broken chain around my left wrist, pulsed every time we crossed paths with anyone.

It didn't care for my father's leather straps meant to hold it in place, destroying them at least several times a day.

The innocent were bathed in a purifying blue light, and the stone did what it could to heal their bruised and broken bodies. I doubted it did much more than prevent death, but a chance at life beat a slow, painful demise on the battlefield.

The rest fell to darkness and became the prey of clan warriors holding a grudge.

Had I been in any shape to fight, I would've joined them, armed with a sword of my father's making, although the weapon wasn't my preferred katana. He'd taken my prized blade and promised I could have it back when I could ride properly, as it'd be a pity if I broke it dropping it onto the cobbles like a fool. I struggled with staying in the saddle, and it was well enough I wasn't armed with a sword I wanted to use. Falling wouldn't do me any favors.

Exhaustion beat death, although I feared I only breathed with the help of a meddling Starfall stone. When it tired of me, the end would come quickly. My father, sometime after the Blade Clan had joined us, confessed he'd almost killed me by taking the stone to see what would happen if we were separated.

I shivered at a dim memory of a deep darkness coming for me. The pain of death no longer frightened me; living hurt a great deal more than the brief discomfort of my failing lungs and stuttering heart.

Because of the Hope Diamond, I lived.

"Are the pulses hurting you?" my father asked while the rest of the clan cleared the street that would take us to the Lancers' Alliance. The red barn still stood, a miracle as far as I was concerned. The rebels had gotten a hold of at least one combustion stone, and they'd torched part of the city already, aware few knew how to stop hungering flames anymore.

"No." I ran my fingers across the Hope Diamond's faceted surface. The stone warmed at my touch. "I'm just tired."

I expected I would be tired for a long time while my body recovered from the toxicity of the nuclear weapon and my time in the ocean's churning waters.

"You have brought the clan great honor."

As far as my father was concerned, I couldn't be more perfect if I tried. Without my tiger and the others having showered me with their affection, accepting his love would have tested me far more. Still, the old shifter needed a qualified mystic to examine his head. "And if it weren't for your art and skill with steel, the clan would have long tossed you off the peak of the nearest mountain to restore the clan's pride and dignity."

He laughed. "I see you have not forgotten our ways."

"Somewhat. Some things I've opted to discard and forget at my leisure."

"And that is for the better. From the moment I laid eyes on you, I knew you would change our world. I had not anticipated for you to change the world, but I am proud of what you have become. Your mother is, too."

"You keep saying that, but according to my aunt, my mother is a terrifying demon of a grizzly who could take on the entire rebellion without breaking a sweat." I had vague memories of my mother helping my father care for me, but she'd left as soon as she was needed to make the final preparations for Charlotte's defense.

I found it amusing my mother loved to fight with my father. I looked forward to meeting her properly when coherent enough to really comprehend who she was and what she was like.

"She is a magnificent bride and wife. I will only be beaten slightly for my failure to keep you in perfect health."

I worried about that; I couldn't remember them actually physically fighting in their verbal sparring. "Most people would be filing for a divorce over that."

"While I am not a Siberian, my species is very similar to yours. Your mother is very skilled with her sword, and when I do not fight to her standards, I endure my beatings as is proper. It is a matter of pride. That is where the Blade Clan—and the other clans—have it all wrong. There is nothing more special than a woman who follows the way of the sword. In the hands of a woman, a blade becomes far more than a tool of war. That is what I had hoped for you from the very beginning. The first time you found beauty in a sword, I held hope that you had more depth than the other children in our clan. I held hope I could forge you into something truly special. Then you went and forged yourself into someone who far surpassed all of my expectations."

"Forged is a good word, since I'll probably fall over dead if I'm separated from the Hope Diamond. Anatoly is not going to take the news well. We'll have gone from trying to remove it to trying to make sure it can never be removed. And it will remove itself at its whim."

"It's only a problem if it goes some twenty feet away from you. Its range could be greater, and the instant the stone realized you suffered, it returned to you. It seems to have intellect, but a rather confused intellect. I think I need to have a talk with it about what it means to be healthy. I will have to find a very healthy Siberian tigress as a model."

"Anatoly has a sister."

"I know of her. She would have made an excellent bride for you, but you make a better bride for your groom. You are exactly as you should be, for all there are those within the clan who are still baffled by your choice. For all you had no idea I was your father when you were a child, the proudest moment of my life was when you decided for yourself you should not be like every other child of the clan. I only wish you had not feared what you had become or doubted it. That was not what I wanted for you."

The Hope Diamond burst again, and blue light pulsed over the street, engulfing everyone in its way. The warriors whooped and hollered, and those the Starfall stone marked fell beneath their swords. Part of me wanted to dismount, find something sharp and pointy, and carve my mark into the bodies of the fallen so the world would know they'd been judged by a higher power for their crimes.

I refused to suffer through remorse for their deaths.

They had wanted to poison an entire city of people for the sake of their twisted plans.

While I wanted to wade in and dispatch a few myself, I rode Miracle. My mare regarded the nearby combat with a wary eye, one ear twisted back. In a way, she reminded me of a dog more than a horse, unfailing in her loyalty and courage. Dipshit and Devil Spawn might view leaves as terrifying adversaries on occasion, but not Miracle.

She had no time for such nonsense.

"I feel like an ornament," I complained.

"Consider yourself a war leader, guiding the clan into battle. I am a blacksmith. While I can fight, my place is to make sure the swords I make do well in battle, so I observe." He pointed into the fray at one of the warriors. "Watch him."

The warrior had a tendency to go in close for the kill, relishing in the spray of blood and swift dispatches. He also aimed for the neck often. "He is predictable."

"He has a way about him, yes. His sword is too short. He has accommodated for this with his choice to engage close early, but in reality, he handicaps himself. You would destroy him with your katana, which suits your build and style of fighting. You are also good in close quarters, but when you get close, you are fueled with desperation as much as skill, so you shine more than he does. He is adequate. It will not give him long life should he continue to hold onto his childhood blade. He has outgrown it, but he holds too much affection for the blade. *He* is the weapon but he forgets this."

"Maybe I should remind him of the rules after we're done with this."

"No, Jesse."

"Why not?"

"You are still not well. When you are well, you may battle the entire clan for your right to claim your groom if you wish. Your groom would be crushed, and you would then battle the entire clan as a matter of honor anyway, so we should spare your groom his dignity."

"My groom has been training with grizzlies. My mother's brother and sister to be specific."

"That is concerning for my brothers of the clan. I will wisely go forge a second weapon for my new son to properly welcome him into our family rather than test my strength unnecessarily. Your mother will insist on having her turn with him. She is an opinionated creature."

That my aunt and uncle had been completely tricked by my mother would be a source of amusement for the rest of my life. While amusing, I wasn't sure I would ever understand why they'd opted for subterfuge over openly engaging in a relationship. "I can't believe you two have been visiting with each other on the sly."

"The clan would not understand, and your uncles would have come for my blood upon finding out I didn't properly release her from her duties after bearing you. My bride's sister? She would do terrible things to me. She probably will. I've heard of Madam President's temper. My bride tells me her sister takes after her quite a deal."

"I don't want to know."

"Once you are properly mated, I believe we shall try for another daughter. Daughters are the true jewels of our world, and you would do well having a sister you can teach to walk in your footsteps. Two of you would be a true wonder of this world."

"You do realize I'm a paid killer when I'm not delivering letters, right?"

"I find your desire to fight fate and the circumstances of your birth to be a glorious thing."

My father embraced formality and needed a swift kick in the ass to join modern times—or at least an introduction to contractions. "Wouldn't this go faster if we were helping with the cleanup?"

"We would damage our clan's pride beyond redemption if we assisted them."

"And the other clans, too."

"We have already done that; their Starfall stones desire only you, and they have been persistent on remaining with you through this. We will have to convince the stones to return to their homes."

My recovery, slow by all standards, had left me with a great deal of time to contemplate the Starfall stones. "I think the stones understood what has been happening. The clans are a unified front because they stick with me."

"It does help the Hope Diamond has chosen you."

"I wonder why. I'm not exactly a shining example of goodness in the world."

"Neither is it." If anything, the Hope Diamond brought everything other than hope to most. Except me. Without it, I wouldn't have anything at all.

I liked breathing.

"Right now, it is a symbol of hope. It has kept you alive in this world, and that undoes much of the harm it has done and will do. It helps us to clean this city of the filth polluting it."

Unable to argue with him, I nodded, and I bore witness to the carnage. The Hope Diamond pulsed again, but instead of the black and blue glow I expected, it shed a pure white light. The flash bathed the streets and erased all evidence of bloodshed, washing away the red from the asphalt and stone. While the dead remained, the wounds darkened as though cauterized, and the screams of the wounded quieted. A stunned silence fell over the streets.

"Be careful what you wish for. You might get it," I muttered.

"I wished for you to survive, and you did. I will be forever grateful that the stone listened to this blacksmith's wish."

I considered my father, who didn't seem all that old to me. "How old are you?"

"I met my seventeenth winter shortly before you were born. Your mother is far older than I am, but I am as long-lived a species as her, so we will enjoy many long years together."

My brows raised at that. "You hadn't undergone your second shift, then?"

"No, I had not. You were five and learning the way of the sword when I grew into my true self. I had hoped I would learn who my sire was through my animal, but I am much like you. We became what was needed without care or consideration of those who came before us. I have since learned who my father was —and his father before him. But the rest of our lineage remains a most interesting mystery. The clan whispers legends of our line."

Considering how the clan did its best to eliminate paternal lineage, that my father had learned anything at all about his father amazed me. "They do? I don't remember anything like that."

"Oh, you do. You just do not realize it yet. It is our proud line that brought Steel Heart to our clan, and it is our line that waged war with the stone you wear for the right to claim a shard of its power. Perhaps the

Hope Diamond remembers, and it showers you with its favor to remind us it gave us its child willingly. Or, perhaps, you are simply a magnificent daughter, and it recognizes this."

Once I found Anatoly and the others, I would have to ask them how to handle my father's inability to refrain from praising me every other breath.

I hadn't done anything to earn it, and he barely knew me. And what he did know of me was tainted by illness from exposure to the metal tube and its wretched contents. With a little luck, the ocean would keep the taint from spreading or hurting anyone else. Without the Hope Diamond and Sunder, I would have died.

"I'm hardly magnificent."

"You are."

"We're going to have a fight over this, old man."

"One I will win. I am sure you will fight to the best of your ability, but I have age, experience, and health on my side. I will sit upon you until you surrender and accept more of my care until you can fight with me on equal footing."

My mother must have gotten to my father, teaching him bad habits. My aunt would say something similar upon finding out about my lack of good health—and that I lived only because some Starfall stones decided I should continue to count among the living.

Sort of.

My mare snorted, stretched out her neck, and shook her head. I gave her extra rein, and she sniffed at one of the eerily cleaned corpses littering the ground. I patted her shoulder. "I'd like to see how I stand against you at some point."

"Of course. That is the nature of our clan. We always strive to best our brothers—and we always desire to bring pride to our unknown fathers. I was proud of you from the day you wandered into the forge and pointed at one of my failures and called it beautiful. While beautiful and flawed, it served you well."

Damn it, I missed my old katana despite having not known the flawed blade's history. "But it broke."

"You waged a war against a grizzly with a larger blade of almost equal quality. Flaw or not, that blade would have broken. I saw the pieces and how deeply the other blade struck. The flaw made it break a little easier, but it would have broken all the same. I am of the opinion it held as long as it could, and it saved your life with the resistance it did mount against your foe. You stood triumphant in the end. It protected your life. That was its ultimate purpose."

"The new one is just as beautiful."

"You are a biased daughter."

I grinned at that. "I'm a little sorry I modified the hilt, but only a little sorry."

"Do not be sorry. Your modifications melded your life in the Blade Clan and among the tribes and as mercenary together. I continued those modifications, as you are well aware. Your next blade will honor the tribe who cares for your spirit as much as I. Perhaps I will forge them a true prize, something they can hold with pride unlike the stiletto you were bequeathed. That is a symbol of trials and tribulations. They deserve a symbol of triumph. They became your family when I could not be your family, and when your mother could not be your family. This is a debt we can never repay, although we will try. I do hope Steel Heart will cooperate when the time comes to forge their gift."

"Does Steel Heart often give you trouble?"

"Only when it has better things to do. Lately, with limited exception, it has had better things to do. My new son's sword and yours were finished without incident, although I had to beg for its cooperation lately on other blades. And the blades they have done? They are not my best work. They will be tolerable blades for the youngest of warriors. My new son's blade is a masterpiece the match of yours, and I look forward to you discovering your blade's gifts. I look forward to him discovering his blade's gifts, too. I hope you will bring change to the clan, especially when your groom proves his strength to the other warriors of the clan. They will find themselves shamed by his heart."

Maybe if the clan had valued something more than brides and swords, they would have been able to see their other lost potentials. In Anatoly, I found many things no men from the blade clan possessed. "I think you'll like him."

"I know I will like him. Perhaps I have not been a visible presence in your life, but the moment I learned what had become of you, I kept an eye on you."

That explained a few things. "And you showing up on that beach?"

"Then, I kept a close eye on you. I had not realized you held Sunder in your possession until it was too late to tell you a safer way, or what you meant to do with that weapon the enemy sought to use. It took much courage to do as you did, but I would much prefer if you did not do such a thing again."

"Agreed. I don't suppose you'll neglect to tell Anatoly about that?"

"Neglect to tell me what?" my mate demanded from behind me.

Well, shit. At a nudge of my leg, Miracle whirled around. Anatoly led my champagne mare, and she snorted at me with her ears turned back. "You're supposed to be across the city."

"I was, but then a certain Starfall stone burst, and it decided to start exposing traitors, leading us to an absolute massacre. You wouldn't happen to know anything about that, would you?"

"I'm just sitting here riding my horse. Look! Miracle's coat came in black."

"Did you really need a third black devil horse?"

"I absolutely do need a third black devil horse. You have my Sweetie Pie. She's my angel horse. She is so angelic she makes up for my three black devil horses. Why do you have my horse? You better not have been riding my horse. She's too far along to be ridden."

"She broke out along with Devil Spawn, and she wanted to follow me around, and I was asked to stay out of trouble. I was riding a spare, but then the spare was needed, so now I'm walking."

Sweetie Pie stretched her head towards me, and I rewarded my mare with a scratch behind her ears. Miracle nuzzled the other mare, and the two horses decided they were far more interested in keeping each other company than paying attention to me.

With a little luck, Miracle would teach Devil Spawn and Dipshit some manners, but I had my doubts those two assholes would ever cooperate. As it was, I expected twin tantrums the instant I showed up at the stables.

Neither horse liked lazing about when a fight could be had.

"Anyway, Sweetie Pie didn't want to be left behind, and I was slated to be the rear guard. For better or for worse, your pair of blacks were recruited for today's activities. Madam President rode Todd until he broke his leg, then she rode one of the Secret Service horses. Her damned rabbit is riding Dipshit. Yes, we know Devil Spawn is too far along in her pregnancy to ride, but she broke out of her stall and followed us when the rebellion began. We tried to stop her, but we failed. As usual. I think your horses are the happiest of anyone today, as the last I saw them, they were creating mayhem, taking names, and adding to the bloodshed. Your aunt didn't want you flattening the entirely of Charlotte if something happened to me. She figured your horses flattening Charlotte would be sufficient. As you would try to flatten Charlotte should anything happen to me, I thought I'd cooperate. That plus the First Gentleman gave me an ultimatum. I'd stay in the back and behave, or I'd wake up from a mystic-induced nap sometime after the cleanup was over."

I needed to thank my aunt and her lecherous rabbit later, as I would have been inclined to destroy the entire city if anyone had done anything to my tiger. "You followed the glow from the Hope Diamond here?"

"I did. If I go to where Starfall stones burst, I'm bound to find you in the middle of trouble. I was not wrong. Again. You're pale. What happened?"

"She is ill," my father announced. "She recovers, although she recovers slowly."

Anatoly eyed my father like he wanted to start a fight, which wouldn't end well for me or my tiger. I tensed, and Miracle's ears turned back.

"Who are you?" Anatoly demanded.

"I am her father. As you are my new son, I look forward to beating good manners into you. I will only have the perfect groom for my daughter. Your new mother is eagerly awaiting her chance to meet you, and she will beat you far worse than I will."

Anatoly's eyes widened, and he turned to me. "Jesse?"

"He forged you a Blade Clan sword, so I recommend you accept your fate unless you want him to beat you with it before forcing you to take it anyway. After he is done beating you, he will hug you. He enjoys hugging his victims. It only took a few beatings to learn this lesson. Don't bother trying to escape. It's futile."

I'd earned every last one of his hugs for putting up with his lessons, thinly disguised as therapy to help me recover. Given a few more weeks, I might be able to do something other than barely stay in the saddle, assuming a mystic could figure out what was actually wrong with me and cure it.

I gave it low odds, but I kept my pessimistic thoughts to myself.

My mate relaxed, and he reached up and stroked my cheek. After so long apart, I leaned into his touch, fighting my initial urge to bite his hand and mark my territory again. "Got more exposure to affection, did you? You didn't even flinch that time admitting you accepted a hug from someone."

"I fear I've been acclimated to people hugging me. I no longer try to stab those who hug me before I've evaluated if I'm all right with them doing this. I find this custom of hugging to be strange but tolerable."

Anatoly flicked my nose. I snapped my teeth at his fingers, but he evaded with a laugh. "Excellent. You're obviously well enough for your sense of humor to have survived. We'll work on making sure you maintain your ability to stab those who enter your space inappropriately. What happened? After you gave me the slip at the train station, all hell broke loose. Then, once we figured out what was going on and that they were after you for the Hope Diamond, we played along and pretended you were still with us to lure them off. I'm just glad it worked, but I've been worried."

I'd been worried, too, especially when I'd reached the end of the line and had gambled everything to protect him and the rest of my family. I nudged

Miracle away so I wouldn't assault him while I was mounted. "I meant to scout, and I'd made a guess where they may have taken their weapon. My plans changed when I came across more dead horses. I found and destroyed their weapon, but it made me sick. The Hope Diamond helped Miracle; she helped me carry it to a place it could be destroyed. But it's been disposed of, and they won't be able to use it. After I recovered enough I could ride, we came here. My father and the clan helped with the timing."

My father grunted. "She is only alive because of the Hope Diamond, and should it be taken from her, she will die."

Sucking in a breath, Anatoly stiffened and focused on my father. "How do you know?"

"An unfortunate accident. I went to repair the necklace, which had been damaged, and I took the stone too far away. It returned of its own volition, but it must be kept close to her. It requires a new setting. She will have to keep the stone nearby during the repair. It also needs to be taught what it is for her to be healthy. As far as I can tell, it is maintaining her body, but it is but a stone and doesn't understand how bodies are supposed to work. It learns, as she improves a little each time it observes a healthy person, but it is still confused. I think we need to expose the stone to healthy women, preferably another Siberian woman, to teach the stone what it needs to know."

"Where's the Hope Diamond now?"

I lifted my wrist and showed off my bracelet, and

since I didn't need it out anymore, I moved it to the pouch on my hip, which held my collection of Starfall stones. "If I drop it, it comes back, so it seems to like me. Or maybe it likes you, and it is determine to keep you happy."

Anatoly growled, and he eyed my throat. Reaching over, I placed my fingers on his lips. "You're not allowed to bite until Henry and Cleo figure out what's wrong with me. I don't know if I have much extra blood to spare."

He kissed my fingertips. "All right. If you're admitting that, you're worse off than I feared. Miracle wouldn't mind carrying us both if needed. She is small but strong. I'd say Sweetie Pie, but while she's willing, you'd kill me for suggesting it."

"You will be burying my body in a shallow grave the day I can't ride Miracle while conscious."

"Jesse."

"I'm riding my horse."

My father chuckled. "Unless she improves more than I expect, within an hour, she will be tired enough you can do whatever you wish with her, include carry her at your whim. I have found it is best to wait until she is too tired to argue. It keeps the screaming, yelling, and roaring to a minimum. Of course, after a roar or two, she exhausts herself, so if you go that route, do scrape her from the ground once she falls from her horse."

"Isn't the idea to catch her before she falls from her horse?"

"Of course not. She will learn nothing if someone insists on catching her all the time. Let her fall. Once you scrape her up, that is when you gloat over her, which will make sure she does her best to keep from falling again. Do not weaken her strength on some fool's quest to make her comfortable."

With a scowl, Anatoly considered my father, and then he heaved a sigh. "This explains so much about your tendency to get into trouble, Jesse. It's obviously genetic, inherited from both your parents."

"Have you met my mother?"

"No, but I've met Stephanie. I've also met Gentry. I can't imagine your mother being a wilting lily."

She really wasn't. "She's somewhere around bashing heads in." I gestured to the carnage and chaos around us. "The last I checked, I believe she intends to drag my father to the family and start a fight if anyone has any problems with her keeping him."

"I thought their bride arrangement was finished."

I snorted at that. "They don't agree. In fact, they don't agree so much they've been keeping each other company. The only reason they haven't had any other children yet is because I'm that much trouble."

"It is a rule," my father announced. "We have to finish with the first child before we have a second, and this child is trouble enough. Once we worry less about the trouble this child creates, we shall have a second child."

Anatoly shook his head with a smile, overlooking the vestiges of the battle. "Just have the second child.

This one will be trouble for a long time, and it'd do Jesse some good to have a brother or sister."

"It would?" I regarded my tiger through narrowed eyes. "How do you figure that?"

"Having a doting sibling is pretty enjoyable. I have one. She loves me."

Had I not heard stories about Noona, I might have fallen for his trickery. "She loves beating you."

"That, too."

I turned to my father, expecting my tiger would continue driving me crazy just to hear me roar. "You don't need anyone's permission to do whatever my mother will let you do to her."

"That is a great deal," my father replied, and while his tone was dignified, he smirked at me.

"Some things I didn't want to know. That's one of the things I didn't want to know."

My father looked Anatoly in the eyes and said, "You will need much luck with her. I feel I should apologize for my part in your current difficulties."

"I like her just as she is, but thank you."

I doubted I would ever understand my tiger. "You need to see Henry about that, Ana."

"I do not."

Snorting at the Siberian only irritated him, and he growled at me. Rather than tire myself, I displayed my middle finger for his enjoyment.

The bastard bit me.

As always when it came to my damned tiger, common sense made way for impulse, and I lunged out of the saddle and went for his throat, teeth bared to bite and put him back in his place where he belonged. Anatoly tried to catch me rather than defend himself. I latched onto where his shoulder and neck met, dragging him to the ground. We landed hard, and I grunted without releasing my hold on him.

My teeth hurt, but I ignored the pain to mark my mate as mine.

After a brief scuffle, Anatoly won, pinned me to the asphalt, and freed his throat from my clutches. I'd made him bleed, and he chuckled at my assault of his person. To keep me from tearing into him, he captured my wrists in a hand. Then, as he knew it would drive me crazy, he pressed a finger to my nose. "You score full points for landing the first blow, but you're going to have to do better than that, Jesse."

I licked my lips, which tasted of his blood. "You're delicious."

"When was the last time you ate?"

"I don't see what that has to do with anything." As always when I bit him, the bloodied mark already began to heal, and I'd leave yet another pale scar on his skin. Given time, my favorite place would be a brand no one could erase, and I wished I could purr to express my pleasure over having claimed the tiger as mine.

"I fed her this morning, but she does require sustenance soon. Really, I find her voracious appetite following battle disturbing, but she still heals and needs to eat much. She is tired of the soup I feed her, however. Might you know of a female Siberian? I would like to teach the stone how best to care for my child."

"Noona's probably with her wolf, which means we'd have to take a trip to find wherever she took her brood this time. Any feline should work, and there's plenty of Bengal ladies who wouldn't mind helping." Anatoly released his hold on me, got to his feet, and offered me his hand. Any other day, I might have gotten up on my own out of spite, but I accepted his help.

However much it disgusted me, I needed his assistance to get on my feet and stay there. My tiger pulled me into a hug, kissed the top of my head, and sighed into my hair.

"We will do this. It did not occur to me that shifter humans of different species might suffice for this."

"Bears and cats are different enough you were wise to wait, but in biological terms, there are only minor differences between Bengals and Siberians. But, Noona should be somewhere in the city, and she won't mind helping. Or she better not mind helping. If I can find her. She said she'd be here to help out. But she might have taken the brood somewhere nearby and means to help with the cleanup. Honestly? I have no idea where my sister is. She likes making me guess."

I foresaw trouble, as Anatoly expected to get his way when he set his mind to it. The pair of Siberian siblings might destroy the rest of Charlotte. To stop the chaos before it could begin, I suggested, "Why not talk to Blossom?"

"We could," he conceded.

"And she's not a blood relative, so if the Hope Diamond is literal, there shouldn't be a problem." In a way, the Blade Clan's practices made sense; with an all male population, with me as the sole exception, the bloodlines remained diverse, as there was little chance of brides being related to each other.

"I guess we'll ask Blossom first."

"Maybe we could have Henry and Cleo have a talk with the rock, now that we have a better idea of what's going on." Maybe the two mystics could talk sense into the stone.

Anatoly rubbed my back before pulling away and shaking his head. "We'll figure something out. Convince Sweetie Pie you still love her, and let's find somewhere somewhat safer than here to talk. For some reason, I have a feeling you've gotten into more trouble than I expected."

"It is like you have met her before," my father muttered.

As they were right, I shrugged and went to shower my champagne mare with affection. Unlike Dipshit and Devil Spawn, she didn't put me through my paces before forgiving me. Miracle insisted on receiving her fair share of attention, which left me with my hands full while my tiger talked with my father about the disaster that was my life.

Chapter Twenty

HENRY AND CLEO descended on Anatoly with the same growling force as a pair of grizzlies, and I observed the mystics tearing into my tiger with a raised brow. The conversation degraded to wordless growls and grunts, although I questioned if the mystics howling Anatoly's name could count as a conversation. My aunt, her lecherous rabbit, and Gentry followed in their wake.

The trio regarded my father with narrowed eyes.

With the fighting all but over, I figured the grizzlies and the bunny were still hopped up on adrenaline and wanted to keep fighting, As I wanted my father to survive through the day, I said, "This is my father, and I will resent if you dispatch him. As a warning, my mother is around here somewhere, and she'll resent it far more than I will."

My aunt grimaced. "As far as threats go, that's a potent one, Jesse. Are you all right?"

"No," my father and Anatoly answered for me.

I eyed Anatoly's throat and contemplated if I could land another bite before he pinned me to the ground again. "I was going to answer as fine as I can be considering the circumstances."

"Jesse, go first, and then I'll get the complete and honest answer from the men," my aunt ordered.

I rubbed Miracle's nose. "This is Miracle after the Hope Diamond got a hold of her. I guess she was a black. Or she is now. In any case, the stone fixed her. I guess it had seen enough horses to understand what she needed to be to become healthy again. I have what was wrong with her because I disposed of their weapon. I am probably worse off, as it seems as though the only thing keeping me alive at this point is the Hope Diamond."

Silence.

Gentry inhaled, straightened his shoulders, and thrust his hand out to my father. "Thank you for putting up with my sister, and I'm sorry she's probably been causing you problems. I'd apologize for my niece, too, but she has probably groveled so much you wish you could gag her to make it stop."

While true, I resented my uncle's accurate and blunt description of my tendencies. "I'm not that bad."

"You're that bad," my tiger muttered, but then he smiled, invaded my space, and kissed the top of my head. "When you're feeling better, I'll be biting you. I'm keeping count of how many bites I'm owed."

He would. "You're lucky I'm tired."

"No, I'm really not. How are things going, Steph?"

"Randal is delayed, but he's fine. He'll be available for you this evening. As soon as word spreads down the line, he'll show up, and he'll expect to take your tigress under his wing and hover. We're in the cleanup phase, and most of the residents are gleefully assisting. The Starfall bursts isolating traitors really helped. Jesse, I don't suppose you know something about that?"

I shrugged.

My father straightened on his horse and stared down his nose at the President of the United States. "The Starfall stones sought revenge, pure and simple. The Hope Diamond, mother of all of the clan stones, does not approve of what has happened to my daughter. It has bonded with her and it preserves her life when, by rights, she should have died. Right now, she cannot be separated from the stone. I hope that will change in time as her body heals. Right now, she is too sick to sustain her life without the stone's help. For which I am grateful, of course. But it is a delicate balance. Her tiger says he knows of options, but the Starfall stone needs to learn how she should be, as it is unclear what makes a healthy human."

"Well, I'm sure Henry and Cleo can talk sense into the Hope Diamond if that's the issue, They're both intimately familiar with the human body." My aunt strode over, ruffled my hair, and kissed the top of my head. My big, black, mean horses followed in her wake, and they snorted their disapproval, their ears flattened back. "Dawnfire is intact, so I'll have Gentry settle you there. Anatoly, your house is intact; the fighting missed it by a few blocks. Last I heard, Randal was going to stand guard to make sure it stayed that way. He's winded, so it's a good way to keep him busy. After we're done at Dawnfire, you can take Jesse home with you. But to Dawnfire first. They have a full medical facility, Nate. You do not."

My uncle eyed me as though he planned on settling me by tossing me over his shoulder, hauling me to where he wanted me to go, and sitting on me to ensure I cooperated.

I held up my hands in surrender. "Where's Todd? Anatoly said he broke his leg?"

"He is busy creating trouble for one of my mystics. He took a bad fall while playing warhorse, but he'll be all right. His guild building is a bit of a mess, as a great deal of the fighting took place on his doorstep. He'll be fine, but he is grumpy at the moment. His new lead mare is taking care of things."

"Who is his new lead mare? What about Cleo? Why would Cleo abandon Todd?"

My aunt's brow rose, regarding the pair of mystics who ignored us and grunted at my tiger. "You're getting fussy, little girl. Cleo didn't abandon Todd. Todd told Cleo to go help people who might die without his help. A broken leg won't keep Todd down for long. As for Todd's new lead mare, her name is Kali. I'm not sure you've met her. She joined the herd while you were out west, and she's been handling a lot of matters at the manor while Marie's been bitching about Todd wandering off. Kali's about as headstrong as you are, and she's always butted heads with Marie. For good reason, it seems," my aunt muttered, shaking her head. "Don't worry so much. We're just in the wrap up."

"And your Secret Service agents?"

My aunt and her lecherous rabbit of a husband pointed down the street. I spotted several of the suited men checking bodies down an alley. Randal joined them and paused long enough to discuss something with one of the men before striding over. Unlike in Tennessee, my agent showed no sign of stress or anxiety, and I doubted any of the blood splattered on his suit belonged to him.

I glared at my aunt. "You said he was at Anatoly's house guarding it. You are a liar."

My aunt shrugged. "He, at some point, went to check on the house. I hadn't known he opted against staying there."

"I should leash you," Randal growled, and he gave my aunt a serious dose of side-eye. "As if I would guard a house when it was obvious my charge was here causing trouble."

While I bristled, Anatoly laughed, wrapped his arm around my waist, and pulled me to his side. "I wish you the best of luck with that. We're going to take her to Dawnfire. We're going to need Henry, Cleo, and Blossom. Jesse's gone and gotten herself into trouble. As usual."

"What now?"

"It is best if you do not ask quite yet," my father

replied, dismounting from his horse and taking hold of Miracle's reins. "You need to walk for a while, Jesse, or you will regret your laze tomorrow."

At my wretchedly slow pace, someone would be carrying me before we got halfway to Dawnfire. Rather than complain about it, I sighed and nodded. "Will I regret it because you'll beat me, or will I regret it because my mother will beat me?"

"You will regret it because we will both beat you."

"I solemnly swear I will behave."

My aunt's brows shot up all the way to her hairline. "You've gotten her to actually listen to you?"

"I speak her language quite well. When she misbehaves, she trains. When she continues to misbehave, she trains harder. When she behaves, she trains, but she trains gently. It did not take long to teach her my authority. Her mother roared once, and our daughter decided it was wise to make some effort to behave."

Gentry chuckled. "This explains a lot about how a slip of a girl could become such a talented fighter at such a young age. That was her life in the clan from an early age, wasn't it?"

"I found time to nurture her more delicate attributes, but yes. She survives because of that training, and she shall continue to survive because of that training."

I wondered at that, but rather than talk back and earn more training, I pointed in the direction of Dawnfire. "I'm walking that way now. With luck, I'll make it before it's nap time."

"Do not wish for miracles not even the Hope Diamond can grant," my father chided.

I HAD BEEN BORN STUBBORN, I had grown up stubborn, and I would die stubborn. To make it perfectly clear I refused to quit, I made it all the way to Dawnfire before crawling onto the nearest warm, soft surface my uncle allowed. Later, I'd be ashamed of heeding the grizzly's warning growls without putting up a fight. The oversized arm chairs in the guild's study made an excellent nest, and once I curled up on one, I matched the grizzly growl for growl until Anatoly dumped a blanket onto me.

"You are too tired to take on a grizzly," my tiger said, perching on the arm of my chair. "You're probably too hungry, too. I'll make sure Henry sets up an appropriate meal plan for you again, especially if you're suffering from the same affliction Miracle endured. I'll even let Randal fuss over you all he wants until you're well enough to put up a fight."

Somewhere nearby, my agent chuckled, which did a lot to convince me everything was all right despite having given him the slip yet again. When I spotted him in his usual watchful position near the door, I relaxed. "I haven't lost my hair at least."

"You had, but the Hope Diamond rectified that. It recognized your hair loss was a problem. That is how I figured out the stone was trying its best for you," my father announced. "You were still sleeping most of the time then."

Well, shit. I remembered my anguish while waiting to learn if Miracle would survive after Fort Lauderdale. My horse had been an excellent teacher and example, and I'd make sure she never suffered so much ever again. "Don't remind me how long I slept, please. I have done too much sleeping this year." I cuddled into the blanket, maintaining what little I had left of my dignity through a careful covering of my head. "I'm perfectly healthy, nothing is wrong with me, and I don't need an army of mystics to get me through this latest incident."

Anatoly sighed. "You need the army of mystics, Jesse. This is you we're talking about here. You're not healthy, and I'm very concerned about what's wrong with you. You still have the Hope Diamond, right?"

While annoyed he'd watched me put the damned Starfall stone away, I wiggled on the chair, untied the pouch from my belt, and slipped my hand out from beneath the blanket so I could give it to Anatoly. "Sunder is in there with a bunch of other stones, so try not to set them loose."

"How about you retrieve only the Hope Diamond so there aren't any incidents?"

I grumbled a curse, but I did as asked, pulling the stone and its broken necklace out of the bag. I handed them over. "Sunder disposed of the weapon, but I was exposed to its toxin before it finished its work. It's not the stone's fault. And I'm not sure how the setting broke."

Anatoly took the Hope Diamond, and I retreated beneath my blanket, debating if I should give into my exhaustion or try to stay awake to listen in on the conversation. Before I could decide, my tiger growled.

"Don't pick a fight with the Hope Diamond, Ana."

"If it doesn't take good care of you, I will fight with it until it does."

"Be reasonable."

Everyone in the room laughed, and I scrounged up the energy to hiss at them.

"By your nature, you're anything but reasonable, Jesse. Keep being yourself. Everyone else can whine if they don't like it, and I'll enjoy their misery and suffering. Also, it's worth reminding you that I'm sure Jesse's father would enjoy beating you on her behalf if you floor me right now, Gentry."

The grizzly grunted. "You're getting cocky."

"I have my mate back, the Hope Diamond is living up to its name for once, and once we figure out how to treat her sickness, I can provide for my mate properly. Ferdinand's scheme has fallen to ruin, and while we have some messes left to clean up, Charlotte's safe. Today's a good day, and I've earned being cocky."

"You followed Stephanie around while she bashed heads together."

"That was quite the sight to behold, really."

Gentry heaved a sigh. "I should have stayed with the damned stallion."

"Will you two stop?" my aunt demanded. "Jesse, do you remember what happened when the Hope Diamond's setting broke?"

To a certain degree, I did, but I wanted to shy from the memory of being battered in the ocean, drowning in a fool's suicidal errand to save the world—or at least a small part of it filled with people I loved. "Can we just say it was exposed to conditions unsuitable for a piece of fine jewelry?"

I suspected Sunder had helped the necklace break. Had the Hope Diamond remained intact, had anything been different, I wouldn't have been certain of the weapon's ultimate destruction. Things would have been different.

My body would have joined Ferdinand's weapon at the bottom of the restless ocean.

"How about I compromise with you, and you can give me a very brief retelling of what happened with your promise to elaborate later." When my aunt took on her Presidential tone, she'd flatten me to the mat until I confessed.

My mother and her family bore more responsibility for how I'd turned out than the Blade Clan's ruthless teachings.

Sighing, I considered slithering off the chair and worming towards the door in a bid for freedom. Why had I deluded myself into believing I might dodge the bitter truth? Had I put in any time thinking it through, I would've realized I had no hope of dodging any of them. One day, I would learn.

While blood bound us, stronger and deeper emotions tied us together. Love and friendship played their roles, as did something else, something that I still didn't understand as well as I should. I expected I would spend the rest of my life trying to figure everything out.

But I'd learned an important truth: they would stay through it all.

"I took the weapon out into the ocean, where I believe Sunder broke the Hope Diamond's chain along with the weapon. It was the only place I could think of that might scatter its poison in a way no one else could ever gather and use again. I thought the ocean was my best option." I considered the weapon's initial bubbling eruption in the water before Sunder could finish its dark work. "The Starfall stones worked together, but Sunder destroyed part of the setting in the process. Just carrying that thing for a short period of time made it clear I'd probably not survive exposure to it, just like the horses. By the time I got to the coast, it was pretty clear I wasn't making it out alive. I did it anyway. I couldn't let that thing get into Charlotte."

The silence hung heavy in the room, and I held my breath.

My aunt heaved a sigh. "You were never afraid of making difficult choices. I'm proud of you. It takes a rare person to make that choice for the sake of others. However much I want to protect you from yourself, I will never judge you for making that choice. No matter how much I want to keep you safe, I admire and respect your courage and integrity. I would have done the same. And Anatoly? You best be proud of my niece."

My mate pulled the blanket off long enough to kiss my cheek. "I am. I'm just angry over the necessity of it. We've seen how damaging that thing could be."

Given a few more months, he'd have me trained to expect affection as his way of telling me everything would be okay—and I wouldn't mind it. To maintain some of my dignity, I grabbed the blanket and recovered my head. "You're supposed to be angry with me."

"I have assigned you a punishment of five bites and an hour of nibbling. I will claim my reward for your bad behavior once Henry and Cleo clear your health."

After experiencing how one bite tested my limits and patience, five bites and an hour of nibbling would result in a complete removal of our clothing. He'd only have himself to blame afterwards. "What did I tell you about biting?" I growled.

"I plan on enjoying my reward."

Tigers. Given an inch, they'd take a mile. I'd enjoy the entire trip, but everyone else around us would have their patience tested for certain. Assuming Anatoly's house had actually survived the rebellion, I'd stage my takeover in his bedroom. No, our bedroom.

The lock on the door might keep our busybody family and friends at bay for a while.

"If you two are done flirting?" my aunt asked.

"Never," my tiger replied in his smuggest voice. "I will turn flirting with your niece into an art."

"You can flirt with her later. Just leave any mauling for until we're gone."

"I already said I'd wait for my reward until they gave her the all clear."

I peeked out from under the covers to observe my aunt glaring at my tiger. The pair engaged in a stand-off, which my father interrupted through snagging the back of my tiger's neck, pulling him off my arm chair, and putting him in the corner. "I swear. I thought at this age, I would be dealing with adults rather than overgrown toddlers on a mission of destruction. I remember my daughter's toddler phase very well. It took the entire clan to contain her, and she did not at all appreciate containment. She was such a source of frustration she was locked in the forge to watch me work, as no one else had hope of bending her will. It is entirely my fault she is as she is now, with a little help from her mother."

I didn't remember that, and I regarded my father with interest. He kept Anatoly in the corner, and my tiger grumbled curses over his imprisonment at my father's hand.

"She hasn't changed much," my aunt replied, her tone rueful.

"Never before has a tribe so aptly named a soul. She has run against the wind from the moment she drew her first breath. She brought much change to the Blade Clan. She kept her mother close at hand for the first two years of her life, and her mother learned much from the clan—and taught the clan much. Her mother would not have *her* child drinking any milk other than hers, and she waged a very brutal war with the clan over it. She emerged the victor—and birthed the seed that daughters could be as strong as sons. I merely encouraged what had begun with her mother. We broke many traditions, as for some reason, our clan believed that only I, her true father, could handle the little hellion she became the instant her mother wandered off."

"Sounds like it's the clan's fault for letting my sister escape," my aunt replied.

"She stayed close enough at hand."

Several grizzly growls warned me my mother's family finally understood where my mother had been over the years.

"Are you saying that brat of a sister of mine stuck around? With you?"

My aunt eyed my father, and as such entertainment could not be purchased, I fully uncovered my head to get a good view of the show.

My father, who still held Anatoly by the back of his neck, smirked at my grizzly of an aunt. "My wife and bride is a true delight. Did you think I alone cared for our daughter when she was too ill to care for herself? She is around, likely taking heads as trophies for their involvement in our daughter's misery. That is what she does. She will show when she is ready. But she is worth the Blade Clan sword she wields."

"If she's out for the blood of those who hurt your

daughter, there is a long list, although Jesse does tend to clean up after herself quite well."

"That is the Blade Clan way."

"The Blade Clan way needs a little refinement in terms of teaching its children it's possible to show affection without being embarrassed over it."

"Her tiger seems to be doing an acceptable job of teaching her all she needs to know. He must earn her affections. That is the Blade Clan way, just as her mother taught me. I would not rob my daughter of her chance to learn the joys of braving a difficult road. She values affection now enough to change the world for those she has learned to love. Why would you wish anything but the masterpiece she has become? She is my best work."

I groped for the nearest throw pillow, pulled it out from under me, and flung it at my father. He sidestepped, resulting in the pillow smacking into Anatoly. My tiger sighed and regarded me with a raised brow. As I'd failed to dodge the conversation through sleep, I sat up in the chair and shrugged, wrapping in the blanket to keep warm.

Anatoly smirked.

"If you two could stop flirting, that would be great," my aunt complained.

"They are young and in love. Let them be young and in love," my father replied, releasing my tiger and shooing him out of the corner. "Behave yourself. Make yourself useful and serve as a living chair for my daughter's warmth and amusement."

If my father was trying to earn my approval, he was doing an excellent job. My tiger wasted no time obeying, and I slithered off my chair long enough for Anatoly to sit down before taking over his lap and making myself comfortable.

"And that is how you keep the young ones quiet for a few minutes. Managing an amorous young man with a sickly lady is simple. Give him a job for her comfort, and he will do his job in such a way that best pleases her. And he is smart enough to know not to cross me when it comes to my daughter. I will crush him should he not treat her like the treasure she is."

My aunt tossed her head back and laughed. "Of all the things I expected, I didn't think you'd be a doting parent. Four months ago, I would have laughed if you had suggested she actually crawl onto Nate's lap of her own free will. But it makes sense. There is no way Jesse could have become as caring a person without some form of influence on her at an early age. She has always been compassionate, even in her choice of targets."

"So, now that the tigers will be quiet for a few minutes, tell me about this weapon. While I was tailing my daughter, I missed her direct acquisition of it, and she has been silent on its nature. I saw how badly it sickened her. The Hope Diamond held her at death's door, and it did what it could for her. It still does. But she is very ill, and her body does not recover as it should."

"It came from an energy source we use in the city

to generate electricity. The mystics call it nuclear power. It requires a mystic to shield because it emits something they call radiation, and we require the mystics to swear an oath to keep how it's shielded a secret. We know how toxic it is, but mystic shielding is relatively simple and does an excellent job. That said, we're taking steps to prevent this from happening again. It'll change how we generate power for the cities, but we had no idea it could be weaponized so much even without combustion —and I don't want to even imagine what it could have done if combustion worked."

"May we never find out. I believe the Hope Diamond, while it is confused on what it needs to do to help my daughter heal, understands how badly it damaged her. It is more thirsty for vengeance than even Sunder."

"This is the one civil war nobody wanted except the rebels, who couldn't accept the majority's decision. I have always made certain everyone's vote counted. I have vetoed every law that would make it harder for every educated voice to be heard. I have put steps in place to help make certain anyone who wanted an education could get one. I have struggled to maintain a tolerable neutrality. I have fought to keep this country unified. I gave the man who came before me a funeral worthy of his station despite the circumstances that led to its necessity. I have dedicated much of my time making certain the surviving residents of Fort Lauderdale can adapt and learn about the world they now live in. When their ruby city first awoke, I feared the Hope Diamond had done something crueler than letting them sleep, but I find it has birthed a new hope for people despite the grief it has created." Sighing, my aunt shook her head. "I thought about resigning. Can you guess what I was told?"

I could guess, and I regarded my lecherous rabbit of an uncle through narrowed eyes. "If you haven't already, you have my blessings to spank her for that nonsense. It sounds like she needs it. I hope you told her she should continue to allow the people to vote as always. That's our voice."

"I did, indeed, ensure she had her attitude appropriately adjusted. I will spare you from any discussions of how I adjusted her attitude, but I took care of it."

My aunt bowed her head. "You're never going to let that go, are you?"

"A rebellion of a few thousand who wouldn't be happy no matter what you do is no reason for you to resign. You can't carry the burden of their guilt, and there's only so much you alone can do. I will remind you of this as often as possible. When the people no longer want you as the President of the United States, they will make their voices known. You have a clear majority, babe. There was nothing close about the last election, and we all know those who nominated themselves for your job did so for there to be options on the ballot. You have never controlled our people through violence or the threat of violence, and a rebellion founded on such violence because they couldn't win through diplomacy is a rebellion unfit to serve the people."

It amazed me someone like my aunt could suffer from doubt and uncertainty, too.

Anatoly tucked the blanket more securely around me. "Have the masterminds been eliminated?"

My aunt muttered curses and shrugged. "We think so. Ferdinand, Marie, my brother, and his husband were the primary conspirators, as they had the connections needed to infiltrate the government for the tools required—and the mercenary guilds. Without my brother, they lost a major player in the conspiracy. Had Ferdinand been a little more sane, things may have been different, but Ferdinand couldn't control the rebellion, nor could Marie. Marie's role was to keep Todd from functioning at his best and leave Lancers' weak and ripe for takeover or dissolution. She failed at that, because she forgot Todd is not afraid of making difficult choices."

Todd wasn't afraid of sticking with his friends until the bitter end, too. "She wanted Todd out of politics and the government, and she wanted the guild to go to someone else."

"She was old, stupid, and selfish," Gentry announced. "And her love of being the queen of her herd far surpassed her love of Todd and her children. Todd was blind to it because he wanted to believe Marie was happy, and she played at that with him around. But Kali caught on, and she started working in the background without Todd's knowledge. She convinced the stronger mares of the herd to keep an eye on Marie because 'she was concerned.' When everything started to happen, the herd had figured out something was seriously amiss—and they were ready for her death. Not at the exact moment you killed her, Jesse, but they figured Todd would the instant he figured out the truth. Herd justice can be brutal, and a mare who betrays the herd faces exile or death. And your place as an honorary herd member was never revoked for all you're Nate's mate."

Anatoly rested his chin on the top of my head. "I told Todd if he hurt her feelings revoking her status, I'd beat him, harness him up, and use him as a plow horse."

Anatoly would. "You're terrible. You'll make Todd cry if you do that."

"Gentry promised he'd help."

When I regarded my uncle, he shrugged. "It's true. Todd knows better than to insult *my* niece like that. Anyway, he wasn't offended, so don't worry about that. We were more worried about getting you back." The look my uncle shot my aunt promised some form of retribution or another. "And if you could stop asking her to be an assassin, that would be nice!"

"But I'm a good assassin. I changed my mind about payment, however. Pay me. You owe me for two bodies."

My aunt flipped my uncle off. "I'll have a contract drawn and approved for both kills, and I'll add a bonus for the disposal of that damned weapon. I'll notify the appropriate parties I had requested your assistance with the situation. And, as it will annoy my brother into roaring and terrifying the Secret Service agents, I'll have him run the contract through Dawnfire."

"Make Gentry negotiate in my favor."

My aunt shook her head. "That's harsh, but okay. Gentry, we'll have a fight over it tonight. Sound good?"

"When you should be sleeping and taking it easy on your leg?"

"It's fine. It's barely sore, and the exercise today was good for me. I found today's exercise to be very agreeable albeit a little bloody."

When I thought about it, my relatives were rather bloodied. "Maybe you should go take a bath and stop dirtying the study. Especially the guild leader, as his mercenaries will get cranky if their guild leader looks like he was butchered."

"I got a scratch or two, and that's it. We're just cleaning up at this point, and everyone knows it. I'm fine."

"Your clothing isn't. Don't you practically live here? Get cleaned up, take my aunt with you, and deal with that lecherous pervert of an uncle, too."

"I make one comment, and I'm labeled as a lecherous pervert for life," the First Gentleman complained. "You're a naughty little girl, and I'm going to have a round with you on the mat later."

"To be fair, it was more than one, and you were strutting around like a peacock," my aunt muttered. "And she's not wrong. And you won't have a round with her on the mat until she gets the all clear, so you're just going to have to wait for your next beating. But I approve of the match, as you're a lazy rabbit who needs more exercise."

"You're mean. I'm the First Gentleman! Someone here should treat me with respect."

"You're a perverted First Gentleman who can join me in the shower. If you want respect, you'll have to go earn it from somewhere else. You're barking up the wrong tree for that here."

"I can live with my status as a perverted, lecherous First Gentleman," he announced, heading for the door and dragging my aunt with him.

Gentry laughed, shaking his head. "Don't let them trick you, Jesse. They're both exhausted, and while they'll take a shower together, they'll probably relocate to a tub and take a nap, where someone in the Secret Service will keep an eye on them to make sure they don't drown. A soak will do them both good, as will some downtime. I'm fresh compared to them, so I'll get cleaned up and start making sense of everything that's happened today. We'll need to compare notes. If we missed any major players, I want to know about it."

"I'm not sure I can help you with that, but I'll tell you everything from when we got separated."

"Assuming you are not napping as soon as things become quiet," my father said. "Where would I go about finding something appropriate for her to eat?"

Gentry went to the intercom, pressed a button, and said, "I need a mystic healer and someone to bring a pair of hungry tigers and a guest dinner to the private study, please. That damned niece of mine might eat us out of the guild this time."

The speaker buzzed before someone laughed and replied, "I'll let the kitchen know, and it'll be twenty for the mystic unless it's critical. Please do not eat in the private study, sir. We have a dining hall for a reason. Move your dining activities there."

"Twenty is fine. I'll even think about moving us to the dining hall." Gentry released the intercom button and regarded my father with a solemn expression and nodded. "Don't let the tigers escape. They're slippery, and they love giving us gray hairs."

"All children do. I think I can keep track of them. She is tired and will not wish to move, and he has her where he can defend her and keep her close. All I have to do is look threatening and stab anyone I do not approve of approaching my children. I will enjoy my duties."

"And on that happy note, I'm going to shower. Try not to eat me out of the entire guild, Jesse. Nate, if anyone looks at Jesse wrong, rip them to pieces if your father-in-law doesn't get to them first."

"With delight."

"Jesse, stay put."

Between Anatoly and the blanket, I'd warmed up, and I saw no reason to move. "Don't get me in trouble with my father. I'm not supposed to be lazy."

"You can be lazy for now," my father replied. "You walked twice as far as I thought you would manage, so you get to be rewarded tonight for good behavior. If you manage to stay awake until evening, you will be rewarded some tomorrow, too."

"It's a trap," I muttered.

Anatoly chuckled. "It always is, isn't it?"

"If I manage to stay awake until this evening, I get tomorrow off, to lounge around, eat, and watch you beat everyone else up."

"You will walk a minimum of one mile to continue your physical therapy, but you can have a day off from sword practice and other exercises."

"With a maximum of a mile and a half unless I decide otherwise," I countered.

"Deal." My father rubbed his hands together. "That will give me extra time with my new son tomorrow."

"I feel like I've been tossed under a carriage here, but pride demands I put up a good fight. I'll help you stay awake, Jesse. You deserve some pampering, and we can make your walking time a trip to our house to see what's left of it."

Tomorrow was going to be a good day, and I looked forward to it.

Chapter Twenty-One

I NEEDED to stop lying to myself. No matter what I did, tomorrow wouldn't be a good day.

My mother stormed Dawnfire, waged war against the mercenaries, my aunt, and my uncles, and won without breaking a sweat. Within ten minutes of her arrival, she took the place over. From the safety of the dinning hall table I'd claimed as my territory, I nibbled on my steak. My run-in with Ferdinand's weapon hadn't done my teeth any favors; I counted my blessings I still had my teeth, but it hurt to chew on most things, resulting in a slow, awkward battle with anything that wasn't soup.

I could go the rest of my life without choking down any more damned soup, although a bowl waited for my attention, my father's contribution to my meal.

If my father found out I didn't want to eat the damned soup, he'd force it down my throat after sitting on me. As I didn't want anyone sitting on me, I made certain to have a sip of soup between tentative bites of my steak.

Henry and Cleo showed up in my mother's wake, shooed Anatoly out of his seat, and flanked me.

"I will kill you both if you stop me from having this steak." I pointed at the steak. "This is the first time the dictator has allowed me to try to eat steak."

My father glanced my way and raised a brow. "And I only allowed it because I knew you would have two mystics available to fix your teeth should you break them indulging in food you shouldn't have."

"It annoys me none of us realized Miracle suffered from radiation sickness, but now that we know the full story, it makes sense. And yes, radiation from the nuclear power source is what has made you sick. There may be other things, too, but it's probably severe radiation sickness. That's why mystics shield it at the power generation plant. Even knowing what was wrong, we wouldn't have been able to do much for Miracle," Cleo said taking my plate of steak and pushing it aside. "You will get that back in three minutes if you don't argue with me. We can handle treatments for humans because we know what it does to humans. And we're not really trained for the extensive care of horses. Most just put the animal down rather than try to do organ restoration. But your Miracle is your Miracle, and that means we were going to do whatever was needed for her. We value our lives. Now, open your mouth and don't bite me, or it'll take a lot longer than three minutes to strengthen your teeth and repair the nerve damage so chewing doesn't hurt."

If having Cleo's fingers in my mouth meant I could eat steak, or anything else for that matter, I'd tolerate it for far longer than two or three minutes. I turned my head and opened my mouth.

Cleo pressed his fingers to my tongue and pressed down. "You're a hot mess as usual, Jesse. Henry? Pick your favorite disaster."

Anatoly cleared his throat and presented the Hope Diamond. "Perhaps you could teach this thing how to help you. It likes her, and it's the reason she's still among the land of the living."

Without any evidence of fear, the donkey snatched the stone with his free hand. Unlike the times he'd tried to remove the necklace, the Starfall stone didn't zap him. He frowned, regarding the stone with a considering expression. "All right. Henry, take this and see if you can figure out how to work on her organ failure. I'll take care of her teeth so she can eat without it being an exercise in self-torture. Still, I'm impressed you wanted that steak bad enough to deal with that pain, Jesse."

I pointed at his hand in my mouth.

"You can talk after I'm done."

Right. Henry pressed his hand to the middle of my back while Cleo poked around in my mouth. I'd been to a dentist a few times, although I hadn't gone often enough to make anyone happy. I'd probably get a scolding and an appointment assuming the donkey could salvage what was left of my aching teeth.

"Henry, numb her mouth for me when you get a moment. You're better at it than I am. I'd rather she not scream when I fix this mess, and I have to work on her nerves."

Henry moved his hand from my back to my face, cupping my cheek. Moments later, my entire face tingled. "If you've got to work on her nerves, I'll maintain it while you work. I can take care of my share of the work while she's happily eating as many steaks as she can cram into her stomach. Her stomach is the only organ that's fine, by the way. It was the first thing I checked."

"I am not questioning that miracle." Cleo poked and prodded at my teeth, and despite Henry's assistance, I could feel when the loose ones wiggled. Every time Cleo touched one of those, a dull throb spread throughout my jaw and cheekbones. While it hurt, I'd endured far worse over the past few weeks, and I sat still and waited for him to finish his work.

To my relief, it didn't take him long to finish and take his fingers out of his mouth. "Give it another minute for the nerve pain to settle, Henry. What do you want to tackle next? I'll help while she eats. She's more than half starved, and with those teeth, I'm damned surprised she ate anything at all."

"There were days it involved holding her down and forcing soup down her throat," my father reported.

"Ruthless but effective. Don't blame yourself for her unwillingness to eat. Jesse has ridiculous pain tolerance, but that level of discomfort would turn anyone's stomach. I'm not even sure how she has a functional digestive system at all."

"The Hope Diamond," my father reported. "It tries, but it does not understand the human body."

"Well, that's different. Let's try to teach it what a healthy tigress is, Henry. Jesse, we'll try not to stop your feeding frenzy, but we'll have to interrupt you every now and then. You need every damned bite you can cram in at this point, so act like a proper glutton. Anatoly, your job is to bring her food until she can't eat another bite. And no, you will not have her eat out of your hand however much you would enjoy it. If you want to hand feed her, wait until you're somewhere private."

"Since when has she ever let me hand feed her? I mean, I wouldn't mind, but she tends to look like she will stab anyone who gets too close to her food when she's eating. I'd rather not be impaled with a fork."

"That's because you're smart. Go get someone in the kitchen to start on another steak, and get them to make up a plate of vegetables. And yes, Jesse, you need the damned vegetables."

I snagged my plate, dragged it close, and tested a bite. When no pain manifested, the relief at being able to do something so basic without it being a struggle was almost enough to make me cry. Instead, I took another bite, determined to avoid any tears through food therapy.

Anatoly left with my father following. My mother continued her war against the President of the United

States, and the grizzlies settled into a roaring match certain to alarm every Secret Service agent in hearing range. Gentry sat across from me, sighed, and shook his head. "Jenny is going to turn this place upside down. Like she always does. I should have guessed you were my niece from the first time I saw you following Todd around. I don't even have to look too hard to see the resemblance. I'm just a blind old man at this stage. Only my sister would set her daughter loose and then get upset over the resulting chaos."

Cleo snorted, and he rested his hand on my side. Henry placed his hand on my back, and while I didn't like the tingling sensation, it beat pain. As choking would make it harder for them to work and take longer for me to fill my stomach, I took my time cutting up my steak. "You also didn't think I'd be an assassin, either."

"Yeah. That one caught me by surprise. I expected you to get your hands dirty somewhat; street kids who become mercenaries tend to create trouble wherever they go, but Todd kept you on a short leash. Not a short enough leash, but you're as stubborn as your mother. Of all the damned things to breed true. Jenny, this is all your damned fault!"

"Come say that to my face, you brute," my mother howled before roaring at my aunt again.

Shaking my head, I took another bite of steak, careful with my teeth until I could confirm yet again they no longer ached.

Steak tasted so much better when my mouth didn't hurt.

"I would, but I'm watching your daughter eat. Your mate ran off."

"He's tending to the boy, so don't you worry none about him. Mind your own business, Gentry. I've got a few words to have here with Steph, then I'll deal with you."

The lecherous rabbit joined Gentry, and he sighed. "This was not what I had in mind. I was expecting Jenny to be a little more restrained in her behavior."

Gentry snorted. "You've been hit in the head a few too many times, I think. This is exactly what I expected. Jenny and Steph have been brawling since the first time they saw each other. It's what they do. Don't get me wrong, I love both of my sisters, but they're both stubborn and have a temper. You've seen them fight before. Don't act all surprised."

Between bites, I grinned and said, "They're grizzlies. They have a temper by default. Still. I had no idea Felicity was the Vice President. How did that happen?"

"How else? It started as a damned joke. My sister thought it would be hilarious if she, a grizzly, had a wolverine as a political partner. She figured she wouldn't stand a chance for the Presidency, but she had underestimated how much Americans wanted someone who wasn't afraid of using a little violence and didn't need any damned man taking care of her. Add in the damned rabbit here, who did his best to hide for the first few months of her campaign, and she managed to offend the entire country so much they started paying attention to her. Then it turns out they liked what they heard, and they voted in her favor. The other options were *that* bad, though. President Wilson's demise along with a bunch of other higher authorities in the government really did a lot of damage—but it allowed for a complete change in the system. Then Americans decided they liked the change. She tried to leave after her second term, but the people weren't having any of that. Every state voted to have the term limit overturned, because the options after her just weren't up to their standards. Do you know how she won her third term?"

"No. I never really paid attention to that sort of history," I admitted. "I generally prefer to vote with the mentality of don't fix what isn't broken, and right now, we have something that generally works."

"That's how I vote, too. Most do. Change for the sake of change is a disaster waiting to happen. That plus we're generally lazy, have no desire to see a major overturn of the government when it's doing its job, and otherwise don't want to deal with election campaigns. Hell, nobody even remembers what party Stephanie is anymore. Nobody cares. That plus my wife was from the other party, so everyone has some form of representation at the top. Don't ask my wife what her party affiliation is, by the way. She'll just tell you it's the one that'll kick your ass. And then she'll kick your ass. She hates that question. And right now, the law treats everyone equally. Anyway, Steph was written in on the ballot, and the states voted to abolish the term limits. The government had a choice of changing the term limit rules or face a rebellion. In the next few days, she'll write a speech about the incident in Charlotte and have the couriers work as news mules for a while to make sure everyone finds out about the details. Then she'll, because she's an idiot, open the country to a vote of what they want to see moving forward. I expect the voters will tell her to shut up and go back to work, please and thank you. And we'll have a new surge of Secret Service applicants, because that's what happens every time she calls an out-of-cycle vote."

"Why doesn't she just wait until the end of her term?"

"That was one of the additions to make it so the government—or the President—could jumpstart an election if there was a reason for it. The Clan Council can start an election cycle with a seventy-five percent majority. The congress can also call a session and trigger an election with a seventy-five percent majority. The senate and house can force the congress session with a majority vote on both. Half the time, the senate and house don't want to be bothered with sessions because they have work to do for their constituents, and they'd rather be doing their jobs at the local level unless something needs to be changed at the top."

"So the Clan Council controls just about everything, doesn't it?"

"Pretty much. And when it runs into a situation where they can't resolve it without the congress's input, they call a session. They also send weekly reports to all upper government employees. This generally means the states have more control over their business, but as long as they follow the rules the Federal government puts in, that's what people want. Steph tends to handle the really important matters."

"Gentry, she's going to talk to you if you keep talking to her, and that will slow her rate of steak consumption," Cleo announced, pausing in whatever he was doing to point at my uncle. "Stop distracting her from eating. You can sit and make sure nobody interrupts her if you need a job to do."

"Can I get an update on what you two are doing so I can stop the women and turn on their maternal instincts before they break my guild?"

To make Cleo happy, I rampaged on my steak and devoured it without bothering to chew. Once I swallowed the last bite without choking on it, I said, "I want to know, too."

"Right now, Henry is working on your lungs. When he started, you were down to half functionality at best. The theory about the Hope Diamond helping seems to be accurate; he's making much better progress than I expected. I'm working on your heart, which is working to about a quarter of what it should be. That's part of why you've been sleeping so much; your heart just can't move blood everywhere it needs to go, and you're resting because you're oxygen depleted. Your brain is in good shape; I am refusing to question that miracle, either."

Henry sighed, and he patted my back. "The Hope Diamond is definitely paying attention to what we're doing. It seems to be trying to repair the damage now that we're working to restore organs to their proper working state. I'm going to be working on your kidneys and liver next. Once Cleo is done with your heart, I'm going to have him tackle your immune system. From what I can tell, it's not functional at all. The Hope Diamond seems to be working as a stand-in, likely because it understands *something* keeps making you sick, but doesn't get how antibodies work."

"I'm a mess." I regarded my empty plate with a scowl, hoping Anatoly would return soon. Then I'd have to decide if I wanted him or the steak—or both. "This is going to hurt, isn't it?"

Henry grinned. "No, I don't think so. I've never had to teach a rock about basic biology, but it wants to help, so it is. Good job convincing that stone to like you. It really wants to help. It's funny. It can do so much, but it doesn't really seem to understand something as basic as making someone healthy. It can sink cities. It can freeze cities in time. It can flatten cities. It can raise cities from the ocean if it wants. It can imbue everyone in its radius with magic. But, for all the destruction it can bring, it is really struggling to keep you alive. Now, it's getting the job done, but you're even more of a mess than Miracle was. But, you'll be back on your feet in no time. Unlike with your horse, we know how to treat this in people."

Cleo grunted and shifted his hand closer towards my back. "Depending on how much the Hope Diamond helps, we should have you back on your feet within a week for basic physical therapy. In good news, for the next week, all you get to do is eat, sleep, and snuggle with Nate. Nate needs the affection, you need the affection, and you need rest. I'll have to fight the grizzlies and whatever the hell your father is, but I don't play fairly. You'll be able to do your share of the mental work if you'd like, but your body needs to rest."

I liked the thought of resting for an entire week and getting to keep my tiger close company. "I was supposed to walk to his house."

"You will not be walking to his house. If you're not up for riding one of your black demons, I'll saddle Todd up and make him work the stiffness out of his leg. Breaks are tough on the equines, and he'll be grouchy and sore for at least a week."

Poor Todd. "He's all right, though?"

"Just surly he broke his toothpick leg trying to pretend he's a warhorse when he's better off as a trophy. He's also mad us mystics weren't gentle about fixing the break during combat. He should be happy he can use his leg. If he wanted a gentle pampering, he should have hired Henry."

"Normally, I would be upset I was causing you any discomfort, Jesse, but I checked your pain levels before I started, and you probably don't even think you're hurting at this point. And I can't give you painkillers; your organs can't handle them."

"It tingles, which is far better than what I've been dealing with."

"Well, you'll be tired and hungry most of the next

week, but you'll be in much better shape. After dinner, you can answer everyone's questions, but once that's done, you're on an easy schedule until you're in better health."

Anatoly returned with my father, and they both carried two plates each, which they placed on the table in front of me. My stomach growled, and I wasted no time accepting the plate Anatoly offered.

I gave the steak, mountain of mashed potatoes and gravy, and steaming pile of asparagus, carrots, cabbage, and other green things a lifespan of approximately five minutes. As I expected my damned tiger would withhold the other steaks until I cleaned my plate, I went to work shoveling everything into my stomach where it belonged.

Cleo sighed. "You don't have to inhale it, Jesse. It's not going to escape. You're not at any risk of throwing it up, either, unless you eat too quickly. You're going to burn those calories right off while we're doing our work. Take your time."

My father sat beside the First Gentleman while Anatoly sat beside Gentry. "I have been worried about her teeth. It hurt her to eat, even though she tried to hide that. I tried to tell him she would not be able to handle more than one steak, and the one might be too much. I wanted to offer soup. He said she needs meat."

"I'm glad you noticed, although I question why you gave her the first steak if you knew her teeth were hurting."

"It is a reward for good behavior. Will her teeth recover?"

"I've already taken care of it. She can have as many steaks as she can stomach, and she might get a sore jaw from exercising it so much chewing, but she'll be fine. Jesse, I'm going to start working on your kidney, and you might want to sit still. I'll try to keep this as painless as possible, but it's going to hurt, even with Henry trying to shut your nerves down while I work. It'll be just about as bad as a punch to your gut."

My lecherous rabbit of an uncle grimaced. "Having experienced one of her punches, I don't envy you at all right now, little girl."

As warned, Cleo's mysticism hurt like hell, and I roared in the donkey's face. The pain intensified, and I hissed at him to make it clear I disapproved of his less-than-gentle treatment of my internal organs.

"Well, your lungs are definitely doing better. Good work, Henry. Can you reduce the effectiveness of her lungs a little until we're done here? My ears are now ringing."

"Easy does it, Jesse. He's about done, and the Hope Diamond's figuring out what is supposed to happen. And, unlike Cleo, it's surprisingly good at being gentle. Do her liver next, then handle the gallbladder. I'll tackle the rest of her digestive system. After that, we can work on her immune system."

"That's going to be fun. Not."

That didn't sound good. "Why is that not going to be fun?"

"The immune system is a very complicated beast, and we'll have to fiddle with your bone marrow, a bunch of glands, and parts of your brain to fix that mess. Hopefully, we can get the Hope Diamond to figure it out without a lot of work from us, but I don't think it understands how illnesses work in the human body."

My eyes widened. "Wait. After Fort Lauderdale, I kept getting sick. Is this related?" The mystics fell silent, and I narrowed my eyes. "My immune system broke before this, then?"

"You would have been exposed to radiation from riding Miracle," Cleo replied, and the tiredness of his tone worried me. "It's possible there was enough radiation on the horses that were brought in that your body was already starting to suffer from radiation sickness even then. But we hadn't thought to check for that; we figured your immune system had been impaired due to the severity of your shoulder injury."

"It's not your fault. I didn't even know radiation was something that could make people sick until you all started using the word."

Henry cleared his throat, and Cleo waved for the other mystic to take over the conversation. "It's complicated, Jesse. But some techs figured out how to make it work, and it does a good job, but it's not without its problems. It generates a great deal of heat without combustion, which is why it drew a lot of attention. But I think we'll start trying to find an alternate power source. I think everyone failed to see how it could be turned into a weapon—a very lethal weapon. And while we can heal those sickened with radiation, it's not an ideal situation. And there aren't that many mystics who can handle the work."

"Yet the two healing mystics I know both personally can."

"We're that amazing," Cleo announced before snapping his fingers and pointing at one of the untouched plates. "Eat. If the rabbit could get his wife to settle down and ask Jesse questions while we finish up here, that would be useful."

"Why are you making me split those two hellions up? Do you want me to die, Cleo?"

"Your wife loves you too much to kill you, and your sister-in-law actually likes you enough to keep from killing you."

My father chuckled. "I will take care of this." Turning in his seat, he hollered, "Jenny, beat on your sister later. The mystics are working on our daughter, and they have news."

To my amazement, the fighting immediately halted, and while both women looked worse for wear, they came to the table, wearing identical suspicious expressions. My aunt placed her hands on her hips and glared at Cleo. "Report, donkey."

"It's definitely radiation sickness, it's the worst I've ever seen in a still-living person, and the Hope Diamond adores her. We start working on fixing an organ, and it figures out what we're trying to accomplish, and it picks up the work. We move to a new organ, and it keeps piggybacking on our work. The worst part was her kidney, but Henry's been dampening the rest of the pain. Her teeth were a mess, but that was the first thing we fixed. We do need to rebuild her immune system; I suspect radiation exposure from Miracle is responsible for her immune system difficulties. But with the Hope Diamond helping, Nate can take her home with him as early as tonight. We'll need to do daily checkups and help make sure her organs are functioning properly, but she's already leaps and bounds better off than she was an hour ago."

My aunt came around the table and sat beside Henry, pushing one of the plates closer to me. "You eat, and I'll get your father to do most of the talking."

"What about me?" my mother demanded.

"You are an entity of pure evil, and you didn't tell me you were still shacking up with your Blade Clan man!"

"Well, look at him. Can you really blame me? He's a hunk, and he knows how to use his sword."

"You disgust me, Jenny."

"Don't you say shit about my man when you married a rabbit!"

"At least she didn't call me a complete waste of air this time. That's what she usually does," my uncle complained. "For some reason, being black never bothered her, but me being a rabbit mystic? I have broken every rule on the planet with that one."

"You're *dinner*. You're dinner I can't eat. And damn it, you actually fucking cried to make certain my sister fell into your trap. You'd be great and rewarding prey, and I'm not allowed to eat you. You disgust me."

I stared at Anatoly, who shrugged.

Fascinated by my mother's ruthlessness and almost pitying my rabbit of an uncle, I nibbled on my food while keeping a close eye on the unfolding family drama.

"If you two could stop fighting for a few minutes, there are more important things to attend to." My father waited, and to my astonishment, the grizzly women settled down and limited their dispute to silently baring their teeth at each other. "I tailed my daughter from Charlotte to Tennessee, debating how best to recover her without ruining whatever she planned; I had initially meant to dispatch the wolf, but I realized she hunted someone from her behavior. While the wolf insisted on biting her, she shook off his magic without issue, so I had assumed my new son had successfully bitten her sometime prior. I also wonder if Siberians actually require a bite, as I had noticed some signs of a bond for a while. At that point, I became less concerned, as she seemed to have the situation under control. I have found it is best to leave my wayward child to her own devices. In most cases, she is usually able to get herself out of trouble. When she can't, it is trouble no mere mortal can rescue themselves from, at which point help is mandatory. She was not in that situation, so I did not interfere. I then discovered the pack of wolf women she wanted to protect. I assumed my daughter's kind nature had once again gotten the best of her. I would not ruin her efforts. Then she killed the equine female rather ruthlessly before making her move on the wolf. After your arrival, I waited to make certain my daughter and her mate arrived where they belonged. That, as you know, did not go to plan. I followed my daughter when she slipped away at the station with her horse. She seemed drawn towards the coast, which confused me, but I suspected she had a destination in mind. I lost her trail for a while, and I acquired a suitable horse for me and my bride. My bride met with me, and we began our hunt."

Everyone glared at me. I chewed on another piece of steak with wide eyes before swallowing. "What? Does anything I do ever go to plan? Don't look at me like that. It's not like I wanted to stumble on the convoy with the damned tube. I was just going to check out the one town that got a mention in Ferdinand's file, and you were all fighting over the main targets. I *thought* I'd be in and out by morning. Hell, I didn't even know what was actually going on until I saw their horses and realized they suffered from the same sickness Miracle had. Then Miracle went after one of the men with a strong desire to shed blood. I got mad over all the dead horses and killed the bastards. I figured the tube was the source of the sickness, as that was what they kept moving. I took it, decided I needed to dispose of it, and went to the ocean. That's where things get sketchy."

"By sketchy, she means she danced with death and only lives because of the benevolence of the Hope Diamond and the other clan Starfall stones." My father pointed at my plate. "Eat more and talk less. You were barely conscious for the rest of this tale, so you may as well feed yourself before the mystics get upset with your dawdling."

As my father would find some way to make me pay for defiance, I gave my dinner my full attention.

"She is a quick learner. She understands if she defies me on this, I will find some heinous way of tormenting her later. Anyway, she ventured into the ocean to destroy that weapon. The Hope Diamond, with some help from the raging waters, tossed her back on shore where she belonged, but not before she was too sickened to fend for herself. With a little help from her horse, I found her. By that time, she coughed blood, and the Hope Diamond glowed red. I believe without the stone, she would have died then."

"Honestly, she probably would have drowned long before being spit back onto shore," Cleo said, and the damned donkey pinched my side. "I've a mind to have Todd teach you some manners on the mat."

The First Gentleman raised his hand. "I can help with that."

"Only if you don't use your mystic powers. A shock would not be good for her right now," the donkey replied. "Give it a week. She needs rest and time with Nate. After, you can all take turns beating sense back into her. I'm sure she's done or said something self-deprecating to have earned it."

"There was only a minimal amount of whining about how her chosen mate would view her as hideous and would regret her bite. That was around the same time she was coping with sores. The Hope Diamond needed little encouragement to handle those, although she had a rough first week."

"I was wondering how you'd emerged unscarred, Jesse," Henry admitted. "The sores from radiation sickness can be nasty and hard to treat properly. I've seen them go bone deep in accidents at the plant."

I paused eating my dinner long enough to ask, "Are accidents at the plant common?"

"No. It only took one major incident at the plant to convince everyone there is a reason they need to maintain three shields around the power generation plant. There's one a year, and it is usually because someone is an idiot and wants a closer look. They've been developing other methods of containment and neutralization, but it is slow going. I expect as soon as we figure out a better and safer source, the plants will be dismantled and shut down."

"Anyway, in the following two weeks, her mother and I handled her care until she was well enough to begin rebuilding her lost muscle. But, she had a very difficult time eating anything, and we were unable to get her to progress beyond being able to ride her horse."

I found it interesting my aunt could transform from a family woman to President of the United States at her whim. She straightened and considered my father with a solemn expression. "Do you know why the rebellion delayed their attack? Nate had received missives through the courier network, but we hadn't realized how accurate or valuable they were until the first day we'd expected conflict and it remained quiet. Then we built our plans around Nate's intel."

"When my bride tended to our daughter, I coordinated with the clans to make certain we could do our part. We also sent falsified letters to the rebellion sects to make certain they believed the date of attack was delayed due to issues with transporting the tube and acquiring the Hope Diamond. It was that simple. But sometimes the best solution to a difficult problem is something simple. It was trivial to play their ambitions and greed against them. Their belief in their victory was so strong it blinded them to the reality of their failure closing in around them."

"Should I expect a bill?" my aunt asked, her tone wry. "I'm not sure the government can afford to pay out that many clans for their assistance."

"The clans have no desire for payment. They viewed my daughter's recovery and possession of all the Starfall stones as sufficient motivation to participate. Because the stones chose her, they rallied behind her cause, and she fought for the government that has nurtured us all when the world itself wishes for us to fall. If the clans can keep their stones in control, they are welcome to take what is rightfully theirs—if they can convince them to leave my daughter's care. They are rather smitten with her."

"I'm rather smitten with her, too," Anatoly said,

grinning at me. "I can't blame them for falling for such a beauty."

I regarded my food, and as I had nothing I was willing to sacrifice, I debated if I could live without my knife or fork. Before I could fling one of my utensils at my tiger, my father cleared his throat and regarded me with a raised brow.

Damn. "What?"

"You will not assault your mate with your dinner or your utensils."

"Was it that obvious?"

"Yes. You are a Siberian. It is what Siberians do. Your dinner is for eating, and your utensils are for helping you eat. You can discipline him after you're finished dinner."

Anatoly leered at me.

I flung my fork at him, and the bastard caught it before offering it back. Grunting at being thwarted, I schemed how best I would discipline my tiger. It would involve a bed, a lot of growling and roaring, and demands for a second dinner after I finished with him. As I couldn't get through my plans to dominate my tiger without finishing my dinner, I attacked the rest of my steak with a determination to get it into my stomach as quickly as possible.

Henry laughed. "Good luck, Nate. You're on the menu tonight."

"Well, it's about time. Steph, don't need us for at least a week. I'm on the menu tonight, and I will be very upset if anything interrupts my status as dinner."

My aunt turned to her lecherous rabbit of a husband and said, "You don't need either one of them for a week."

"Apparently, I have no need of you for a week. If you are going to be retiring to your home for the next week, take your Secret Service agents with you. I'll send some extra security over, and I expect you to tolerate them until we're certain the city is truly cleaned out. Otherwise, have fun, don't kill each other, and make sure you feed your tigress at appropriate intervals. Henry? Are you going to be able to handle them on your own, or will you need Cleo? I might be able to find some other spare mystics around this place somewhere if necessary."

"Please don't need me," Cleo begged.

"I'll check on the idiots once a day and handle the treatments she needs, but I think they'll be fine. The Hope Diamond is doing the heavy lifting, so I think it just needs some time and guidance. We'll make sure her immune system is working during the week. Nate, you need to get your overprotective tendencies out of your system."

"No, I don't."

Cleo snorted. "Yes, you do. Anyway, Jesse is too tired to cause much trouble. I'll take care of making sure there's sufficient food for them, and I'll recruit one of the kitchen staff to handle the cooking, Henry. You can handle the rest. Send someone for me if you need any help, especially with her immune system. I think we've gotten the important things taken care of tonight.

Make sure she keeps the Hope Diamond close at hand. Embed the damned thing into her forehead. Maybe that'll work."

Anatoly growled. "No. You will not embed the Hope Diamond into Jesse's forehead."

"It would keep it close."

"No."

My aunt sighed and shook her head. "Don't try to talk sense into a pair of Siberians, Cleo. It's pointless. I'll have a jeweler come to their house and bring an extra setting and reset the Hope Diamond on a new necklace or some other piece of jewelry. A bracelet, perhaps. Or in a gauntlet or wrist guard so it can be useful for her. In any case, keep that damned thing close to you, Jesse. No letting it wander off, and no wandering off. You've already done your share of the heavy lifting, so we'll finish taking care of the rest of the mess. Take Nate as your reward. I say you've earned him. Just try to return him in somewhat comparable shape."

"I'm still expecting a cash payment for both dispatches, and you can make the teddy bear deliver it on your behalf."

Gentry sighed. "You're such a mercenary."

"Yes, I am. You may assign all blame for how I turned out on your sister and my father." I polished off the rest of my dinner in record time and pushed away my plate. "Can I go now? I have a tiger to tame."

Henry laughed and placed the Hope Diamond on the table, which I returned to its pouch. "You can go.

Just take it easy. Well, as easy as you can while taming a tiger. Actually, I shouldn't even bother with talking to you. There is nothing more unreasonable than a Siberian tigress. Nate, be as gentle as she'll let you be, try not to alarm your agents too much, and remember you need to feed her about twice as often as usual. And sorry, Jesse. No alcohol for at least a week."

"What is it with you all and beer bans?"

"Your kidney and liver need a week to finish healing, then we'll see if your body can handle a beer. But until then, you'll just have to cope with your tiger for your entertainment. It's only a week. You'll survive. Just don't run away and go to another damned bar. Bars get you into trouble."

Judging from the glares everyone leveled at me, I had no hope of defending myself against the unfortunately true accusation. Technically, tattooing Anatoly in a bar had created a great deal of trouble for me, but all things considered, I would do it again without regret. "No, bars don't get me into trouble. Smug tigers in bars get me into trouble. I'm an innocent bystander in all this trouble. All I wanted was a beer!"

Anatoly chuckled and grinned at me. "I can't say you're wrong. Let's go home, Jesse. It seems we have a week off work, and I know exactly how I want to spend it."

I did, too. I had a tiger to tame and a second lease on life to enjoy. Everything else could wait.

Afterword

Dear readers,

Thank you for your patience while waiting for Steel Heart. I appreciate it so much.

This book was hard to write. I, rather lovingly, call it the feral book. Part of the delay in writing this was due to my inherent understanding this would not be an easy book for me to write.

You may have noticed that Steel Heart is shorter than Water Viper. There's a reason for that. When I initially planned the 'series,' it was going to be two books only. After I finished Water Viper, I made the decision to turn it into a quartet.

I'm happy with that decision, as I didn't feel like I needed Steel Heart to be this epically long novel out for my blood. Turns out it didn't need to be epically long to be out for my blood, but that's all right.

The next book in the Jesse Alexander series is titled Stone Bound, and while I'll make no promises on its release date, it is coming. There will be four novels total in the series plus one anthology. The anthology will consist of short stories, novellas, and perhaps even a short novel. I am undecided about when I will release the anthology, but it will include stories from more character perspectives than just Jesse.

If you wanted to see Nate's perspective from that fateful day in Miami, you'll find it in the anthology. If you're curious about how Jesse caught her two blacks, you'll find that in the anthology, too. If you want to see Jesse find her way straight into trouble, well, you're in luck. You'll find that in the anthology.

Thanks for reading.

P.S.: While Steel Heart is a feral little brat, probably rabid, has bitten, and will undoubtedly bite again, it's also one of my favorites—I just had to finish writing it before I could love it.

(There's always one...)

About the Author

Want to hear from the author when a new book releases? Sign up here! Please note this newsletter is operated by the Furred & Frond Management. Expect to be sassed by a cat. (With guest features of other animals, including dogs.)

For a complete list of books written by RJ and her various pen names, please click here.

RJ Blain suffers from a Moleskine journal obsession, a pen fixation, and a terrible tendency to pun without warning.

When she isn't playing pretend, she likes to think she's a cartographer and a sumi-e painter.

In her spare time, she daydreams about being a spy. Should that fail, her contingency plan involves tying her best of enemies to spinning wheels and quoting James Bond villains until she is satisfied.

RJ also writes as Susan Copperfield and Bernadette Franklin. Visit RJ and her pets (the Management) at thesneakykittycritic.com.

Follow RJ & her alter egos on Bookbub:
RJ Blain
Susan Copperfield
Bernadette Franklin

CPSIA information can be obtained
at www.ICGtesting.com
Printed in the USA
BVHW041652270120
570628BV00009B/81